S. A. CLAREMONT

The House of Roosevelt

Contents

1

Angelic Chloroform

It's weird the things you think about in the throes of a crisis. Here I was about to bleed out and I kept wondering, *Who the fuck gets attacked by guardian angels?*

I drew in a shallow breath and watched Eli's face, trying to interpret what he was feeling. His eyes, so unnaturally blue, fixated on mine. His black hair was unkempt and wild. He held me gently as he leaned back and kicked open the heavy wooden doors of the tremendous house. They burst with force, and he carried me over the threshold in haste. It felt like a romantic post nuptial moment, except that it was twistedly all wrong and I was dying in his arms.

I was awed by his startling beauty, never diminishing, lost in a reverie of amazement he remained so calm after everything.

"How's your leg, August?" Eli called somewhere over his shoulder.

I could make out a rough grunt. "Better if you hadn't attacked me. You should've let me finish him."

My best friend August limped up beside me, eclipsed by the man holding me.

She was adjusting well considering she just encountered an angel carrying her half-dead friend in the woods.

This wasn't exactly the way I'd imagined introducing my best friend to one of the guys I'd been secretly dating. Me, a bloody heap of flesh being held together by his arms as he fought his way through members of heaven's Legion while they tried to murder me.

"You'll be okay, Lily. Eli thinks he can fix you." August's turquoise eyes attempted reassurance. Her bright blond waves tangled and blood matted. A blackened bruise encircled her right eye and spread down her cheekbone, jaw, and into her neck. I didn't want to see what other damage had been done. She stopped and waited diligently to be told what to do by him.

My vision was too cloudy to understand where we were. All I knew was it was a house. A big one.

My eyes fluttered with the flickers of pain dripping from my back. My breaths were wet and every exhale gurgled.

An enormous mahogany table lined a far set of windows and glass doors. With one sweeping arm and he thrust whatever was acting as a centerpiece aside, throwing chairs back hastily clearing the way.

"August, hit that switch." Eli jerked his chin at something I couldn't see.

He leaned down carefully and gently laid my limp body across the table top. On my side I could feel my limbs spill out in front of me. It was so cold. Everything was cold.

Bright light flashed overhead. I blinked to adjust, and liquid spilled down my cheeks and nose, little flowing drops hitting the table. The pink tears pooled near a knot in the grain my cheek lay against. Blood in my tears? That wasn't good. A radiant chandelier hung overhead. Thick black iron held dozens of soft yellowing orbs illuminating anything beneath, like something out of a turn-of-the century hospital gallery.

I'd never had an operation in my life and here I was about to undergo combat surgery on someone's dining room table. And not just any *someone.* A guy I was kind of dating who hadn't been completely honest about *what* he was.

"Take this and go get all the candles you can find underneath there. We'll need that kind of light." He turned to me. "I'm so sorry, Lily, but this is going to hurt."

Eli kissed my eyelids gently. His warm massive hand cradling my neck dissipated and the arm he held underneath my knees pulled away.

A hot flash of pain shot down beside my spine over my ribs and surged deep into my chest. Until the day I nearly drowned in Eli's hot spring, I had only associated pain with the minor injuries I'd endured up to this point in my life. Most of which took place in the presence of August's wild brothers.

This was something else.

I couldn't swallow the blood pooling in my throat fast enough, and it was stealing my ability to speak. My stomach lurched in revolt from the over consumption of the syrupy substance. I wrenched forward with a sudden pull of my spine, like a rip cord opening a cattle chute. I involuntarily purged a clotted stream of dark burgundy across the surface.

I screamed through broken sobs, "Eli, help me!" My fingers fumbled across the table reaching back for him.

"Light them all!" Something slammed down behind me.

"Shh. It's okay," he whispered in my ear and placed a soft palm on my side. The pain retreated with his touch and I was saturated with numbness. My shaking subsided.

Every breath was a chore, and I strived to keep my eyes focused. I couldn't die here. But when I tried to think, the cold haze filtered any coherent thoughts out like a thick morning fog coating my mind.

Fleeting images of August's blond hair as she ran at Eli's heels, firing rounds over her shoulder from her *borrowed* rifle capered across my memory.

"So that's what you meant when you said, 'If I stop touching her'?" August stood frozen, a tall ivory candle in one hand and a tiny black lighter in the other.

His touch was keeping out the pain, but it also was keeping out any tangent of coherence.

"Keep lighting."

I watched her shakily grabbing candle after candle, trying desperately to light one after another while tremors rocked her fingertips.

I wanted to comfort her. Tell her not to be scared or worried. I wanted August to know she was brave and beautiful. Tell her that if I died to bury me in the forest somewhere without a funeral. To be nice to Ethan, my other best friend.

I wanted to let her know that she could do better than Mason, who used her, and to put it frankly was an asshole. But the damned fog was thickening like a heavy roux.

"Why candles? Why can't we turn on all the lights? I thought you said you lived here?" Her eyes darted around the room.

"I do. That doesn't mean more of them won't come." His voice was firm as he peered through the window behind him, searching through the black outside.

"August." I croaked her name.

She set the candle down. "Don't say anything." She smiled nervously. "you'll be okay."

I sucked in hard, trying to gain strength. "What happened?"

She looked to Eli to give an answer and then back to me. "You were attacked by guardian angels."

A snort was all I could manage.

She laughed as tears welled on her bottom lashes. I held my smile as best I could. I didn't want to scare her. I whimpered when I caught sight of the large gash under her forearm while I watched her light another candle.

"Those weren't the Guardians," he said. "Take this and roll it out in front of her."

I watched as a leather-bound pillar rolled into what looked like instruments of torture. My eyes widened and fear brimmed in my throat.

"No, don't worry. Eli, do something! She's scared." Her hands fluttered nervously, afraid to touch me and unsure of how to soothe me. "If it makes you feel any better, he kept the bigger ones behind you." She grimaced, reassuringly.

"Hand me the scissors, fifth from your left." I watched as his shadow cast across the wall, hunched behind me, holding my neck with one hand pointing while working with the other.

"Oh my God, Lily, this is so gross." She stopped pursing her lips after making eye contact with Eli. "What are those? Diamonds?"

"Shrapnel." His words were solidified with tiny clinking as he dropped pieces into a small metal basin. "Go into the bathroom and above the sink is a cabinet. Get me a small silver case on the top shelf in the back. It has an *E* engraved on the front."

"Got it!" I watched as August jogged into the rim of shadow and her footsteps echoed further and further away.

"Okay, I'm lost! I can't see really—"

Thump.

"Look out for that little step up!" There was a moment of pause from her. "Okay, I don't know where the bathroom is." Her voice was muffled.

"Turn right in two steps," he called down to her.

"Okay, I got it this time." She shuffled around momentarily before her footsteps grew louder as she broke back into the light.

The small silver case she held sloshed with an unknown liquid inside.

"Set it down and dip the linen into it lightly. Hold it over her mouth and nose," he instructed, the clinking endless.

She did as she was told. "Chloroform?"

The smell was warm, sweet, and pure. I had nothing I could equate it to.

I felt like Dorothy Gale fighting against the pull of the poppies as the room darkened. Flashes of the horrors I had just witnessed swept through my mind before vanishing altogether.

"Better," Eli whispered, letting go of me and leaving no pain behind.

2

Beautifully Marred

Sunlight warmed my closed eyelids, illuminating them pink. I took in the savory, fresh smells surrounding me. A light breeze blew gentle strands of my deep russet hair over my neck and collarbones. I didn't open my eyes.

Songbirds congregated closely welcoming the morning. The backs of my hands swept lightly over the sheer silk pooled around me. I wasn't sure where I was, my senses clearer than they had been in days.

I'm alive. I wiggled my toes. In someone's house. In some stranger's bed and it smelled like cedar and hints of amber. The last conversation I recalled was one of August telling me I had been attacked by supernatural beings. *Try and remember, Lily. Men had taken you.* I scrunched my eyes in thought.

They wanted me to die. What had they done? Warmth streamed beside the length of my spine. With a slight twist against the bed, I felt nothing. Hadn't they ripped my back into a bloody mess of flesh? Why?

A human defense mechanism was fighting me. Blackness was throwing a veil over the memories. I exhaled slowly.

A high-pitched squeal interjected my thoughts. A fit of laughter followed.

August.

I opened my eyes slowly and the haze gently subsided. Thick beams and wide planks of darkened wood ran parallel along the ceiling. My vision was obscured by the edges of deep navy silk lining a pillowcase. Golden yellows refracted by the sun danced across the ceiling.

I sat upright, taking in my surroundings. A large bedroom with luridly green walls. The ceiling matched the hardwood flooring. A rich rug of intricately woven reds and gold, large tassels tangled the edges. The headboard behind me was a dense mahogany with delicate carvings of birds camouflaged throughout. A collage of photographs and paintings framed together within inches along the connecting wall. Massive shelves were floor to ceiling thrusting inwards, hundreds of antique books overwhelming some shelves while gold and copper trinkets crowded others. The other "walls" weren't walls at all but wood-framed paneled glass folding away, opening to an impressive balcony. A large cushioned chair sat in the corner of the room with fabric so beautiful it was certain to have been imported. Beyond the folded glass were railings of wood with sizable chairs surrounding a wrought-iron bowl holding a pit of sand. Lush persimmon cushions were tightly bound to the furniture. Refreshing honeysuckle and ivy clung to the outer edges of the escape. Tall trees cloaked in moss concealed the hideaway. A wind chime clinked gently in the cool breeze.

I looked down and noticed I wasn't wearing my own clothes but an ivory silk robe tied loosely around my waist. Her laugh cracked upwards to me again. I looked at the expansive doorway and edged past the sheets and warmly-plush silk comforter.

I dipped to the hardwood timidly, like toes testing cold water. My fingers clutched the bed for support, standing for the first time in days, unsure yet of how many it had been. Crossing through the wooden double doors spread open loosely.

I slipped along the length of the wall, walking on the balls of my feet, carefully peeking in rooms as I went. I headed down the steps quietly following my best friend's voice chattering away at some poor soul.

A wide staircase opened over the living room acting as a veranda over the huge space before splitting to the right and left. There, across the room, an open kitchen tucked in the corner brandishing dark cabinets and cement counter tops. Perched cross-legged on one end of the angled island was August, spouting what she most likely deemed important information. On the opposing end, smiling casually and listening patiently while one hand worked a sizzling frying pan, was Eli, my black-haired Apollo. His striking blue eyes had a semblance of safety about them, soft yet influential. His presence left an impact in his wake. I could feel the magnetic *pull* in my chest and drifted towards him.

The feeling I'd discovered a few months prior whenever we were near one another.

I met Eli sporadically over the last two months. He seemed troubled and held reservations in getting to know me more. I didn't know why at the time, but it turns out, he was an angel. Apparently, there were rules he had decided to ignore by engaging in a relationship of sorts with me.

He looked up through his lashes, noticing me and quietly peeked sideways at August who wasn't aware I had arrived. He smiled ever so slightly.

"What?" She shrugged, noticing his change in demeanor. "I eventually told her. It's not like we lied about it forever to her. My brothers and I are mean sometimes, E, but not cruel. Besides, the damn thing would have started to smell eventually when we pulled off the..." She turned, following his gaze. Her eyes widened in shock.

I braced myself against the back of the leather couch, I could smell it, softer than would appear to the eye, so many crinkles aging the piece of work. She flew from her high-top post and leapt over to me. Her arms wrapped around my neck.

"You're not dead. He put you to sleep." Smothering me with her excitement. "I thought he euthanized you! I sat with you every day and every night and now you're here!"

I looked at her, puzzled. "How long was I asleep?" I was shocked at how smooth my voice sounded.

"Almost four days. You look so well," she said, almost disappointed. "No pouches under your eyes, pink cheeks, and your hair is shiny. It's the stuff he gave you. Like a steroid for pretty. I wanted some, but *someone* was being selfish," she called loudly back over her shoulder. "He hid it when I wouldn't stop asking. He could have trusted me," she scoffed.

August Bayne. My best friend and shining beacon of hope. I met her freshman year at CSU here in Fort Collins, and she quickly became the little sister I always wanted.

"Apparently not when I caught *someone* looking through one of the guest bedroom drawers," he mocked.

"I had a tummy ache! But I don't get any because I'm not Lily, I guess! I'm expected to suffer." She threw up her hands.

"Then why did you proceed to eat all the—"

"White puffy things with the creamy crunchy stuff on top? I *wanted* to stop eating them." Hand on one hip she pointed at him with an attitude.

"Does the same go for—" He eyed her skeptically.

"I'm not going to have you attack me here in *my* home because you're some kind of food dealer. Look out for that bacon. It's probably laced with delicious temptation!" She nodded curtly.

"So, you won't be joining us for breakfast this morning?"

"What do you want me to do? Go through withdrawals?" She

smirked. "I'll even save Lily one and eat it all."

"So gracious," I whispered.

"Right?" She nodded eagerly.

Eli walked around the corner of the island. Slipping a soft, massive hand into mine, he stealthily whisked me away from the addict that was my friend, leading me over to one of the tall dark wooden stools lined with an ivory cushion.

"Breakfast?" He leaned in close and inhaled deeply. "You smell lovely," he whispered.

"Gross! She hasn't even showered in like a week!"

I shot her a look.

"But you look *nice* in a back from the dead kind of way." She shrugged.

"What did I ever do to deserve a friend like you?" I rolled my eyes.

"You must have been really good in a past life, and now I'm your reward." She hopped up beside me, one leg tucked underneath while the other swung casually. She plucked a biscuit from the plate behind her. "Yep."

"Did they find you in a box of cursed objects?" One brow raised, I eyed her skeptically. She opened her mouth, appalled and ready to fire back her witty retort.

"Bacon's ready." Eli pushed the frying pan between us, sidelining the conversation.

"Humph." She chewed the bacon.

* * *

The hot steam rose and swelled around me. My hair limply hung in damp waves along my face. I didn't know what I feared more—that it didn't hurt or how terrible the wound would look. A slow breath blew past my lips as my eyes closed.

"Just look." I whispered the words to myself.

My palms were outstretched against the edges of the porcelain vanity and my shoulders dropped. What was the big deal? I wasn't a vain person, and it was only a scar. A big, ugly, jagged, purple scar most likely. I shook the thoughts from my head. I wasn't ready to see it. I didn't want to turn. I tried to take deep breaths preparing myself to witness my pale flesh marred horrifically.

My skin glistened in the mirror, mist clinging to small follicles covering my body. The evening sun streamed into the open windows overlooking the forest behind the house. I glanced sideways. A perfect Colorado summer.

I closed my eyes and let my hands drop to my sides. Turning slowly, I faced the massive tiled room, condensation dripping down all the walls. Thick and plush ivory rugs were soft under my toes. With my back towards the mirror, my eyes parted slowly.

I kept thinking about Eli saying the word *shrapnel* and didn't want to see the damage. Anticipating a monster reflection, I glanced over my shoulder and gasped.

I quickly brushed my hair over my shoulder to see it all. Running the length of my spine was a line so thin I had to turn continuously to and fro to see it in the lemon glow of the setting sun and heavy lanterns hanging on either side of the mirror. It wasn't colored at all how I expected. I never saw anything like it. Instead of the deep colors and bruising I anticipated, it was almost invisible except for a pearly iridescent sheen that appeared almost silvery when I moved. That was the less surprising part. It was beautiful.

The line shooting upwards was brilliant, tiny, with delicate spirals straying outwards from the central line along my ribs before it plunged sideways below my neck, twisting downwards over my shoulder blade into four vivid lines appearing to have a leafy appearance. Tears moved down my cheeks slowly.

"I told him you would like the leaves. They were my idea."

I jumped at August's voice in the doorway. "Thank you," I murmured.

"Get dressed. I robbed the booze room, and this shit looks expensive. It'll taste delicious and free. I'll go start the fire out on the balcony." She smiled gently and backed out of the room, closing the door behind her.

I stared for a little while longer at my new battle wound before tugging a T-shirt over my head and buttoning the jeans hanging from my hips. My standard go-to.

Eli appeared suddenly behind me, his fingers pulling the collar of my shirt aside gently. "I'm sorry about the scar. I did what I could." Hurt plagued his face. "I'm sure you have a lot of questions."

"A few."

"We'll have time. Right now, I want you to make yourself at home. I think it's best if you stay in here. I'm going to reach out to some people who may be able to help remove you…" His shoulders dropped and he looked away ashamed.

I searched his eyes and waited for him to continue.

"…from my brothers' *fixation* with you. In the meantime, I believe August found the Dom." He smiled half-heartedly.

He disappeared quietly down the hallway. I turned away, anxiously wishing I could have comforted him, but I needed to see her. I needed to apologize.

* * *

I was curled in the wide chair outside, staring hypnotized at the fire rising from the sand unnaturally between us. Small lights illuminated underneath the bed and the bookcases inside. The fire cast flickering shadows out into the night.

"So, I didn't see any of *this* happening." I sipped my drink that indeed tasted quite expensive.

"Yeah, it's a lot bigger than my brother and our best friend's love affair you were cooking up. Does Ethan or Jarrett know?" She acted as though it hadn't bothered her I hadn't divulged everything. "Does *he* know?"

Jarrett was August's oldest brother of six. After years of flirtations and hopeless crushing, we were finally something. What that *something* was, I wasn't sure. It only became more complicated when August caught me kissing our best friend, Ethan, notorious heartthrob and womanizer who now had confessed he was in love with me. Which strained our relationship to say the least. I thought August was never going to speak to me again until four days ago.

I had decided not to tell anyone about the stranger from the forest. So much for keeping that on the hush. Eli was more than I had ever expected.

Honestly, I hadn't told anyone anything. Maybe because I had no clue what I was doing?

"—and I was like, 'Can I see your wings?' And he gave me this cocky look that went like this." She squinted her eyes and tightened her lips into a crooked smile. "So, I took that as a no. I tried for three hours to catch a peak. I followed him out back and he took off his shirt. Honestly, I kind of hated you in that moment! There was nothing there! His back is smooth. I don't get it. That was challenge number one." She gulped the liquor eagerly, excited to continue.

"There are more?" I prodded lazily.

"Yeah. If I hadn't seen it with my own eyes, Lily, I would never guessed he was who he was." She looked out into the trees pondering an errant thought.

I couldn't finish her sentence. I wasn't ready to admit out loud what he was. I didn't know whether it was me or everyone else I couldn't say it to.

"Did you know this whole time?" She turned serious.

I shook my head slowly and looked away.

"Why didn't you tell me about him?" Her bright turquoise eyes sparkled in the flames. She was crestfallen.

"I didn't know what to say. I was confused, falling in love with Jarrett...with Ethan. Maybe even with him..." I couldn't look her in the eye. "I didn't want to hurt anyone. I was trying to figure everything out and after all the drama between you and Ethan, I needed time. I didn't see Eli coming. We kept crashing into one another, and I wasn't even sure he was real. I thought I was losing it." I shuddered. "And then I caught his brothers and him fighting and it scared me so bad. I ran away and fainted that day near Grizzly.

"When his brothers showed up and found me, they were spouting stuff about me I didn't understand. How they needed to get rid of me because Eli couldn't. I figured I was going to die. You weren't talking to me, and you were so mad at me. Jarrett was up in Washington, and Ethan was hurting so much after seeing me with him, I was avoiding him." I sniffled. "I didn't know what to do. I was alone."

"You'll never be alone, Harper." She reached a hand over to me and wiped a tear away.

"So, what's the plan?" I tried to divert the conversation safely.

She paused mid-sip. Staring at me, her eyes saddened around the edges. "I was hoping you wouldn't ask so soon. He said you were going to be pretty coherent."

"I'm sorry?" I replied. I had remembered what happened, but I wasn't clear on what the outcome was. We had gotten away and it was all I knew.

"Lily..." She took a deep breath. "I thought you were going to die."

"I know," I whispered, leaning forward around the fire to place a calm hand on her knee.

"You were so pale." She was speaking so softly, it was hard to hear her over the dull whip of the flames. "Your blood was everywhere."

"We don't have to talk about anything right now." I smiled in reassurance.

"Yes, we do. Eli is not just an angel." She stopped for a moment in thought. "Maybe he should tell you all of this?" She closed her eyes.

"Tell me."

She bit the inside of her cheek. "He made it sound like he wasn't supposed to speak to you, but…" She chose her words carefully. "He's a Guardian, Lily."

I wasn't quite sure how to respond.

"The only one in this part of the world," she breathed slowly.

"So how many are there altogether?"

She was quiet.

"Thousands?" I turned to look directly at her.

Nothing.

"Hundreds?"

"Nine," she murmured somberly.

Shock overwhelmed me. "That's it?"

"That's it." She smacked her lips together, savoring the taste of her drink.

"For the whole world?"

"And he royally fucked up by involving himself with you."

"So, what does all this mean?" My lips found the edge of the thick glass I was holding and I began to gulp nervously.

"You or him. The bounty on you is priceless. Those swift pricks who gave me this shiner"— she pointed to her eye which still harbored heavy bruising— "are members of the Legion. From what I understand, they aren't quite as prestigious as Eli but are still heavy hitters. Eli said he's not concerned until their numbers grow, but his brothers definitely want you gone." Her head dropped and she continued to fight off tears.

I didn't want to tell her about his brothers thinking I was something called a Lost One. She had enough to digest already.

"Well, this sucks." I searched the wooden planks of the balcony for some understanding while leaning back slowly in my chair.

"Sucks a lot. But it's not the worst part." Small salty drops inched over her beautiful thick lashes as she pushed her blond hair behind her ears.

"Of course not." A bounty on my head from the earth's personal hounds would simply not be enough.

"We can't go home." She stifled small sobs. "I can't believe all this is really happening."

I hushed her quietly.

"They won't stop until you're dead. We won't win this."

"*We* don't need to worry, only me. And I'll figure this out. We just can't tell Ethan." I smiled encouragingly.

She chuckled mildly.

"Or your brother." I looked over, imagining his beautiful sienna eyes and sandy blond waves. His golden skin flashed across my thoughts. His face warmed my memories. I blinked away the image. "So we can't go home. I accidentally started dating a heavenly being, who I may or may not have strong feelings for, and now we're running from heaven's army. Got it."

"And tomorrow night is the meeting," she said.

"Meeting?"

"Eli's called on people who are supposed to help."

"Who?" I asked, bewildered.

"Oh, this is going to be some crazy shit." She grinned.

3

Convergence of Ethereals

August stood firmly. I, on the other hand, couldn't make the tremors leave my hands and feet. Eli had planned on keeping us hidden away upstairs during the meeting, which only gave me the afternoon for my crash course on Ethereals. Intrigue and trepidation wove through my nerves about the impending gathering.

Eli stood directly in front of me, his build looming, in the room I had awoken in on the top floor of the house. *His* house. It was impressive, with rooms lining the hallways.

I was hopelessly lost in his arctic blue eyes. His face was soft yet serious as he reached up and tugged the thick bulletproof vest down over my head tightening wherever it needed to be.

My socked toes curled as fear pricked my nerves. He leaned over pulling a heavy, but too short shotgun out. Bending the weapon he exposed the opening of the barrel and fed the heavy shells into the end. The ammunition was odd in color, a tarnished copper. Slinging the weapon upwards, snapping it closed, he thrust it into the holster he strapped to my thigh moments early. Lingering as his fingertips grazed my skin. He sighed slowly.

Bending down into the heavy chest at the foot of the bed we were crowded around he pulled out a small silver cylinder.

He hesitantly handed the glimmering item to August. "Use it carefully."

"She gets a sawed-off shotgun with magic bullets and I get a damn lighter?" she asked, dumbfounded. "What the hell am I supposed to do with this? Throw it at them?" She feigned a false throw. "Stay back, or I'm going to do some light bruising!"

"It's very useful."

"How?" she asked. "If it fails, Harper, at least you got your antique bullets."

He took it from her and gently grabbed her wrist. Walking out onto the balcony he let go of her and kicked the furniture away. "Stay back, Lilian." He looked at her once, then flipped open the top of the small device. A tiny green flame flickered with the motion. Closing his eyes, he raised it inches from his lips. Tilting his head skywards, he exhaled a slow hot breath.

A monumental flash of neon green flames erupted dozens of feet above us. Loud cracks of hot white lightning splintered from his hand. It snapped back as swiftly as it appeared. My heart stopped at the show. A small flame flickered lightly before he clicked it shut and handed it to her. "You'll be fine."

She was frozen to where she stood. He walked past her, intent on completing his tasks.

Well dressed in an all-black casual suit, his collar lay open and his neck and chest were exposed.

"I thought these people were supposed to be on our side?" A pleading tone laced my words.

His eyes softened when he heard the worry under my tone. "Not necessarily," he murmured. "I need you two to stay here until I can speak with them. Don't unbolt the doors. Don't be afraid to use your weapon. Run if you must."

What did that mean? Why would I run if we had weapons and if he was here to protect us?

"He means this won't stop them. Only buy time to get a small head start. Because they've killed him. And these most likely won't save us in the end." Shaking her lighter. And for the first time I sensed the nervousness behind August's sarcasm.

"It's time. Stay quiet and don't draw too much attention." He eyed August when he spoke.

With a small wave of her hand she wandered out onto the balcony and twisted her tiny metal toy between her fingers. I would have to make sure that didn't get used unless necessary.

He and I were alone in the bedroom and my head dropped. I didn't want to cry but I could feel the tears welling behind my lids. I wanted to apologize for doing all of this to him. For causing all of this trouble.

He walked over to me. Taking a deep breath, he cautiously put a knuckle to my chin and lifted my head. "I'm choosing you because I want to. I'm sorry I've done this to you."

I sniffed lightly, trying to stop the tears from coming.

He stepped closer, his body inching dangerously near. His warm hands palmed each side of my face lightly. He put his lips to my hair and whispered, "Lilian, the hold you have… Nothing is going to change that for me. They won't take you again. I won't let them…" He trailed off. "Stay with August. They're close now."

He was gone. I locked the doors behind him and her hand slipped into mine. "Come on. Let's wait outside."

* * *

August stood to my left as we faced outwards overlooking the front of the house from the balcony. The two of us were motionless in the evening sun. The mountain breeze was absent. The silence of the

20

forest was deafening. Her breath was barely audible over my own. We stood for ages. Straining our ears, willing them to hear something. We never let go of each other's hands. My other arm hung limply at my side and my fingers trembled continuously.

I had no clue how or where to run from anything that had wings. Was that even possible? I hoped that it wouldn't come to it.

A faint crack echoed into the fading light. Our grip tightened as both our heads turned towards the sound.

"They're here," August whispered.

I was scared, and we edged closer to each other.

Leaning into my ear, she said, "Don't be afraid. I'll chuck my lighter at them if they come at us."

I smiled. I couldn't do this without her.

Headlights turned the corners of the long weaving blacktop drive. Neither of us could make out the vehicle through the dense trees surrounding the house and lining the driveway, only the white lights drawing them closer. A black suburban appeared first, followed by a motorcade of three others.

They rolled into the crescent-shaped entryway, ready to leave at a moment's notice. Everything angled away from the extensive front porch for a swift exit.

All in well-timed unison, dark figures rose from the vehicles. Several colossal men and two tall and lean women gathered in a circle. Their beauty couldn't be washed away by the setting sun. Most of them were tucking large, curved knives into boots and hip holsters. Some cocked their rifles before slinging them over their shoulders to swing from their backs.

"They must be the Fallen ones," I said.

She nodded slowly. "Stunning."

"They're angels. Or used to be..."

We listened as their heavy footfalls disappeared up the front steps and into the house. It was really happening.

A slow, rhythmic thumping drummed against our backs. We turned our heads towards the other side of the balcony, gazing into the thick Ponderosa pines swarming behind the house. The drumming grew in strength.

August let go of my hand and began walking towards it. The floors pulsated against the soles of our feet.

Her hands gripped the railings.

"Lily." She spoke without turning.

Rich cobalt-blue satin flitted between the trunks of cinnamon-colored trees, the watery fabric flowing outwards from their backs and gripped their necks. Lucid pale faces with soft features turned downwards in a brave assurance. Carried on the saddles of heavy-hoofed black stallions spread in all different directions. I drifted towards the corner to see them better as their scattered paths drew to one tight-lined formation heading directly toward the expansive back veranda.

"The Saints," I whispered as though they could hear me over the roar of the ground being punished beneath their thunder.

Her eyes grew wide as she peered down to the back patio. I followed her line of vision. My mouth hung slightly agape as slow-coasting people in odd clothing erupted before us with no hint of their origin. These must have been the Residual beings Eli told us about. Something halfway between a ghost and a person.

The horses weaved around them with ease as they rushed danger-ously near the house, slowing in the final moments. The cloaks of the Saints fell around them masking their delicate demeanor as they dismounted. Leaving their horses to walk aimlessly, rearing their necks, and whinnying.

The number of people grew so quickly August lowered her hand and stopped counting. The scent of burning lavender and lilac wafted from the small pots Eli had surrounded the house with earlier. Flames glinted while faint violet smoke wound around the timber and spread outward pulling people in. An attractive pheromone meant to call to the ghosts. The conversation among everyone was barely audible.

A bellowing growl was making its way up the drive, so loud we both yelped. I didn't wait for her. I jogged to the opposing side, clutching the ivy between my knuckles. A bass you could feel reverberating in your muscles.

Motorcycles. Less than a dozen or so ripped over the blacktop, screaming towards the house. They came to a stop and I cringed. Booming men, immeasurable in size, stood beside them. Tipping them over and thrusting down kickstands with substantial coal-black boots. Thick darkened leather tautly bound every colossal muscle on the formidable group. Their features were so daunting I ducked when one gazed upwards toward the skies, exuding dark intimidation. They walked towards the house. A thin, blue-cloaked girl climbed the steps timidly towards the front door.

"Move, Saint," a massive man growled down at the girl as he passed. I cowered and August mirrored my actions beside me. The girl paid no mind, only stepping aside, head cast down.

"The Condemned," I murmured, leaning into her ear.

"Scary bastards."

No kiddin'.

"Probably why they were Condemned," she said.

I understood what Eli meant when he said the Condemned favored no sides.

People flowed from the trees pouring into the doorways when headlights cast over the house again. Night had fallen. Only the light shone from inside and illuminated our surroundings.

High-dollar vehicles stopped before reaching the head of the drive and parked away from the rest. It was difficult to make out the outlines of people as they approached. In several large groupings, however, one thing was unmistakable—a red-ringed *glow* burning beneath several peoples' clothes.

My breath stopped cold in my lungs, and I automatically reached for August's arm.

"August, it's the Legion."

"No, they're not," she replied coolly, patting my hand gently. "It's the royalty, remember? Almost all of them have the Legion for hire as their personal security detail. Don't worry, they can't go against their obligations. Strictly protect the nobility's life, that's all." She snorted. "Bitches… They don't look so tough. I could have taken that one, Lily." She rubbed her bruised eye tainted with a hint of bitterness.

I patted her shoulder.

She didn't have time to interject as they drew close, moving all in a synchronized motion. As the last of the three groups headed up the steps, one man's eyes locked on mine, and I couldn't move. We stared at each other as he made his way inside. His irises were a tumultuously hardened brown, and when he disappeared below, I felt as though I could sense his glare drilling upwards through the floors of the house at me.

We waited until conversations were the only noise spilling out from inside. All chatter of the woodland fell silent yet again.

They were all here. To talk about what Eli and I had done. To figure out what the Guardians were planning to do to us. To find out if anyone was willing to help.

"Where the hell are you going?" My thoughts were interrupted as August was swinging a leg over the railing tightly gripping the ivy.

"Do you think I'm honestly going to wait up here in the tower of the castle standing idly by while real live angels are downstairs? We are going to spy, Harper!" She grunted and huffed as her head disappeared.

I leaned over the railing. "*We?*"

"Yes, *we*. C'mon they're going to be starting soon."

I paused for only a moment before I realized I, too, was following her.

* * *

"August, where are you?" I whispered loudly into the darkness as I tried to keep close to the wall of the house, unable to fully see the bouncy blond.

August was the type of friend you called who was up for anything. The girl that you wanted by your side when shit started hitting the fan. She did well under pressure and rarely let stuff get to her. She was the girl that you wanted next to you when you were attempting to spy on a giant meeting of supernatural beings.

She jumped out in front of me suddenly. "Right here." Then without hesitation, she reached forward and ripped away the long sleeve covering my left arm.

"I like this shirt," I scoffed.

She began tying a makeshift bandana around the crown of her head, knotting it tightly in the back. "You shouldn't. You'll never get a man in that color."

"I have three more than you." I cocked my head.

Her mouth dropped. "I was going to make one for you too. You can forget it! C'mon, we need to catch a horse." She stomped away. "Come here, pony, pony, pony," she called quietly to the grazing animals as she glared back at me.

"Why do we need a horse?" A stupid question once spoken aloud. I was dealing with a Bayne. There was no method to the madness in this equation. They were wired for wild. I followed while thinking about my stolen sleeve knotted around her head.

The large horses backed away from the tiny blond attempting to lure them closer, hands outstretched. One finally turned and quickly trotted deeper into the trees away from the little blond storm cloud. I watched with odd amusement for a moment while I kept my back to the wall of the enormous house.

"Just great!" She slapped her hands down against the side of her thighs in apparent frustration. "Your giant footsteps and split ends scared them off!"

"They're not giant." I peeked downwards at my feet.

"Now we have to use my backup plan, and it's a little sketchy, Lily." She sighed, placing heavy hands on her hips and looked at the ground surrounding her feet.

"No! No Bayne plans. We're doing it my way." I turned on my heel, heading back around the corner of the house toward the front.

I didn't want to admit it, but August was right. I wanted to know what was happening in that meeting. It was, after all, about me. The thought sounded strange. To think that a grouping of Ethereal beings had amassed to discuss me and someone I was maybe dating was insane.

I backed against the wall, listening for any hint of someone nearby, being sure to crouch below the windows lining the library at the end of the stone house.

I only had a day to explore and with August as my guide it was a lot to absorb in a minimal amount of time. The expansive home was brilliantly intimidating. A modernized cabin that spanned thousands of square feet under the guise of a rustic lodge. Set deep in the Roosevelt National Forest on a sweeping piece of property grandfathered into the park over a century earlier. Different-sized stones blanketed the exterior. Huge porches with beams as large as tree trunks supported the balconies jutting out from above. Dark woods, rich leathers, and fine imported objects filled the house. Every room was adorned with beautiful decor. It reminded me of one of those houses people with old money would buy in the mountains and use to go skiing once every five years.

Wooden shutters tilted the high altitude summer sunshine away. Sheer silks and linens sprawled over every bed. Lengthy halls were clad with original art pieces. Wandering about while August asked questions and gave me information on Eli I didn't know.

"This is your lame spying attempt? We're going to walk up the front steps and slink along the front windows? So much thought must have gone into this for you." August stood up right next to me, arms crossed.

"Get down, you idiot!" I tugged at the corner of her bulletproof vest. "And be quiet. I can't hear them." I squinted through the aged and wavy glass into the living room full of people, half looking for Eli, half avoiding him so he wouldn't be upset I hadn't listened to his instructions to stay upstairs.

"Why would you possibly want me to get down, Lily? Are you not confident in your super-secret spy plan?" She leaned her back against the wall and rested a heel.

"Shh!" I pointed.

"Would you like to hear what they're saying?" she eyed me skeptically.

"No, I don't need some August scheme to listen." I rolled my eyes and leaned my ear close.

She reached over and lifted the window slowly.

It was unlocked. I stared at her while smiling impishly and shrugged. "Sorry."

She slid down beside me muttering her caustic comments as voices began to gravitate in our direction.

"I'm in agreement with Amelia. No decisions are being made at the moment. I think we all can accept this has never happened." A young man spoke fluent English with a thick unknown accent.

Well, there went any hope that some kind of precedent existed to help guide us. I tried to listen closer.

"Bringing her to the Garden like that... I think we should ask ourselves why they've reacted in such a heated manner," a petite girl added.

I peeked over the sill just enough to peer inside, and two people stood with their backs hindering my view. I tried to see past them. Tried to get a glimpse of the voices discussing my grim fate, but I couldn't.

"Is it true, Elijah? They believe she could be one of the Lost Ones?" a voice suddenly called from the far wall.

A flurry of murmurs broke out across the crowd.

This made my ears perk. Eli's brothers had referred to me as this when they kidnapped me. I had no idea what it meant.

"They think she could be." Eli's deep voice rose above the noise. "But I haven't seen anything that would allude to it. I truly believe their anger is directed more at me for intervening with the fate of a human."

"How so?" another voice chimed.

"I saved the girl from drowning in a hot spring on my property. She would have belonged to the dead had I not intervened," Eli explained.

"Who cares?" a loud voice rang from the back. I could see one of the Condemned standing with his arms crossed. His dark hair cut close to the scalp and his thick brows shadowed his rough face. "Aurelius's involvement during the Dark Ages with Antoinette, the human, didn't cause the Legion and all nine brothers to converge. And I think we can all agree that was far more egregious than a drowning!"

Hums of approval brewed among the throng.

"Is it true the brothers stabbed her with one of their mortal daggers and she did not die?" a small robed Saint posed.

A hush fell over the room.

"I intervened before she bled out." Eli paused for a moment. "But no, she did not die after contact."

Gasps broke out.

The memories of the attack from Eli's brothers and what followed with the Legion still refused to surface. When I tried to bring it up earlier to August, her stare became distant like a shell-shocked soldier who'd couldn't wipe the horrors away of what she'd witnessed. I hated that she had to endure something so awful. Hated such a memory was living within her.

She grew white with fear thinking about the surgery she was forced to help Eli perform along my spine. And he told me that she sat by my bedside for two days watching and worrying that I wouldn't wake up.

"How do you know she isn't a Lost One then?" an angry voice chorused.

"Because they haven't been seen in thousands of years. I believe if she had been a Lost One, upon provocation, the brothers would have been mortally wounded—" Eli was cut off.

"Not if she hasn't reached full strength! She may not have found her mate yet! And if she is one, not a single one of us in this room would be safe from her wrath."

The room fell silent, and icy fear lurched through my veins. This was why the brothers had wanted to kill me? Why everyone did? All because they thought I was some ancient being? Not possible. I was only in my twenties, and I think I would know if I had been around that long!

"Anything good?" a smooth voice whispered beside us.

August jumped and I froze. A silver-haired man with tanned skin and icy gray eyes was crouched next to us a few feet away. He was young, in his late twenties or early thirties. He had sinewy arms and a lean build.

August reached for her lighter, nearly falling backward with the effort and frantically began blowing, but she couldn't manage to get it open in her haste.

The guy reached toward her, but before he could, I had the shotgun pushed into his ribs.

"Dark brown hair, vivid green eyes, and beauty only bestowed upon the beings of the Garden. I'm guessing you're the *her* we're all here to discuss. The girl who has the first brother in some heat up in the Garden." The guy calmly stuck out a palm, "Tristan."

"August!" August thrust her hand past me quickly into his.

"August, what the hell are you doing? We are supposed to be spying!" My mouth was agape.

"He seems nice." She grinned sheepishly. "And I like his silver eyes. You're not one of the assassin types in there are you?"

"August!" I snapped.

"She likes my silver eyes." Tristan gestured toward her, smiling smoothly.

"She's upset I'm ruining her 'super-secret spy plan,'" she said while making air quotes.

"It looked like it was going swimmingly." Tristan nodded. "But I think if you can, you should head back to the safety of wherever Elijah told you to wait. Some of the company kept in there would rather see you dead than risk war among the regions."

"Roger that. I got her," August whispered. "Bye, cute Tristan." She began pulling me away along the side of the house.

"Bye, August." He gave a casual wave.

"You never saw us." August gestured between us.

"You are going to get us killed." I glared at her as I scaled the ivy trellis.

"What's new?" She shrugged beside me. "But you're going to have fun doing it, won't you?" She winked.

4

The Other Best Friend

I slid over the edge and walked to the chair I had laid some clothes on earlier. The meeting should have ended hours ago, but Eli hadn't returned. I pulled the white T-shirt over my head, in too much of a hurry to untuck my hair. I had decided I needed to see Ethan. The last time we'd spoken he'd blurted, "I love you," and I fled. Hopefully, he'll be willing to forgive me. I needed my other best friend.

Tiptoeing over to August's nightstand while she slept and picking up the small silver lighter Eli had given her, I assumed I would use it for protection should I encounter anything. Doubting it would help much, it was more for peace of mind. I assumed the modified shotgun would be too conspicuous. I wasn't going to let the fear rising in the pit of my stomach deter me now.

I didn't want to risk being seen by Eli or anyone else for that matter, so I thought it best to exit over the edge of the balcony again. When the lights of the house burned bright earlier, I could see where I was climbing. In the dark of night it was a lot harder. A trickier feat than I had assumed. Struggling and trying desperately not to grunt loudly, I had to settle for cursing under my breath.

Walking the center of the blacktop driveway, I slipped my bangs behind my ear as I scanned along the tangle of forested growth for danger. The driveway was a half-mile walk with a wrought-iron gate at the quarter-mile mark from the access road. Since the looming house was seated deep in the forest, at under eight square miles, the property had no neighbors. The house had two natural springs and a river etched behind it barely in view of the guest cottage. It housed a horse stable, renovated miners' cabin, countless trails, caves, and miles of thick forestry.

Listening carefully for any imminent danger, my fingers caressed the lightning lighter I was rolling nervously in my hand. My footsteps echoed against the trees. I was nervous when my eyes were adjusting too slowly. If anyone happened upon me I would pull an August and blow at the lighter frantically in all directions.

By the time I reached the road, I was no longer looking over my shoulder, paranoid I was being followed. I walked only a few paces when I stopped cold.

"Headed out for an evening stroll?" A dark figure spoke, leaning against a motorcycle.

My lungs halted filling with fear. Worried a member of the Condemned had wandered across my path or followed me. I stood still. Should I turn and run or face them?

Eli had warned us prudently to stay away from them. Gruff men who would rather cut your throat than hear you scream. He called them *barbarous vulgarians.*

"Beautiful night for it." I gestured wide with my arm as I tucked the other behind my back that was harboring the green fire lighter.

"Pretty far away from the house wouldn't you say? Someone could find you easy prey." He coiled a piece of gum into his mouth.

"I'm not afraid." Evening my voice was the best I could manage. I flicked open the top of the lighter and slowly drew in a large breath. At least it might be enough to distract him and run back to the house.

He coasted towards me, stopping only inches away. "You girls and this fire." He sighed, reaching behind my back and plucking the lighter from my hand. "You're going to hurt someone." As I drew back from the shadowed man, the fear in my chest swelling, the moonlight caught his sterling eyes.

A small smile played on the corners of his lips.

"Tristan?"

His eyes were surprised at my realization. "Well, who else did you think it was?"

"One of the Condemned." Relief washed over me.

"Those ruthless heavy-handed grunts? Hardly." He smirked.

"Whatever they are, I never want to be in their way." I smiled politely. I still wasn't sure what part he played in all of this.

"I'm sure I could get you there a lot quicker." He patted his bike. "It's the middle of the night, and I'm not as dim as you might think."

"I need to go see someone…in town."

"Alright." He swung a leg over and held his helmet out for me. "Get on. No questions, and I promise I won't tell."

I took a deep breath before my fingers gripped the leather jacket he wore as we took off, looking back in time to catch the dim lights of the porch disappearing around the corner.

* * *

My arms bound tightly around Tristan's waist, and I watched as the yellow streetlights glowed against the pavement. Fort Collins looked different after all that happened in such a short time. Nothing had changed, but everything had shifted.

I looked up at the dark condo. "He's going to be mad."

"Well, you said he was your best friend, right?" Tristan leaned on the bike I was standing next to.

"Hopefully." My shoulders drooped.

"Ah. Something more perhaps?"

I turned my head to the side. "Friends. That's all." *I think.*

I walked towards the front door and shook my hands out several times before I felt like I could ring the bell. Cracking my neck from side to side slowly in wait. The roar of Tristan's bike pulling away behind me as the door swung open.

Holding a bowl of his favorite ice cream in one hand and a spoon wedged in his mouth with the other. A pair of boxers clung to his tanned hips. I hadn't seen Ethan since the night he confessed his feelings.

His vivid blond curls were loose and they were getting so long. His hazel eyes had a sallow tint and dark whiskers corroded his jaw.

He straightened his posture at the sight of me.

I could do nothing but wave timidly, awaiting his angry tirade. But he was worn down.

"A wave?" Ethan stuck the spoon into the bowl. "It's the middle of the night and I haven't seen or heard from you in weeks, Lilian."

"I know. I'm kind of in the middle of something right now." I bit my lower lip. "So, you're mad then?"

He sighed. "Go home."

I knew he was mad, but it still stung. Only weeks before this I was lost in Ethan's kiss, further tangling my thoughts towards Jarrett. I'd known Ethan for years. Most of them he spent satiating his massive appetite for women. However, August often said the only tender spot the guy held was for me.

Apparently, that statement held little ground now. I didn't want to argue with him, and when his mind was made up, it was usually beyond reason.

I looked up at him with pleading eyes and held in the tears I felt pricking at the corners.

"Okay," I whispered. I walked away slowly. Swallowing the lump in my throat.

I realized I was unarmed, being hunted by guardian angels, and was unaccounted for by the only people who knew anything about my current situation. My ride had left, and at this moment, I honestly didn't know where *home* really was for me. My small apartment or the warm stone compound in the woods filled with my bubbly best friend and Eli.

I stepped off the curb into the street. My feet made the decision before my mind had. Walking towards the mountains. This was going to take a while.

"Where are you going?" Ethan called to my back.

I paused. A smile warming my face.

"Home."

"Home is across town. Where's your truck?" He attempted nonchalance, but I could hear the concern.

"Like I said…middle of something right now." The tears were quietly flowing again.

I could hear an irritated grunt and bare feet jogging towards me on the warm summer pavement. "I was trying to stay away from you, Harper. And I told myself if I saw you, I would stay mad." He was speaking to my back while standing beneath a street light. "I have never said the L word to any woman ever. And when I said it I meant it. I knew you were confused, but you…" He paused, and I could imagine him clenching his fists at his sides and closing his eyes the way he did when he was frustrated but needed to say something important. "You panicked and ran. It hurt…" I could tell he wanted to say more but he trailed off.

I turned to look up at him. Broad shoulders shadowing me, eyes pinched shut. I didn't need an invitation.

"I'm sorry," I whispered into his ear as I reached past his clenched fists encircling his waist with my arms. "You're my best friend and I was scared." I paused, really hearing what I was saying. "I'm scared right now. Some things are happening, and I don't know what the right thing to do is. I care about you." I closed my eyes and laid my head on his chest. My pale skin was a stark contrast to his.

He waited, still trying to make up his mind. I felt the warmth of his reach around me. He bent his head and gently kissed my forehead. "Stay here tonight?" he whispered.

"I was hoping you would ask." He took me by the hand and jogged back to his house.

"Wait." I stopped on the front step. "I really am sorry. Still best friends, right?"

His head dropped ever so slightly. "Right. Best friends." We slowly walked through the door. "Besides I'm sort of out of your league, Harper." He grinned.

Now *that* was my Ethan. I felt safe here. Would the stone house feel safe tomorrow when I faced Eli and August? The funny thing—I was honestly more scared of August.

* * *

"So, tell me again, why am I dropping you off here?" Ethan looked up the long driveway trying to glimpse the hidden house through the morning light of the trees.

"I wish I could tell you, but things are complicated right now." I sighed heavily. I wanted to tell him everything, to get it outside of my head. I decided I wouldn't risk sounding like an insane person. Last night was incredible. I didn't want to muck anything up with the truth.

"Alright, babe. I know you'll tell me when you're ready." He grinned. "Married couples aren't supposed to keep secrets from each other."

Ethan had decided years ago we would be married one day. My input was not pertinent in the final decision. I laughed.

"I have to go. August is already going to kill me." His shoulders dropped as he came to stand in front of me outside his truck. "I'll call you." I nudged him.

"Lily…" His voice broke. "I want to…" He leaned forward.

I pushed my palm to his chest.

"Let's not complicate things any more than they already are right now." I felt guilty for not kissing him. I wanted to. I wanted to taste his lips on mine, inhale his smell, and pull him into me. "Sorry," I whispered, eyes cast downward.

I turned away unable to look him in the face. I began to walk the long drive and couldn't ignore it when I heard him slowly pull away. I paused to draw in a brave breath. Puffing out my chest it was time to face her.

"She's here!" I heard August's high-pitched voice before I could see her through the trees.

She stood in front of the large garage, arms crossed, and Tristan standing beside her. I gave a feeble smile towards him. "Hi," I calmly called.

"Hi?" she questioned, marching directly at me. "Where the hell have you been, Harper? We've been looking for you since dawn!" She grabbed me by the arm and drug me towards the front door of the house. Some of the attendees of the meeting were standing scattered about.

"I needed to see someone." I wasn't sure if I should mention it was Ethan, and it was obvious Tristan had kept my secret.

"Who?" She turned on a sharp heel and eyed me skeptically. "There are people who want you dead. Does that little chestnut-covered head of yours comprehend that fact?" I shrugged. "You could have been hurt! Who is so important you would run off…" she scoffed and her eyes widened at the realization. "Ethan!" She threw her hands up and immediately stomped into the house, yelling incoherent obscenities and his name over and over again.

Up until a few months ago, August was hoping we would be sisters when her brother Jarrett and I had finally crossed over the crush veil we had been hiding behind for so many years. How things have changed.

Tristan was leaning on the frame of the front door behind me. I turned to look over my shoulder in time to witness the grin he was wearing.

"She's something else," he said.

I rolled my eyes. "Yeah, I can think of a few things she is right now."

"And now you're insulting me?" She crossed her arms angrily and cocked out a hip. "Wearing *that* outfit?"

"Where's Eli?" I decided this was getting nowhere.

"Your hot piece of angel meat left when you started walking up." She rolled her eyes and started to walk away.

"He went out back." Tristan thumbed over his shoulder.

"Thanks."

"Don't help her! Her hair is a mess. Hair like that happens when you sleep at houses you shouldn't!" She held up a hand indicating I wasn't going to be allowed to respond and stomped out the front door.

She would never get on board with Ethan.

I casually began walking towards the back, ignoring the crowd that had gathered to witness my homecoming. August was walking so freely I came to the conclusion these would be the people helping us.

Closing the glass doors behind me, I caught sight of him. His back was towards me and shoulders were tense.

"Hi," I murmured. He didn't move. "I'm sorry I took off last night. I should have told someone." Nothing. "Are you going to ignore me forever?"

He started walking forward slowly and automatically I began to follow.

"Stay here."

I had no choice. He had disappeared into the trees, and I was left standing alone to feel guilty about absconding.

5

A Spitting Image of Her Father

Eli had been absent for days, and I made no attempts to go and seek him out. Instead, I took it upon myself to gain information on the new people inhabiting the house. After the meeting, a little over a dozen stayed behind while the rest left.

Some wandered about the expansive house and surrounding woods all hours of the day and night. Some would politely nod while others continued on their way. The soft whinnying of the Saints' horses nearby kept everything constantly abuzz. They made it clear they weren't here for me and only for Eli.

August had turned her attention onto Tristan, and he found her to be equally appealing. Usually, when you found one, it was less than difficult to come across the other.

Tristan was extremely helpful in explaining who everyone was and why they would be beneficial to us. All the Condemned stayed with us and were members of the Legion who had been banished to wander the earth indefinitely. With nothing to lose, their hot tempers were volcanic more often than not. Easily irritated, they maintained a shoot-first attitude. Frequently breaking out into fights with others. I gave them a wide berth.

40

The Fallen were more than hesitant to stay. The group only left behind two of its members. They used to be in the Legion and now had been cast down to earth, serving a sentence that could last millennia. They had no intention of breaking parole. It meant a great deal for the two of them to stay.

The Saints were pleasantly friendly. Although most were small, appeared delicate, and were timid, they were skilled fighters. Able to inspire the masses to fight in their wakes.

The Residuals were more complicated. Although they came across as solid to the naked eye, August discovered quite early this was not the case. For all intents and purposes, they were ghosts, but step too close and they were capable of adapting and sapping the life from you. A dangerous trick. They glided gently about the house and stood in small clusters beneath the red candles dangling from several corners in long hallways. The purple smoke was burning lavender, a scent that attracted them. These were people who had been executed by the Legion—wrongfully or not we may never know.

None of the nobility stayed behind and Tristan said this made sense. They wouldn't risk being sanctioned by the brothers and stripped of their titles and wealth.

"So are you two ever going to speak again?" August sat on the railing of the balcony outside our bedroom playfully. She had been staying in Eli's room with me. Tristan leaned nonchalantly in one corner, chewing on a bright green apple.

I leaned back in my chair, legs tucked close to my chest, and I tilted my face skyward, letting the sun wash over my skin. "It's obvious he doesn't want to see me."

I decided to leave out that I knew he was close by since I could feel the tug in my chest. A low burning ember below my collarbone letting me know he was nearby.

"I think you should say sorry," Tristan said around crisp bites.

I couldn't figure out what his angle was. Because when August would prod with her questions he would become evasive with his explanations.

"For what?" August chimed before I could respond.

"For sneaking out of the house and not telling anyone. Lily could have been hurt or worse—most likely killed. Something like that would have haunted him forever." He pointed with his apple.

"I thought you were on my side?" I glared at him. The double meaning was obvious behind my tone.

"I don't play sides. I'm free." He grinned with a hand to his chest.

"You wouldn't understand. He's one of my best friends, and sometimes just being around him can put things in check for me. He can level me out in ways August can't," I said.

"Hey!" She pointed. "I'm a wonderful friend. I introduce you to hot guys. Remember your twenty-first birthday?"

"When you threw up on my back? As far as hot guys go… Well, you know." I nodded, gesturing at my surroundings with my brows raised.

She scoffed, "One time! And Jarrett still thought you looked amazing that night!"

"Jarrett?" Tristan turned to August.

"Jarrett's my big brother. He's her primary boyfriend. Ethan's her side piece. And Eli's her secret boyfriend. Did I forget anybody that I don't know about yet?"

"Wouldn't want to leave anything out. Yeah, that about covers it." I stood and walked away doing my best to end the conversation. August paid no mind and hopped down grabbing Tristan by the hand and following wherever I might be off to.

* * *

I had cheated death once and decided to make a second attempt.

Except this time I wouldn't be going as far. I tossed and turned last night thinking about Tristan's statement and how I should apologize.

Slipping on my incognito outfit of jeans and a plain white T-shirt, I tiptoed down the hallway foregoing another attempt to scale the length of the house.

"Evening." I whispered politely to a Saint. A young man with sharp features and warm brown eyes. I wasn't sure of names but faces were becoming more and more familiar to me.

A gentle nod and he was behind me. I continued on, assuring my purpose by walking with a determined destination in mind. As though I were meant to be headed wherever I was going. This was the unsure part. I didn't exactly know where Eli was hiding out, so I decided to test the theory I'd conjured yesterday afternoon and follow the constant pull in my chest. I was hoping I could find him simply by the severity of the feeling. A silent game of hot and cold.

I wasn't nervous until I reached the trees beyond the back door and the heads of dark figures slightly turned, keeping watch. They didn't follow, and I was surprised. Perhaps they assumed I would be fine as I had been previously. Perhaps they were better off without me. I was, after all, the catalyst to the war of the brothers.

I tried to push the damp thoughts from my mind and continue. The moon was covered by hazy clouds and the darkness pressed down on me with a penetrating force. I couldn't hear the soft whispers of voices or see the dim glow of lights. I couldn't keep ignoring the fear simmering in my stomach.

I stopped when the pull was at its height. He had to be close by if this was right. After several minutes of walking, I stood still and closed my eyes.

Was I supposed to call out to him? I wasn't exactly sure how this was going to work. I let my lips part to say his name—

"What are you doing out here?" A deep voice vibrated longingly in my bones and I smiled.

"It worked," I whispered, opening my eyes carefully.

He was inspiring. A creamy thermal clung to him with rugged jeans and heavy boots occupying his feet. His thick black hair was unkempt, giving way to a tired look, but his eyes were fierce. He was angry.

"I asked what you're doing out here." Eli's voice slowly grew and his brows furrowed as his fists balled.

"I was—"

"You were being reckless. People are risking their lives. Do you understand?" He was so close. I could feel his nerves standing on end.

Half of me was elated my plan had worked so flawlessly while the other half was slowly becoming angry he wasn't giving me the chance to explain myself.

"You should have asked me! You know I would have taken you," he barked and ran a frustrated hand through his hair.

I could feel the heat of his breath, making it difficult to concentrate. Despite that he was fuming, I wanted nothing more than to reach out and soothe him.

"You're lucky it was Tristan who found you and not one of my brothers. Did you think you had a chance? Of course you did!" He turned his back to me, hands on his hips. "I've sheltered you from what they can do." He came to stand in front of me. "Close your eyes," he murmured, frustration in his voice, brimming on the edge of anger.

I tentatively closed them.

"Okay. Open," he whispered.

I opened my eyes and jumped in shock, gasping. My hand flew to my mouth. I was staring directly back at my emerald-green eyes, except it wasn't me.

"Dad?" I whispered to myself. He looked how I remembered him, stunningly handsome. However, the feeling quickly dissipated and anger seeped in.

I hadn't needed a cruel reminder of the reaches his brothers would go to. I had a scar stretching the length of my spine not letting me forget.

I did everything to keep my face even. At a glance or from a distance, it could easily have passed for my father. But standing this close and the longer I looked, some things weren't exact. The shape of his eyes were a bit off. And his nose, like Eli's, was infinitesimally longer.

"Point made, Eli." I knew it wasn't my dad. I was hurt and to avoid showing my tears, I turned quickly to walk away. "I wasn't trying to sneak out again. I was coming to find you and apologize for not telling you." The lump in my throat was thick as I started to sprint. I wasn't exactly sure where I was. I just knew I wanted to get away from the feeling.

An angry growl. "I'm sorry," he called to my back apologetically. And I could hear his boots jogging to catch up. "I'm just..." He placed a hand on my shoulder gently and pulled me back.

"Mean?" I wiped at the tears spilling down my cheeks with the back of my hand.

"I'm"—his hand dropped— "scared."

I looked up at him. "Of what?"

"I couldn't forgive them if they did something to you. I'm trying to make them see *this* isn't wrong." He shook his head.

For the first time I felt his fear under my skin, raising my hairs on end. "We will." I raised a palm to his cheek making him smile softly.

A sharp scream sliced through the silent forest. Eli's head cut upwards immediately in the direction it echoed from, and I followed his gaze.

"Come on!" he yelled. He grabbed me by the hand and pulled me along quickly.

My feet were hitting the ground hard, and I couldn't help but notice I didn't hear *his*. I watched his boots thrum against the dirt but still no sound and the house coming into view distracted me.

"Why are all the lights on?" I panted.

"Someone's hurt," he called.

My heart beat erratically. What if it was August? How could I have put her in this mess? Or anyone else for that matter? Eli let go of my hand and bolted up the back porch into the dining room. I stood still.

I froze at the fear of seeing her mangled as *I* had been. I could hear the roar of voices and running footsteps throughout the house. Time stood still, and I slowly walked up the steps and relief washed over me at the sight of August standing next to the immense dining room table crowded with bodies. She was biting her nails nervously.

"Who is it?" I asked.

She looked up, her eyes pink with tears, "Tristan," August choked in a small voice.

"It's okay." I went to put my arms around her but she pulled away.

"Don't." She turned and went to stand at the edge of the table.

I stared at her unsure how to soothe her as she went and stood by his side. I couldn't see past the people milling around him so I turned my attention to the front door.

"What are you doing?" I questioned a large Condemned, a wad of tobacco crammed into his gums.

"Bringing in the casualties." He pointed with his eyes at the body lying next to the door.

"Who did this?" I asked, shocked at what was in front of me.

Another member of his group filed in with a limp body he pulled from his shoulder and slung over the other lying by the front door. A petite girl with blond hair cropped into a pixie cut. Her thin face was covered in dirt, and narrow trails where tears had made their way down her cheeks were all that was visible of her pale complexion.

"Time to go!" a Fallen yelled at the others. Looming men swung large rifles over their shoulders as the wood groaned under the stress of their heavy boots.

"Where?" I questioned the same Saint I had passed earlier this evening.

"To find her and kill her." The Condemned smiled, placing a reassuring hand on my shoulder.

"Who?" I was shocked at how frank he was.

"The member of the Legion who did this." He walked away.

"One woman did this?" I looked at the world surrounding me, a dozen with weapons fearlessly leaving to fight for Eli's cause in the dark of night. My best friend crying over her new beau. Others leaning against the walls panting from the unknown battle they had seen.

Stricken with devastation, I set a quick pace past everyone out the back door. I needed to get away. I wasn't thinking about the danger outside. I couldn't believe this was happening.

* * *

Sitting nestled into one of the canopy swings on the tremendous back porch I clutched the macrame-like webbing threaded through my knuckles. Why would his brothers send someone from the Legion?

I didn't know any of those people whose bodies were heaped near the front door. Didn't know anyone who attended the gathering. And now they were suddenly dying for Eli. And maybe even for me.

The whole thing felt like some hypnagogic hallucination and I was just wandering through its dreamlike scape.

My fingers trembled at the thought. I hadn't wanted any of this. I was never one of those people with aspirations of something more. I liked that I was quiet and unassuming. And I liked Tristan too. Now my actions may have caused harm. Whether it was through any fault of my own or not didn't sit right with me. I was beginning to see what

Eli had meant before about me not understanding the full scope of what they could do. What all this had meant. I was out of my depth, and it was making me uneasy.

"I thought I saw you come out here earlier." Eli's smooth voice floated towards me.

The Colorado summer night had set in, and a cool breeze was rippling through the tree's tops, making way for starry skies overhead. I pulled my arms around me and began to sway to and fro in the swing.

"How's Tristan?" My eyes stayed focused on my feet drawing circles on the weathered redwood porch.

"Tristan will be fine, and August is a lovely nurse. Can I?" He gestured to the open space beside me.

I nodded.

"Don't be upset," he whispered.

"I can't believe any of this is happening."

"Everyone understands what they're facing. I'm sorry for the way I acted earlier. This is new to me."

"Well, we can figure this out together," I breathed.

"Would you like to go on a date with me?" I looked up at him, suddenly picking up on his nervousness.

"What?"

"I should have asked you earlier, but it never seemed like the right time."

"And now people are dying, it does?" I asked, puzzled.

"Well, if they're risking their lives then shouldn't we?"

He was right. These people had come together because they believed what we had done wasn't wrong. How could I deny them what they were standing up for. To be with whoever someone chooses.

"When?"

"Tomorrow night. Wait, where are you going?" he called.

"If I've got a date, I need to scour this place for a curling iron and something to wear," I calmly called over my shoulder.

I was nervous. What the hell do you wear on a date with an angel?

***

"We're walking?" I stood facing Eli on the edge of the property, the house fading into night behind us.

"Mm-hmm." He nodded slowly, smiling. "Is that a problem?"

"Nope." I smacked my lips together. "I love hiking." Not in a dress, but apparently I haven't figured out dating-angel-etiquette yet.

"Are you nervous?" I blurted.

A thick smile spread across Eli's face. "Yes." He stopped walking. "Angels primarily don't date."

I hadn't thought of it from his perspective. "Me too. What do you wear on a date with a…person like you?" I tugged at the bottom of the dress and pulled loose threads from the pale yellow lace.

"That dress is inspiring." He reached over and paused before withdrawing his hand.

It was a calm summer night, and we slowly walked down a well-worn path before we arrived at a river. It babbled and rushed over jagged rocks, hissing mist along its edges. He climbed a large boulder and reached down with a welcoming hand. I took it shyly and climbed up beside him. His black wavy hair and intense blue eyes were accentuated by the moonlight.

Ponderosas freckled the water's edge, and the Colorado woods hummed with the scent of cool pine and hints of sap.

We both sat in silence for a while, listening to water. "Are you sure it's okay to be here?" I asked, peering into the woods around us.

He turned, smiling at me sympathetically. "Promise." His palm gently caressed my upper arm before he pulled away.

I smiled, blushing and immediately felt calmer. His words were warming.

"What are you thinking?" he asked.

"Nothing," I yelped.

"Tell me."

"I don't want to ask. It might be rude."

"You can ask me anything." He twisted the lace on my dress between his fingertips.

"Anything?" I cocked my head sideways skeptically and he nodded. "Where are your wings?" I asked timidly.

A small laugh escaped through his nose. "Do you have a conscience?"

"Yes." I nodded, slowly wondering where this was leading.

"I can't see it, even though it's a part of you. Some things are intangible. And you can only see them when you need to use them. I see you make decisions based on that conscience, but it isn't something you wear all the time." His eyes focused on the lace between his fingertips. "May I ask *you* something?"

I nodded slowly.

"Who is Ethan to you?" His eyes turned to look over the water.

"My best friend." It came out naturally.

"He loves you though…more than a friend?" His fingers played while his look hardened.

"Yes," I whispered.

"Do you feel the same way about him?"

"No." I bit my lower lip nervously before I took a deep breath. At least I didn't want to.

His head dropped and he grinned wide before looking up at me to make eye contact. "Alright."

"Can I ask another one?" I looked at him curiously. "Will you explain the halos to me? Why aren't they floating above your head? Why are yours blue and the Legions' red?"

A soft chuckle escaped his lips. "It's rather simple. My *halo*, as you call it, is blue because I am one of the Guardian's *nine*. The placement on the arm shows rank. Ours aren't as close to the chest. Our rank is higher"—he used his fingers to encircle his forearm—"allowing freer roam. We can move between places with ease where the Legion cannot."

"How do you turn it on?" I interrupted. "Sorry." My shoulders drooped in embarrassment.

"They're attached to our nervous system. When things excite, anger, or sadden us, they change." His palms were spread wide across the rock and I couldn't help but stare at his forearm. But I saw nothing.

"Here?" I whispered as my fingertip grazed his pale skin.

"Yes." His eyes closed.

I couldn't stop. I *wanted* to touch him. My skin was raised, and a thick current pulsed over its surface. My fingertips slowly drew loose lines around his arm. Then suddenly, I could hear a low hum drumming in my ears. His fingers drew back gripping the rock. A blue glow of lightning pulsed through the inside of his forearm where my fingers had been, shooting into his palms. I stared hypnotized at his skin. I could see him biting his lip and I couldn't stop, I wanted more. The pull in my chest grew, rising at the sight of his halo reacting to me.

"How am I doing?" His voice broke my internal chatter.

"With?" Tilting my head to one side.

"Our second date." He swallowed, smiling.

"Beautifully." A warm grin flashed across my face.

I felt shy around him. His gaze held so much intensity it was unnerving.

"Lily?" he spoke softly.

"Yes?"

"I wanted to apologize. I'm sorry you're in the middle of this." A mixture of embarrassment and anxiousness washed over his face. "I knew better. I knew better from the moment I saw you watching me from the side of the road while I was hunting deer. I should've left, but I chalked it up to you being alone and human. I knew no one would believe you." He shrugged. "So I decided to stay. I knew better after our encounter in the park, but intrigue drove me to wait."

He stood up shaking his head in frustration. "We have etiquette we follow about interactions with humans. Relationships are out of the question. After Aurelius's *indiscretion*, it was clear why we couldn't—"

"Indiscretion? This has happened before?" I looked at him in surprise.

He sighed through his nose, thinking carefully before he spoke.

"Yes. Once with my brother Ecclesias. He was involved with an elderly man. A scholar during the fall of the Roman Empire. He'd grown to love him. And again during the early years of the Dark Ages. Aurelius and a woman named Antionette. It resulted in… It doesn't matter. A rule is a rule." He shook his head.

"Being born an angel sounds lonely." I changed the subject, feeling sorry for him all of a sudden. "A life where you can't get involved with the people who surround you sounds isolating."

"Forged," he corrected.

"I'm sorry?"

"We're not born. Guardians are forged. They imbue us with the power, our bonds." He touched his halo. "It's an honor." He smiled as he noticed my surprise.

"What were you before? People?" My mouth was agape.

"No one remembers, so they learn from those that came before them. The Forging abolishes your previous life. Alokin was a Saint, Aurelius a general in the Legion's army, besides Lucian, the others were lieutenants in the Legion." His brows furrowed with stress and quickly he pulled his lips up into a half smile. He continued before I could inquire, "Lucian was a rarity—he came after me—a Fallen."

My eyes widened, stunned. From what I understood, the Fallen rarely redeemed themselves, having committed egregious sins, and when they did they often rose to the lowest ranks of the legions. I couldn't imagine what could be so terrible to cast them to Earth when getting involved with a human was so wrong.

"What were *you*?" I asked quietly.

He paused for a long while.

"The first."

"You were the *first* guardian forged?" I leaned into him with empathetic eyes, astonished.

"Yes. There was no one before me to tell me of my previous life." He went silent.

"How long ago?"

"I don't know. I no longer remember that either. We should get home."

I looked up to see his eyes peering into mine. I noticed for the first time what was around us. The water in the river had pulled away from the rock we were perched upon and the mist was backing away, spiraling beyond where we were, as though everything was purposely avoiding us.

"It's already midnight." He stood and reached down for my hand.

"We've been here three hours?" I looked around, confused.

Eli dropped softly to the grass and turned. His palms wrapped gently around my waist, picking me up effortlessly and lowering me lightly to the ground. We tentatively stood chest to chest, and I let out a slow breath.

"I want this," he murmured sadly.

I nodded, worried words might steal from the weak breaths I was holding onto. My arms hung limp at my sides, and my fingers trembled. The last kiss we shared almost drew the life completely out of me. Maybe humans weren't meant to kiss angels? I didn't care.

One of his hands swept upwards holding my face, his palm warm against my cheek, the other wrapped around into the small of my back. He didn't pause as he had before. There was no hesitation. Effortlessly, he lowered me to the damp grass. I arched my spine against the wanting pull in my chest. He hovered over me, his palms pressed into the ground on either side of my head. His body cast heat down onto mine.

I wrapped my trembling thighs around his waist pulling him closer, allowing my hands to cup his jaw. I pulled him to my lips. He tasted sweet and warm, I drew in the frigid air, pushing it towards my lungs, willing them to keep going. The pull below my collar bone roared louder and louder. My heart was frantic, erratically beating behind my sternum. His tongue found mine with ease and his chest pressed into me as his arms wrapped around my torso. I vaguely heard the wind pick up around us. The trees creaked as though stressed from the breeze.

I didn't think about hurting Ethan or Jarrett or how they felt. This wasn't the same. My fingers curled into his thick, inky hair. His chest hummed and I could taste the electricity burning between us. I could feel the air in his lungs begging for more. We couldn't breathe but we didn't want to stop.

One of his hands pulled away and reached down to my thigh caressing the length to my hip. Reaching under my dress, his fingers lightly grazed my ribs before moving around to my back, clutching my shoulder blade. Our hips thrummed against each other.

His pulse gained speed, matching mine, and then suddenly, it was like our blood synchronized in our veins. Followed by our lungs breathing in time together, tongues swirling in perfect chorused unison.

"Eli. I…" I arched my neck back, my eyes open, breaking away for breath. "I want more," I whispered. I closed my eyes as he kissed the length of my neck. His halo glowing an impossible blue, illuminating a ring around us. I could feel the earth begin to tremble at my back.

His heartbeat echoed in *my* ribcage. He paused looking up. "We're not alone." His voice grew dark.

He shot up, forcing me upright, I scrambled to my feet, clutching his hand helplessly. "Who is it?" I begged, terror making my vocals tremble.

"I don't know," he growled.

He quickly turned to face me, bending slightly to look directly into my eyes. He was soft as he addressed me. "Listen to me, Lily. Trust nothing." His voice grew and he let go. "Get away from here!" He looked somewhere beyond the trees, seeing something I obviously could not.

I turned to run and hide, understanding what he had wanted me to do. Feeling his wishes burn into my core. I leapt around the boulder and into the water, splashing along the edge stooping to stay hidden among the mist until I found one curving over I could crouch underneath.

I kept my lips tight, breathing heavily through my nose. I covered my mouth with my hands, afraid they might hear something. My back pressing into the wet rock, I looked the way I had come, too afraid to inch outwards for a better view. The water lapped against my ankles as it streamed past. The mountain run off was still icy. It was early in the summer and it made my feet ache. I tried my best to ignore the pain rising up my shins into my knees.

Angry voices began to grow and reach back toward me. I couldn't make out what they were saying, and I closed my eyes to help me focus. Still nothing.

Tears silently tumbled down my cheeks and my stomach burned with fear. Not for my sake, but for Eli's. What would they do to him? Kill him? I wanted to scream out and distract them but a voice inside me urged me not to.

I didn't know how long I stood crouched there. Hours? Minutes? The ground shook around me and crashing limbs made the rock I was holding onto tremble. I pushed my head back into the stone.

Then as suddenly as it began, it stopped. Everything was blanketed with a quiet void. I didn't move. My heartbeat shook with fear as heavy footsteps drew closer.

"Lily?" Calm washed over me as Eli's voice broke the darkness. "Everything's safe. You can come out."

Trust nothing echoed into the depths of my stomach. Reaching out, I realized the pull in my chest felt distant, not the ache I typically felt when we were near. I wiped the tears and pressed my back further into my darkened hiding spot. I stood cold and still atop my numb soles.

The stranger's footsteps, pretending to be Eli, moved on. On the brink of collapse, I pinched my eyes shut trying to keep in the wracking sobs I felt.

Moments passed and a hand flew over my mouth out of the darkness and an arm wrapped around my waist. I tried to scream but the grip was too tight. I was horror-struck.

They spun me around and my eyes found soft hazel ones staring back at me. His hand dropped.

"Ethan?" I asked, astonished.

"Middle of something?" Ethan leaned sideways and peered around the edge of the rock. "Let's get you out of here."

Shock mingled with relief, and my voice twisted into a whimper. "How are you here?"

"Because my condescending mother shacked up with my arrogant father. They're gone. Let's go," he whispered, holding me by the arm and tugging me along through the water.

I was relieved and confused, I looked back and there was no evidence of any of the brothers, Legion, or Eli as I clambered up the hill at Ethan's heels. I swallowed hard and hoped Eli was going to be alright.

6

The Unborn

"He's not here yet?" I was pacing and rolled my shoulders to push away the anxiety.

"No. Why would they have come?" the slim Fallen pondered aloud.

August came to my side. "It'll be okay." She patted my back gently trying to assuage my fear. My hands were still shaking from the encounter.

"I am surprised they're acting so soon." Tristan pinched his chin in thought. I cringed at the sight of his misplaced shoulder and wondered what they would be doing to Eli.

"Who?" Ethan piped in behind me.

"Ethan, go home." I turned to him again.

"I'm not going anywhere until you tell me what the hell is going on!" He raised his voice.

"Ethan, you heard her! Go home!" August snapped at him.

"Listen, blondie, I'm not going anywhere!" He pointed a heated finger in her face, edging closer.

"Who is this guy?" Tristan asked, putting himself between Ethan and August.

"Lily is almost my wife!" Ethan called back from behind me.

The room stood still. August smacked her hand to her forehead, shaking her head back and forth slowly in disbelief.

I groaned, "No, I'm not. Ethan, *leave*," I pleaded through gritted teeth at him as I pulsed my hands gently at the crowd.

"Yeah, Ethan, leave!" a bulky Condemned called casually as he lounged against a countertop.

"Who the hell are *you*?" Ethan shot caustically.

"Marcus. Why? You want to get into it, pretty boy? Maybe I can teach you something." A slow smile flashed across his face.

"No!" I screamed. The buzzing chatter in the room stopped. I spun on my heel and placed both hands on Ethan's chest pressing him back through the front door and out onto the porch slamming it behind me. "You need to go home." I stood in front of him with arms crossed.

"I'm not going anywhere! I want to know what the hell happened out there. Who the fuck are all these people, Lily? Why is August here?" He continuously looked through the windows while he spoke.

I realized then he wouldn't relent. "I was on a date." I braced myself for the backlash of hurt. But I needed him out of here before something happened to him. It was the only thing I could think to do. I watched him stop.

"You were..." He repeated it slowly, trailing off while he processed what I had said. "After the other night?"

There it was.

I looked at him and caught the hint of anguish in his eyes. "Yes. I told you I was in the middle of something right now, and you chose to ignore it. Leave me alone," I responded coldly. "I don't want to see you."

He stood still for a moment and then opened his mouth to say something, but paused and turned, quietly walking away. I stood still until I could no longer see the taillights of his truck down the road before I walked inside.

"Where is she?" Eli's voice cut through the bodies and hit me square in the chest. He jogged through the room and straight towards me, without hesitation he wrapped his arms around me kissing my face. "Oh, thank God. I thought everything was okay until I saw Zacarius break away as we were leaving and started looking for you."

"I'm fine. He pretended to be you. But it didn't feel the same, so I didn't move." I whispered the last part.

"Why were they here?" Marcus called. I now had a name for the face.

Eli sighed, his arms never left my waist, "Aurelius was displeased with Tristan."

August and I both looked at him at a loss while others around the expansive room were unfazed with the revelation.

"Why?" August shrugged, confused.

If I hadn't been looking I wouldn't have caught the exchange between Eli and Tristan. "Aurelius cares," I murmured slowly.

"I heard that, but why?" August repeated.

Tristan was important to him. "Because you're something to him." I pointed.

Tristan chimed, "They *will* find out sooner or later." He was speaking loud enough so everyone could hear but was talking directly to August.

"They haven't been telling us something, August." I watched her face grow with worry.

"I'm his son," Tristan stated matter-of-factly.

A small gasp caught my lips as I looked to Eli for answers. August on the other hand was immediately frantic.

"So we're already in hot water with these guys because of these two lovers over here." She thumbed over her shoulder. "But let's add to the fact one of them has a son who is on our side, risking his life?" Anger pierced her vocals. "You have to be fucking kidding me! Why don't we chum the water a little more?" She threw her hands up, marching away towards the stairs.

"I'll go up and talk to her." I reached behind Marcus and snagged a bottle of wine from the rack on the counter. "I'm happy you're okay." I smiled toward Eli before I walked away ready for the day to be over.

* * *

I felt a poke at my cheek. "Tired. Kill me another day," I whined into the pillow. They poked again. "Ugh. Seriously," I grumbled. I opened one eye to see August standing poking my cheek repeatedly as she crouched down on my side of the bed. "What time is it?"

"Five a.m.," she whispered.

"What the shit, August? Go back to bed."

"Come on, get up," she pleaded in a whisper. I glanced back over my shoulder to notice she was fully dressed.

"What time did you get up?"

"Seriously Lily, please get up. I need your help…and hurry." I noticed her face for the first time. It was white with a hint of fear.

"What's wrong? Where's Eli?" I bolted upright in the bed.

"The guys are fine. Please get dressed." She handed me my jeans as I swung them under my feet, pausing frequently to yawn while she waited by the door, constantly glancing down the hallway.

She lured me through the house, swatting at me when I shuffled my feet and didn't follow suit tiptoeing. The morning sun was bright, and I was surprised so few people were milling about. I was more alert once we went outside and she headed purposefully into the woods.

"Okay, now we're being stupid? Running away from the prodigal son is not going to help our situation, you know. I thought you were over this? After talking last night, you know…dating the world's *only* Nephilim, *hybrid-angel-babies*, and all that?" I quoted some of last night's conversations to her back, continuously rubbing my eyes and stretching. I didn't attempt to keep up with her brisk pace, instead shuffling along. She would stop to look around and change direction suddenly.

"They're going to get mad if they find us missing." I continued to call remarks up toward her.

"Shut up!" She shushed me. "Over here."

I stopped, bending to tie my shoe when I stood to find her gone, "August," I droned in a monotone. I heard rustling and followed it. I spotted her up ahead talking to someone behind a tree. *What the hell is she doing?* "Seriously, Miss Bayne, what is wrong with you?"

She turned to me, smiling awkwardly with wide eyes. "Surprise."

The breath left my lungs. "Jarrett?" I whispered.

August was nodding.

There stood August's oldest brother Jarrett Bayne. My—the *other* thing I was in the middle of. I hadn't had the time to think about him.

"I thought I would come early." His hands were tucked in his pockets. He was wearing a faded gray T-shirt, jeans, and his sienna eyes were cast downwards in a bashful manner while his sandy hair was perfectly combed.

I stood for a moment processing what was in front of me. I couldn't fight it. The attraction was instant—it always had been. I was elated he was here and my heart sang in his presence. My cheeks flooded with color.

Jarrett was my boy next door. My good guy dappled with cute freckles across his perfectly sun-kissed cheeks. He made me feel warm and happy. This wasn't the serious Eli, my dark star hypnotically pulling me in. This wasn't the sweet Ethan who listened and flirted shamelessly.

This was Jarrett.

My Jarrett.

After everything that had happened with me and Eli, I had overlooked him. I was so wrapped up in the chaos I was tangled in that I hadn't thought to call him. To tell him we should cancel. He shouldn't be here. It wasn't safe. I had completely forgotten he was flying in to visit, and now it was too late.

But the truth of the matter was, after seeing him standing here, in the golden light of the morning, I didn't want him to leave. The fluorescent light of my old life began to flicker on again.

"Well, are you going to say hello?" August demanded.

I yelped and ran to him, jumping up. He caught me as my legs wrapped around his waist, and I kissed him excitedly.

"I missed ya, Lily Bear," he whispered as we pressed our foreheads together. "A lot."

I could feel my throat hum in approval. Jarrett was my heart. I didn't move. I closed my eyes and inhaled his smell so deeply, hoping it would stick to the insides of my lungs.

"Excuse me? Yeah, we have to go!" August interjected, wide-eyed.

"Go?" I asked, clearing the hypnotized haze he created.

"I have a plan," she spoke over her shoulder as she looked for something. "Aha!" She yanked a small backpack lodged under a root and fished out a cell phone. She continued to speak. "Here, change into these clothes. Hopefully, enough saw you in your poor outfit choice as we left." She marched around holding the phone out searching for a signal.

"Um…" I held the jeans and slim-cut shirt she picked out in front of me. "You want me to wear this?" I looked at Jarrett.

"I won't peek." He grinned, placing his fingers over his eyes moving one aside.

"That counts as peeking." I giggled and turned to change.

"Hi, honey." There was a long pause as she looked at me giving a thumbs-up about the outfit she had picked. "No, I'm not mad. I needed to clear my head and wanted to go for a walk, but I got lost. Can you come find me alone? I think we should talk." She winked at me.

I stood next to Jarrett as my hands found his. "Crazy morning."

"Yeah, August said that. I probably should have let her know I was coming early, but my brothers are always suspicious, and I didn't want to risk a leak in the plan." His smile was golden and intoxicating.

"I'm happy you're here." The words fell from my mouth. "I missed you." I could feel my cheeks blush red as I inadvertently spoke the sentence. "I meant—"

"I missed you too." He smiled, bending to scoop my face into his palms and kiss the tip of my nose.

"Alright, he'll be here in a second." She smiled.

"Who?" Jarrett asked as he played with my fingers.

She looked at me unsure of how to answer. "My new boyfriend."

Surfacing for air for the first time, it occurred to me how we were in unsafe territory. Shit. What the hell were we going to do? It's not like I could stay at Eli's with some guy I had been dating.

"Umm?" I pondered out loud.

August picked up on my subtle realization.

"Okay, don't panic! I have a plan. It can go one of two ways. I'm really inching towards the good way!" She nodded, grinning in approval.

"What are the two—" I started before Tristan's voice cut me off.

"I thought you said to meet you out here alone, Lily doesn't count as being alone." Tristan approached, brandishing a playful grin. "Whoa." He looked over, suddenly realizing Jarrett was here. "Who are you?" He pointed and I watched as his eyes followed the length of my arm and come to rest on Jarrett's hand holding mine.

"Oh, sorry. Nice to meet you." Jarrett thrust forward his free palm smiling wide. "I'm August's oldest brother"—nodding a head at her and then me— "and Lily's boyfriend." I didn't want to deny it felt wonderful to hear him say the words and my cheeks burned pink.

"No kidding. August, Lily's boyfriend is here." He swung an arm around her shoulders, her blond curls bouncing under the weight. "I met her husband and now her boyfriend," he said through the corner of his mouth.

"What was that?" Jarrett asked, looking confused.

"Inside joke. So"—he turned to her—"how do you suppose you two are going to pull this off?"

"With your help." She grinned. "Please." She glossed on her best pleading eyes.

"What?" He stepped back. "You want me to help. Uh-uh! I'm not going against *him*." Tristan nodded his head back toward the house. "If this is your brilliant plan, then you better get a backup."

"Who's *him*?" Jarrett questioned at my side.

"Listen." August turned to face Tristan. "If you help us, I will forget the dad fiasco. But if you don't…" She crossed her arms slowly, and I wondered how someone so small was so capable of appearing this menacing.

He exhaled slowly. "Has she always been this bossy?" he asked Jarrett.

"Since she could talk." He grinned.

Tristan chuckled along with Jarrett and for a moment I was lost in how normal this was.

Tristan tried to stare her down, arms crossed, but the odds were against him because August didn't waiver. "Ugh! Fine! Lily come here." He waggled a finger at me.

We stood huddled together tightly as he began to speak, barely above a whisper. "Listen, Eli leaves in a little bit for some business and should be gone for a few days. I'm meant to look after the two of you. He's assuming you two are both sleeping—which you should be. I'll head back to the house with August so he can see her while you head that way towards the road with Jarrett. We'll come around the corner and pick you up. If anything happens to you, this isn't on me." He pointed a stern finger at both of us.

"Here's my handy dandy lighter in case you come across *unwelcome* guests." She pushed it nonchalantly into my back pocket.

"Thanks." I smiled as Tristan turned, grabbing August by the hand and spinning her back towards the house.

"See you in a bit!" She grinned, waving excitedly. "Knew he'd do it!" He tugged at her as she spoke the last sentence.

"What was that about?" Jarrett's casual voice blew the haze towards me again.

"Nothing. August being August." I grinned, trying to change the subject quickly.

"Tristan seems nice." He reached down and plucked my hand up as we walked side-by-side.

"Yeah, they're inseparable." I tried to keep up the conversation while I kept looking around periodically for danger.

"I'm happy for her. Hope she doesn't put him through the wringer." He played with my fingers while I kept a casual pace.

"Yeah, me too. August seems to be taken with him."

"His eyes are kind of weird." He looked down at the ground pondering his statement.

"The silver? Oh, yeah. Eerie, right?" I shuddered involuntarily, remembering Aurelius's gray-blue eyes so clearly from my memories. Watching for them and expecting them to appear between the trees at any moment.

"Yeah, they almost look unnatural. I bet his parents are foreign." He kept talking, unaware I had laughed amidst his comment.

"We're here. They should be coming around that corner up there."

"Maybe she was Finnish?" He rubbed the whiskers on his chin.

"It shouldn't take long." I was becoming impatient.

"Don't the Finnish have light eyes?" He looked up at the sky in wonderment.

I turned and looked at him. He wasn't nervous they might appear from somewhere between the trees and end us effortlessly. He didn't care a massive house up the road was filled with deadly people risking their lives. He was here surprising his *girlfriend* at what he believed was her work. He was untouched by it all. I couldn't help but let the Bayne warmth that envelopes you take over. My eyes misted as I felt the smile warming my cheeks.

"What's wrong?" he asked, becoming concerned for the first time.

"You're here," I breathed.

* * *

I stared off, reliving the day's events with a smile playing on the corners of my lips. Tristan felt that we might be safe with Jarrett around. Since human intervention was frowned upon, he felt the brothers and anyone in the Legion would be unlikely to attack. They would wait for him to be gone before moving in.

I insisted we stay at our apartment to keep Jarrett from suspecting anything was amiss, and Tristan agreed to watch over everyone while keeping his finger on the pulse of danger. If anything picked up or a hint of something unsafe flickered, we were immediately to tuck tail and fall back to the Eli's house.

As far as explaining to Jarrett that I was dating an angel named Eli? Well, August felt that it was better we left it on the back burner for now. We didn't want to drag him in to any of this. Hard as it was to see me with her brother, knowing Eli and I were together on some level too, I think she was just as happy to be in the comfort of our former life as much as I was.

It made sense.

It was familiar.

Easy.

Safe.

So I was going to take a page from August's book and just figure it out another time. Right now, I was going to enjoy myself.

"Chew, August." Jarrett laughed at his little sister.

"You would think we don't let her eat." Tristan, too, stared at the tiny blond forking everyone's plate on the table.

"Hey!" she garbled. "Don't worry about it. Tristan's paying." She grinned at her brother.

He gave her a sideways look and then pulsed a hand at the table. "Yeah, guys. Apparently, *I* got this."

"Well, it's not like you can't afford it. You've been around forever." She paid no mind to her statement and continued to eat.

Tristan and I stared at her, surprised.

"How do you mean, *been around*?" Jarrett interjected, politely making conversation.

We all paused. "I mean he's well traveled." She took a big bite of pasta hanging from her fork and nodded energetically towards me while elbowing Tristan.

"So, what do you want to do tonight?" I diverted. I could honestly say I didn't hear his response. I only could focus as his palm came to rest on my thigh underneath the table.

My mind wandered playfully, daydreaming about the many moments like that one. As his fingers played with mine while he talked to everyone during the car ride. When he placed an arm comfortably around my shoulders and gently tousled my hair when we curled up to watch a movie. Or when he kissed me on the forehead softly before falling asleep.

I listened to him breathing slowly, a hand barely resting on his chest, the other tucked under his pillow.

I inched away from his side and tiptoed from the room. Sleep evaded me tonight. Was it guilt? I had somehow acquired two boyfriends with no idea how to go forward from here.

I shook my head as I passed the muffled giggles of August and Tristan in her room. She would say not to worry about it and just have fun. Everything felt so normal back here at the apartment. August *entertaining* in her bedroom, me unable to sleep. But how could I have fun when so much was on the line?

"How often am I going to have to track you down?" Eli stood shadowed in the dark living room. He wore an expensive watch that glittered in the moonlight and loafers to match. His ensemble tied his impressive look together.

"Breaking and entering is illegal," I whispered, folding my arms and cocking out a hip.

"Do you see anything broken?" he spoke softly with a wave of his hand.

"You didn't need to come."

"The fact I'm standing here is proof I did. Tristan is too busy with Miss Bayne to be watching over you." He stepped closer and his voice began to rise heatedly.

The ache below my collarbone rumbled, sensing his frustration. I closed my eyes, trying not to get distracted from his exceedingly magnificent blue ones.

"Listen, we're fine. We are *all* fine." My vocals were barely audible.

He pulled my face into his massive palms. "Open your eyes." Anger brimming through his words. "This can either be simple or difficult."

My eyes shot open catching him staring directly into mine, I quickly pinched them shut and continued, "Simple? Nothing about this is simple, Eli! I'm trying to figure out what I am to *you* and what I *want* from Jarrett. Up until a couple of months ago, my biggest concerns were how to keep my job, who I should date, and if I was getting enough sleep. Now, I'm illegally making out with some angel on a river bank, while his brothers are trying to start a war I may or may not have instigated between a bunch of beings, who I still am trying to comprehend being real! So I'm sorry I want a couple of nights with my old life!"

"Eli?" August whispered, shocked, from the hallway. "You're supposed to be out of town!"

"August, stay out of this!" I pointed at her.

"Well, then stop yelling." She combed through her hair with her fingers.

"Will you talk to her and explain Tristan can't watch all of you?" Eli pursed his lips.

"We're not yelling!" I ignored his statement.

"You're whisper-yelling!" She pointed back at me.

"Hey, what's going on out here?" Tristan tiptoed into the living room nude, firmly holding a strategically placed pillow in front of him. "Eli? I thought you were out of town. You're back...very early."

"I'll deal with the two of you later!" He pointed over my shoulder and then walked towards the door turning on his heel in the darkness.

"We're going to be alright." I did my best to pacify him. "I'll come back in a few days." If he wanted me to after this.

He placed a gentle palm below my ear caressing my jaw with his thumb and bent to lightly kiss my neck. He sighed through his nose.

"So willful." The warmth of his whisper lingered in my ear as I walked back towards the living room after he left.

"Great, Harper, you just got my boyfriend killed! Wonderful! You know sometimes you can be really selfish," she scoffed unapologetically.

"This was your idea," I murmured, astonished.

"Irrelevant!" She flicked her hands at me in disgust, walking away down the hallway. "Tristan, get in here and drop your pillow. This might be our last night ever, thanks to Lily!" She shut the door with a quiet force, and I stood in the dark living room alone.

Why did I get the feeling Eli wasn't going to stand idly by while I figured this out? Tomorrow my answer was about to come hard and fast.

7

When Blood Runs Green

"I'm afraid," I breathed, my eyes opening to stare straight into the blackness of a night sky. Untainted by city lights, the stars flickered brilliantly.

"Don't be frightened, Sparrow. They will pass," her voice whispered beside me.

My back was pressed into a crescent of dirt. I could feel a hand clutching mine at my hip, slight trembles shivered through my fingertips and the hand squeezed mine gently. We looked through a cage of branches above our foxhole, leaves rustling in the breeze of the night.

"Temper your breathing. That arrow was tipped with ancestral blood," she murmured urgently.

"A tracking dart?" I tasted the panic behind my realization.

"They're gaining wisdom." Her hand suddenly clenched mine.

"We are the night. We are the ground," I reassured and her hand relaxed.

There was no room. I couldn't turn to see with whom I was speaking or where we might be. When a twig broke nearby, I inhaled through my nose slowly and my eyes knew to look the way we had come.

I listened, hoping for it to be an errant animal pausing while they grazed.

My jaw tightened as the sight of a man rose above us into view. He held an arrow at ready, the end illuminated green as he scanned the forest surround.

It happened so quickly in the fashion that dreams do, where you don't fully understand how it came to be. One moment we're lying still, and the next we're bursting from the grounding running so fast wind was rushing past my ears.

I looked down at an arrow that was broken, puncturing between the soft tissues of my lower ribs. I feared further damage by removing it, so I continued to run. The sounds of him grunting in our wakes, his heavy footfalls a fierce reminder he was not far behind. Arrows soared past our heads with a definitive whistle when pain seared hot through my shoulder blade. Looking down, another arrow exited below my collarbone, and I knew I was not going to keep my pace for much longer.

Turning back I saw her, the one who referred to me as Sparrow. Clothes slim cut and a hood pulled over her, she turned her face before I could see and the hood fell exposing vivid auburn hair, a pale jawline reflected moonlight. She held a gun arm's length and fired.

"Run!" she screamed. "Sever our paths!" Her frantic vocals echoed as she dropped a clip and swiftly snapped in another.

Without pause, I turned and hurdled over a downed tree. I continued until my own footfalls broke the stillness, yet I refused to stop until her scream yanked my chest backwards and I halted immediately. My head snapped in her direction, and I stood, exhausted, with a heavy breath through my nostrils.

Had he won? Was one of us captured? My body ached, drawing me painfully back to her, but I slowly jogged onward and kept my eyes forward.

* * *

"Wake up." I could feel Jarrett's hands pressing into the pillow on either side of my head as he hovered over me. "Open"—he kissed my eyelids softly, and I fought the smile growing in my cheeks— "your eyes. I miss you too much, and I'm jealous of sleep for monopolizing you this way."

"Even though I'm dreaming about you?" I whispered, pulling him into a soft kiss.

"She's here." He grinned, kissing me around the words. "What are we going to do today?"

"What would you like to do?" I asked, twisting my legs between his as he pulled me closer. We lay on our sides, the fluffy down comforter I hadn't felt in weeks pulled over our heads.

This felt good. Being away from the powerful beings in the forest. Maybe I would never go back and they would just leave me alone eventually?

"Be with you," he murmured into my neck.

"I agree." I grew rosy with his compliment.

I could hear the water running to the shower as I slipped a sweatshirt over my head and fluffed my hair walking out into the hallway.

"Me now." August sat curled into Tristan's side on the couch as he held a bowl of cereal they were sharing. She popped her mouth open at the waiting spoon he held.

"Morning, Lily." He didn't turn when he greeted me.

"Did you guys have a nice—" A brisk knock on the door threw all our heads in that direction.

Tristan pushed the bowl into August's hands and pulled a thick curved knife from between the cushions. "Both of you get in the hallway."

"What for?" I asked.

They stared at me momentarily. "We don't know who it is, Lily," August whispered. "Where's my brother?"

"In the shower." I thumbed over my shoulder. "Do you honestly think anyone we should worry about is going to be courteous enough to knock on the door first?" I crossed my arms, staring at them skeptically, while I walked to answer it. "Seriously, I think we'll be okay."

The knock repeated. They both stood frozen facing my back as I swung the door wide and my breath went cold.

"Lil!" Their voices hit in unison. "Where is he?" they yelled back into my apartment.

The remaining five of August's brothers were standing crammed together in our entryway. I stood in stunned disbelief.

"You can't be here yet!" August was astonished as they all appeared.

"We got your text last night. Jarrett flew down here before us!" Grey craned his neck to look further into the apartment, hoping to catch a glimpse of his oldest brother.

I hadn't texted anyone.

Fuck.

Eli.

So this was his grand scheme? The Baynes had already planned to come down for the Fourth of July. August and I had decided days ago she would go off to entertain them, explaining away my absence with an emergency at work. But with the meeting and his brothers showing up during our date and my fleeing to see Ethan, we had forgotten everything. There was no way I could duck out now, and Eli knew I would never put my family in danger like this.

"He's..." My mouth hung agape, and I wasn't quite sure how to respond.

"Dammit!" Grey clapped his hands together.

"We've missed you, Lily!" Trip elbowed forward through the

doorway and wrapped both burly arms around me. "She smells like flowers, guys!"

One by one I was smushed in burly hugs.

"Hi, Lily." Bennett smiled warmly and bent to politely peck my cheek. The youngest of all her brothers, he was by far the largest, towering over everyone and thing. "I tried." He shrugged sweetly, his personality mirroring Jarrett's the closest.

"It's okay." I gave an empathetic look. "I know how they are." I closed the door and joined everyone in the living room.

They dropped their bags to the floor, and it was hard to hear over the hustle and bustle of voices.

I stared at the intimidating group before me. Trip and Tate were identical twins and usually the criminals of the group. They often spent more time moderating Bayne games than applying their skills to something more practical.

Grey and Logan were mostly referred to as the playboy twins. Blond hair and blue eyes women were weak to resist, they often sent disheveled girls parading through the morning light after a night out.

I looked to August for help and realized quickly there would be none. Her and Tristan's mouths hung open in shock.

"What's up with the sketchy neighborhood, Lil?" Tate was peeking through my wooden blinds. "Those bros look shady, like a motorcycle gang."

"We should pledge!" Trip shoved at his twin as he, too, peered through the window.

"I bring leather to life." Tate clicked his tongue approvingly.

"I have never seen—" I poked my fingers through the blinds and spread them. My heart skipped in my chest as I saw who they were referring to. There on the street below were three massive men I recognized, Marcus, and two others I didn't know yet. All members of the Condemned leaning against heavy motorcycles chatting casually.

"Subtle, Eli," I snorted under my breath.

"Lily, can we have a word with you?" Tristan chinned me in the direction of August's bedroom. I glanced towards the boys raiding my refrigerator and followed.

"Eli has some of the *family* perched out front," I chuffed and discreetly attempted to speak in code.

"Good." Tristan nodded, pacing back and forth in August's room.

"Good? Are you kidding? I tell him we'll be fine, and this is his solution? Secret service crap?" I shook my head, folding my arms angrily at the idea.

"Yeah, Harper, *we'll* be fine." August motioned to the three of us. "Tristan can't look out for this many bodies. Think about it!" She was pulling on a pair of jeans hurriedly.

I hadn't thought about that. One bodyguard for nine bodies isn't going to be enough. I didn't want to admit they were right.

"I get why he did it. This many humans would make any Ethereal reluctant about intervening. And if you weren't willing to go back to the house, this was his only option." He rubbed his whiskers anxiously.

That didn't sit right with me either. I didn't like the idea of using any of the Baynes, let alone almost all of them, as some kind of protective boundary to me.

"Well, what are we going to—" August started.

"Hey, what the heck—" Jarrett's voice cut down the hallway.

"There he is!" Trip yelled.

I pulled open the door and ran to the living room with August and Tristan at my heels. They had dog piled on Jarrett and all I could see was his hand poking out of the pack over their shouts.

"Who is this guy?" Grey was standing next to Tristan comparing himself in height.

"Yeah?" Logan chimed from a barstool with a mouthful of *my* frozen waffles.

"August's boyfriend." I grinned at August and Tristan, knowing they had wanted to finish our conversation.

"August has a boyfriend?" The twins popped up. "Auggie, why didn't you say anything?"

"It'll be the perfect weekend to break him in!" Grey grinned.

"No!" August spun around the room pointing at everyone. "He will not partake in this weekend's activities!" she scolded them.

"What's this weekend?" Tristan asked, confused.

"Um, only the greatest extended weekend of the year!" Trip stood next to me swinging an arm around my shoulders. "It's our time to shine. This is the weekend when we can really be ourselves. It's 'Freedom Weekend'!" He palmed the air as if the words were written in it.

"What's that?" Tristan asked.

"Fourth of July." Bennett leaned back into the couch unamused.

"Oh God." I panicked.

"What?" Jarrett asked.

"Bayne boys…" I didn't want to say it. "And fireworks."

"Huzzah!" they all called. "This is about to be the greatest weekend of your life, Lil!"

* * *

I groaned into the mattress. "No more," I croaked.

"I'm sorry," Jarrett whispered while he lay beside me. "It's been a long day. Why don't we lock the door?"

"Uh-huh." I nodded face down.

I could feel him slide from the bed beside me. "You know, maybe this whole thing won't be terrible. I could lie and push back my flight, stay a day or two longer, and we could be alone." He shrugged.

I smiled meekly at his adorable attempt to comfort me. "Well, that would be nice. I don't want to share." I pouted sitting upright to face him.

"I'll call the airline in the morning." As he was shutting the door, a hand stopped it.

"Calling the airline to stay a little longer, big brother?" Grey strutted in, and Jarrett's shoulders dropped.

"He was going to call the airline?" Trip asked. "See, Grey? I told you it would be a good idea to sneak in. We would've never heard if Bennett had been here crying like a baby." He thumped his brother's chest in triumph.

"Where is Bennett?" I disappointingly changed the subject.

"We got back first. He's probably moping about what happened at the brewery." Grey nodded.

"It was cruel," Jarrett interjected.

"It was a joke. Besides we didn't think the waitress would actually get him the booster seat." Grey defended their actions.

"The bib made it golden." Trip high-fived Grey, and they both doubled over in laughter.

I looked at Jarrett in time to catch a glimpse of a smirk. Despite his mellow demeanor, in comparison he still had the heart of a Bayne.

"Are they here?" Logan called from the front hallway.

"In the bedroom!" Grey hollered a hand beside his mouth.

"Phase two! Everyone, time to get man pretty. Except you, Jarrett, you're wearing what you have on." Logan shoved at his brother as he entered my room that was apparently becoming the meet-up area.

"What are we going to do now?" I snapped my mouth shut. I didn't want to know.

"We're going out to the bar." Logan grinned enthusiastically as he fished for something in his brother's bag.

"I'm not going to go. I think I'm going to hang out here." I faked a yawn and stretched pretending to be tired.

"That's too bad. It would be really fun. It's always fun going here, fresh meat, and *he* always attracts women like honey." Logan held a shirt up to his chest and quickly dismissed it, tossing it aside.

"Who?" I pondered the out of place comment.

"Ethan! Mom swears she never had an affair, but nobody pulls in the girls like that besides Grey and I." His arms poked through the holes in the T-shirt he decided on.

My face grew white, and I could feel the anger swelling in my gut.

"You're cool with that, right, Jarrett? Ethan always had that little flame burning for your girl, you know," Tate jabbed.

"You guys almost ready?" August called. She walked into my room which everyone was using as a mass dressing area. She was wearing apple-red heels with lipstick to match and a white dress so tight it could have been painted on. Her bouncy curls that were usually strewn about were sultry. "Are you wearing your customary jeans and T-shirt outfit, Harper?" She cocked out a hip and smacked her lips together as she stared into her phone camera she was using as a mirror.

"You're going too?" I asked skeptically.

"I haven't been out in forever. Shit yes, I am! I need my clutch." I could hear her rummaging around in her bedroom a minute later.

I knew that meant I either had to stay here with the brutish bodyguards outside, or I would have to go to a bar with all the Bayne boys.

"Knock knock?" Ethan's smooth voice called out.

Grey and Logan hopped to their feet jogging to the door. "He's here!" They beamed like starstruck fangirls.

"You invited Ethan here?" I asked the remaining brothers in the room.

"Yeah, we're all walking together," Trip said.

I couldn't help but roll my eyes and assume Ethan played some part in all of this. *He can never stay away when I ask him to.* I strolled into the hallway as the anger filled my gut, ready to tell him off.

"I thought I made it clear…" I looked up surprised.

"Hey, Harper. This is Amanda." Ethan smiled caustically as he strolled into the apartment.

"Alexis," she corrected.

"That's right…sexy Lexi." He winked, and in turn, she giggled.

"Sexy Lexi?" Trip looked at Logan. "Do you have a sister as cute as you?" I scrunched up my face in disgust from the outpouring of flirtation.

"You ready?" Logan nodded at me.

"Lily's going?" Ethan was amused.

"Oh, I wish I didn't care about my appearance like you. I've always been envious of those types of girls." Alexis smacked her lips together, as she looked at herself in the reflection of my microwave, fluffing up her hair.

I could hear my heart thundering in my ears. I was furious at the turnip-faced twit, turning on my heel as I headed for my bedroom.

"What's wrong?" Jarrett questioned.

"Nothing. Just going to change quick." I knew exactly what I was looking for hanging at the end of the closet with the other gifts from August I never wore.

"Alright." He kissed the top of my head as I crouched, digging for the shoes I wore for a wedding ages ago.

I hurriedly shut the door of the bathroom and quickly undressed, holding out the royal blue dress in front of me. "'I wish I didn't care how I looked.'" I mocked Alexis's comment. "Please fit," I whispered to the dress. I tugged it upwards and zipped it before spinning it around to see how it looked. Slipping on the slinky heels that matched, I reached into the bottom drawer for some makeup. I bent over and flipped my hair backward as I stood up.

"Is everyone ready to go?" I called walking down the hallway.

"Yay!" August screeched. "You never wear any of the things I buy you."

"Lily, I love you," Trip blurted as Tate elbowed towards me.

"Marry me?" Tate countered.

Jarrett came to stand beside me. "I think you look beautiful." He smiled warmly.

"I think you look cheap," Ethan chuffed. "Okay, let's go!" He clapped his hands together.

I laughed to myself that I had succeeded.

* * *

The bar reeked like fried food, and someone kept playing the same song five times in a row on the digital jukebox about going out on the weekend. Murmuring voices and intermittent hollers were punctuated by the clap of billiard balls breaking in the corner, and I watched as drunken girls leaned into overly flirty guys from their bar stools.

"One more time and then I won't ask again. Please?" Trip batted his eyes as Alexis gleaned from the boys surrounding her. I sipped my drink spitefully as she nodded energetically.

She placed both hands behind her back and dipped her mouth into one of the tall glasses scattered on the high-top table, pulling out the cherry hiding among the ice with her lips. Tilting her head back she sucked in the red orb and chewed, the smile never diminishing. After a minute, she began to wiggle her jaw around and close her eyes. The boys all leaned in closer.

"If she can do it this many times in a row, Ethan then you gotta wife her up!" Logan nudged Ethan's side.

"Talent is an important part of a relationship." Ethan turned and smirked.

"Done!" She put her manicured fingers to her lips and pulled out the stem that was tied into a tiny little knot.

"Isn't that cute?" I pushed the straw aside and emptied the glass into my mouth, chewing the ice bitterly.

"I wish I could do that," August muttered airily. "I like her. I think she's spunky." She smiled at me.

"You would. Your type tends to run in herds." I raised a brow at her.

"Okay! How about more drinks?" Jarrett looked to Tristan.

"Great idea!" Tristan ducked backward.

"Are you seriously this jealous? Your acting surprised he's being himself!" August pointed in my face. "Don't be shitty with me because he's on a date."

"A date at the bar does not count as a date. And I'm not angry about that. I'm irritated the one-percenters over there followed us." I looked to the bar where Marcus and two members of the Condemned sat drinking and casually attempting to blend, despite that all the customers weren't stepping within a ten-foot radius of them. Like a cancer at the end of the bar.

"Bullshit. You're upset because he's being Ethan and ticking you off, and your dressing-up act faded." She grinned sipping on her straw seductively eyeing Tristan waiting at the bar to order beside the other patrons. "You can sulk, but I'm having fun tonight." She bumped her head to the beat of the blaring music and ignored any further conversation.

I watched for an hour and a half as men from around the bar flocked to watch the *Amazing Lexi* and all her cute little tricks.

"You almost ready to go home?" Jarrett brushed some loose strands of hair behind one of my ears and peered into my eyes.

"I don't care," I replied, annoyed.

"You look great." His eyes ran the length of my dress as his hands moved down my sides and came to rest on my hips. He swayed lightly with the music begging my body to do the same.

A shrill giggle cut through the massive room and echoed against the wood-paneled walls of the dive bar. I turned to see Ethan dragging Alexis onto the dance floor, pulling her into him she beamed with every movement. His hands wrapped around her sides, one teetering close to the belt line while the other tilted her head sideways. He reached down and kissed her neck. My stare hardened when he looked up to connect his eyes with mine. She reciprocated and leaned into his chest, swaying, before kissing his neck passionately. He closed his eyes and smiled.

"Well, they look like they're having fun." I turned back to Jarrett who was watching Ethan and Alexis.

"Who cares?" I smiled darkly at him.

"You are so gorgeous, Lily." He twisted me around, pressing my back into the wall. I could feel his hand resting on my spine while the other rested on the wall above me. He began to hover closer, and I didn't care that we were in public.

He kissed my neck lightly. I let my head fall to the side as I closed my eyes. And then he moved to my lips. I reached up to place both hands on his shoulders as I let my lips part. I exhaled slowly and hummed approvingly.

"Jarrett…" I whispered as he kissed the front of my throat while his hand pulled my thigh to his hip.

"Yeah?" he whispered, his tongue dancing around the edges of my ear.

"Take me home." I curled my fingers into his shirt.

His hands twisted into my hair, and his lips ran along my jaw while his tongue lingered before finding mine.

My chest purred, and I held onto him as I let out a weak moan.

"No!" Voices broke out around us, and Jarrett was being pulled backward. I opened my eyes to see Logan and Trip tugging at their brother who was beaming red and grinning boyishly.

They were chastising him as I fixed my hair. I looked up to notice Alexis standing on the dance floor alone and scanning the crowd for Ethan. I didn't see him anywhere until I looked in time to catch him exiting the bar.

I excused myself from the stir and headed towards the door, shoving through it out onto the sidewalk. I looked down the street to catch Ethan walking away, his shoulders drooping.

"Ethan!" I called. He didn't turn. "Seriously?" He didn't pause.

"That was low, Harper." August passed by me with Tristan in tow. "Even for Ethan." The group poured out as he rounded a corner in the distance. I couldn't deny the guilt I felt.

8

Confessions in a Cursed Parking Lot

I walked around the corner into my parking lot. August's and my place was on the end, squished against four other apartments on a single floor. The lot was deserted for the summer holiday. A college town whose population dropped when spring semester let out. The other dwellings were empty and dark. I liked when everyone left for all the holidays. It was quieter.

August and I had gotten lucky to find the garden apartment last year, and being here made me miss it a little.

"My truck keys are locked inside." Ethan sat slumped on my bottom step.

I didn't want to hurt him. I didn't want to hurt anyone, and the way he sat there with his sweetly sad face made me feel terrible. What the heck was I doing? I was being petty. Kissing Jarrett like that in front of him.

"Ethan—"

"Lily, I'm begging you please don't say anything." He closed his eyes and sighed hard.

I looked down, fighting back the tears in the corners of my eyes.

"I know you're mad, and…"

He stood up, his eyes cast down. "Lily, please let me in before everyone gets back from the bar."

I nodded as I led the way inside. He silently jogged to the counter and snatched his keys, turning without saying anything. I didn't want to leave it like this.

"Ethan—"

"Go to hell, Lily," he shot coldly walking out the front door.

It was a kick to the chest. The words spoken with such animosity I feared he meant them. I followed out the front door not wanting to leave things this way.

"Listen to me, dammit!" My hands balled in fists at my sides. "You have no right to be mad at me!" He didn't? "I have been here for how many years, Ethan? I have listened to your weak excuses for not wanting a relationship with countless girls. I have watched you date and hurt some of the nicest women. You...are nothing more than a flirt and heartbreaker. No one can live up to—"

"You?" he murmured with his back to me.

"I will not be that girl in the light of morning scooping my clothes up to get in the car *you* called. I'm not her. I'm not the bone you toss aside after you're done with the meat!"

"Lilian Blue Harper, you are the girl I have hopelessly pined for since the first time I saw her." He was close now, within inches of my face as his voice dropped an octave. "You think the first time we met was when I pulled that little car out of the snow up in the pass? You're wrong." His eyes caught mine as his face grew soft. "You were walking through the woods on a trail not far from my post. You had the cutest little smile on as you spoke into your recorder while twisting a pine needle between your fingers. You didn't know I existed, lost in your little world among the trees. You had leaves stuck in your ponytail and every other minute you brushed your hair away from your eyes while the afternoon sun caught your chestnut hair so perfectly you looked like an angel walking in the forest." He smiled at the memory as his eyes welled with tears. "I knew in that moment I wanted to be the person who made you smile, pulled the leaves from those strands, and drew you back from the tree limb you almost tripped over. You don't get it. It was always you. Every minute of forever was you." He sniffed hard and wiped at his eyes as his blond waves rustled in the breeze.

I swallowed hard and felt like something was about to break inside my chest.

"So, Lily, I do love you. I have loved you. I'm going to love you—no matter how much I want it to stop." He looked away.

"I'm sorry, Ethan, but—" A hand came up around my waist.

"Hey, guys, you got out of the bar awfully quick." Jarrett smiled at us.

Ethan shook his head looking between both of us, the anger returning. "I'm going home."

Jarrett looked at me in confusion. "Did I say something?" I was unsure how to respond as the distance between Ethan and I grew.

Fuck it.

"Ethan!" I pushed Jarrett's hand away. "Don't leave it like this, please. We're best friends."

He turned. "We're not best friends. We're less than strangers now."

I felt the wind leave my lungs. "I'm not some temporary fix for you to feel better about your commitment issues," I snapped.

"You're right, Lily." His eyes grew dark. "I didn't feel better about anything after being with you."

I sucked in a small breath.

"Ethan, you need to cool off. Maybe you had too much to drink?" Jarrett came between us trying to defuse the hostility. I could see Tristan and August jogging toward us from down the sidewalk. The rest of the Baynes were laughing and drunk, further yet.

"Oh, that's fucking rich. C'mon, Lily, the guy deserves to know!" He laughed caustically. "You fucking Baynes are thick. That girl right there"—he pointed angrily over Jarrett's shoulder to me—"the one you think is your 'girlfriend'… is a hypocrite."

I choked on the tears spilling freely down my face.

"Ethan, go home!" August yelled as she and Tristan arrived breathlessly.

"Anywhere away from Lily I will gladly go!" He laughed sarcastically, turning to leave.

"She chose me. Let it go," Jarrett countered.

I closed my eyes, too afraid to watch the blow back.

"She chose you?" he replied darkly coming close to his face, a fistfight inevitable.

"What's going on here?" Grey asked as he came up.

"She chose *me!*" Ethan violently pounded his chest. "She chose me years ago! She chose me again and again. She chose me when she was lonely on the holidays, me when she didn't want to fret about dating, me when she was happy, and me when she was sad. I was the one that picked her up back when your sister found out she chose me and she had no one to turn to!" he yelled angrily before breaking to heave through his flaring nostrils. He began walking away before pausing and turning back. "And it was *my* bed she chose three nights ago in the middle of the night." He looked at me, "I don't know what's going on with you lately, Harper, or what trouble you might be in, but when you finally chose *me* the other night—really chose me"—he put a hand to his chest—"that was the best night of my life. Being with you…" He coughed on his tears. "I fucking love her. I'm in love with her." Tears lined his cheeks. He turned, jogging down the street and abandoning his truck.

The group stood quietly still before August broke the silence.

"We're going to be staying at Tristan's house up in Roosevelt. There's more room. Everybody, go pack your shit. We're going now," August quickly ordered. "Lily—"

"I need to go for a walk…" I wiped at my cheeks and coughed on the lump in my throat. "Alone."

As a pained Jarrett stood in my wake, I turned the corner out of view and collapsed on the grass of an unknown boulevard crying. I could feel my Condemned onlookers quietly watching me from across the street.

* * *

I heard footsteps drifting down the sidewalk toward me and didn't bother to look. *Kill me now, angel brothers. Who cares?* My messy love life had caught up to me. I didn't deserve any of them and I was right to have them ripped away from me. I was being selfish and playing all sides.

Ethan wasn't a best friend. Whatever semblance was left of that was now dead. The pain I inflicted on him felt horrific. Seeing him break down was too much for me to bear. I guess that was over now. I had set fire to all of it.

Eli, a selfishly unexplainable craving. A mysterious addiction and burning desire running so deep I could feel it buried in my very marrow. I ran off on him again and again. Rationalizing to myself I had had a life until he came along. A life I couldn't just abandon.

What was I going to do? Break up with Eli? We're we even *together*? It's not like we had really had any formal conversations about where we stood. He had shunned his brothers and gone against all the laws of his kind to be with me. You don't exactly just walk from that with an *I'm sorry*. And did I really want to? Whenever I was around him I wanted nothing but him. And when I wasn't with him, there was the ache burning in my chest like an open wound that wouldn't heal.

Then there was Jarrett, who was going to hate me now, and it was warranted. I was his sweet Colorado *girlfriend* who he had been in love with for years. Finally, the woman he had been waiting for.

So where did that leave me? *Do I end things with Jarrett and run back to Eli?*

I didn't like that either. Jarrett was so sweet. His charm made me giggle and his fun personality made me feel light, happy.

I wished there was a way where I could have them both without hurting the other.

I could smell him sitting down beside me.

"I'd be lying if I had said that wasn't terrible," Jarrett's smooth voice said quietly.

"I'm a terrible person," I whimpered into my forearm while I lay face down. "You deserve some cute little lumberjack girlfriend, not me. Not this shitty mess," I sniffed.

"You gotta give it to him." I turned to peek at him. He was staring ahead into the street. "At least you knew how he felt. I'm jealous."

I flipped over suddenly. "Of what? Ethan and I? Don't be—"

"Of his honesty. At least you knew where he stood. I should have told you how I felt. He's been here proclaiming his feelings, and I've been taking my time. Afraid I would scare you. At least he's telling you he loves you…" He shook his head angrily at himself.

"But I couldn't say it back to him," I whispered into my palms.

He pulled my hands from my face and turned to look at me. "I'm not like him. I'm not…smooth. But I'm honest, Lily. I want to be with you. I should have said it before, but I'm saying it now." His eyes searched mine.

"Then you deserve to know something." I held my breath for a beat. I'd been thinking this for awhile, inhaling, I mustered the courage. "I think I'm falling in love with you, Jarrett. All of it. The warmth, that you smell like sawdust. Everything."

"Good. So we're in love then. The slate is clean. Everything starts now for us."

I leaned into him and let the tumultuous thoughts eroding my mind slip away. I'd figure it out later I guess. Perhaps this bout of honesty would be the first step in absolving me.

"Let's get to Tristan's. August said it's big enough for everyone to have their own room." He pulled me up into his arms, hugging me. "Sawdust, huh?"

I shyly smiled and nodded. I didn't deserve him.

* * *

"Rooms are up those stairs and down the hall," Tristan said.

"Tate? Did you see the climbing wall outside?" Logan grinned excitedly.

"We'll have to find some gear around the house," Tate said.

"That's not a climbing wall, you idiots. It's just the house." August called.

"Aug, it's a wall of rocks. How is it not for climbing?" Trip wondered.

As August rolled her eyes at her brother, she gently grabbed my hand and pulled me onto the privacy of the back porch. She turned to face me. I was bracing for the inevitable blow back of hearing what Ethan and I had done together.

"Do you remember that New Year's Eve when Mason got so drunk he broke your favorite necklace and threw up all over the coffee table in the living room?" August asked.

How could I forget?

"I lied to you. I told you I was the one that cleaned everything up that night and fixed your necklace. I didn't. It was Ethan. He was up until the sun came up trying to fix that damn necklace for you. I remember him cursing because his hands were too big and the clasp was too small. That was the first time I ever understood what all the other girls saw in him... Tonight was the second. I don't know how you're going to get out of this without someone getting hurt. Even Ethan."

I remembered that night perfectly. The three of them closed our favorite bar down. I had spent the last hour begging August to go home when I got tired of watching Ethan cozy up to some redhead. When we all finally got back to the apartment, Mason vomited on the table, spraying the blue liquid everywhere, before he stumbled in it and tugged my necklace away, breaking it. I was fed up. I broke down. Retreating to my room in a fit of tears. Despite Ethan's soft pleas through my bedroom door, I refused to come out. I thought he had left that night. I had no idea.

"I hope that *someone* is me," I murmured softly.

Tristan blocked August and I from closely following her brothers upstairs after we came back inside. "Alright, Eli's *guests* are out behind the stables in the cottage. Most of them should stay out of sight. No unchaperoned excursions off property unless you're going into town. And you are not"— he was speaking directly to me now— "to go anywhere alone."

I found myself suddenly nervous. Knowing the childlike curiosity of the men ahead of me and some of the wonders out in the woods. We would just have to get through this weekend.

Thankfully, the Baynes would keep away any of the scarier things that were looking to hurt me. Tristan felt with so many humans around, they were less inclined to make themselves known.

"Nice try." Trip's voice drifted down the hall followed by a loud *thump*.

"The baby always gets the smallest room," Logan quipped.

"You don't want to be down here by the breeding grounds anyway,"

Tate called.

"You're disgusting. The farther away I am, the better," Bennett said calmly.

"Lil, you came to check on me. That's so sweet." Trip smiled as he poked his head out of the first room and winked.

I rolled my eyes.

"What do you think is behind *this* door?" Tate asked as he leaned over and tried to turn the knob of the locked door directly across from us.

I shrugged. I never asked, and it had been locked since I arrived. In fact, I hadn't spent much time exploring. It didn't feel right since I was a guest.

"I'll bet that's Tristan's vault," Logan said softly as he glanced around.

"Vault?" I asked, perplexed.

"Makes sense. A guy like Tristan. A house like this," Grey said as he strolled over and put his ear up to the door.

Tristan. I'd forgotten! The story was this was *his* house for the weekend.

"I'll bet he's got some great stuff in there," Tate said longingly.

"Or creepy," Grey said.

"Maybe it's where he keeps all his gold!" Logan replied eagerly.

"He's not a leprechaun," I chided.

"He does have weird eyes." Trip widened his eyes.

They all nodded.

"That's your sister's boyfriend you're talking about," I said.

"Not that I would be interested in that sort of thing! With a treasure like Lily here, who would need more?" Tate said as he wrapped an arm quickly around my shoulders.

Treasure? Oh man. Trying to make me feel better after Ethan's outburst, I was guessing.

"Oh, best fri-end! I need you down here in my room." August's joyous voice rang from the room at the end of the hall.

The room that was *ours* until the night before last.

I dropped away from Tate's arm and moved through the crowd staring at the forbidden room.

"Your room?" I whispered as I reached her.

"Tristan's house, primary bedroom? Do you really think I'm going to let you sleep in your angel boyfriend's room...in his bed...with my brother? Your other boyfriend?" She looked smug as she said it.

"I didn't think we—" I began.

"Save it. I know. It's not happening. So Tristan and I have decided to help you out by taking on the burden of sleeping in the primary suite of amazingness. For your own good. Of course." She turned on her heel and walked away.

"Right. So where am I sleeping then?" I asked.

"Wherever they've decided I guess," she called over her shoulder.

"You're enjoying this a little too much." The words were barely audible to my ears, and I doubted she'd heard me.

A hushed whisper of my name caught my attention from my left. Turning, I saw Jarrett hiding in the shadows of a room.

"Why are you hiding?" I asked as I stepped inside.

"Because if they see me in here, they'll banish me." He smiled.

"Banish you?" I grinned.

He reached out and pulled me gently into the shadows with him.

"From you," he said before his lips covered mine.

I wrapped my arms around him.

"Whoa! Not this again." I heard Logan's voice behind me, and my grip on Jarrett tightened.

He sighed against my lips as he stepped away and threw his hands up in surrender.

"Looks like Jarrett infiltrated Lil's room already," Grey said as he pulled Jarrett into the hallway.

"I believe I was invited." Jarrett grinned as he looked at me.

"Always," I answered with a smile.

"She's still under his influence!" Trip called as he rushed straight to the window and lifted it wide open.

August's brothers had always gushed over me and playfully played for my affections since the first time I visited their woodland farm all those years ago. I guess it started after they discovered Jarrett had let slip his crush on me. In the beginning I found it annoying and occasionally overwhelming, but soon learned to love it after an uncomfortable encounter at a bar there when we were visiting once.

A much older man kept trying to dance with me and buy me drinks. Despite nearly being double my age and my courteous *no thank yous*, he cornered me while I was coming out of the bathroom. I politely tried to rebuke him, but he blocked my exit and angrily grabbed my arm before pinning me to the wall, his intentions terrifyingly clear. I screamed out in fear.

I had never known anyone to come to my defense so readily and fiercely. I never had siblings growing up. No chivalrous brothers to fend off would-be bullies. Nearly all of the Bayne boys rushed in and dragged him back. They had the man against the bar, shouting in his face threateningly while August held me and wiped my tears.

"You rapey fucker, don't you ever touch a woman like that again!" the usually playful Logan seethed.

"No means no, asshole!" August shouted over her shoulder.

"Call Pete, Janet!" Trip shouted for the bartender to call the local sheriff.

The guy kept justifying his actions proclaiming he had done nothing wrong.

"Tell it to Judge Charles on Monday!" Grey wrestled against the guy trying to get away.

"You alright, Lily?" Tate asked, seriously checking my face over.

I shakily nodded while cringing at the sight of the greasy-haired man they restrained.

"Dumb bitch," the disgusting man spat.

The boys dropped their grip on the man. "Bennett!" Tate whistled.

Bennett took one massive step forward and landed a crushing blow to the man's jaw with one of his bear-sized fists.

"You do anything like that to another woman around here or come near her again, we'll drag you out back and do worse than a broken nose." Grey nodded curtly.

Blood dripped from the man's face.

"Lily's family, and you don't touch our fucking family," Logan growled.

That's when I learned the Baynes weren't just the playful and mischievous town troublemakers I thought they initially were. In the face of moral wrongdoing, all jokes were set aside and justice was served.

Back slaps from other patrons and beers were doled out to the Baynes from the bartender once the dust settled.

I would later learn that Daryl was a convicted sex offender who hadn't registered in the next county over. He was arrested and I hate to think what would have happened had I been alone that night.

I never looked at the Bayne's the same way again. They would always be my fearless and playful protectors, and I saw why August spoke so frequently of them.

I sighed as I watched Jarrett vanish.

"He's gone now. You'll be okay," Trip said as he brought my hand to his lips.

"What happened? Who's gone?" Tristan interrupted as he came into the room.

"She was attacked," Logan piped up.

I saw the seriousness take hold of Tristan's eyes.

"No," I said in alarm.

"What? Who was it, Lily? Did they—" he began.

"We're used to this, Tristan. Jarrett thinks he can do this," Trip said.

"Jarrett?" Tristan asked in confusion.

"Comes in here and puts his moves on our girl." Logan beamed.

"No," I said.

I couldn't recall a time when I'd felt more embarrassed.

Tristan cracked a smile and laughed.

"*This* is not funny," I said seriously.

"Yes. Yes, it is," he said and turned to leave.

A thought crossed my mind, but I quickly dismissed it. I wasn't going to think about the terrors that lie beyond the treeline outside.

Jarrett sat with his back against the wall at the top of the steps. His eyes caught mine, and he smiled softly. Where were they sending him to?

I waited until they all went to sleep and then snuck off. Trip and Tate attempted to sleep in the closet of my room in case of "intruders." I actually laughed at the fact they had no idea how close they had been to the truth. But I needed to finish Jarrett and my conversation from earlier. I needed a chance to explain everything or mostly everything.

The car ride here had been loud. Most of the brothers were still drunk, and all awkwardness ceased when they discovered they would get to vacation at "Tristan's mansion." Jarrett spoke very little and held my hand politely the entire time. But I needed to know that everything was okay. I crept down the steps to find him, not realizing the trajectory I was about to send both of us on.

* * *

"Tristan's house is… August really outdid herself with this guy. What does he do for a living?" Jarrett turned to look over his shoulder from eyeing the great span of books in the library.

"Um, government…warfare-related things." I spoke slowly, trying to create a plausible explanation on the spot.

"No wonder my brothers think he's amazing."

Jarrett had been waiting patiently on the first floor. I brought down the extra pillows and comforter off my bed for him and made up one of the two colossal couches in the study.

"I've been thinking," I began. "I think we were hasty before, and I'll understand if you want some space." I sat perched in front of him on the edge of the makeshift bed.

"No, I want you here with me." He pulled me close to him.

I slowly curled up with my back to his chest on the couch. The library had deep leather couches and a small wet bar at one end. The same bar August raided my first night awake. A soft fire was crackling in the fireplace from whatever business had taken place in the "war room" before our arrival.

His breathing was uneven. I could tell he was thinking something, but I lay there quietly. I wish I could know what was going on inside his head. He must've been hurting. It was late. A golden clock hung to the left of the wooden door reading 2:30, but I couldn't sleep.

He drew a tentative breath. He wasn't sleeping either. His hands were trembling gently around my waist. Then carefully he pulled my hip back towards him and his thoughts were clear. I could feel him swelling under the cotton of his boxers. I pushed my hips against him and began to move slowly in circles. His breath was loud in my ear as a satisfied sigh passed his lips. His hand trailed slowly down the front of my knit shorts and settled between my thighs. His fingers began to explore the soft peaks of my lips, carefully drawing rings, dipping inside of me and pulling them out.

"Is *this* okay?" he whispered into my ear from behind.

"Mm-hmm." My self control wavered under my desires. I fantasized about kissing and touching Jarrett a lot over the years. Now I only wanted one thing. To feel him inside of me, making me shake like a bass drum trembles a stage.

He kissed my neck as my hips began to move with the rhythm of his fingers. I could feel him rock hard against my tailbone.

"You're not his, ya know."

And I knew he meant Ethan.

"Tell me you want me," he growled into my shoulder, his free hand down the front of my tank top massaging and gently pinching my rigid nipples.

I reached behind and pulled down his boxers.

"Say it," he commanded.

"I want you," I whispered to him. He pulled aside my underwear and using one hand to guide himself, while the other spread me open, he thrust himself forward without hesitation. Moving his hand up to my hip, pulling me down onto him until he was fully seated inside me.

"Oh God, you're so wet," he moaned. "Say my name." His teeth gripped my shoulder.

"Jarrett," I called. He pumped faster and harder.

He was rough and untamed, like making love to a wild animal. He wasn't careful or worried he would hurt me. He was turned on by me, and it showed.

"You're mine," he growled loudly into my hair. He wasn't hurt or broken. He was staking his claim.

He shoved me forward and off of him. I ripped my tank top over my head dropping it beside him. He twisted me around. I kicked off my damp underwear, and he pulled me back down to face him. My knees pushed into the cushions on either side of his lap as I mounted him and expertly used my free hand to lead him back inside of me.

His eyes burned, and he licked his lips. His forearm wrapped around my waist and his other palm pulled my tailbone forward rhythmically.

His fawny skin was a stark contrast against my pallor.

We moved like this until sweat glistened like hot oil on his neck and chest. The shadows of the flames danced across the ceiling.

I could feel him slowing, I was getting close, and so was he. He shuddered with every stroke I brought down onto his lap. I dropped forward, my breasts brushing his face with each movement. I clutched the back of the couch and rose and fell with determination as he began to shake. I could feel him pulsing inside me.

"Come with me," I whispered, tongue dancing along his ear.

"Lily," he called out slowly through labored breathing. His husky voice echoed lustily. He knotted his hands into my hair and kissed me frantically through gritted teeth. He pushed deep inside with every pulse, and my head fell back as my orgasm gripped his swollen cock until we were both trembling. My lips came to rest on his and our cheeks relaxed against each other as we struggled to catch our breath. We slowed to a still and he let out a winded laugh. "I love you, Lily. You're amazing."

I kissed him passionately around his smile, and I was completely happy in this moment. I was also certain everyone in the house and the woods tonight *heard* who I belonged to.

9

One of the Dead

I didn't know what time it was, but the sun looked to be mid-morning through the windows of the library. Jarrett was still asleep with his forearm draped over his eyes while the other cradled my head. He looked sexy lying there, breathing softly. The sandy brown hair of his chest was highlighted blond in the sunlight. I slipped away from his side, careful not to wake him.

Plucking his T-shirt from the floor, I tugged it on, not bothering to find my things and crept out of the library closing the door behind me. The house was quiet and most of the boys were still asleep. Thank God. I was making a line for the shower when a hand grabbed my wrist and yanked me back.

I turned to see August with a giant grin on her face and wide eyes. The excitement was coming off her in droves.

"You're so welcome." Bobbing her head slowly. "Tell me everything. Wait." Her hand shot up. "Nope. That's my brother." Shaking her head no. "Tell me nothing."

I rolled my eyes at her and opened my mouth to speak.

"Wait. Did you make a love child?" She put her hand to my stomach and scrunched up in excitement. "I want a niece," she exclaimed, practically vibrating with glee.

"Shh, you dummy!" I clapped my hand over her mouth to shut her up, "I don't need any of *them*"— I pointed with my eyes at the other rooms— "to hear!"

A wicked smile grew wide on her cheeks. "There was no one in a ten-mile radius who didn't hear you two last night, Harper. I think we're a little past that."

I winced.

"I honestly think wild wolves are quieter when they mate." She raised her eyebrows, smirking. "I need to up my game, Lily. No wonder they're all in love with you! Also, my brothers left a half hour ago to go get breakfast in town." She shrugged. "Oh, don't worry, I told them you ran back to our apartment for some stuff you forgot last night. Except..."

"Except?" My eyes slowly grew wider with horror.

"Bennett went to wake up Jarrett for breakfast, annnnnd you're welcome, because he came back from the hallway with a big fat smile on his face. You owe him. He covered for your ass."

"You said *everyone* heard?" I grimaced, talking around my toothbrush.

"Like potentially mammoth-sized angels? Yup, I'm guessing so. You really have a knack for being unable to keep your lovers out of the loop. You really shouldn't play the field. The universe wants you with one person I think." She laughed as she lay back on the bed.

"Your brothers are never going to let me within a mile of Jarrett." I called over my shoulder as I stepped into the shower. "When are they going to be back?"

"About an hour. Why?"

"Keep your brothers busy. I need to go find Eli. I have to be honest with him about Jarrett. Then maybe this whole thing can end." My hands hovered over my thigh while holding the loofah. I didn't know how much of that I believed but the idea my life could go back to normal was an enticing one.

"Lily." August pulled at the bottom of her eyes and scooted closer to the vanity, examining her dark circles in the mirror. "I'm all for not being wanted by Eli's brothers, but I have a feeling if it were just a matter of you dumping an angel, they wouldn't be trying to kill you."

She was right. But I had another confession I didn't want to tell her. That I was struggling to admit to myself. I didn't *want* to end things with Eli. As much as his life was soaked in danger, I felt the most like myself when I was with him. He didn't send my mind on daydream tangents like her brother did. He wasn't my novocaine the way Ethan could be when I was upset. Eli was something else altogether, and I was only beginning to scratch the surface on it. I wasn't sure if I was ready for it to end.

"At the very least, he should know I'm in love with your brother." I twisted the towel into my hair.

"Tristan and I were talking last night—don't make that face, we have conversations—and he told me about his mother. Aurelius did everything to protect Antionette, but it wasn't his call. They chose to execute her anyway. I guess he pleaded with his brothers and it didn't matter. There aren't second chances with this sort of thing. I guess they stabbed her with some special knife, and it was over." She shrugged.

She was referring to the mortal dagger, the one Eli managed to protect me from. If he hadn't marred his halo and used some of its power to keep me alive, I would be dead now. I shuddered at the thought.

August went on to explain how Aurelius didn't fight his brothers to keep Tristan alive, but it sounded like his childhood was dreadful. He was raised by one of the Ethereal nobles, some duke of sorts in Austria before he became a teenager. He joined the Legion when the duke died and rose through the ranks. I guess he was a general. Aurelius had grown to tolerate him, but Tristan thinks it's because he sees him as more of an asset than his *son*.

"I don't think this is all going to go away because you love Jarrett. It already happened."

I agreed. I knew no matter what I said this was already in motion. But I still felt like I needed to try. "Do you think that's why Tristan is helping Eli?"

"I don't know. I guess he owes him." She hopped down and looked serious. "Do you really want to leave Eli?" she whispered.

I pondered for a moment. "Sometimes I don't know if I have a choice…" Because when we were together, it never felt like it. It felt like he was the only other person alive on the planet. And when we were near enough to one another it was almost like we synchronized. I couldn't deny the way I was around him.

"I don't think you want to hurt anyone. I know you want to do the right thing." The corner of her lip pulled up in a half smile.

"Well, I got one thing right." I pulled my T-shirt over my head as she made a face at my comfortable choice. "I kind of told Jarrett that Tristan was in government warfare for a living."

* * *

I headed towards the cottage on the back half of the property. It was more like a second home that was nestled into a rocky outcropping almost a half mile from the main house. I wasn't worried Jarrett would catch Eli and me. Firstly, he didn't know Eli existed, and any interaction could be explained away as some stranger that worked on the property. Something I'm sure Eli would agree with given that Jarrett was a human. He would be just as inclined to stay hidden.

I was tired of trying to keep everything from tangling up. Keep this strand from intertwining with that one. It's why I needed to come clean and tell Eli everything. Before any more damage could be done or hearts could be broken. I paused, remembering the pain that crossed Ethan's sweet face.

The cottage had a heavy forest surrounding it with tall firs a foot from the stone walls. It reminded me of a grander version of some French fairy-tale cottage. Its femininity contrasted the main house's darker woods with its white shudders and light stone exterior. Eli and the remainder of his proselytes were outside in serious conversations, and I wondered if I should wait, not wanting to interrupt. But Eli looked up at once. The draw in our chests grew, and a soft smile curled his lips. A smile I was about to remove.

"I need to talk to you." I ignored the looks of distaste ranging in the faces around me. "Alone."

He gestured for me to follow him through the arched side doors. The glass in the matching wood-trimmed windows practically undulated, it was so rippled. Once inside, the decor surprised me. It wasn't the masculine leathers, deep woods, and golds of the main house. The walls were a bright white plaster with thick wooden beams running along the ceilings, and the furniture were soft earth tones. It smelled strongly of honeysuckle, like perpetual spring indoors.

I wasn't sure where to begin, but on the walk along the bark-dust trail, I had made up my mind.

"I don't know what you heard last night—"

"I wasn't here." He stood in the morning sunlight, his features breathtaking. "However, some of the others outside enlightened me."

Okay, full disclosure. Here I go. I took a deep breath.

"Before I met you, I was involved with some people." The term *involved* was foolish. "I was dating. Specifically, August's brother Jarrett." I stopped, trying to gauge his reaction. He was watching me with a small smile of amusement. My human drama felt trivial cascading from my lips given our circumstances.

"I was also, not on purpose"— I shook my head and furrowed my brows— "dating my best friend Ethan." I rolled my eyes. *Not on purpose? Full disclosure!* I chanted. "Let me start over. I was dating two people when I met you. I didn't plan that, and frankly, it wasn't going great." I remembered Ethan catching me with Jarrett. Then August caught me when I was with Ethan. I shuddered and pushed it away. "It was a little messy and confusing. That all didn't go away because I met *you*." I kept my eyes cast downward. "I still care about them both. Maybe even falling in love, I don't know. But I don't think it's right to be dishonest with you." I was playing nervously with my fingertips. "So in full disclosure, I think you should know everything. I was with Jarrett last night. I care deeply for him, but he also doesn't live here and that brings about its own challenges. I never really thought of myself as someone who could do a long-distance relationship.

"I also have unexpected feelings for my best friend Ethan. But I struggle trusting him. Sometimes I think it's an Annette Hargrove and Sebastian Valmont conquest for him. And then there's *you*. Sometimes I wish my life could go back to the way it was…" I opined softly.

His expression saddened, and he seemed slightly anguished. I could *feel* his ache in my stomach. The regret he wrestled with and the confusion at why he didn't understand it.

"But when I'm with you"— I moved so we were only a breath apart, but I still couldn't look at him—"I feel strange. Whole? Connected? Nothing matters except *this*." I spoke in a small voice gesturing between us. "Not like the desire I feel with *them*… It's *more*. Almost—"

"A compulsion?" he whispered.

I looked up to meet his icy blue opals that had been haunting me for the last few months. His breath blew warmly in my face, and he smelled like everything I craved.

"Then I should be honest as well." He took a step back and closed his eyes. "Do you remember when you were hiking near my hot springs?"

He didn't wait for me to respond, but I nodded.

"That was one of the first times I saw you. The springs lead along a river to an underground bathhouse into the main house." He saw me connect the dots to the beautifully tiled and steamy cavernous room on the lower level.

"I never imagined I would see you again. But time and time again, there you were. I had hoped to keep a reasonable distance until the night you were upset when you came to the grotto. I had never felt more compelled to intervene. When you slipped into the water, I didn't worry at first. You were strong and I had seen you climbing the trees so often, but when you didn't resurface I felt something I had never encountered before." His face twisted in discomfort. "Fear.

"I have never been concerned for a human, even in their hour of death. It's the way it's intended, and I've seen it so often it means very little to me. But watching you, *hoping* you would be alright, consumed me, and in that moment I made a choice. I chose *you*. I didn't choose to follow the canon that had dictated my existence since I'd been forged. I acted before I could consider another path. I knew I didn't want you to be a part of the dead." His head fell in defeat.

"The dead?" I whispered.

"Yes. People who die of their natural accord become the dead. A dream-filled multitude. Their souls drifting in the Ethoes. I didn't want your soul there. I wanted it with you. Here. It was selfish to take that from you, the serenity of rest. I knew your father's soul was there, and I robbed you of that reunion." He looked away, ashamed.

"Speaking of my father"—I took a furtive step toward him— "I have to ask you something. Something I've never said to anyone. Why was Aurelius at the scene of my father and my accident?"

He looked at me stunned.

"He was standing on the street corner, and I remember looking into his eyes before the crash."

"Is this the only time you've ever seen him?" His expression grew agitated.

"Well, no." I paused, speaking quietly again. "There are the dreams too."

This also surprised him.

"What dreams?" He placed both hands on the points of my shoulders, forgetting our discussion of feelings.

"The dreams I have about your brothers…"

"How long has this been going on?"

"My whole life?"

His eyes curiously searched mine.

"What does *that* mean?" I worriedly asked.

"I don't know, but I'm starting to think there's more to Aurelius's crusade to end you than we all understand. Can you tell me more?"

So I did. I told him how I had dreams that felt real since childhood. Dreams of the Herculean men who carried large swords. Sometimes I could see them wander in unknown landscapes alone, and other times gathered around a beautiful table in a moonlit garden. How I could hear their conversations and deliberations and how they scared me. That I hadn't drawn the parallel between seeing Aurelius at the accident until the day they kidnapped me in the forest and took me to the *dream garden.*

I hadn't shared any of this with anyone. I felt vulnerable and scared. I then decided to tell him something I had only ever shared with Ethan. I had other dreams that felt *real* or something like it, more akin to memories. The dreams of a girl I felt connected to. The one who called me Sparrow.

He put up his hand gesturing for me to wait. Walking to the door, he spoke quietly before coming to face me again.

"What do you need? Hey, Lily." Tristan grinned and plopped down on the edge of a desk near the adjacent wall after walking in. He must have been waiting outside.

While Eli rehashed everything I had told him, Tristan was contemplative and quiet. His face grew more stern as the details unfurled.

"She's having former life recalls? Well, that only happens to a reborn soul. I mean, the odds are astronomical." He was trying to remember something. "Practically non-existent."

Thankfully, Eli saw my confusion. "When someone becomes one of the dead, their soul is set free into the Ethoes. Rarely do they come back. I'd heard times of it happening before my Forging, but even then, it wasn't something done often. A soul has to *choose* to come back and no one does. The nirvana achieved is beyond anything. To *wish* to come back would mean something is lacking there. It explains your connection to the Garden and its occupants though. How you're able to view it in almost real time or near to it."

"She must have a paladin then?" Tristan rubbed the whiskers of his jaw, silver eyes narrow with concern.

"A pala—what?" They were trying to include me but I was lost among their conversation.

"Din." Eli, again, wanted me to understand. "A Paladin is your personal bodyguard. The universe tries to correct itself when a person has to be reborn. Help them achieve the completeness they need to rest in the end. This person is imbued with great bravery, strength, and otherworldly fighting skills. Their sole purpose is to protect the anomaly." He turned to Tristan. "I'm thinking it must have been her father, which would explain why Aurelius was present at his death. I can't say for sure whether or not he was involved though." He turned back to me. "This person can be a parent, sibling, close friend, or confidant."

"So, I'm basically an anomaly soul that's not supposed to be here?" I shook my head in disbelief. "And my dad, who could have been my knight, died?"

"Paladins are not souls tied to the Ethoes. When they die, they move onto another corporal form because they're bound to their duty. If their duty lives, they live. They are made of your proverbial rib and would be close to you."

Who the hell would that be?

"You said dreams. Plural. What are the other ones about?" Tristan interjected while Eli contemplated.

And for the first time in my life, outside of the half truths I gave Ethan, I told someone about the vivid dreams I had about the girl and me.

"Can you describe her?"

"Easily. She has very long burnt-red hair. Fair skin with freckles across the bridge of her nose and cheeks. Round faded green or blue eyes, and she's tall. She has a square face and soft pink lips." I rattled off the face I had seen thousands of times in hundreds of nights.

"When you see her, do you see it from her perspective or an onlooker?" Tristan continued.

"Always myself with her." I shrugged.

Eli's head snapped up suddenly, and he darted quickly into a connecting study before coming back holding a large leather-bound book. It smelled ancient, and the pages were so yellowed I couldn't be sure what material it was written on.

He dropped the book onto the table forcing Tristan to swirl and face it. Quickly, he paged to something he was looking for.

"Does the girl look like this?" he demanded in a fierce tone.

And there she was. The girl. Not a likeness of her, but her. The girl I had known since I was a child. She couldn't have been older than twenty and even in this crude sketch she was beautiful.

"That's her!" I gasped, pointing.

Both of the men backed away from me and stared wide-eyed with fear and disbelief.

"Who is she?" My mouth was agape and a sick feeling of fear flooded my gut.

"Hesperia." Tristan whispered, blown away. "Is *she*—" Tristan began.

"No one utters a word of this!" Eli growled. "I need to get to Durrës."

"Zacarius's region? Why the—" Tristan wondered.

"A Scribe." He took two strides and then held my face in his hands. "Lily, listen to me. I don't know what's happening. I wish I had more answers for you. I'll be back here in an hour or less. I need you to be careful and stay close to Tristan or hidden among the Bayne family. Do not go off on your own without him or one of my acquaintances as a liaison. Trust no one." And he gently brushed his lips to mine. They felt electric but worried.

"Tristan, I need to talk to the others. Take Lily back to the house." He turned to me. "I'll see you soon." And then he disappeared into another room while he pulled out a cell phone.

* * *

I quietly pondered the feeling that Tristan was now afraid of me. Honestly, I was afraid too. Nothing made sense. I was alive before? I never believed in reincarnation, but this was too much. And who was Hesperia? Why was she in that old book? And worse, why were they terrified of her? More often than not in my dreams, we were running from people, but sometimes the dreams were happy too. Eating wild raspberries together in a sun-drenched field, riding horseback through a mountain valley or swimming in an idyllic pond. Always smiling, always happy and peaceful. I never felt threatened by her. She was always helping me.

"Hey, Lily Bear." Jarrett came up and wrapped his arms around my waist. He kissed my temple with a smile. "August said you and Tristan went for a walk. We were eating a quick brunch before the rest of the boys got back from town."

They were both standing in the kitchen casually eating breakfast.

August immediately noted the serious expressions on both Tristan's and my faces, and concern furrowed her brow but she was quick to dismiss it when she caught Jarrett's gaze.

"What's on the agenda for today?" I quickly interjected before any questions could arise.

"Now, babe." Jarrett squared his shoulders to face me. "Don't panic!"

I groaned. Whenever a Bayne reassured you, it was sure to be something troublesome.

"We're going to head to the lake this evening and play ring toss," August spouted happily.

"Oh no," I grumbled.

"Sounds fun. What is it?" Tristan looked between us for an explanation.

"See, I knew we were meant for each other!" August practically beamed.

"A game Trip and Tate invented on Fourth of July weekend when we were teenagers after we were banned for life from the city pool. It involves rope, beer, and swimming!" Jarrett grinned with excitement.

"You'll see, babe. I'm the champion four years running." She winked at Tristan.

"It's because you get a longer rope!"

"Oh, hush, you're just a terrible swimmer. We all know it," August spat at her brother.

I took a hardened breath and listened to August and Jarrett banter back and forth while Tristan relaxed and laughed at the two of them. I had a sinking feeling. I wished I could talk to Ethan. To call him and explain everything and have him comfort me, but any hope of that was snuffed out outside my apartment last night.

August put her hand up. "I'm going to go get my purse. They'll be here soon to pick us up and go get supplies."

"Lily, could you help me on the back half of my property? I have a tree I would be deeply indebted to you if you looked at it?" Tristan was trying to keep me here while the Baynes went to do their errands.

"Absolutely," I replied with a polite smile.

"Fantastic. August, you and your brothers can go and get your essentials and maybe pick up some food for us to grill up this weekend, and Lily can help me do a quick chore or two while you spend some time with your family." Tristan inferred more with his words, and August immediately picked up on what was between the lines. She nodded sweetly.

Jarrett pulled me outside by my hand gently while August and Tristan were discussing the nuances of how to win at ring toss when he turned to face me with worry creasing his brow.

"Are you mad at me?" His voice carried a note of a plea.

"Of course not."

"I was worried you're trying to avoid me because of the way I behaved last night." He looked at me remorsefully.

"Jarrett, last night was"—I took a deep breath and scooped his sorrowful face into my hands— "incredible. You were passionate and sexy. It was better than when I imagined it."

"You imagined it?" A sly smile crept into the corners of his lips.

"Many times. For *six* years." I nodded slowly. "I hoped I lived up to whatever you had in *your* head."

"You silly girl." And he let out a deep laugh and wrapped his arms around me, kissing me with a happy smile. "I think it'll take a year for me to get the full feeling in my limbs again you made me so weak."

My cheeks flooded red and I beamed at his praises.

"I love you, Lily Bear. I want to be with you," he breathed into my hair. "Always."

"I love you too, Jarrett. That sounds like a dream."

And it did sound like a dream. One that was getting further away with every truth I discovered. Could I really subject him to this violent life of danger? Running from savage angels for the rest of our lives? I knew I couldn't, but I wasn't ready to send him away. Not yet anyway. Not when I needed his warmth so much. I buried my face in his chest and squeezed tighter. No, for this weekend, I would be with him and he would be with me.

10

Acquiring Pony Potpourri

Tristan and I headed back to the cottage after wishing the Baynes farewell. They would be gone for hours. I could see the worry creasing his brow as we walked shoulder to shoulder quietly.

I never thought the dreams I had were strange. But everyone thinks they're normal until someone shows them something different.

Questions swirled in my mind like the snow of a shaken globe. Eli had gone before I had a chance to formulate a coherent thought. How does someone digest that they may have lived another life? Or that they may have some fierce protector watching out for them? This and many more questions started to bleed into the forefront of my mind as I pasted a smile on in front of my visiting family.

One question, however, rose above the rest.

Hesperia.

She clearly struck fear among Ethereals. So what was more powerful than *them*?

"She's one of them," I reassured him with a smile watching my footing as we headed uphill.

"Pardon?" His strides lengthened.

"I can tell you're worried about August, and don't be. Her brothers are intense but remember she's a Bayne. She can go toe-to-toe." I patted his arm.

"She's so small." He attempted a brave smile as he gestured her little height with his hands, but I could still see the uncertainty tugging at his gray irises. It was nice to see someone who worried about her the way I often did.

We rounded the bend and I saw the edges of the cottage come into view. "Why does he do that?" I asked nervously.

Tristan cocked his head sideways at me.

"*Trust no one?* I trust *you*."

"You shouldn't," he stated soberly. "Afternoon, ladies." Tristan gave a casual wave to two women grooming horses in the clearing in front of the cottage.

"Hi." I smiled politely to a tall, slender girl with lengthy blond hair almost white in the sunlight. Her blue eyes were bright as she returned the smile. She was brushing one of the massive black horses belonging to the Saints.

"His name is Clover." She must have seen me in awe at the size of the beast. "Amelia, do you need any help?" she called over her shoulder to the other girl brushing an identically large horse.

"Be done in a bit, and then I'll be ready." Amelia came into view, petite framed and black hair. Both wore clothes hugging their thin hips.

"Wait here, Lily. I need to see what's going on." I nodded at Tristan and turned my attention back to the girls as I took a seat on a nearby tree stump.

"I'm Lydia." She stood in front of me and I reached out a hand to introduce myself.

"Lily." She stared at my hand, then at me.

"Residual." She looked apologetic. However, I caught something unusual. What was it? Intrigue perhaps?

"Understandable." I lowered my hand. I didn't understand at all. *They can possess, but they can't shake a hand?* Something was off, but I wasn't about to appear rude. I hadn't quite learned all of the nuances of each grouping. Tristan tried to help August and me learn so we would be better prepared, but it was a lot to absorb. Something about them needing a life force for physicality was tingling in the depths of my memory.

"He's still not back yet," Tristan interrupted, appearing next to us. "How are the Centuries doing?"

"Fine, we were waiting for the mortals to leave and now we're heading out to get feed." she motioned over toward the stables.

"Centuries?" I spoke softly, unaware I had said it aloud.

"Century stallions." Amelia came to stand next to me, wiping her hands with a rag. "They live for a hundred years." She beamed.

"Whoa," I exhaled.

"Extraordinary, really." The horses shook their heads as they cast their manes aside. Their coats were so black a navy tinge appeared in the shine of the early July sun.

"You should come along, Lily." Lydia, the blond, pulled me from my mesmerized stare.

"Where?" I turned to her.

"With us." She smiled sweetly.

I looked to Tristan for reassurance.

"Go ahead, I'm going to discuss some things with Marcus and the other Condemned. August will be gone with her brothers for hours and it's only a few miles." He turned to head back inside but paused. "It's time you get to know Eli's *friends* living in the woods… Have fun, ladies." And he was gone.

* * *

Inside the SUV was silent. Amelia drove and Lydia occupied the passenger seat, both tight in their posture. I couldn't be sure whether they were always like this or if undue distress was caused by my presence. I noticed their eyes frequently scanning through the forests, and I was sure I could assume why. Every so often I caught sight of Amelia's eyes watching me in the rear view mirror.

"So, how do you two know Eli?" I asked, nervously trying to attempt mild conversation.

"I fought for him once during the Nordic Wars before the times of the North Sea Empire." Amelia smiled. "The Guardians call on the Saints to inspire the soldiers."

I was stunned by her words. This young girl who couldn't have been older than seventeen fought in a war? Rallied it like a Joan of Arc? During a period some twelve hundred years ago? I was astonished. At seventeen I was trying to figure out parallel parking, and this girl had mastered a cutlass in close combat.

"Oh" was all I could manage. "And Lydia, how do you know Eli?" I shakily asked.

"I met him when he was staying with Lucian in Colombia. The guardians rotate. It keeps them impartial to any *one* region. That was back when Eli guarded the Kingdom of Prussia. I think it was a tenuous time for him." she turned to look over her shoulder at me.

I felt completely inept at how little I knew. Ashamed. The depth of who I had become involved with. I should have been asking Eli more questions. The profoundness of his choice rang clearer in my ears, but it was still too difficult to grasp someone who had been alive for such a serious amount of time. I was struggling to grapple with everything and the overwhelming urge to retreat to my previous life, my easier life, was getting more intoxicating by the minute.

What was I doing here?

I felt like I was a teenage girl again standing on the edge of Goldman's

Pond in the woods of Vermont. Watching the girls from school, who had convinced me to come along, drink from a stolen bottle of vodka, and use the old rope swing tied to a dead limb. Afraid we would get hurt or something bad would happen and remembering I just wanted to go home.

"Why are we heading deeper into the mountains?" Uneasiness crept into my chest. The feed store was just outside of town. I looked through the rear window of the SUV.

A sly smile took over Amelia and Lydia, and I clutched the leather of my seat. Tristan knew I was with them so they must be safe. Right? *Breathe, Lily. You sound paranoid.*

"He lives *here*." Lydia stared straight ahead.

We came around a bend and slowed, turning onto a dirt drive with weeds growing up in the center. We weaved around trees and over the bumps slowly climbing further into the dense timber, making it difficult for light to peek through.

A man waited on the sloped porch of the log home. Thick ivy encroached on every corner.

"Good morning." Amelia approached, hopping from the oversized vehicle. "Thank you for making time."

"Everything you need is inside." The man gripped the railing for balance, an elderly tremor shook his weak frame.

Inside were bundles of exotic-looking flowers stacked on the thickly wooden table, bound together by twine. The aroma saturated the air with a sweetly floral scent. It reminded me of the fragrant gardens of the greenhouse at an estate I interned at in college.

The tropical fuchsias and deep violets coiled into one another and their perfume fused with the scents from the bundles of dried lavender and rosemary hanging from the beams of the low ceiling. A cacophony of nature surrounded us.

"It took me a bit to find everything on your list and I apologize for the delay, it was a great deal you were asking for." His stare went back and forth between Lydia and Amelia, who now hovered over the table looking at everything. They didn't respond. "I had to order most of it because they are all very rare." He reached back and pulled out several pairs of gloves that were arm's length and leather.

Amelia and Lydia slipped them on while appearing to be doing a mental inventory of the array.

"So, can you tell me why you three needed so much?" The man squinted a skeptical eye.

"No," Amelia replied firmly.

"It's all here." Lydia stood straight.

We loaded it carefully into the back of the SUV.

"No small children, never handle any of it with your bare hands, and keep it away from animals," he instructed.

"Why?" I pondered his odd instructions. This is what we would be feeding to the Century stallions? August would love to see this, a strange "pony potpourri" she would probably call it.

"Because it's all extremely poisonous." He looked at me sideways.

"Thank you. We greatly appreciate the effort into finding all we asked for. It was prepared exactly as we instructed." Amelia came around the side of the vehicle holding an envelope. "You may count it if you wish."

The man quickly peeked inside, and I watched his eyes grow wide.

"We compensated you for the trouble you went through. And you're discretion."

I didn't know all the things we had gathered, but I did recognize some and they were prohibited from anyone growing them. Since they weren't native here, I imagined this man had somehow procured them illegally. This only made more sense when he made an offhanded comment that he had never been asked to acquire illicit flora before.

I'd never met a smuggler. Not that I knew of at least. What else could he secure if someone asked? It made me wonder how he came about this profession. He seemed so sweet and frail, like a little grandpa who fed pigeons in a park somewhere and always carried butterscotch candies in his pockets.

"Thank you." His eyes misty.

"No, thank *you*. We'll keep you in mind for the future."

He nodded at Lydia's gracious statement as she pulled her gloves off handing them to Amelia to return to the man.

"You ladies have a lovely afternoon." He thrust a hand towards Lydia. I froze and Amelia did the same. I stared as I stood by her side unsure of what to do, but before the thought was finished forming, things happened quickly.

Lydia reached with her left hand for my bare forearm and wrapped a cold palm around it tightly. With her right hand she shook his quickly.

A cold breath escaped my lips, and I felt faint. My heart throbbed and thudded erratically before calming to a slower pace. The world around us became muffled against my eardrums and the edges of my vision faded to dark.

"It's cold." I held my hands, which were involuntarily shaking out in front of me. They were almost alabaster. I was in the back seat of the SUV, and we were driving fast through the winding roads, but I couldn't recall how I had gotten there.

"Why would you reach for *her*?" Amelia's temper boiled.

"I don't know," Lydia stammered, staring back at me over the headrest. "Do you think he'll notice?"

"Yes, he'll notice. Her lips are blue, Lydia! You're lucky you didn't kill her!" Amelia growled across the console.

"Take deep breaths, Lily," Lydia instructed. I couldn't focus on anything.

"What's...wrong with me?" I pleaded.

"Residuals need life to touch another human, so instead of taking *his* and getting caught, she instinctively grabbed the next available one!" Amelia yelled, staring straight ahead.

"Me?" I whispered sluggishly to myself.

"I'm so sorry, Lily. She's pale." She turned to Amelia.

"Yes, Lydia, because she was almost dead." Dark eyes reflected at me in the rear view mirror.

I looked out the windshield and felt the familiar turns of the driveway as we arrived. Driving around the side of the house we accelerated uphill and parked behind the stables.

"*You* stay back!" Amelia instructed.

"Amelia?" I could hear Tristan, but I couldn't make out the words. "What happened! Lily?" Tristan was palming both sides of my face. "I thought you were going to get feed up the road? How did this happen?"

"Lydia needed a more *corporal* form for the interaction. The guy went to shake her hand, and Lily was all she could think of." Amelia was standing beside Lydia with a stern set to her jaw.

"Really? *Her*?" Tristan spun to face Lydia.

"I didn't know what to do." Her tone was desperate.

"What happened to her?" Eli roared suddenly behind them. The gathered people fell silent, and I could feel him getting closer.

"Eli?" I called softly.

"I'm right here, Lily." He scooped me close to his broad chest and turned towards the stable. I could hear a dozen footsteps following and I closed my eyes.

"I'm sorry," I replied.

"This was not your fault. Can you look at me, Lily?" I opened my eyes and gasped at the wild blue irises that sent shocks down my spine. He smiled lightly. "How are you feeling?"

"Better." He wanted to set me down but I tightened my grip. "Not yet," I whispered. I felt faint.

He stood still, breathing slowly, his eyes closed as mine were.

"I'm alright." I smiled softly after many minutes, standing, looking up at him.

"You're still very pale." Worry pressed his brows together.

"I had the life sucked from me." I smiled, trying to make light of the situation.

"I *know*." His voice lowered and his eyes embraced new darkness as he cast his stare behind me. "You!" He walked around me and the bodies that had gathered hung their heads. He made his way to Lydia.

Tears coated her words as she pleaded for him to forgive her. You could sense the terror she felt as he closed the space between them. Never once had I feared him. Even after knowing what he was and seeing what his brothers were capable of I didn't shy away.

"You could have killed her!" he bellowed, and it echoed inside the vast stable reigning down on us all. I shook from his strength and averted my eyes.

"I didn't mean—" And before she could finish her sentence, his hand ripped upwards, seizing her neck, and turning her ashen with the grip. He raised her from the ground slowly as she clawed at his grasp. Her feet dangling, tiny choking gasps escaped her mouth as her eyes rolled backward.

"I don't care what you *meant* to do." The people pressed their backs into the walls now, while some were crouching down. Like bowing before a king the people obeyed. He had her raised above his head, his arm outstretched, the weight an effortless extension.

However, I wasn't afraid. I was growing angry *I* might have been caught. I leaned forward, discovering I wanted him to do this. I licked my lips in anticipation and the thought frightened me.

What was going on? I knew she hadn't meant to harm me. She was only reacting.

She almost killed you! My conscience screamed inside me from another corner.

A low growl rose in my chest, and I felt his strength pulse in my neck and back.

"Kill her."

The thought that erupted from my mouth drew a strange reaction from the crowd. My hand clamped across my lips. What was I saying? Kill her? Was I serious?

Eli turned towards me, my words breaking through his anger and he dropped her. Tears filling my eyes I shook my head to and fro.

"I…" The words struggling. "I don't know why I said that." I looked to him for answers. "I'm scared," I murmured.

He turned and stared at a whimpering Lydia who was clutching her neck nervously, crumpled at his feet. "I want you away from here," Eli commanded as his fingers laced through mine while he guided me from the stable.

Tristan was close as we passed the cottage and started trailing into the trees. "Are you bringing her with us?" he inquired with a hint of worry.

"I can't trust them to take care of her when I'm away, so I'll bring her with me." Eli's jaw was tight as he spoke. We were now accompanied by others as we cut through the forest: two of the Condemned, two Saints, and one Residual, all behind us except for Tristan who was at our side.

"Are you not concerned, Eli, this could be harmful?" the blond Saint pondered.

"I can take care of her!" Eli yelled, rotating quickly.

The group of men fell quiet.

"Eli?" Tristan stepped forward bravely. "We are on your side and do not question you. We worry equally for Lily's safety more than we do the rest of her kind. Her mortality and vulnerability are difficult for all of us." He placed a reassuring hand on Eli's shoulder.

The remainder of the journey was silent, except for when I almost tripped at the sight of weapons being drawn once we reached a certain distance past the grounds of the house. The danger lurking beyond the perimeter seemed distant, like another country, but here now, on the fringes of the property, it was very real.

And while I had been playing house with Jarrett and grappling with my feelings toward him and Eli, I ignored the fact that we were under threat. Maybe *ignored* was the wrong word. I had outright been in a state of denial. Unwilling to accept what was happening around me.

"Why are we here?" I turned to look into his intrusive eyes.

"Results." Leaning in, he whispered in my ear, "Wait here. Marcus?" He motioned to Marcus with his hand. The Condemned who argued with Ethan in the kitchen.

Marcus took two small steps forward and leapt into the opening surrounded by wispy willows. My underground waterfall crashing over the opposing edge, a hearty turquoise burning green in the warming sunlight. This had been the place I took Jarrett to, a place I sought out for refuge when governed by confusion, where Eli pulled me from the warm black depths. When our paths so faithfully began to twist and bind.

He swiftly bent one arm underneath my legs, the other firmly around my ribs. Effortlessly, he flung me into the gaping hole. No scream could escape my lips before two more arms were firmly holding me below.

Marcus gently placed my feet atop a mossy boulder. A moist blow to my left, and Tristan began to stand upright. One after another they leapt from the edge and landed muted around me.

They all walked to the water's edge.

"No one draws weapons in the water. Not with Lily here." Eli instructed, and they all nodded. "Keep her surrounded at all times. Is this clear?" He made eye contact with everyone.

"She's mortal. Understood," the other Condemned shouted. "Everyone stay alive!"

Where I was confused. What did they mean, *in the water?*

11

Breaking Vases

Rifles, swords, and weapons littered the mossy floor of my hidden oasis. A heavy reality weighed on me for the first time, and I found it daunting. What we were about to do was dangerous.

"See anything, Andy?" Tristan looked to Andy, the Residual, who had been walking around the cavern for a few minutes.

"Nothing close enough to worry about." Andy shook his head as he looked skyward, the beams of light ambling across his young features.

The way I understood it was that Residuals walked both sides of the veil, here and in the Garden all at once. They could watch for people coming. Tristan was telling me this while they prepared small drawstring bags. You could see both plains but could only focus on one at a time. Like hearing two different songs at once, he explained, you had to listen to differentiate the tunes.

"This time is as good as any then." Tristan began to unbutton his shirt.

The other formidable Condemned, who I learned to be Bjorn, began to unbuckle the thick leather belt tightened around his waist, simultaneously using his toes to pry off bulky leather boots.

Every time I saw Bjorn he seemed to be glued to Marcus's side. I wasn't sure if that was because they both hailed from the Condemned or something more was between them. Ethereals had a casual take on life, death, and love. Holding a fluid nonchalance toward all mortal tendencies. Everything seemed to be *less* with them. Death was a fact that came and went. Life was a finite and insignificant human flaw. And love was whatever they felt it to be.

I was distracted by the Saint with the golden crown of hair pulling the shirt he was wearing up over his head and quickly stuffing it into a black pouch that was velvety in appearance. One after another they began to undress around me.

I turned, not wanting to gawk at the five angelic men disrobing in the sunlight next to my misty waterfall. The scene that lay in front of me was unexpected. Eli stood with his bare back to me, his shirt tucked away in a similar velvety pouch. He was looking down, unbuttoning his jeans, and I bit my lip as my heartbeat grew irregular. His skin was flawless in the light of day. Unable to look away as he spun them into a small cylinder tucking them away into his bag.

I could hear nothing except the thundering pull tearing through my chest desperately reaching towards him as he stood in his underwear. The hesitation to mimic the group derailed, and I pulled off the clothes keeping me from him, standing in my cropped camisole and underwear. My jaw was shaking and all muscles were taut as a painful ache took over my heart. A thick want grew in my throat, and I needed to cry out to him.

"Warden," I spoke the words barely above a whisper. He turned in the blink of an eye. Our stares were hypnotic.

"Lily?" He stepped to within inches. "I..."

"Can feel it?" Our eyes didn't break.

He nodded. "How do you know that name?"

"What name?" I whispered leaning into him.

"Warden…" He trailed off searching my eyes. His face had an abundance of familiarity I had never known.

"Because you are their ward, are you not, my Eli?" My voice was low and soft as he nodded. "Will you not follow me?" My arms reached up around his neck.

"Lily. Eli. Are you guys alright?" Tristan erupted into the forefront. "This is *interesting*." He was staring down at me. "How did you do that?"

Suddenly, it was as if I finally noticed the men standing closely. All of them surrounding me with blank expressions and a trance-like stare. Lost for a moment. They wavered and awakened as I blinked away my own haze filling my head. "Do what?"

"That voice?" He cocked his head sideways while looking around slowly at the men.

"What voice?" I looked up, blinking in the sunlight as I too fell from my trance.

It felt like I just awoke from the most perfectly calming nap. Relaxed and needing to stretch, I wanted to crack my back and yawn.

"That voice where you called out to him using their other name. You don't remember it happening?" He looked closer. His silvery eyes squinted in skepticism.

I had no idea what he was talking about. One moment everyone was undressing, and the next I remembered seeing Eli and feeling a drawing desire to be nearer to him.

Unable to form an answer, I held my silence. "No one knows how to call them unless you're…" He took a few steps back with a trace of fear constricting his pupils. The same fear I had seen this morning when I confessed my dreams of the red-haired girl.

"We need to move," a Saint called from the water's edge.

"He's right. They're getting too close," Andy said, his eyes focused on the treetops.

I felt a hand on the small of my back while another gently gripped my forearm, urging me into the warm water. I didn't have time to figure out what Tristan meant. We were on a timetable.

"Eli?" A frightened whimper called out to him, recalling the night I had almost drowned here. I had never willingly swam here, let alone, downstream into the caves beyond the opening.

"You can do this," he encouraged.

I paddled frantically while my lungs briefly seized and recited his words to myself. My eyes were fixated on his face as my head weltered below the surface.

"Easy, human, this isn't even the hard part," Bjorn smiled. Amused while leading me by the forearm to Eli.

They all swam effortlessly as I struggled beside them. One of their strides was three of mine. Each stroke would lead you to believe the waters were still for them.

Tristan, occupying my other side, encouraged me.

I managed to thank him before water rushed through my mouth and I was sent into a fit of coughing. "Sorry," I garbled before my head dipped underwater yet again. Eli was there to quickly pull me upward.

"Let's pull to shore here." Tristan nodded.

Eli tugged me lightly to the sandy edge bathed by light where time had eroded holes in the forest floor above. I sat perched on my knees heaving, my arms a numb weight dangling from each shoulder socket. I shook hard, tasting the cold blue radiating through my lips while in the cool shadows of the cave. Eli pulled the black pouches he had carried, and one after another shook them out into beautiful silken robes, our clothes suddenly absent. He draped one over me and rubbed my shoulders for warmth.

"These should help." I felt his concern and reassured him with a weak smile. "Take this." A small charcoal handgun lay in his palm.

"You're going unarmed?" the lanky Saint pried nervously.

"Lead." He raised a brow. A small order not meant to be ignored.

We walked for some time. The cave's crystals sparkled among the rocks from the refracting shine above. I shuffled along at the rear of the group as we passed through light shafts like ghosts. When we slowed in a widened area the pack of men began cocking the rifles they held over their heads while swimming. I couldn't see what we were getting ready for, until I heard a feathery voice in front of us.

"You brought friends," a woman articulated delicately.

Tristan walked around me. Another barrier as he stood shoulder to shoulder with Eli taking away my complete view.

"Shall we pick up where we left off?" A reserved yet arrogant tone took to the mysterious woman's vocals.

"Still a prophetic whore I see?" Marcus layered his reprise with thick sarcasm.

"Prophetic? How sweet of you to think so." Her voice sprung higher, a smile rounding her words. "Eli?"

She sounded surprised when she uttered his name.

"Josephine. Exile has been treating you well I see." Eli started toward her. Tristan moved into his place diminishing my view. Whatever she was, they weren't going to let me get close enough to find out.

"I never fathomed you to be a turncoat to the guardians. Gabriel and his independence perhaps. Even Alokin's aloof ways would lead one to believe." She clicked her tongue disapprovingly. "But Elijah, the prodigal son? The first. Now moved to kidnapping? I believe humans refer to you as a *fugitive*."

"Zacarius never was one to hide his collectibles well," Eli said.

A foreign accent played on her words. An elegance hiding there. I wanted to see the woman the men feared who spoke so caustically. Was this the reason they were so heavily armed? I learned not to underestimate the power of one Ethereal. Their stature alluded little to the strength they wielded.

Peaking around Tristan's waist, I leaned closer to the wall trying to get a glimpse of her. I was stunned. The young voice did not match the face. She was older with long silver hair and cloudy blue eyes. She held a small smile at the corners of her thin lips, and she wore a linen ivory dress while she sat cross-legged in the sand. Her hands resting in her lap as sunbeams enshrined her. Each wrist shackled heavily. Chains heaped in tiny piles for the slack she was granted.

This was a cell.

If anyone were to attempt an escape, they would be swept downstream to the house or drowned in their efforts to get back to the grotto.

"So, she's real?" Her eyes met mine abruptly as she whispered, "You really are doing this for her." A furtive smile pulled the edge of her mouth upwards.

Tristan moved to hinder her field of vision again.

"Trying to stifle my view, Tristan?" I could feel her stare moving past him still connecting with me.

I gazed at her once again, and she slowly pulled a bony index finger in front of her gesturing for me to step forward. I walked cautiously toward her. The squelch of sand moving around my toes with every footstep.

"A bold move, Elijah, to bring her while you do this." She tilted her head to one side, contemplating me. I wondered what she meant. "Provocation." She smiled, reading my mind. "For whom? All," she answered my questions before they were formed.

"Wars have touched many shores of all regions by humans. Some by members of our own Legions, but *none* by the Guardians." She held a grim tone as she spoke in an echoing voice. "You, my love, will be here to witness the first. A deed that will prove costly for many in the end. This will be an act of *true* war," she murmured reverently as she slowly closed her eyes. "The pain you'll collide with will be reality."

A strange calm clung to the air and then it happened. The barrel of the gun was pressed to the crown of her head, yet she remained still while harnessing a soft smile on her lips. There wasn't a bright flash, but a deafening bang, no scream to accompany what took place. The cave filled with the smell of iron from the spray of blood that soaked the sponge-like walls. I heard her cranium crack from the fracture of the bullet. Eli's hand released the trigger, and he bent seizing the thick chains and wrenched them from the ground with a clang.

"Andy, be merciful. Finish her."

The gentle Residual moved forward swiftly and placed a palm on the reddened woman staining the sand. A minute lift of her chest and an exhale escaped. I understood what Lydia, the Residual who grabbed me at the smuggler's cabin, had done. A soft touch pulling away the final strands of life. Absorbing it. Taking it from the living thing and becoming corporal themselves.

"Apostate." Eli suddenly clenched his jaw and cocked the trigger. Quickly firing a round into the chest of the Residual as he came to stand. My eyes widened as this Andy fell to the sand and a soft breeze blew the stolen threads of life away from him. He had become tangible. More prescient on this plane, and it was used as a trick to kill him.

Eli walked past pausing to gently kiss the top of my head. Crimson tarnished his skin. "Move quickly."

The men ripped the black robes from their shoulders and jumped into the water waiting to head the way we had come. I looked to him for answers. I could barely swim downstream, let alone up.

"Tristan, take her back to the house. Marcus, dispose. We have a guest." Eli jumped into the water and suddenly they were gone from view.

"Let's move." Tristan reached for my hand and immediately we took off in the opposite direction.

"This is not good?" I called as we jogged through the fleeting light.

"If you mean by murdering our own or slaughtering a Scribe? Then yes, not good," he called. "We should run faster."

"Scribe?" I called. "What the fuck is that?"

"A big deal," Tristan laughed through his nose.

***

My arms were wrapped around Tristan's neck as he stroked downstream. We were moving with the rush of the water, and I was afraid of who might be behind us when suddenly he veered off to the right into a large off-chute. The waters instantly calmed and grew hotter. It was dark, but there was a light glowing yellow up ahead and drawing closer. Suddenly, the cave changed and we swam through what appeared to be a brick-underground-aqueduct.

He pulled me through a second archway, and we were inside the bathhouse in the basement of the main house. Steam filled the room and rose to the domed ceilings where Edison lights filled the space casting an amber hue below. White-tiled steps had been laid into the edge of the gentle swirling pool and I climbed up.

Tristan ran into the glass-paneled sauna and snatched two robes, tossing one to me.

"She was clairvoyant?" I panted, a little out of breath.

"I forget how much you don't know," he exhaled and pinched the bridge of his nose. "Yes, in a sense."

I was lost.

He went on to explain how the first Forging was foretold in something humans would probably think of as scripture. "Scribes foretell events recorded in our sacred writs. They can only be read by *real* priests. Unfortunately, I don't know any of those. They haven't been seen for some time, and my ability to find a Scribe is above my pay grade."

We washed the grime from our faces before we headed up in case the house guests had returned home.

"So, they are likened to prophets and wrote what? History of…?" I searched for the answer.

"Us. Accurate ones can be challenging to find. If scribes could be classified, Josephine was an icon. It's why she's willingly stayed in Zacarius's care." He rolled his eyes, insinuating something else.

"Then why did we execute her? Shouldn't we have asked her more questions?" I still felt sick rehashing the scene I'd witnessed.

"We didn't want her for intel. She was retribution or our first move, depending on how you view it." He was unfazed. "Killing a scribe is egregious. Sacrosanct if you will."

"*Don't worry about the vase,*" I whispered to myself.

"What?" Tristan stopped short. He was staring at me.

"The movie *The Matrix.* The Oracle tells Neo not to worry about a vase and he turns and inadvertently breaks it. But the bigger question was, would he have broken it if she had said anything?"

He was still confused.

I sighed. "Josephine said for the first time the guardians will start a war involving themselves, and *I* would be there for it. What if everything we're doing is wrong? What if we're telling people not to worry about the vase?"

"Eli's right. You are brilliant." He shook his head.

"Who's coming?" I asked.

"And highly observant." He began to walk the long hallway to head upstairs. He wasn't answering any more of my questions. "The Baynes fly out after tomorrow. They're acting as camouflage for now. No one would come close while this many mortals are here. Let's relax and deal with this later."

Before I could pepper him with any more questions, I heard music blasting from upstairs. The muffled guitar vibrated the floors. We opened the door to the main hallway and CCR's "Fortunate Son" was ringing out through the house's built-in sound system.

"Lil! Tristan!" Tate spotted us first.

Bennett was flipping burgers on the grill out back, and the boys were scattered about the space behind the house playing some ridiculous version of volleyball where one of them was blindfolded. The entire scene was a striking difference to where I'd just been. It felt strange, as though I'd witnessed a crash no one else could see or hear.

"Where have you guys been?" Logan piped. "We got home an hour ago and couldn't find you."

I kept flexing my hands and taking slow breaths. I could see August eyeing me and I shook my head minutely. She knew something was going on, but now was not the time or place to share it.

My head was spinning, and I wanted to talk to Eli. What was happening? What did Tristan mean when he asked how I knew Eli's other name? Why did he kill that Residual and that scribe, Josephine? The questions were stacking up.

I was worried about Eli. Worried about everything the Scribe had just shared. It felt like someone had taken hold of the threads of my life and began running wild with them.

"We were down in the bathhouse. It's on the lowest level of the basement." Tristan walked past the counter and plucked a beer from the ice chest cracking it open. It was as though he had completely moved past what had happened in the cave.

I tried to take a page from his playbook, but I felt edgy and nervous about what I may have just been a part of. Like I lit the wick of something volatile and I didn't know which direction to brace for the impending explosion.

"God, I love this house! It's giant! Auggie, marry this son of a bitch!" Grey hollered, facing backward on his side of the court. It was his turn to be blindfolded. Three on three with each team having one player blindfolded to make it interesting.

"We figured when you two got back, we'd eat some lunch. Then drink some rum and head to the lake to play some ring toss this evening." Bennett pushed a corn cob farther back on the pit.

"I made my homemade fruit salad," August beamed while she dropped to her knees and volleyed the white ball back across the net.

"You mean your sangria?" Tate corrected.

"It's fruit salad, ass hat! With my special ingredient." She shoved her brother.

"The secret is moscato." Bennett smirked.

"Just like mom used to make." Logan sighed wistfully.

"You both don't get any now!" August chided.

"You smell nice." Jarrett appeared at my side and kissed my cheek. He could smell the bergamot soap I had used to hastily wash the blood speckles away downstairs.

"Thanks. You do too." I smiled weakly.

"Sawdust?" He grinned.

I nodded and forced a half-hearted chuckle.

"I'm gonna go change and clean up. I'll be ready to leave in a bit," I said as he kissed my forehead, and I headed back into the house. I was taking slow and even breaths. The shock was wearing off, and now I was grappling with the next step.

To pretend I didn't witness a murder that was the nascence of a war.

12

We're Waterproof

I f there was anyone who could disassociate, it was me. I learned the skill as a child after my father died. Learned to shut off the feelings fear and grief could incite. I adapted the behavior quickly in the wake of his death after my mother would snap at me for crying. She would tug my hand, pulling me in close, and murmur in a clipped tone how I must be a *big girl now* and to *just stop it*.

Forgetting was a survival tactic I picked up to endure my teenage years under the reign of my mother. The woman thrived on appearances.

I was applauded for my resilience. But all it really did was make it harder to share my feelings. More difficult to ask for help when I needed it. I could compartmentalize in ways others couldn't. Stay focused. Driven. However, it also made me feel another thing—alone.

I closed my eyes and focused on my fingers laced through Jarrett's. He was laughing heartily at something Bennett said. I felt the warmth of his palm and safety pouring from him. I folded up the horrors I'd seen this afternoon and neatly tucked them into that place I kept everything which could gnaw at me or unravel my composure.

"Hello, girls!" Tate stood on a cooler addressing the group. "And my beautiful Lilian. Another year has passed since our last Freedom Weekend, and to kick off this celebratory time we must start with our annual event—ring toss!" He grinned, holding his arms wide, and cheers erupted from the group. "Okay, so everyone knows the rules. August won't let Tristan play with us and Lily is easily breakable, so they will be our honorary referees. Everyone, suit up!" Tate jumped off the cooler and jogged to the shores of the beach.

Tristan and I stayed seated in the trunk of the Tahoe. The doors hung open as we watched.

"Why the invented games?" Tristan leaned over to me questioningly. I think he could sense my uneasiness and was trying to calm my frigid nerves.

"That's easy! Because the *law* is too scared to allow real games!" Grey raised a fist as he and the rest of the group began to undress. "Avert your eyes from my man glory, little sister. I brought a secret weapon this year!" He bent to the ground after removing his jeans and pulled on a pair of biking shorts he had bought while they were in town.

"That's nothing!" Trip and Tate yelled, turning towards each other, and dipping their fingers into a jar of petroleum jelly before caking it on their bodies. "We're waterproof!" Tate called over Trip's shoulder to Logan.

Their antics helped me relax, and the invented games made me laugh. And a shirtless Jarrett was distracting me in all the right ways. I started to lean back onto my hands and watch as August tied her hair up while others snapped on swimming caps. They pulled up belts with a single ring hanging from each hip and tightened them around their waist. After all were secured, they clipped a rope to each side of the rings.

"What are they doing?" Tristan murmured out of the corner of his mouth.

"Turning it into a Bayne game. They hook the ropes to themselves and then the person on either side of them," I explained nonchalantly since I'd seen it a hundred times. "August is a girl so she gets a handicap—a longer rope to even out the odds." Tristan huffed a laugh fondly. "She insists she doesn't need it."

"Of course I don't!" August retorted, hand on her cocked-out hip. "Are we going to do this shit or what?" She motioned at her brothers.

I scooted off the vehicle and headed to the cooler of ice where they were keeping the beer. I pulled out cans and handed one to each player while speaking.

"Everyone finishes the beer first. No cheating! That means crunching the can! Know your colors! You move a player's ring you know the penalty. I'll call the fouls as I see them." I reached into the ice and lifted out the dozens of white translucent rings.

This was good. Normal. As normal as things could be around a Bayne.

"Alright, we need the best and the worst from volleyball earlier today," Logan yelled as they crowded around. Jarrett and Tate came to stand face to face. "Ready?" They each nodded, stern looks accompanying their features. "Tate, you call it."

"Tails!" Logan flicked a silver coin into the air, catching it on the downfall. Quickly flipping it onto the back of his hand. He covered it.

"Tails!" He peeked quickly. "Sorry, Jarrett, you lose." He shook his head.

"You didn't show everyone!" Jarrett called with his mouth agape.

"You calling me a liar?" Logan pointed. The boys huffed out their chests. "Deal with it. You lost. Grey, get the ankle weights!" He thumbed over his shoulder.

"Guys, let's keep focused. First to finish the beer gets to use the cheat." I waited as they bent and strapped the weights to Jarrett's ankles. I looked at him sympathetically as he smiled and rolled his eyes. "Ready? On three. One—three!" I screamed.

They all gulped frantically. The yellow ale dripped from the corners of their mouths and ran down their necks. Some were serious while others side-eyed and chuckled through their swallows at their adjacent siblings. A smile warmed my face at the sight of Jarrett's chest giggling between swigs. A can crunched to my left, and Trip thrust it into the air. Shortly after, others crushed their cans in defeat. Grey finished his last, throwing it to the ground irritated.

"Don't be sour, Grey. Maybe next year!" Jarrett winked. I couldn't help but smile.

"Shut it!" he growled.

"You all shut it!" Trip instructed, boasting an air of confidence at his victory. "Lily, my love, the rings please?" He waggled his brows. "Can't wait, sweetie, until I can really say that to you." He held out a hand as I gave him the translucent white rings I was holding. "Know your colors!" He cracked the rings and tossed them out in the shallows of the darkening water. An eerie glow taking over. "Everyone line up," he spoke sternly. Then he reached down and snatched up his prize.

"What is he doing?" Tristan asked as I went to take my seat next to him on the tailgate.

"Whoever chugs the beer gets the *cheat*." I rolled my eyes. "An underwater flare. It burns bright and smells terrible, but they strive like hell every year to win it." I shrugged.

"Because it makes us look cool!" Trip yelled over the burning of the flare he was holding out, the strong scent of sulfur growing.

"I'm pretty sure it's illegal," I uttered under my breath. As if that even mattered to them.

They lined the bank of the lake looking for their rings, some laughing, most yelling, and all stumbling slightly from the self-induced head rush they had guzzled.

"Go!" I shouted.

They madly rushed to the water. Grey and Logan, standing on both sides of Bennett, tugged on their ropes and held him back.

"You can't swim, Bennett. You're too little!" Logan grinned. "I hope you brought your floaties at least!"

Bennett kicked his heels into the sand and dug in trying to pull people forward while he searched for his rings. Yanking his brothers slowly closer to the water. I laughed, watching him drag the lankier Baynes at his sides.

August was already out with a bright pink ring in one hand heading to her bucket at a run when, suddenly, Tate appeared out of the water. He had one hand tightly gripping her rope attached to his left hip. He yanked it backward, causing August to whip in the opposite direction of her run, smacking flat on her back in the sand.

Tristan immediately stood at my side.

"She's fine. It's part of the game to hinder your opponents." I smiled at his tender gesture and pulled him gently to sit down. I once saw August cold cock a guy in the throat at a bar who grabbed her boob. She could be feral if you wronged her or those she cared about.

"Haha, you suck!" Tate flipped off August as he dropped the ring in his bucket. He sprinted towards the water but she was too quick on the revenge. Jumping to her feet she tossed the ring into her bucket and ran hard, leaping onto Tate's back as he was about to plunge below the surface again. Wrapping their shared rope around his neck and shoving him underwater. Every time bringing him up to yell, "Don't. Pull. My. Rope." Uncoiling it she dove sideways and disappeared before coming up with yet another bright pink ring. Tate was still recovering. "Yeah bitch!" August wagged the ring and danced her way to the bucket. "Me, two. You, one!"

Tristan and I both chortled from their escapades. It was nice, an outsider alongside me, bathing in their warmth. Laid back and laughing together at their amusing wildness they brewed.

These people didn't murder supernatural beings. They were kind. In fact, one summer Grey and Logan found a batch of orphaned kittens they raised up. They even trained them to come when they sang the chorus of a song. I smiled, remembering the sound of their off-key rendition they would call out, while the tiny mews of mismatched tabbies trotted up for a meal.

"See?" I gestured to Tristan. "They'll clothesline each other, get tangled, hold one another underwater, and cheat in every way they can think of."

"Oh yeah, what?" Tate chucked a pink ring back into the water.

"Foul!" I called. "Tate waits thirty seconds."

"I love it when you talk dirty to me." Tate licked his lips at me.

"Golden rule: don't touch the other's rings," I explained and we watched in silence for a while. Now and again Tristan would laugh loudly at the antics unfolding in front of him.

I stared, lost in the Baynes. I wasn't being hunted. I wasn't getting the life sucked from me. And I wasn't facing imminent death. I was me, with them, warmed by their bright lifestyle. I was *safe* again.

And the darkness on the fringes of my life suddenly fell out of focus and the happiness they brought washed over me. I didn't want them to leave. I needed them *here*.

"I see why you care so deeply for August…and Jarrett." Tristan spoke more softly now.

"I can't help it." I watched Jarrett.

"Nor can I. It's the strangest thing…all of this," Tristan speculated. "But how will Jarrett feel when you break his heart?"

"What do you mean?" I looked at him sideways.

"How does Jarrett fit with Eli?" Tristan stared ahead.

I was quiet for some time. "I don't know." And I didn't. Jarrett was safe and warm. Eli was elusive and mysterious. How do you choose when you care so deeply for both? "I haven't thought it through. The train started to move so I got on." I picked at the dirt flicking it away from the truck.

"And your...*husband*? Where does he belong?" A small smile grew.

"Ethan *was* my best friend. He's passionate and sensitive." I sighed heavily.

Tristan must have understood I was confused and this wasn't helping. "Well, I'm going to water a tree. Would you like me to get you a beer?" He stood brushing his hands along his jeans.

"No, I'm fine," I replied lightly.

"Lily?" He bent to look me in the eye. "You don't have to know the answers right now."

I nodded while smiling, and then he disappeared. I tried to re-focus on the games. I normally would talk to August during these situations despite how few there were. But I didn't know which way her opinion would lead. I felt the gnawing of guilt swell in the pit of my stomach. It was unfair to Eli, Jarrett, and Ethan.

Ethan. I missed him. I closed my eyes and tried to shut out the hurt I felt for pushing him away last night. How relieved I had been to see him.

I floated away to the night I ran off to see him and tried to grasp something of my life prior to the ruins it now was becoming.

I awoke with a shudder.

"One of your dreams?" Ethan whispered through the darkness. White moonlight seeped through the blinds of his bedroom.

His arms gently cradled me. I nodded and reached up to wipe away the tears.

"Are you going to tell me what it was about?" he spoke softly into my hair as he kissed my forehead gently.

"That you know I have them is enough. Why aren't you asleep?" I tried to get away from the darkness lurking behind my lids.

"I have this feeling something is going to change with you and me now."

Our eyes met, and I watched the torment teeming in his.

I looked away. He was right. No matter how things ended, they would be different. Ethan could never know about Eli. Especially the danger that came along with him.

"Ethan… If I left…" I closed my eyes searching for the words I needed. "If I couldn't come back here, I always *want* you in my life. Always." I smiled into his side as my fingertips caressed his bare chest. Slowly drawing lines over his exposed ribs. I was trying to tell him that even if I couldn't be around him to keep him safe, he should know I would always want to.

He was quiet. I peeked through my lashes expecting to see resentment. Instead, his eyes were closed and silent tears flowed over his tanned temples coming to rest in his bright blond waves.

"I…" My chest ached at the sight of his despair. I wanted to stop it and tell him everything. I couldn't.

I leaned into his side and let my lips form the kisses. A cold sigh slowly escaped my nose, and I felt his hands tremble. I let my tongue run along his collarbone, finally kissing the base of his throat. A desire grew between my thighs as he arched his back into the pillow. I moved a leg over his pelvis to sit atop him.

"Lily…" Ethan murmured.

I didn't respond. Both of my hands grasped the bottom of the T-shirt he had lent me, and I pulled it up and over my head dropping it to the floor beside the bed.

My breathing intensified as I sat motionless. The moonlight casting across my bare breasts. I reached for Ethan's shaking palms resting on my thighs and brought them to my chest. My breathing quickly turned unsteady. Ethan sat upright, kissing my neck, letting his tongue play across a nipple gently as he cupped a breast. He tilted his head back and groaned while my forearms rested on his sun-kissed shoulders.

I found his lips and let mine part while our tongues twisted and my fingers played with his hair.

I pulled away and watched while I lay on my propped elbows as he dragged the lacy underwear clinging to my hips away. He hastily tugged his boxers to his ankles. They caught around his left foot, and he cursed under his breath. Once free, he leaned forward and pulled me upwards with a hand under each of my arms. He had done this so many times with women. But for someone so seasoned there was an air of tension about him. He was being careful with me.

Our kisses evoked a hard ache in his groin. I could feel it brushing between my thighs. There was a moment of pause before he lifted me gently with one hand while using his other to guide himself. Pulling me down slowly, our bodies carefully began to pump and fluctuate. My head rolled back and a moan rose from my throat. My hands tightened while clutching his shoulders.

"Am I hurting you?" he asked worriedly.

I smiled at him. "No," I said airily.

His hands were hot against my hips as his lips trailed my naked skin. Sweat beaded and trickled down my spine. Hypnotized by the ecstasy, our friction created. Moving faster and harder as he tossed me to my back I clutched the bed sheets. Feeling him within me moving deeper as my eyes rolled back. Every throbbing movement drew the pinnacle closer as his body shook.

"Ethan…" I pouted.

He paused momentarily looking into my eyes and then pulled my face to his. His kisses became frantic as he moved faster.

"I love you, Lily." His arms wrapped around me and—

"Yoo-hoo! Lily!" August's voice cut through my flashback snapping me into reality. "What the hell were you thinking about?" She cocked her head sideways.

"What? Nothing." I shrugged the remaining thoughts floating away behind my eyes.

"'Kay, well then, whose foul?" she questioned.

"Tate?" I hadn't been paying any attention.

"Yes!" Jarrett pulled down an arm in victory.

"Haha. Told you she would pick her boyfriend!" August grinned while jogging back towards the water.

"I forgive you, Lily." Tate stood next to his bucket. His bucket which was nearly full now. How long had my mind wandered?

I looked around for the first time. Where was Tristan? I slid from my seat and stretched before rounding the edge of the vehicle.

He wasn't anywhere near the cooler beside the front of the truck. I looked around, hands on my hips, and listened.

Nothing. Had he gone back to the house? He wouldn't leave us alone out here. I continued walking farther into the surrounding pines when I heard it. I inched closer and my mind whispered to listen.

"She's different. She's never alone, and Elijah never places trust in only one person to watch over her," a dark voice murmured.

"And his travels? Has he confided in you?" another man replied.

I kept my back to a tree with my head turned sideways as my ear was gathering as much of the conversation as possible.

"Unfortunately, he's not shared this with anyone. I'm unsure if he stays in his region or even takes someone with him. He is wise and knows what he's up against. I assume he may be gaining information on their interest in the girl." Tristan's voice rose.

Fear encased my nerves.

Desperate to know who he was swapping details with, I edged my head closer as I held my breath.

"Their determination to succeed is infallible. It's a desperation few have witnessed rising from them." My head broke into view, and I almost gasped in terror. Tristan's back was to me, and I looked on in horror at who the other voice was.

"It's a shared desperation." A toned young man with auburn hair and red halos encompassing his arms and burning bright beneath his jeans.

He was speaking to a member of the Legion.

WERB LITCHOOK

13

An Answer For Murder

After a speech no one listened to by August, the self-proclaimed winner, we cleaned up the beach and headed back to the house. I was doing my best not to side-eye Tristan through dinner, who was laughing alongside the boys with a casual arm around August's shoulders. Already an honorary Bayne. My intuition wasn't sending up a warning, but I felt wholly uneasy about seeing him talking to a Legion soldier.

I liked Tristan. I didn't want him to be a double agent so I was trying to be rational about what I'd seen. He *was* a general in the Legion so it would make sense for him to talk to those red-ringed barbarians. But on the other hand, Eli pressed again and again to trust no one. Even Tristan himself advised me not to trust him. Was he warning me? Or was something else happening here?

"Lily, they drank too much. There's no way they won't sleep all night!" I smiled hearing Jarrett call from the bottom of the staircase. I wanted to go to sleep next to him. I wanted to cuddle up and keep the horrors away, but some small part of it was beginning to feel wrong. Maybe it was what Tristan had asked me when we were talking, or maybe the Bayne high was growing less and less with Eli's new reality bleeding onto my life.

It would have to be a problem for tomorrow. I was too tired after today, so I drifted to hollering Baynes and footfalls.

Opening my eyes, a dark hood clouded my periphery and my heartbeat thundering in my ears focused my erratic thoughts. It was a dream and I was already running when I peered down quickly to notice weathered cobblestones. The small passageway narrow and foreign in appearance was shrouded in nightfall. Dangling lanterns flickered flamed shadows high across the stone walls.

I could hear the distant drunken singing and echoing footsteps.

"Be swift," a warm voice whispered frantically.

I looked ahead to see a person cloaked in black running with me as well, and I quickened my pace. I knew danger was pressing on my heels, and I watched in wonderment as the one in front of me was silent while their feet pummeled the ground. The black cloak draped over them lapped at every corner we hastily turned.

I felt fear aching in my stomach for something. What was it? The thoughts were abruptly halted when the cloaked figure reached back and pulled me forward pushing me into a gap between the stones.

"The both of us can't fit," I whispered urgently. A hand forced me downward as their head whipped sideways watching the way we had come.

They leaned close. "Be still." Deep auburn hair and the tip of a small creamy nose were all that was visible of the girl.

Hesperia.

She vanished without another word. I panicked as her silence and the comfort of her presence evaded me.

Only a moment elapsed before another cloaked figure appeared. I cringed into the shadows as fear seized my lungs.

They stopped, scanning the alley, before pushing their hood back and letting it spill onto their shoulders. A young man with short hair cut close to the scalp and tanned skin heaved an angry sigh through his long thin nose. His ochre eyes were captivating, and he had an odd symbol tattooed along one side of his neck.

He cursed under his breath in something I could only assume was Slavic. I remained statue-like. He clenched his hands into fists and rolled his head in a circle. Then as suddenly as he came into view he faded. As though veiled in a gossamer curtain, he turned ghostly before he melted into the opposing wall like a mirage.

My eyes shot open and I was staring at the ceiling. Sweat beaded my temples and I blinked away the nightmare.

"A Residual?" I rubbed the ache below my collarbone. "That was weird." I whispered. I was getting names for the beings I had seen in my haunted dreams. Or perhaps the better word was *memories*.

Keeping on the balls of my feet I froze when I saw Logan leaning with his back towards me sitting on the top step. I bit my lower lip and waited.

Slow deep breaths echoed back toward me. Jarrett was right. They had drank a lot. I smirked.

It was different this time to sneak out of the house. Once in the living room there were no more people. No Condemned smoking on the front steps or soft Residuals flowing about. Life felt slightly normal.

I walked with a triumphant smile towards the stable laced with excitement to be alone with Jarrett finally. We had agreed to meet here after a hushed conversation following dinner. The smell of hay eroded the lavender of the house away and soft light warmed the night as I stepped through the large open doorway.

Realizing Jarrett hadn't arrived I plopped onto a waiting hay bale and leaned up against the weathered wood. Closing my eyes I floated away on the sounds of the evening trees and the crickets serenading the night. Hesitant footsteps severed small blades of straw, and I smiled.

"Finally. I was beginning to wonder if you could find the…" I opened my eyes and sat straighter in surprise. "Lydia. I thought you'd left."

Lydia, the Residual who hurt me at the smuggler's cabin stood nervously before me.

"I wanted to speak with you," she said with courage and practiced affirmation. "I was glad when I saw you headed back here alone."

"Well, uh, I was actually going…" I looked back to the other open doorway and saw the windows of the house were black.

"Today when I reached for you…" Lydia sighed through her nose, adding a hint of nervousness. I could see dim bruises around her neck where Eli had choked her.

"Don't apologize. I was angry earlier but now…" *I'm too excited to freaking see Jarrett.* "Now I'm over it." I smiled.

"No, that's not it. Today when I reached for you, something strange happened." She was soft with her words and her silky hair fell in front of her face when she cast her head down.

"Strange?" I edged closer to the beautifully nervous girl. Her blue eyes hidden beneath her thick lashes.

"When I touched you—"

"Thought I was sleeping, huh?" a deep voice cut through the seriousness.

"Logan?" I turned suddenly, shocked. "Please go back to—"

"Who's this beauty?" He grinned a crooked smile towards Lydia.

"Logan!" I scolded his obvious flirtation.

"What? I was just asking who she is." He smiled. Peering around me for a better view.

"I'm Lydia," she replied politely.

"Lydia, huh?" He licked his lips like a lion readying for the kill.

"I tend to the horses a few times a week. Sorry to stop so late, but I let Tristan know ahead of time." A darker smile spread through her reddened lips, "Logan, right?"

He nodded. Encouraging the flirty banter.

"Having a good time?" Lydia was inching around me in the direction of the hypnotized Bayne. Her beauty emanating around her like a mysterious glow.

"No!" I pointed a finger in her direction. "Stay away from him." I spat through gritted teeth. Narrowing my eyes, letting her know she had overstepped her bounds.

"Whoa!" Logan beamed. "I knew it!" He puffed out his chest. "You can't deny this forever." He looked me up and down and motioned to himself.

"Lily?" Lydia's voice chimed behind me.

"Not now!" I pulsed an errant palm in her direction.

"Look at the house!" I whipped my head towards the house and saw what she was referring to.

"Something's going on. Why are all the lights on?" I squinted my eyes and listened when the shouting reached us. Lydia didn't follow when we bolted towards the house while Logan made comments the entire jog.

"You know I always saw something with you and me." He smiled despite the possibility of something wrong developing inside.

"Logan, shut up." I rolled my eyes pushing through the back door into the large living room.

We skipped the steps side-by-side. I was met by plumes of blue hazy smoke billowing through the hallway as the voices of the awakened Baynes cut through the low visibility.

"What is this shit?" Trip yelled.

"Lily, I'll save you!" Tate's feet ended abruptly.

"I'm here for you, Lily!" You could hear the grin behind Grey's words. "Let my hands guide you!"

"I'm your sister." August's voice was accompanied by a swift smack.

"Ouch!" Grey's voice yelped suddenly followed by running and what appeared to be two dark figures hitting the floor.

"Who was that?" Bennett laughed.

"Grey and Tate." I smirked at the two of them lying still at our feet.

My tongue tingled as the blue haze tickled my nerves.

"Where did you guys find this stuff?" August swatted her hands at the smoke trying to clear an area.

"Downstairs in the weird room today," Logan answered excitedly. "Tristan, what is this? How do you have smoke bombs?" Logan lurched towards his disabled brothers.

"Where's Jarrett?" I asked.

"He's never been chivalrous," Logan called back toward me.

I planned to roll my eyes, but I found the movements made me feel off balance. My nose felt stiff and my muscles were weak. I reached for the wall only to discover my depth perception was playing tricks on me. I stumbled backward as I grasped my throat. I couldn't breathe, and I could hardly see or hear.

Tristan was walking towards me wearing only a pair of boxers. His mouth was covered by his gray T-shirt. He scooped me up in his arms and thrust the T-shirt in front of my nose and mouth like a mask.

I was about to speak when he looked down at me with his brow furrowed in what appeared to be amazement.

He leaned in close. "Is your throat and chest experiencing a burning numbing sensation? Don't speak. Only nod."

I nodded weakly yes.

"Can you see clearly?" His head was cocked sideways.

I shook my head no as he bit his lip questionably. We were through the doors of the large bedroom and he quickly closed them behind me. Not stopping until he laid me gently in a cushioned chair out in the night of the balcony.

I removed the T-shirt from my face and pulled cool untainted air into my throat. The feeling dissipated. My thoughts cleared I spoke. "What's wrong?" My voice was raspy.

He didn't answer while pacing to and fro in front of the glowing room. He had his fingertips caressing the whiskers of his chin and his eyes distant as he pondered something seriously.

"Is it Eli's brothers?" I whispered.

He turned to face me as though suddenly realizing I was present. "What color was the haze?" He squinted while waiting for my reaction.

"Blue," I answered with a shrug. That was odd. "Why?"

His jaw hung and he stared at me sternly. "What did the smoke taste like?" he asked slowly.

I looked around thinking before I answered. "Sweet?"

"Holy shit." Tristan whispered. "And could you—"

"Is she alright?" Eli's voice interjected. He appeared mysteriously on the opposing side of a railing swinging both legs effortlessly before he silently landed. "What happened?" He came to kneel beside me. "I should have known better. If they were anything like their sister, they wouldn't hesitate to *experiment*." He kissed my cheek softly then turned to find Tristan. "Thank you for keeping her safe."

"Eli?" Tristan held up a hesitant palm. "Lily—"

"He works for the government!" August slammed the bedroom door, locking it, and then turned to join us on the balcony.

"Everyone alright?" Tristan rested a hand on her shoulder.

"Yeah, they're fine. They think you're mad at them and there's all this sooty shit on the floor now. Oh and you work for the government." She giggled. "That's why you have that stuff. How's Harper?" She turned. "Hey E." She smiled sweetly. "Having fun *camping*?" She winked and slipped an arm through Tristan's while letting out a yawn. "Back to bed?"

"No. We'll have to clean that up before it catches fire. Can you corral them into their rooms at the very least?" He looked at her.

"Are you kidding?" She turned and marched back to the bedroom doors, swinging them wide open. "Everyone to bed! He is super pissed!" She stomped out into the hallway and a collective groan echoed while doors slowly closed.

"I don't think I'll be able to sleep." I looked up at Eli for the first time realizing how much his presence soothed me. "Nightmare." I whispered.

"Come with me then." he smiled.

"Where are you off to?" Tristan cracked his back and rolled his neck releasing the tension.

"To see a priest." He held a darkly mischievous look.

"One's here?" Tristan moved closer in awe.

"Arrived late last night." He nodded.

"I haven't seen one in…" He looked to the ground in thought.

"Eight hundred years." Eli looked over his shoulder, hearing something I couldn't, "Let's go." And he pulled me up by the hand. Before I knew it, we were jogging down the darkened driveway, away from the Baynes and back into my mystical lifestyle.

14

Priests and Cherubs

I followed quietly behind him. Unwilling to speak of the horror I saw in the cave earlier. He didn't look back as he led the way. I couldn't stop thinking about what he'd done to the Scribe and how he'd killed her with the very hand I was now holding. I didn't want to ask questions I was confident he wouldn't answer.

I had told August to let Jarrett know I went to bed and the blue powder everywhere had given me a headache. She'd looked at me funny, but I was beginning to think I was the only one besides Tristan who could see what color it was.

"Follow me," Eli said as he stepped between two large trunks.

I sidestepped the wood and he stopped.

"No. *This* way," he said as he motioned *through* the trees.

"I'm right here. What's the difference?" I backtracked a few feet and went the same way he had gone.

"You have to step between them. Otherwise you'll end up somewhere else. The apertures have a very specific entry and exit path." He chuckled as he said it.

"Apertures? Like in cameras?" He took my hand in his again and for a little while I forgot to pay any attention to the trees around us.

"Yes." I took a moment to enjoy the feel of his skin against my palm.

"And this is how you travel all the time?" He felt as cool as marble.

"Indeed." His voice was low.

"How do they work?"

He glanced at me with reluctance. "Another time."

"Where exactly is this priest we're going to see? Because this is not my forest." I was surprised by the tone of my voice. We were somewhere else. Another state perhaps? I couldn't be sure, but it was somewhere in the south.

"Georgia. Stay close through here. The path gets thin." I found myself wrapping my free hand around his arm.

"The country or the state? Don't let me go." My voice had gone soft with concern.

Immediately, I felt his thumb stroke my jaw. Grounding me and stealing away every ounce of fear creeping through my mind.

"I'm not letting go," he whispered. "The state of Georgia. Not the country." He smiled softly as his grip tightened while we moved through a constricted stand of fragrant trees.

"Gram lived there. My dad's mom. She used to bring boiled peanuts and homemade peach preserves at Christmas time." I smiled at the memory. She had a stroke when I was sixteen and never recovered. She ended up passing away the following year. I remember feeling like the last remnant of my dad was suddenly gone.

Only moments later we stepped into a clearing and a path stretched out ahead of us.

"We're here."

I turned to see a crumbling wall spread out in front of us with no end visible in either direction. Only a single gate-less opening.

We stepped through the stone archway and trees surrounded us with thick, low branches that were barren of flowers but dense with leaves which obscured my view. Though silence allowed the sound of tumbling rocks to reach my ears from somewhere high above us, I could see only a large dark door at the end of the dirt path on which we walked. I glanced around the grounds to see small plaques blanketed in moss. Some darted from the ground as though being swallowed by the earth around them. Rows of stone markers with rounded corners deteriorated after years in the wind and rain. Consumed by the shaggy mosses that assaulted the tombstones. Shadows danced through the filtered moonlight around us.

The door ahead of us opened with a slow groan.

"I almost gave up on you." The voice was light and teasing.

"My apologies." Eli smiled as he squeezed my hand.

I watched as the priest's robes swished against the dusty floor and couldn't help but notice the tattered hem.

What kind of priest was this?

"I must admit I'm pleased you brought her along." He addressed me without a glance.

"It seems to be the theme of the day." I gave Eli a sidelong glance.

He let out a laugh as he turned to face me.

The priest's face was thin and covered by a short, ragged beard. His eyes were bright with mirth and his mouth thin but smiling. I watched as his bony hand rose to pull the robe from his shoulders. Tossing it aside, he sank into a large wooden chair behind him.

"I have something for you," he said, as he reached over to the stone table beside him and picked up a small book.

His collar sat loose and askew around his neck. His shirt was half tucked, and a belt hung open at his waist. A hole was almost worn through one knee. I glanced around the building. The simple pews around us barely stood. Most with missing legs and cracked benches. There was not a neatly tended row within the room. The broken windows held no colorful images within their arched panes. The cracked and flaking paint on the ceiling was faded and water stained. It was a place that was not veiled in grandeur meant to attract a flocking society of devotees. Yet, this made me feel more at home than any other place of worship I'd ever been in.

"This must be a very old church." A serene smile played on my lips.

"Church? You would label this sacred place with that putrid word?" His voice was firm as he stood.

My eyes snapped to him. "A putrid word?"

"This is a place where faith lives, Lilian, not idle, passing fascinations with religion." I felt no threat from his thinned lips and taut jaw.

"She meant no insult, priest," Eli defended as he moved in front of me. "She's still learning."

"She'll need to learn quickly," he said.

"I'm sorry." It eased from my lips.

He looked at me curiously as I stepped around Eli.

"Care to join me?" He flipped open the front cover to reveal a hollow center. Inside was a small glass case of marijuana.

I declined with a flip of my hand.

I looked at Eli. "The priest is getting high right now."

He smiled wistfully as the priest smiled broadly.

"Sanctuary can be a physical place or a state of mind." His hand motioned around the room.

He was definitely not your typical priest, and the thought made me laugh.

"I can see why you're drawn to her. I only wonder why she's drawn to you." He never took his eyes off mine.

"That's why I've been looking for you," Eli said softly.

"Let's see what we can find out for you. I've always been a bit of a rebellion supporter." The priest reached over and picked through a stack of books beside him.

A contemplative look crossed my features.

"It's not a rebellion." Eli reached out and took my hand in his.

"I don't understand." I felt completely lost in this conversation.

"There are stories from the dawn mentioning sovereign ones, but few today believe they ever existed," he mumbled as he flipped through the pages of a book.

"Sovereign? What does that mean?"

"Nothing you need to worry about." Eli's eyes were dark with unease when they turned to my face.

"There are some passages in this one, and there is one more here somewhere…" the priest said as he shoved the small book into Eli's hand while paging through another.

Eli took the book and ran his fingers over the branded images on its cover. "Where did you find this?"

"It's been with me since its expulsion by your brothers." He continued to search as he spoke.

"Do you have others?" Eli's voice was soft.

"The sacred writs are safe." The priest smiled coyly. "Here it is." He handed a book to me. "This may have some answers."

I angled it in my hands and had no idea what language the characters on the cover came from.

"Can you read it?" The priest's head tilted as he asked.

"I don't know the language." Looking at the cover as I spoke, the words became clear to me. "*Of the Sovereign*," I said.

Eli reached out and looked at the book briefly before staring at me.

"Interesting." The priest smiled.

The blue smoke, and now this? I pondered as I looked between the two men.

"It's time to be on your way, angel. I believe there are those who wait for you to return," the priest said.

"There are." Eli nodded.

"We're leaving?" I hesitated as I spoke. "All we have is more questions now." I hoped he could see my distress.

"I don't have the answers, little Lost One. Today we've seen you can read the sacred writs." He paused as I took a deep breath. "And that'll have to be enough for now." The priest rested a hand on my shoulder. "Rest easy these nights. For the darkness looming ahead will be treacherous," he said before turning to walk away.

"Come now, Lily," Eli answered as he swept a hand down my back.

"Thank you…" I paused for a moment. "I didn't get your name," I called after him.

He looked at me over his shoulder. "*You* may call me anything you like." He winked.

And then he was gone.

"Your fame precedes you," Eli joked softly as he leaned into me.

"Oh, like you should talk," I scoffed.

"Let's get home."

"Yes, please," I replied quickly after the priest's ominous words.

Home. And it was beginning to feel that way.

The smooth leather of the book in my hand served as a distraction, and I couldn't keep my fingers from tracing over the title burned into the darkened hide.

We walked the path through the trees that slowly spun from the deciduous oaks of Georgia back to the comfortable pine-needled grounds of Colorado. So this was how they traveled so quickly? Holes in the veil? It was only minutes before we stepped into the yard to find a crowd looking up at the house.

"What's happening?" Eli asked immediately as his steps quickened.

"Marcus is inside with Tristan," a hushed voice said.

"Doing what?" I asked as I wondered how I'd explain him to the boys.

Although they'd probably think the biker gang had come to recruit them.

The thought made me laugh.

"I don't see the humor in the presence of a Karuv."

"No, I wasn't…" I paused as I noted the serious tone around me. "What's a Karuv?"

"A Cherub," someone informed me in a quiet growl.

"Like a baby angel cherub?" That didn't seem serious at all.

"Humans are so clueless," I heard Marcus say as he appeared from the darkness.

"By all means enlighten me," I countered.

"Not my job. Maybe ask one of your boyfriends."

"Mind your tongue!" Eli sharply snarled.

Marcus immediately flinched while the gathering of people recoiled. I may not have completely grasped Eli's authority, but they clearly did.

"Guardian." Marcus dropped his head assenting to the order before turning to me, "Cherubs"—he spoke in an overly tender tone— "are not plump naked babies you've seen depicted in fresco."

I noticed he held a hand over his bicep and his sleeve was torn at the shoulder. "It did that? You're not bleeding out."

"Immortality will do that to you," he grumbled. "Sure you get to live forever, but it still fucking sucks when you get torn apart."

"How did it get to the house?" Eli asked as he stepped closer to take a look at the arm.

"Interrupted her. She wasn't happy about it. Did Kase go in?" he asked.

Eli nodded as I finally looked at the injury.

I gasped. His arm hung limply at his side. In the darkness I could see the blood pouring down what remained. It was barely attached by strings of a torn muscle. A wave of queasiness crashed in my stomach looking at his dislocated shoulder and broken collarbone pushing sharply against the skin.

"Interrupted what?" a small voice asked.

"She was about to"—he paused and cleared his throat— "introduce herself to one of the guests," he said as he glanced at me.

August? Jarrett? My heart raced at the thought. Were they hurt? What if…? I couldn't finish the thought.

"Who?" I asked as my feet began to move toward the house.

Large hands held me in my place.

"They'll be alright, and you know I can't keep all of your boyfriends straight." Tristan's hand reached out and squeezed my arm lightly.

The fear ebbed as anger flowed into my veins.

"We need to get it out of that house," I commanded.

"That was the plan before she shredded me," Marcus grumbled.

"We're working on it," Eli said as he watched someone pull a large, curved needle through the tissue surrounding Marcus' injury.

"Found her entry," a voice called through the darkness as sticks crunched under advancing feet. "Entire front guard was taken out."

My eyes were glued again to the house. As the moonlight punctured the windows, we watched the shadows. It was like an elegant dance but judging by the hisses of sucked-in breath and muted cheers of triumph, it was much more than that. Sparks of light flickered among the obscurity, and I wondered which silhouette they were supporting. I couldn't see any difference in them.

"It shouldn't be long now," Eli noted as he leaned close to me.

I merely nodded as I scrutinized the windows. The flashes of golden light had become rhythmic and prolonged while gaining brightness and speed with each charge. The hushed excitement around me told me this Kase must have been winning the oddly silent fight.

"Kase has her," I heard Marcus say quietly.

Squinting in the darkness my eyes caught the now constant glowing as the two figures emerged from the house and began to move through the yard.

"Did Tristan head inside?" Eli asked.

"He's cleaning up the mess she made in the house," Kase's tenor voice murmured across the emptiness as he was closing the distance to us now.

"How bad is it?" I nervously wondered.

Knowing Jarrett and August were alright calmed the anxious fear coursing through my veins, and all that remained was concern. Watching as the Cherub encroached on the group, I couldn't help but notice the fierceness of her demeanor. Her long, thin fingers clawed at a rich golden chain around her shoulders and neck. A weapon? As she leaned away from Kase, he simply tugged on the small and shining balls anchoring the chains around her, and she cringed under them. A painful leash. If there was a sound, it was imperceptible to my ears. The strands of her hair tangled together and fell across her face, leaving little to see but smudges of filth across her cheeks. Her pale eyes darted from face to face. Her lips lifted in a snarl. The muscles of her arms and legs were lean and taut, as though she were ready for an escape if given the slightest chance.

She was neither the sweet toddler I'd originally imagined nor the Amazonian warrior I was sure she must have been to cause the damage she'd delivered to Marcus. She was thin and young, appearing perhaps thirteen years old at most, but strength emanated from her. As though she were wild and untamed. Feral even.

The thought caused me to shiver.

She locked her eyes on mine and her lips formed into a thin slow smile. A fire of hatred flared in my chest, and I felt the need to watch her die.

It was darker than usual as we stepped through the door.

"Spread out and find it," Eli commanded quietly.

I took the steps two at a time and met August about halfway up.

"She didn't make it past the landing," she whispered as she swept past me and gently nudged me to turn and head back downstairs.

"Everyone safe?" My feet padded across the floor behind her.

"As safe as ever." Her voice was chipper.

"That's not really encouraging," I mumbled mostly to myself.

We headed towards the kitchen, eyes surveying everything around us. There didn't seem to be much out of place considering the "mess" description I'd heard.

"Don't touch anything. Let one of us know if you see something." Marcus' deep voice was soft in my ear and before I could turn to look at him, he was gone.

"What…?" I paused my steps and my words.

"Lily, no time for breaks. We've got to find it," August said as she plucked a banana off the counter and peeled it leisurely.

"What exactly are we looking for?" I asked it softly, embarrassed by my ignorance.

"Oh. Lily doesn't know what we're looking for, guys." August had a blatant disregard for my shame. "So clueless." She nibbled at the fruit as she strolled around the room opening cupboards haphazardly.

"It'll look like a vine," a hushed voice called through the house.

"A vine, Lily, keep up," August loudly whispered.

Eli would later explain a Cherub's vine could decay anything organic or not in a matter of hours. The Cherub Wars of the once lush Southwest led to the demise of what we now know as Death Valley today.

I was thankful for the light of the moon as I searched. Scanning the room for signs of life that didn't belong.

"Here," Eli's muted voice rang through the house.

Turning towards it, I watched as people moved toward him. The moon's rays were glinting off the varied weapons in their hands. Curiosity pushed me in the same direction, and I watched as they sliced around the room. Small delicate leaves and large, bright tri-petal flowers fell to the floor wilting before they reached it.

"More in here," Tristan called softly from the study.

Jarrett's room? My heart seized.

"He's okay. I checked on him already," August whispered as her hand swept over my shoulder.

I took a breath.

"Make sure he doesn't wake," Tristan murmured as a few slipped past him.

Heads nodded in understanding.

I followed them and a hand around my wrist stopped me.

"Now is not the time to check on him," Tristan said.

His tone allowed no question, and I turned away, eyes lingering towards the door to Jarrett.

"I'll go. I'm tougher than you anyway," August offered.

"Like hell you will. Go with *her*," Tristan said.

August huffed in disbelief and opened her mouth to retort as I smiled. Tristan was becoming my favorite August handler.

"No," he said and then kissed her soundly.

A moment later she floated behind me as we made our way through the yard back near the cottage towards a torch-lit area. A group had gathered there and peered down at the ground. As we got closer I could hear the growls of the Cherub and vaguely wondered if she was still smirking. I watched as they helped a small Saint from a hole in front of them and then proceeded to pour flasks of liquid over what I assumed was the Cherub below. Nudging my way through the crowd I peered over the edge.

"Watch it. She's still dangerous," Marcus said.

"She's crying," I said softly as I watched trails form in the filth of her face.

"The water burns, and she wants your sympathy." Kase said.

None of this seemed real, and I was still trying to digest yet another of today's unimaginable circumstances I faced. Between the Residual's touch, the deaths in the cave, speaking to a thousand-year-old priest, and now, here I stood on the edge of this pit. I was so far out of my depth.

"Did I miss the bonfire?" August asked cheerily as she edged in beside me.

"Bonfire?" My question went unheard.

"Nope." Marcus grinned.

Hissing echoed against the dirt below us.

"You're going to burn her?" I swallowed hard.

"It's the only way." Kase, the Saint, pulled a small golden tin from his pocket. Inside were black sticks.

Screams rushed to our ears, and I flinched at the fear they carried.

"Matches? But she's soaked with water," I said as I reached out to touch them.

"You'll light them all if you do that." He inched the case out of my reach.

"Sorry." I drew back my fingers.

"They're not meant for humans, and they aren't particularly fond of holy water." He laughed.

Holy water? How does that burn? Questions plagued my mind.

He ran the match over his palm, and it sparked to life. Arms automatically emerged in front of us and gently pushed us back from the edge of the pit as vines hammered against the ground at our feet.

"Shallow breaths when the smoke starts." Eli's voice was soft behind me as his finger traced my shoulder blade. Ever patient with my constant state of fledgling knowledge.

I watched as the blue flame of the match fell into the dimness of the hole and jumped back as it hit the writhing body below. Thin, cobalt flames spread quickly across her and bright white smoke climbed the air in front of us. The vines begged for salvation as they reached out to us before slipping into death and dropping into the fire.

"Oh, pretty!" August clapped.

In the light of the flames I could see the chain tethering her to the ground and wondered if Kase had another of the weapons on hand. The delicate fabric she wore melted quickly in the heat. Her porcelain-like skin silvered. I trembled under the force of her pain. Her screams slowly softened, turning melodic and beautiful.

"She smells like roasting marshmallows." August drooled as my eyes darted to her face.

"I like you more every day, August." Marcus smiled as he pointed at her approvingly.

"Of course you do," she dismissed happily.

Eli kissed my head.

"That pretty song you hear? She's signaling the others." His voice was firm.

"More like her?" I asked as I watched her thrashing limbs grow still as the music continued.

"Worse than her. And every one of them will pull at your heart to rip it from your chest. So don't be fooled by the sweet disguise," Eli said.

Branches snapped in the distance, and it reminded me we were always being watched.

"Get her covered. Marcus, grab Tristan and follow me," Eli bade.

I felt the smoke in my lungs go heavy as his hand left my back.

I stood silently watching as shovels of dirt were thrust upon her and a memory of my father's funeral flashed through my mind.

"Wait! I need to capture that smell!" August pleaded as she dashed towards the house. "Someone grab me a Tupperware! Quick!"

15

Mortars and Baynes

"This is Ethan. Leave your number and I'll call you back if this—"

I hung up again. I had lain awake staring at the ceiling for over an hour. It was close to three a.m. and I couldn't sleep. I called him twice, too afraid to leave a message. August had completely embraced the alien life we were now living. Talking to her didn't feel like what I needed.

Tristan and August had decided to spend the night in my former guest room, seeing I needed the space. I was sleeping alone back in the primary. It had been a little over a week and a half since the abrupt fissure in the life I knew and the life I was rapidly barreling down now. It felt a little strange to think about. How your life could completely capsize in such a short time. One moment you and your best friend are working your dream jobs in the forests of Colorado, and the next, guardian angels are trying to rip you apart and murder you because you dated one of their own.

If someone had told me two months ago, seeing blue eyes between the trees while on the back of an ATV would lead me here, I would have had you committed.

171

This past week felt nothing short of surreal, and I wanted to talk to Ethan about all of it.

Today felt like a straw had broken a back somewhere, and tonight after the Cherub I made the decision I needed to make. Hearing her weeping screams in that grave, I knew I could no longer continue this way. I would spend tomorrow happily with Jarrett and his brothers and then safely send him back to the asylum that was Maple Falls. I resigned myself to my new life, but I couldn't subject anyone else to this. I would demand August go back to our apartment and continue with work, and I would put in my formal resignation letter with my boss this week.

I had plenty of money in my bank account. My job allotted me more than enough, and I still had the settlement from the accident with my father and the police department to be comfortable for life.

I would pay out the lease on the apartment, so August wouldn't have to worry about trying to find a roommate right away. I would put my belongings in storage and confide in Eli where it would be the safest place on the planet I could move to. Maybe a hut in Bora Bora on the water? Some obscure town deep in the heart of Mexico? I shook my head into the pillow. I could address that later.

All in all, I was coping pretty well with everything. They say people who are exposed to trauma become numb to it when it happens again. Something about the way they're always in a heightened state of alert? I think it might be happening now. I was growing *immune* or something.

But Eli knew better. He could tell I was depressed with a false smile. He could *feel* the truth. Taste it even. The look of concern framing his features when I trudged back to the main house tonight was apparent.

My decision was made. I would break up with Jarrett tomorrow and then say goodbye to any semblance of my old life.

I was making a choice. I was choosing, as Eli had.

I cried myself to sleep, and I could tell somewhere, beyond the fringe of trees outside Eli was watching and feeling my ache. Wishing, but unable, to come to me.

***

"Hey, sleepy head," Jarrett whispered. "Are you going to spend this holiday in bed all day?"

I exhaled softly and smiled. Fourth of July with Jarrett and the Bayne bunch.

He kissed me gently on the cheek. It was sweet, but as I became more aware, it was coupled with sadness. I knew tonight I was going to break his heart. I had made up my mind last night, and I pushed the thoughts from my head.

"You don't have a headache still do you?" He searched my eyes, concerned.

"No, just…sad you're leaving tomorrow morning," I whispered.

He scooted me over and came to lie by my side. "Do you want me to stay?"

Yes. A thousand yeses. Argue with me. Make love to me. Be with me.

But I guess that would be for another lifetime.

"Jimmy needs you," I whispered.

"I have five other brothers. I think he can manage the business without me for a minute." The corner of his mouth quirked into a smile.

I then did something I never thought I would do to Jarrett. I lied. But I knew this would be the first of many. To save him. To protect him from the horrors unfolding in my world.

"If I could tie you to my bed and keep you, I would. But I've run out of vacation at work, and it wouldn't be fair to you. I would be working all day and since my injury with August, I'm behind on a lot of paperwork." I turned to face him on my propped elbow.

He was hesitant and his sweet sienna eyes were worried.

"What?"

"Are you sure this doesn't have anything to do with Ethan?"

"Absolutely not! I haven't spoken to him since the other night. It's over, and I doubt he would want to talk to me." He hadn't even answered my middle-of-the-night phone call which used to be our thing. *No, this is because a Cherub had broken into the house last night while you were sleeping and nearly killed everyone while I was away talking to a cryptic medieval priest in Georgia.* "Didn't one of your brothers have something happen last night? August was telling me about some girl in the house. I was half asleep." I hastily changed the subject.

Jarrett rolled his eyes. "That?" He smirked. "I guess Bennett saw some creepy girl in the house, but he claimed he heard a whistle from the dining room? Tristan thought it was a side effect of the powder the guys got into. He thinks he'll be okay though."

"Well, that's a relief. Sounds like there was a lot of excitement last night." I hesitated.

"We were all pretty drunk. I was bummed you weren't feeling well. I should have snuck up here to cuddle with you, but I thought you would need some sleep after last night." He pressed his lips into a line. "I know you're thinking something, so tell me what's up." He pulled me close.

"Tonight when the boys are distracted"—reeking of gunpowder thoroughly riveted by their celebrations—"and they head out to the bar, can we stay behind?" I asked in a small voice. "Maybe take a hike? Just you and I?"

"I was going to ask you the same thing. I feel like we've hardly had any time together this weekend. I should have suspected with my brothers here. So much for flying in early." He dismissed the thought and turned back to me.

"How about I shower, and we head down for some lunch?" I smiled. I was determined to soak up what little time I would have left with him.

"How about"—he leaned in and kissed me—"you take off that T-shirt and we make some naked memories?"

"Your brothers though? They're going to come looking. And the doors? The noise?" I looked over my shoulder.

"Hungover on the back porch. We'll be quick. I locked them on the way in. And I can be quiet if you can." His breath was hot in my mouth as he spoke. "I wouldn't worry about them. I think they're beginning to accept defeat on *this* front."

His fingers were pulling down the underwear I'd been sleeping in.

My heart ached. I didn't want this to end. Not when it was so perfectly right.

I reached down and feverishly began unzipping his jeans and shoving them down with the heel of my hands.

I began stroking him, running my thumb over the tip of his head until it dripped, using it as a lubricant. He trembled with every downward thrust of my palm. He leaned back, pressed his lips together, and watched my hand work.

I wanted to forget the murder and fear. I wanted the hurt and ever-present ache in my chest to quit. I wanted to be consumed by him.

Hell, this was the guy I had had a crush on since I was a teenager, and now we were finally together!

He shifted his body to hover over me for a moment, meeting my eyes. His breathing had become low and heavy. Slowly, he used his fingers to reach down and spread me open. I lifted my hips so he could gently work his way inside. I may not have been a pro at this, but with him everything felt easy.

His breathing hitched and his eyelids closed halfway. He was focused on slowly breathing through his nose.

As he pushed the length of himself inside me, I instinctively let out a weak moan and his palm flew up to cover my mouth.

"Open windows," he mouthed with a smile.

I bit down on my lower lip and mimicked his breathing and movements.

This wasn't the carnal desire that had been the other night. This was tender. At this moment we belonged to each other.

His lips tasted like desire as he sunk further into me. His tongue explored my mouth. I arched my head back, and he kissed his way down my neck.

"Am I hurting you?" he whispered, moving back up to my ear.

I shook my head no.

He surged deeper, exploring me further, and I let my thighs fall open.

I was consumed by him. His smell as he moved above me, gripping the headboard. I pulled his face to mine and kissed him. Crushing my lips to his. Knowing our kisses were limited.

He let out a small groan and then reached behind my back sweeping me up into his lap. His hands on my ribs.

My hips vibrated forward and back, and his breathing suddenly pitched. I'd found the spot.

"Lily, I'm getting close," he murmured in my ear.

I moved faster to catch up.

He stopped moving entirely while his gaze bore into mine. He was trying not to come. My hands trembled and suddenly I let out a whimper at the mounting pleasure. It barely escaped my throat.

He placed one forearm around my waist and pulled my chest to his, lifting me up and down to ride him faster. "I'm coming." His mouth fell open.

My eyes rolled back, and I had to bite his shoulder to stifle my groan as my own orgasm followed.

He pulled my face up to look at him, and I licked my lips while my eyes crinkled into a pout. He pushed his forehead to mine and kissed me. I could feel us rocking slower. Until the movements shook. We breathed through our noses trying to quietly catch our breaths.

"I love you, Lily Bear," he whispered.

"I know." I smiled. Me too.

* * *

"Why are you both so smiley?" Logan groaned with a raspy voice.

"If I didn't feel like my stomach was going to lurch past my lips every time I stood up, I would do something about this." Tate wagged a finger at us. He was draped limply in an Adirondack chair.

"See." Jarrett pulled me closer. "Hungover." He grinned.

"Not for long!" Trip tipped a beer back into his mouth and slumped forward with his elbows on his knees. "A little hair of the dog!" he spouted with a hoarse voice.

"Amen." Grey clinked his beer can to his brother's in a weak cheer.

"That's why it's always important to hydrate," August chided while sipping a margarita and tanning herself. "I feel great today!"

The boys were casually in T-shirts and shorts. All had on sunglasses and were slung over the chairs on the porch and back patio.

"I could get drunk on the stink alone coming from all of you." I smiled.

"Lil, it's a man scent. It's our essence you're smelling." Logan and his twin brother held up a palm and they high-fived weakly next to each other.

"Maybe you guys should relax today?" I suggested thoughtfully.

"What? On this magical day?" Tate let out a careful burp blowing it past his lips. "Besides, the girls will be here soon."

"What girls?" I asked skeptically.

"We met some girls at the butcher yesterday when we were picking up stuff to grill. We invited them up to come swimming and light off some fireworks at our mansion." Trip sat up and shook out his face trying to knock off the hangover.

"You guys could meet women in a pitch-black room." I shook my head in disbelief.

"You can achieve anything if you believe hard enough, Lil!" Grey raised his beer above his head and took a big gulp.

"August, can I talk to you for a minute?" I changed the subject.

She popped up, and we went inside. I gave Jarrett a look that I just needed to talk to her quickly and I'd be right back, before giving him a sweet peck on the cheek and making my way to the kitchen.

"After your brothers leave tomorrow, I need you to go home." I faced her. I had made up my mind last night that no one was going to be a part of this anymore.

"Sure, what do you need there? I've been wanting to get my straightener." She nodded in agreement.

"No, August. I need you to *go home*," I said the words with more force to make her understand.

She searched my eyes trying to see why I would be saying this and the smallest hint of hurt flashed across her face before her brows furrowed in anger. "Are you joking, Harper? No."

"After the Cherub last night, I've made up my mind." I crossed my arms, determined to maintain my resolve. "It's too dangerous and I can't have anything happening to anyone that matters to me. This is my mess. *My* mess alone, and I'm not going to put you at risk like this."

She was angry, shocked I would even suggest such an idea.

"I'll pay out the rest of the lease on the apartment so you don't have to worry about a roommate, and I'll figure out what to do with my stuff after I can talk to Eli about a safe place to go until all this is over. You can go back to Mason, and I won't judge you for it. Heck, I'll attend your wedding one day. I'm also going to resign from my position at work. I'm sure I won't be able to work out in the woods alone again for a while, and I don't think I'll be missed there, what with my constant absences lately. I haven't talked to Ethan since the other night after the bar, but I've decided that's a good thing. He's safer away from me. It's best that we broke up. Your brothers leave tomorrow, and they'll be safe too. That includes Jarrett. I'm ending things with him tonight. I can't have something happen to you too… You're my sister. I wouldn't be able to—"

Her hand shot up to stop me from talking. I could see the indignation roiling in her eyes.

"If you think I'm going to walk away from this, you're delusional. I caught a peek behind the wizard's curtain and there is no going back for me. If you think I would leave Tristan to go back to that cocky shitbag Mason, then you don't know me at all. I'm falling in *love* with Tristan, Lily. He's… Doesn't matter.

"I paid up the lease on the apartment the second day you were in your angel coma, and I sent resignation letters for our jobs five days ago after that meeting—which were accepted immediately. Congratulations on our new humanitarian jobs in Bosnia, by the way. I've been doing withdrawals from our bank accounts for days to make sure we have cash on hand. I got our passports and IDs stashed in a go-bag upstairs in the room with the scary butterfly wallpaper. I would never abandon you.

"You know what hurts my feelings the most? How many people underestimate me. I didn't expect that from you. I didn't get a full-ride academic scholarship because I'm an idiot! I didn't letter in two sports in high school, was captain of the CSU debate team, and ran the agronomy club because I'm *dim*. I'm a god damn scientist for shit's sake! I know people think I'm incapable. They see me and automatically assume there's nothing more. That's fine because I know I'm a wolf in sheep's clothing."

"Maybe a coyote…or honey badger…" I smiled softly.

"And when those assholes kidnapped you that day"—she pointed in the direction of the cottage, indicating Eli's brothers—"I was the one who tracked you down. You know I called everyone that day. Shit, I tried to call Ethan! No one believed me you were in danger. I tried to convince them you would never take off like this. Other than when you hid at the Bethany Hotel last month, but I did *Find My Phone* and figured you were drinking too much wine and watching Hallmark movies again. Like the time you were sad because you thought Katie Garcia kissed Dean, that lacrosse player you sort of dated in college. I went and got your rifle, and immediately hoofed it out to the park that day. I thought some meth head took you, or you fell hiking, or a *real* bear got a hold of you. You have no idea how worried I was when I found your phone out in the woods that afternoon. And don't get me started on when I found Eli standing there with you!

"I'm going where you go Lily. That's a fact. Now, let's go spend the day with my brothers because I'm not sure when—or if—I'll see them again." And she pursed her lips and cocked out her hip.

I grabbed her, hugging her. I loved her. Like Jason Bourne, Marie Curie, and Aphrodite all wrapped up into one. Her ability to amaze was endless.

"I love you, August." I smiled.

"I love you too, Harper. Now, let's go get drunk and light off some fireworks!" And she marched out the backdoor with a fist in the air.

* * *

I stood on the edge of the river. The Bayne boys were scrunched down in the water splashing and chattering loudly with the gaggle of coeds that had rolled up to the house a few hours earlier, their hangovers cured.

"You comin'?" Jarrett called from the cool water.

I slipped my shorts to the ground and pulled my tank top over my head. I didn't have a swimsuit here, and I was about to strip down to my bra and underwear.

I reached down and shrugged at the pink polka-dot bra I was going to use as a bikini, promptly dropping my top near the coolers and clothes on the shore's edge. I reached into the Yeti, grabbed a beer, and plucked the tab open before taking a swig.

"Now I am." I smiled at him.

His grin was wide.

"In the name of all things that are holy." Grey had spoken quietly. His brothers had stood up in the river and were staring at me.

"I didn't know girls could look that perfect," Tate spoke softly.

"I did." Jarrett grinned.

Logan began slowly clapping and his brothers followed suit as I waded into the river. Cheers, whistles, and hoots erupted from them.

"Best Freedom Weekend ever!" Logan laughed.

"Avert your eyes, Baby Benny," Tate called sideways.

I smirked and rolled my eyes swimming until the water came up to my collarbones.

The other girls followed suit, pulling off their tops and chucking them to the sunny shore while bearing swimwear, not to be outdone, while laughing.

The guys stared dumbfounded around them before clapping louder. Jarrett swam to me and wrapped me in his arms before he laughed loudly.

"You've made the rest of their lives you know." He kissed me warmly.

We spent the afternoon swimming, drinking beer, laughing, and playing loud music while the boys had a normal enough game of Marco Polo in the river before we headed to the house to for some *explosive* excitement.

"I don't think you're supposed to use a box cutter to dismantle fireworks," I interjected watching Tate and Trip opening one of the roman candles.

The sun was getting low enough in the sky. After a hearty meal of barbecued ribs and a quick game of volleyball Jarrett and I watched, we settled onto the front driveway into lawn chairs to witness the chaos that was the Baynes and mortars.

We had to break up the game of tag the devil duo was attempting with Roman candles.

I cuddled between Jarrett's legs on a blanket and snuggled with my back to his chest. He had his chin on my shoulder.

"Lil, you can't make super fireworks if you don't assemble what you buy," he retorted.

"They come pre-assembled! You guys are going to lose a finger!" I chided.

"I apprenticed at a firework company back home. I think I know what I am doing." Tate put a palm to his chest.

The group of girls were giggling and flirting with the boys. A girl named Madison was being shown how to use a sparkler by Logan, and August was murmuring lovingly to Tristan on the far end of the porch.

Bennett walked out after having gone in to call Adele back home. "It was a firework stand in a gravel parking lot, and you were asked to leave after you kept telling the customers they could make most of this stuff at home."

"Real patriots know—"

"Oh, shut it, and let's get this light show going. Ashley and I want to get to the bar." Grey pulled a little redhead closer to his side.

"Ladies and gentlemen…Freedom Weekend." Tate gestured before twisting a wick over three feet long away from a long line of stands containing mortars they had braced using rocks. They finagled some of the purchased pyrotechnics to be larger, but Jarrett assured me Tate and Trip had been doing this since they were eleven.

The first concussive blast was louder than I anticipated. A hoot and cheer rang out in the little crowd as gold sparks reigned down overhead. And one after another massive mortars erupted in the night around us, and I didn't want it to be over. I didn't want the jokes and the Baynes to leave. I wanted this moment to be forever. I was happy here. Why did this have to end?

After forty minutes of booms and sizzles, Jarrett leaned in. "Want to head out?"

My face smiled, but my heart sank. "Yeah, let me grab a backpack and some boots and I'll meet you out back," I assured him.

The boys were standing hollering plans loudly back and forth to one another about who was going to ride in which girls' vehicles.

"Yup, I just have to go grab something. And I'll be right behind you." He smiled.

I looked at August, and she knew before I could make the face what I was about to do. She smiled encouragingly and gently nodded before turning back to the group to figure out the logistics before they all left.

It was time. I was going to break Jarrett's heart.

16

Goodbye, Jarrett

Jarrett grabbed my hand and walked along the river. His mood was gleeful. My heart was searing with the ache of what I was about to do. I wasn't sure how to begin.

Once everyone had left, we set off to be alone. I was running over how I was going to phrase it in my head as we marched. How do you end a relationship that has burned so brightly for so many years?

He was too happy to realize I was being quiet.

"I have a surprise for you." He grinned excitedly.

"A surprise?" I absently murmured.

"You'll like this surprise I know it." A thick smile lit up his face.

"A little confident, aren't we?" I raised a skeptical eye.

His only response was to turn and grin.

"Hmm, a Bayne surprise. I generally find I don't like those." I cocked my head sideways.

"This is a *Jarrett* surprise, Miss Harper. Those tend to be a little different." He didn't hint at anything further. "Come on."

"What are you up to, Bayne?" I followed him as he took off into the woods now, careful to make sure we weren't going too far. The moonlight glowing blue on his white shirt. Fireflies illuminated the darkening forest around us. Their soft blinks glowing in rhythm. He turned, and I caught a glimpse of a grin over his shoulder.

He started jogging. "Come on, Lily!" He waved for me to follow.

I giggled.

"Here?" He shook his head quickly, grinning and grabbing me by the hand. "Nope."

"Maybe I can help you find—"

"Here?" He looked up at the tree limbs above our heads and I followed his gaze. "Nope!"

"I think you're lost." I laughed.

"Never!"

After a few minutes, he abruptly stopped below a dazzling Ponderosa pine I didn't recognize.

"She's gorgeous," I whispered, staring up at it in awe. The limbs on the outer edges were so close you could reach up and hang from them.

"I knew you would love it." He eyed the giant rising above us. "I thought it would be perfect for your surprise." His face was growing soft, and his smile was no longer playful.

"*This* isn't the surprise?" I looked back into his golden eyes in amazement. Staring at the cute freckles dotting the edges of his perfect lips. Trying to remain focused on my task ahead.

"Lily." He paused. I had never seen him so nervous.

"What's wrong?" I threaded concern through the words.

His palm rested on mine. "Nothing." He looked directly at me. "I love you."

My breath caught in my throat. How was I going to find the strength to do this?

"So much. Everything you do to me…" He shook his head, smiling. "Nothing has ever done this to me."

He reached into his pocket and unfolded his hand in front of me. There in the center of his palm lay a simple gold ring lined with delicate little diamonds.

"Jarrett?" I whispered.

He stooped with one knee to the floor of the forest, the white moonlight washed over his features.

"Lilian Blue Harper, you had me since the first time we met. You make me uneasy in all the right ways. Please be my wife." He smiled as his hand holding up the ring trembled.

He was proposing. *This* was his surprise. My insides were awash. Fighting between exaltation and agony from his kind words as I took the ring from his open hand smiling through the tears I felt rising.

The ring was perfectly simple. A thin gold band lined with petite sparkling diamonds that glittered under the light of the moon. A solitary stone graced the center, beautiful in its classic simplicity.

So much of me wanted to slip it onto my finger. Shout yes through the forest and crush him in a hug. Not spending holidays *beside* the Baynes, but as one of them. I wanted all of it.

I swallowed against the lump in my throat and drew on my composure. Used my years of practiced rationalization. An ounce of pain now was worth a pound of heartache later. This would save his life. This would protect us *both*.

The ache under my collarbone gnawed at my chest. Reminding me of what I needed to do and why.

Because the unfulfilled want that was Eli that consumed me. The tearing pull thundering through my life like an avalanche, no matter how scary at times, was the dominating feeling overshadowing everything else. I knew what I needed to do. What some small part of me maybe *wanted* to do.

End things.

I closed my eyes. I couldn't look at him while I did this. I wouldn't be strong enough to continue if I saw the hurt I inflicted.

"Jarrett, I—" Just as the words began to surface, my chest rocked.

My eyes snapped open, and his face grew worried. "Lily?"

Run.

The ancient voice boomed across all the nerves inside me. The same voice I heard before when the brothers had come for me. My head shot up looking behind Jarrett while he rose.

"Zacarius?" I threw up unprepared hands. In the shadows behind Jarrett, I could see Eli's redheaded brother. His face twisted with rage.

"No!" I screamed. He crept quickly from the shadows as he simultaneously pulled the arched sword the length of my body from his back and swung it upwards in one fluent motion thrusting it through Jarrett's chest toward me. I watched in horror as Jarrett was lifted from the ground. I staggered back, screaming at the top of my lungs as the crack of his ribs echoed loudly against the bark. He wrenched the massive sword backward in a sweeping motion and turned quickly in a run.

I watched as he leapt into the lowest nearby tree, climbing higher before the crack of his wings and a rush of warm summer air blew downward. He had fled. He did what he had wanted to do.

"Lily?" Jarrett whispered. "I taste blood." His hand went to his chest where a wound was so deep and long it was hard to tell the complete damage from the shredded flesh lopping loosely around it.

I reached my right hand under his arm behind him to push on the entrance wound in his back as my left palm pressed to his chest.

"Jarrett!" I yelled his name frantically.

His opposing hand reached above his head grasping a low-hanging limb for balance as he faltered. "What was that?" he garbled in a wet whisper. Dropping to his knees as his face contorted with a mixture of incredulous pain.

I dropped to mine as well and ripped the backpack from my back. Tearing open the little first aid kit I carried. Its contents spilled to the ground. Whimpering as tears were running down my cheeks. My hands shook with the adrenaline of fear frantically trying to grab a bandage among the pine needles of the darkened forest floor.

"My hands are too slippery." The blood was making it difficult to open the gauze and I tore at it with my teeth. I ripped his shirt open and shrieked, but the bandage wouldn't adhere from the lake of blood coming out in droves.

I knew I needed to get help. Oh God.

"I'm going to get someone!" I yelled. "Hold on!"

I wheeled around to run, turning for a moment to catch a glimpse of him as his mouth flowed bright red the length of his chin and neck. He sat back on his haunches staring into my eyes, his face overwhelmed with fearful sorrow.

I choked on my wracking sobs. I was gasping while trying desperately to navigate the feeling in my chest. I needed to get to Eli.

The fear and panic roared violently through my bones, and I felt a vibration I had never felt before.

"Somebody help me!" I bellowed, tripping over my own legs. "Eli!" I screamed into the forest as hard as I could.

The tears were so thick in my eyes, the trees began to blend together as though I were running through a water-colored painting. I felt like I was in a nightmare. Some demented horror movie where the man in the mask was pacing slowly behind me. The edges of my vision were going dark from lack of oxygen, but I refused to stop. When I thought I was about to collapse, I smacked into a looming figure.

"Marcus?" I coughed. "Zacar—Jarrett." Pointing back the way I had come.

He placed two hands on my shoulders. "We know!"

I looked around to see Marcus and some of the others ready for a fight. Weapons loaded as they jogged past me towards Jarrett. My shoulders slumped, and I placed my hands on my knees. Coughing and dry heaving onto the ground. I stood still and alone for a moment.

Before turning to see them spreading in a wide protective arc in the distance in front of me.

My fingers were numb, and my legs shook miserably as I tried to run back in a state of uninhabited shock.

I'm coming, Jarrett.

The daze was so consuming I didn't notice when others arrived and ran past. My hair blowing forward as the Saints' horses thundered within inches of my shoulders.

Then through the darkness, trees, and people, where I had left him lying, with his face turned to the side and his arm reaching out in the direction I had gone was Jarrett.

"Jarrett," I called softly. Tripping over my feet as I walked mindlessly unaware toward him. "Help him," I called to the people standing over him and kneeling beside him looking up to watch me coming. My mind refused to believe what I already knew to be inevitable.

"Lily." Eli came from nowhere blocking my path to Jarrett. "I'm going to take you home now." He was speaking in an eerily soft voice.

All I could manage was a feeble finger to point shakily. We needed to *help* him.

He palmed both sides of my face. "Jarrett's been killed." He spoke it with a stern firmness.

I looked around suddenly to realize no one was moving. No one was trying to perform CPR or stem the flow of blood. Jarrett's beautiful sienna eyes were fixed, his breath absent. His perfectly thin lips were coated in blood and his tanned skin was gray. His hand was tucked under his chest still holding his wound. All the people stood still.

I felt as though I were suffocating. This couldn't be happening.

"Eli?" I whispered, looking to him to help me. His words hit me like a freight train and my heart stopped. I could feel the overwhelming anguish running through me and my knees buckled.

"I got her!" he called to someone behind me as he scooped me into his arms and chest and began walking.

I didn't care that everyone was staring, but the silence they exuded was eerie. I kept questioning what the odd sound cutting through it all was before it dawned on me.

Me.

My wailing sobs rang through the forest as I limply hung in Eli's arms.

* * *

You know that moment before you've fully awakened, and reality hasn't had its chance to seep through? I never wanted it to be finished. For the first time in my life I would rather have been asleep than here in the waking world. Rather walk among my haunted nightmares than feel the crush of inevitable pain I would face upon waking. I kept my eyes closed hoping it would change the outcome, but I was foolish to think it would.

My lids slowly parted against the sun radiating through the windows. The painful ache erupted in my chest like a bomb, and I couldn't stop my face from twisting into tears. The agonizing sobs thrummed against my ribs so painfully hard I felt they could break.

A sharp stinging emanated from my fisted palm, and I slowly unfolded it. There clutched in my hand was the ring Jarrett had proposed with only hours earlier. I hadn't let go and the diamonds had been cutting into the soft flesh of my hand, leading it to bleed. The bright morning light sent rainbows dancing up my forearm from the various blood-covered stones.

Slowly closing my hand, I turned my head into the silk-covered pillow and let out a wrenching scream, arching my spine with the breath exhausting from my lungs. I panted through the sobs.

"Lily, what can I do?" Eli's quiet voice whispered to my back in a pained tone.

I couldn't understand how the world was still moving now that he wasn't here. I couldn't possibly answer. Because I didn't know. I pulled the blankets over my head and let my shoulders shake with the sobs.

Once I heard the door close at my back I sat upright in the bed and pulled out my necklace tucked into the collar of my T-shirt. I unhooked it and slid the ring down the chain to land next to the typewriter key my father had given me.

"Death charms," I whispered.

I fell back and stared at the ceiling. The tearing twinge in my heart felt lethal. I closed my eyes and flashes of his face ran through my memories. This couldn't be happening. Jarrett was dead. They had killed him.

17

Deep in the Ethoes

I loathed funerals, they made me uncomfortable. Gave my skin an anxious itch. The nervous conversations. The strange pomp and circumstance or deeply shaded colors of attendees to illustrate their mourning. This weird ritual shrouded in silence and grief.

I wanted to run.

I sat in the second row of little black folding chairs. August at my right and Tristan on hers. She donned a navy fitted pantsuit, and I wore a black dress I had used for weddings with Ethan. The coincidence wasn't lost on me. Here I sat at my *almost-* fiancé's funeral, wearing a dress I use to listen to teary vows laced with love and sipped champagne in.

I'd never really thought about marriage. But seeing Jarrett on bended knee sent bouyant images sashaying through my mind. A future burgeoning with possibilities. It all felt too painful to think about now.

August clutched tissues while constantly dabbing under her sunglasses at her puffy eyes. Her crying had been an endless stream since the inception of this dreamlike nightmare. I'd worried she hated me, would blame me for what happened—and rightfully so—but she didn't.

She would tepidly smile with wet cheeks and sigh heavily before her face would crinkle in on itself and the tears would start again. Too soaked in grief to hate.

Jarrett's brothers were all solemn in dark tailored suits. It felt wrong. To see them so despondent, missing their flirty spark and running stream of banter.

But the worst part was the look they gave me. I couldn't bring myself to meet Nell or Jimmy's depressed gazes. I was always met with pity. Like it was such a shame to be near me. I remembered the feeling too well.

And I hated it.

The story was we had gone hiking that night and he had fallen from a cliff, catching a tree branch through the chest. I had rehashed it to the local officials for over an hour before Eli finally carried me to bed. The screams of August and her brothers when Eli told her to come home, having explained what happened, were something that would haunt my nightmares forever.

My mind drifted away from the painful memory to another one.

"Good." Grey nodded with pursed lips. "It's good he went fast. No suffering." His voice broke as his chin quivered.

The guys faced me in their woodland yard after we arrived for the funeral a week after it happened. It took time to get Jarrett home. I was met with a round of lukewarm hugs and half smiles. I bit the inside of my lower lip and held back the tears as I rehashed the story again for them.

Making sure to cautiously edit the gruesome details of the pain and fear Jarrett experienced. I wouldn't do that to them. That was *my* judgment. To live with the truth of the horrors I had created.

They kicked the dirt and nodded. Their thin facade of bravery evident.

Tate's chest started to shake, and his sweet face crumpled. The

Bayne's lively commentator reduced to tears as he collapsed into his twin's shoulder and broke down.

"How'd you do it, Lil?" Trip choked while the others started patting the shoulder of their devastated brother, lost in his grief.

"I don't know. I just climbed up and ran for help," I answered calmly.

"No," Logan said. "How'd you get through losing your dad?"

In all the years of knowing the Baynes, I had never been asked what it was like. To lose a close family member. My father. Nell always told them if they wanted to know, they would need to talk to me. Only Jarrett dared once, and I wouldn't touch the sting of it for him.

Here now, seeing their usually playful faces anguished and steeped in despair, I owed them. I took a reserved breath and reached for the moment I kept firmly buried away my whole life.

The old memory developed into focus. One I never let my mind revisit.

Suddenly, I was staring at the ugly green carpet of Menchkin's Funeral Home. It was an old house in the town center that smelled like wax inside and had been used for the business of death for decades. Their sign out front boasted, *A Family Business of Dignity*.

I was swinging my legs on the red-cushioned chair with the itchy fabric. Staring at the ruffles of my pink socks around my ankles. My mother sat perfectly poised beside me. A cold look of indifference glazed over her pointed features. I had her umber-colored hair and fair skin.

She wasn't what you would call a warm mother, but I did remember her smiling when my dad was around. I think he softened her. But that was gone now.

I let my head loll back and stared at the ceiling. The stained-glass window behind my father's casket was casting beautiful colors across it. Reds, blues, and yellows that reminded me of those pretty rocks people polished.

"Eyes to the front, Lilian," my mother stated coldly while looking ahead.

I dropped my chin while my gaze wandered to the men in suits standing in the corner looking at me from behind my father's casket. A twinge of pity settled on their faces. Everyone that day looked at me like that. The poor, little girl who lost her dad too young.

Compassionate hands patted my mother's shoulder and she politely nodded and thanked them. Commending her for her brave composure. Confessing how much of mess they all would be given the circumstances.

It wasn't until my grandma, my dad's mom, commented about the tragedy of the accident that my mother's collectedness faltered.

She leaned into my small shoulder and slowly whispered the words I could never forget.

"He's dead because of you. And I will never forgive you."

And she hadn't. She treated me with as much warm regard as an ice sculpture growing up. The looks of pity never ceased from those who learned of my history. In her mind my father would have somehow survived had he not taken the time to toss me aside. Something I still didn't even understand myself. His death, in her opinion, was wholly my fault.

In that moment, a coping mechanism was born. The ability to forget. To shut it off and not look at it.

After seeing Aurelius at my accident, her words might have rung truer than she knew.

I think she was happy when I left for college. She wasn't forced to keep up the charade anymore. The act of being the brave widow and loving mother.

I shook the memories of grief aside. A carousel of pain I was struggling to keep out.

I stared at the jade blades of grass in the sun at my feet remembering that carpet. Not listening to the officiant standing at the podium before me now. Not remembering the sobs of the Bayne boys in all their brokenness last night when I got here. Not thinking of my cold mother.

I couldn't make myself look at the maple casket. I averted my eyes to the grieving faces. I was numb. This would get me through it.

Bennett carefully arranged a piece of paper on the black podium and cleared his throat nervously. "Thank you all for coming today." He smiled politely. "When Jarrett was six years old, he walked out to the yard stark naked and proclaimed loudly he was going to be a Buddhist. He meant nudist, but he'd heard the word on TV and didn't get it quite right. Every year Mom tells us the story of how she couldn't get clothes on him for a whole week that June.

"When he was ten, he got lost in the woods by our house for two days. It took seventy-three volunteers, two police agencies, and a bloodhound before he casually wandered back into the yard himself and proclaimed he loved camping.

"When he was fourteen, he peddled Tate on his handlebars nearly twenty miles to the clinic in Sumas when he broke his arm while mom and dad were in Hawaii. He proclaimed then he needed to learn how to drive in case something happened again. Dad took him out in the truck the next Saturday to teach him.

"At graduation, he turned down a football scholarship with the Huskies and proclaimed he would help dad with the business to take over when he retired.

"When he was twenty-three, he proclaimed he was going to propose and marry the sweet girl my little sister brought home from college. Despite how difficult my brothers jokingly vowed to make that for him, on July fourth of this year, at the age of thirty, he was doing just that when he died."

I looked up, my chin quivering.

"Jarrett was a man of his word. If he was disappointed in you, you knew it. He was better than all of us at everything. The best of the Baynes. He was kind, loyal, responsible, and *calm*." The crowd chuckled. "He was someone you wanted to be. I'm not saying that because he was my older brother. It's who he was.

"If Jarrett were standing here, he would tell you he wouldn't want you to worry or cry. He would tell you everything was going to be alright. He always told me he wanted a quiet cabin, enough food to eat, a loving wife, and a kid or two. He didn't ask for much from this life. He was a simple man.

"To say he'll be missed doesn't do the feeling justice. He kept the Bayne boys reined in. He always managed to make mom smile and was the only person who could get a real laugh from dad. He adored his little sister and spent most of his time in high school warning the boys to stay away." August sniffled a laugh beside me.

"He was an important member of this family, and it will forever be different without him here. Jarrett didn't get to start his life and that doesn't seem fair right now, but I know my brother, and I know if he were standing here today, he would probably say to us:

"I'm gonna miss all of you. When life starts to get tough…just remember…keep your waders clean."

A song softly started playing in the corner, and I pulled in a tight sob as he gathered his papers and joined his brothers in the front row. This was all my fault despite what August said. She held my hand through the airports and followed Tristan as he led us through the terminals here. Eli said he would follow in his way using the apertures, and I knew he probably wasn't far away now. I'd been numb with grief, unable to formulate a coherent thought since that night.

I replayed Jarrett asking, *What was that?* over and over again.

A killer angel, I would scream in my head. A psychotic monster I wanted to tear limb from limb. I could taste a burning in my throat when I thought of the hatred I felt toward Zacarius. But every time the guttural reaction reared its head, I was immediately overcome with defeated grief and the hatred washed away.

None of it mattered, because none of it would bring Jarrett back.

As people drifted to leave, I didn't move. I kept my gaze fixed on the ground frozen in my seat.

"We're headed back to the house for lunch. Are you coming?" August spoke softly by my side.

"Go ahead," I replied flatly.

She didn't wait to see if I changed my mind or urged me to come with her. She would go on ahead, and Eli would wait some distance back to watch over me. I didn't care.

I don't know how long I sat there before I finally looked up. The casket sat on the platform, and I choked back a soft cry at the sight. I slowly walked up to his resting place.

Sorry wasn't enough. There was no amount of apologies to fix this. My fingers caressed the edges of the polished frame. I blew out a breath as the tears ran down my face. I should have sent him away before this could've happened. I'd been selfish.

The breeze blew in my face, and I turned to the sky of the Pacific Northwest summer letting the tears amble past my temples in the sunshine.

I let out a shaky breath and did my best to gather the strength to say the words I had been thinking of all morning.

Leaning forward I put my lips to the casket. "Jarrett?" I spoke barely above a whisper. "I don't know if you can hear me where you are right now, but *please* know this," I begged quietly. "I wanted to say yes."

I knew it didn't matter but I hoped beyond hope, somewhere deep in the Ethoes, his soul could've heard my answer. My longing to be with him again. And know I loved him madly.

"Goodbye, Jarrett." I kissed the casket and walked back towards Eli who was waiting between two redwoods to take me back to the House of Roosevelt.

18

The Final Burn

"Lily, it's late. You should come in. It's going to be getting dark soon," August whispered gently behind me.

I didn't move. I pulled my arms tighter around my waist and stared aimlessly through the trees behind the house. Everyone was unsure of what I was waiting for. Honestly, I didn't know either. I stood facing the impressive span of bark in the days since the funeral, it was the only thing that felt right after all that had happened.

"You can't stand out here all night. Will you please come in and eat something?" she pressed again.

August, aware of how horrific the ordeal was, still held a calm facade. I felt selfish. Although it was her brother who had been lost, she was consoling me.

"No," I whispered with a slight turn of my chin.

I heard her walk down the back steps of the house and toward me. I didn't care that faces were constantly peering through the windows. She folded her arms beside me and joined in the staring.

"I don't understand," I croaked, my voice harsh after days of misuse.

"I know. I want to find that ginger bastard and shove his sword through his skull. You think they'll just quit with him? What's to say they won't hunt down Ethan next? Or *me*?" she whispered. "Want me to find you a vape pen?"

I cocked my head sideways at her. "I don't smoke."

"We're best friends, Harper." She raised a skeptical eye.

I shrugged.

"Okay, give me a few minutes." She was gone, off around the corner of the huge house.

I could hear him better when I was alone. I closed my eyes and inhaled slowly through my nose tilting my face downwards imagining his voice.

"I miss you," I whispered. The lump in my throat I continuously fought rose again.

You never know when it's almost over. You think about what you might have been able to do differently. They tell you not to blame yourself, but it seemed impossible given *these* circumstances. Jarrett was dead because I couldn't stay away from Eli. The entire situation was my fault, and the weight of the looming truth made my stance shake.

"I'm so sorry," I breathed into the quiet.

I opened my eyes slowly and couldn't swallow the pain. I needed to leave. I couldn't be here right now. I turned on my heel and skipped the steps of the back porch two at a time heading through the back door. I ignored people as they stood still to stop and stare as I passed through the house. I continued through the front door around Marcus and Bjorn who were sitting smoking on the front steps and leapt to the ground in front of them.

"Where ya going?" Marcus called. I ignored him as Bjorn placed a hand of pause on his shoulder.

I swung a leg over a motorcycle, completely disregarding how I didn't own the bike, and kicked hard while twisting the throttle and shooting off pulling my feet upwards to rest.

I twisted through the mountains away from the house. I wasn't sure where I was going, all I knew was I wanted to ride away from the pain causing my chest to cave in. I needed to move, or everything would crumble over me.

I slowed when the warming ache of Eli grew apparent. I eased to a stop without looking up, slowly stepping off the bike while I faced away from him in the middle of the road.

"I…" The pain I was outrunning caught up, rushing into my back and pushing me forward. "I don't know what to do." I finally glanced up.

Eli stood still in the center of the road. His face was expressionless. I pushed out the kickstand and came to stand in front of him staring into the icy blue eyes that had rapidly spun my life into a reel of nightmares. He said nothing.

"I…" The tears flowed, and I could feel his sorrow aching for me and surging stronger. "No." I shook my head. "Stop." His sympathy only made it worse.

His lips parted and I put a hand up to halt him. "Listen." I couldn't look at him while I spoke. "I've never questioned you. What you are or how you came to be. I know you're from *there*. I know you are capable of things science simply cannot explain. I know you are aware of things greater than my human self can comprehend. I have not gotten angry, bitter, or loathing at you for the way things have come to be." I pointed a finger at him that shook with the pain growing in my voice. "I have *never* pleaded with the questions *why me* or *why this?*" I gestured wide with my hand. "I have asked nothing of you ever, Elijah." I choked hard on the tears. "But this…" I closed my eyes and clenched my fists, making my nails bite my palms nearly to the cusp of drawing blood. "I can't do this." My lips quivered with the words.

I stood directly in front of him trembling as I continued. "I cannot have only feet between him and me! That's it, Eli. Only a few feet separates Jarrett from me forever." I sucked in the thick tears drenching my words. "So I am asking—no, I'm begging you now, please…" I rasped desperately. "Please fix this. Please bring him back for me!" I succumbed to it.

"I can't," he said quietly.

I pulled in a broken breath and pressed my lips into a firm line.

"I know," I replied calmly, shoulders slumping. I turned before he could continue and mounted the bike spinning it around to head back toward the house.

I knew he wasn't far behind. I could feel him near as I parked the bike in the driveway. That ever-present ache inside me. Staring at nothing as I shuffled back up the pavement with him at my back. I ignored the crowd in the front of the house watching and couldn't bear to look at August. I had ruined her life.

Stopping and waiting for them to give way so I could go inside. I couldn't warrant eye contact with them.

A soft Saint reached a gentle hand towards me but quickly withdrew.

"Let her be," Eli spoke.

I climbed the steps slowly before stumbling a little. I didn't want to go inside. I wanted all of this to end now. I wanted to go home. I wanted my life back.

But I was never going to get to go home again. All of that was gone now.

I faced the door thinking of when Eli had kicked it in after the legion had tried to kill me. The emotions I felt then were overwhelming. I remembered the worry he exuded, and I smiled gently. I turned to face him slowly, making eye contact with him. I maintained a soft smile as it slowly fermented into weak breaths. I pulled in thick gasps of air, uncaring about the small grouping of witnesses behind me. They had thinned after Jarrett's death. Killing humans was a level of conviction most were afraid to face. I looked at Tristan and watched his face grow with sympathy from my breaking grief.

It hit me hard, so incredible it was unrivaled to anything I knew. I dropped to my hands and knees, praying it would stop, and I pulled a scream from painfully deep within, so loud and hard my head arched skywards. I sucked in a breath and heaved another scream, trying frantically to expel the painful broken feeling.

Suddenly, I felt a warm palm pressed to my shoulder blade, and I looked up to catch a dark-haired woman with gentle eyes. One of the Fallen and the last person I expected to come to my side. Often staying on the back half of the property with her friend.

"Evelyn, stop. This will end for her eventually," a man urged beside her. The only other Fallen willing to stay behind, no matter how little they contributed or were present. Maybe he was a lover? Possibly a sibling? They would come and go or keep their distance. Afraid to break their parole. "This is how it has always been for humans. Her grief will end eventually."

"No, she must know *we* are not all like that. Cruelty is not the intention. If she is what they think she is, we can't have her hating all of us. We still have friends there." She raised her other palm and placed it on the lower half of my ribs.

"It's your choice." I heard his footsteps back away.

"It will be over soon," she whispered gently into my ear.

I shook with the sobs. Suddenly feeling something strange. Glancing back I could see her halos slowly illuminated in the dim porch of the setting sun. Except there was one noticeable difference than those I had seen on Eli or the Legion. Her halos, a bright golden color, were secured around her neck. The biggest difference was the cracks. Tiny fractures of broken fissures ran through the glowing ring below the surface of her skin. This could explain why so many legends said angels had golden halos, because the ones who wandered *here* did.

Fallen angels cast from the Garden.

Her head bowed slowly, and I was distracted for a moment when I looked up to watch Marcus push people back. Evelyn drew a low deep breath, and it was as though I was taking in a deep breath with her despite my lungs keeping rhythm with my own breath. When she exhaled, I felt like I was exhaling and I felt my heart grow stronger, working harder to excavate the immense grief coating it.

After several minutes, the grief felt strangely distant, as though it had taken place years prior. I was surprised when I felt a happy calm seep inward, and I sat back noticing Evelyn's halo dim. She backed away suddenly and I did the same.

"Did that ease it?" She appeared to be weak.

"Yeah," I whispered, my lips barely parting with the word.

She was helped up slowly before stumbling into the waiting arms of the Condemned who ushered her into the woods. All who stood facing me were August, Tristan, and Eli.

"What happened to her?" I asked.

"Does she only have one left now?" Tristan spoke softly as he stared at me dumbfounded.

"One what?" I looked to Eli for answers.

"One burn." Eli's face was solemn.

"Burn?" August appeared to be as confused as I was.

"Halos burn finitely when you have Fallen."

"What happens when they use them all?" I whispered in shock.

"They Condemn themselves here." A thick solace hung in the air for a few moments after Eli spoke the words.

"So Marcus and the others…" I didn't quite know how to react.

"Yes, they're more compassionate than they first appear." He turned to gaze into the woods as August and Tristan were now doing.

I slowly began to stand.

"To answer your question Tristan—none," Eli stated.

A Condemned had been born.

* * *

It was hours before anyone reappeared back at the house. I craned my neck when bodies slowly trickled in, but after awhile, it seemed she wasn't coming back.

The chatter was minimal, and people scampered off quickly. "I'm honestly okay." I patted August's arm again.

What the newly Condemned Evelyn had done worked. It felt like someone had washed the ache away from me.

I wandered off towards the back door having heard where Evelyn was. I decided not to wait for Eli to come back from the gathering in the study he was having with some of the dismal group. Tristan would let him know I was out on the grounds.

The night air was warm, different than it had been earlier. I didn't fully understand everything that happened today, and I didn't think it was right to bother people with questions.

A smile embraced my lips from the breeze moving through the tree limbs, and I strolled with a casual purpose to the cottage when I abruptly caught sight of Evelyn standing a ways off behind it.

Her customary black ensemble complimented her slender physique well. Her thick auburn hair was woven into a tight braid between her shoulders accentuating her perfect posture.

"Don't apologize," she said softly, her back to me.

I closed my mouth.

"Will you walk with me?" She nodded into the woods as I followed her flowing footsteps. "It wasn't a difficult choice."

"I'm sorry?" I continued.

"I was simply a conduit." She was looking up at the stars, paying no mind to what was in front of her. Her scent was sweetly riveting. She wore thick high-heeled leather boots rising to mid-thigh, and I was mesmerized when she navigated the uneven forest floor with ease.

"So what I felt was…" I held onto a nearby trunk for balance trying to follow in her footsteps.

"Jarrett. *He* alleviated your grief." Her gentle voice flowed back toward me as she continued onwards. "He's happy where he is, past the pain, relishing in the comfort."

"That was him?" My heartbeat quickened with the pain of hearing his name. Then, instantly, it warmed and slowed. I stopped, staring down at my chest.

"You will always be connected when you have pain for him." She stopped in a small flat clearing to face me, where pine needles littered the ground by the thousands.

Her eyes glazed over all my features. "You are delightfully stunning. I'm truly apologetic for what has happened regarding Zacarius. I hope you will come to understand there will be ramifications for what he has done. To end one without discussion is unheard of…in another's region…" She trailed off, and her eyes saddened. Something sparked when she said that.

"Without discussion?" Eli's brother's decision to take me out of the equation was a group effort. Noted. However, Zacarius had decided to eliminate Jarrett all on his own.

"Of course. Unanimous decisions happen on all accounts." She smiled, and it felt reassuring. It made me smile in reply. Every portion of this woman was alluring. She had a radiant comfort about her I hadn't felt with the other Condemned.

I glanced back towards the house momentarily to realize it wasn't in sight. "He won't hear this." She smiled again, and the warmth immediately followed.

"Hear *this*?" Her words were odd. I was wondering what she meant when I was distracted by a heavy beat pummeling the ground behind me. It sounded distant, and I turned to see what it was.

"Lily? Would you like to *see* Jarrett?" she asked me gently.

My head snapped back to stare at her. "You can do that?" I could feel the tears lining my eyes.

"Yes." Her brows exuded tenderness for me.

"I miss him." I choked on the lump rising in my throat. The old pain resurfacing.

"Of course you do." She reached out and placed both hands on either side of my face. "Then let's not wait."

I weakly shook my head, unable to bear words. I was going to see him. My mind raced with all the things I wanted to say.

One of her hands reached slowly behind her back as I tried desperately not to be distracted from the ever-growing thundering behind me.

A dense wind grew in the night trees. "How long am I going to have with him?" I whispered.

I realized my legs were quivering from the loud hammering and an emphatic roar vibrated in my bones.

"Gabriel!" A deep slow growl tore through the wind. I turned slowly to see Eli straddling a black Century stallion as its mouth foamed white from the extreme pace, his wings creeping up and away from his back as his arm reached over his shoulder, pulling forth the same sword I had seen him use once during a fight with members of the legion.

He was glorious, his halo illuminating and blazing through the night, so bright it was almost impossible to stare directly at him. A deep ire held over his features.

"Do not touch her!" he roared.

In my peripheral vision, Evelyn blurred and vanished. Now I stood next to a man, tall and muscular. Anger brimmed from his thick chest he pushed outwards. His wings exploded from his back with a crack and he pulled a beautiful silver dagger from behind him and wrapped a thick forearm around my shoulders pulling the blade to the wide artery in my neck.

The archaic voice boomed, *Run*, but it was too late.

The horse reared its head back and forth whinnying as he paced in front of the both of us.

"She's suffering," Gabriel spoke smugly past my ear, his breath sweet.

"Her choice is *me*," Eli exhaled through gritted teeth. "Lily, when I tell you, get to the horse."

"She's a human! She has free will, Elijah! You do not!" Gabriel's words were tight and punishing. "You know the law! The *only* law!"

"Then Condemn me!" Eli howled.

"It's not your choice, brother."

"Brother? You're no longer his brother!" Tristan appeared at his side with Marcus and Bjorn.

"Tristan, you always were rebellious. The mistake your father bestowed upon humanity… Marcus?" Gabriel was surprised.

"Let her go, Gabe," he instructed authoritatively.

Gabriel leaned his head back and lamented a painful cry.

"She does not belong here!" he roared.

"Lily?" August's tiny voice cut through the shifting men that faced us.

"Go home!" I yelled at her.

"Lily?" She peeked over Tristan's shoulder as he turned and began to usher her away. "No!" she screamed.

"Forgive me, Elijah." Gabriel's voice was grim.

"August!" I called. "Close your eyes."

She shook her head furiously, her blond waves bouncing with the motion.

Now! The ancient voice inside me rose from the depths and my body moved on its own. Opening August's lighter while I pulled it from my pocket and exhaled hard. A flash of green erupted from my palm, melding with the blinding halos, the full force of the silver lighter billowing towards him as he retreated.

"Get away from them!" I screamed at him. When all my breath evaporated, I stopped, gasping for air, blinking away the sparkles dancing across the darkness in my eyes. Gabriel had gone.

When my vision adjusted, I stood facing my friends, their expressions white with fear.

"I'm sorry. I reacted." I looked from face to face. I'd been carrying the lighter since Zacarius. "I could feel the blade tightening." They stood still, saying nothing. Even Eli appeared to be shell-shocked by my reaction.

"What?" I finally blurted. "Why are you all looking at me like that?"

August broke past Tristan's reach and ran to me. Marcus put a hand out and grabbed her upper arm pulling her back.

What was going on?

"Is it a trap?" Marcus looked to Eli for answers.

"No, it's *her.*" Eli lowered his sword, walking to me. He palmed both sides of my face and searched my eyes. "Lily?"

"What's wrong?" I was worried.

"She's tired. Let's get her back to the house." He threaded his fingers through mine and pulled me through the parting crowd. Eli shook his head to pause whatever questions people were about to ask.

"Who is she?" a Saint questioned Marcus quietly.

"I think you mean *what* is she?" Marcus corrected.

What did they mean? Hadn't anyone fought against a Guardian before?

19

The Sanctum of an Angel

I sat on the couch in the living room cradling my steaming cup of tea. The clock on the stove read 1:17 a.m. and I could hear the rain falling steadily outside. It was one of those steamy July nights.

I stared at the blank text screen on my phone and debated what I should say to Ethan, but nothing seemed enough. It had been a week and half since the funeral and the incident with Gabriel. Evelyn and her Fallen friend had left not long after. My grief had proven to be all but gone. A distant memory residing in the same place where I kept it for my father. Surprisingly, it seemed to be helping August. My anguish was hindering her healing. Now it was gone, and she was slowly getting back to herself. Even making friends with our new acquaintances who resided here.

Some of the people chose to sleep in the house, but most either stayed in the cottage or the loft of the stables. They were now spread out covering more of the grounds. August and Tristan slept in the second largest room, and the primary suite had been bestowed upon me without asking.

The house felt darker these days. The light of the Baynes had vanished. August, the last little beam of their warmth, had dimmed after Jarrett. I wondered if she would ever be the same again.

"Why aren't you asleep?" Eli spoke softly as he came to sit across from me. I hadn't heard him come in.

He was wearing cream drawstring pants and no shirt. I hadn't seen him at night, and I hadn't seen him in this state of undress since I watched him kill a Scribe. In fact, I wasn't certain where he slept since I was occupying his room. Maybe he didn't sleep.

Sometimes it hit me how little I knew.

"I can't sleep in that room anymore—your room." I spoke sorrowfully into my mug. "It's not just *him*. It's the angel coma, and the missing Baynes, Gabriel, Zacarius, and I just can't sleep anymore."

"The angel coma?" He carefully moved closer. Afraid to touch me since Jarrett's death. Always avoiding me or constantly keeping a careful distance, not wanting to jostle the landmine.

"August," I whispered.

"And when's the last time you slept?" His elbows were on his knees, and he pressed his palms together into an anxious clasp.

I was an insomniac without August's stash of Valium. When I didn't answer, he looked up at me. "Lily?"

I leaned forward and set my mug on the table. "Two days." I looked away. "I try to sleep, but when I close my eyes…"

He let out a pained sigh.

"Do you have any more angel chloroform?" I joked quietly, nudging his shoulder with mine.

"Maybe I can help another way?" he whispered tentatively.

He stood and I followed. We headed up the stairs to pass the landing to the second floor of rooms. He turned the corner and walked quietly to the door that had been locked since my arrival. The same door the Baynes were convinced had to have amazingly fun things hidden behind. He turned the knob and pushed it gently and gestured for me to go first.

A set of winding wooden steps, bowed from heavy use, ascended in front of me. Golden lights lit beneath them. I turned the corner into a large attic bedroom. Larger than my suite and August's put together.

A massive beam ran the length of the vaulted ceiling and met a looming stone wall opposite me with large joists running down the angled ceiling. A great chandelier of antlers and lights faintly cast a shimmer throughout. A wood stove seated in the corner next to a stack of dried birch. A simple desk was pushed to the stone wall with books and a laptop scattered about while an oiled-leather chair sat crookedly beside it. A large, deep-brown rug of fur sprawled the wooden floors, the same wood ran up the ceiling and most of the walls. A platform bed with pooled white sheets and a soft down comforter, looming in size, pushed against the wall to my right facing a massive, black-framed window running vertically along the roof. I could hear a composer's cello soft and melodious from a speaker hidden in the wall nearby. The only artwork was a large yellowed atlas of the world above the head of the bed and the entire room smelled softly of a bonfire, ink, and something I couldn't put my finger on.

"*This* is my room," Eli whispered beside me.

It was beautiful.

"You've been using the main guest suite. I didn't want to be presumptuous when I brought you here. But if it will help you to sleep in a quieter place, you're welcome to my room." He walked to the nightstand and moved a timepiece to set it on the desk. He then scooped an overturned book off the floor next to the bed to place back on a small shelf. Tidying his space I had never seen. It felt private, intimate, like I was seeing *him* for the first time.

"It's not much. There's a bathroom with a shower in the far corner behind the wall there and the door at the bottom of the stairs automatically locks at all times, but I can show you how to get in." His face was bashful, worried it would be enough for me.

I turned to peer out the window. "It's beautiful."

"It's yours," he said barely above a whisper.

"Thank you." I smiled tenderly.

He picked up a few more books scattered about the floor to place back onto the shelf while I climbed carefully into the bed. The sheets were fused with his scent.

As he turned off the chandelier, little lights beneath the bedframe blinked to life. He then twisted to walk down the stairs.

"Where are you going?" I sat upright.

"You should get some rest."

"Aren't you staying with me?" I asked nervously.

He thought about it for a long moment and then apprehensively came to stand beside the bed. After several more considerate minutes, he began crawling in with me. A large space flowed between us, the only sound was our breathing. He stared at the ceiling from his back while I lay on my side to gaze at him, my hands in prayer beneath my cheek.

The rain was fading to mist on the enormous window above us and the night clouds parted enough for the waning moon to shine through.

"You can sleep, Lilian. My brothers won't make another move for some time, I promise." I watched his red lips in the moonlight.

"Even Zacarius?"

His face hardened and he turned to look at me, his head propped on his palm. "He won't get close enough to you again. I underestimated their desperation. If they saw you had a human you were involved with, I thought they would relent. I'm sorry." He rolled to his back and his face creased with pain.

He had chivalrously stepped aside and let Jarrett through. Despite his *choice* he proclaimed to his brothers. I realized at this moment our shared sameness. Somehow we could find a way to end his brothers' obsession with me. But if I was being honest with myself. I had never truly let Eli go. I hadn't wanted to. And maybe his brothers knew that.

"Eli." I hesitated. "I know you can't bring him back for me. I'm sorry I begged such an impossible thing of you." I swallowed hard, not wanting to revisit the pain now residing somewhere in the deeper parts of my ocean of grief.

"I've never wanted to give a mortal something so desperately." He closed his eyes against the memory.

I wasn't sure what he was capable of. I hadn't taken the time to get to know him. I had selfishly tried to keep them all as long as I could, and it had cost me.

"Could you…" I trailed off. "Never mind."

"I promise you. I'll keep you safe."

"That's not it." I drew in a tired breath. "Could you hold me?"

He didn't move at first. I could feel the conflict warring within him, but the drawing pull pushed harder, and slowly, he slid his way forward and I did the same.

He was unsure. Carefully, he put his immense arms around me, but he didn't relax.

"I understand if you don't want to," I whispered into his broad chest.

He looked down to me. "It's not that I don't *want* to. I don't know *how* to be with you."

"How 'bout we start here?" I curled into his chest and lay my cheek against his skin.

"Are you cold?" he whispered. "You have goosebumps."

"No, your skin does that to mine." Like it's trying to get closer to him. I could feel his arms slackening, becoming more comfortable as he rested his chin on the crown of my head.

"Is it strange I don't want it to stop?" Eli whispered.

"I think that's what got us here in the first place," I mumbled, yawning into his chest. He shivered. "I can't seem to stay away from you."

"And I, you."

I had so many questions, so much I wanted to understand, but my brain was running on fumes, and I couldn't make the words form into sentences.

I didn't feel anything afterward because, for the first time in as long as I could remember, I slept dreamless and deeply.

* * *

His right hand rested on his bare chest at the base of his sternum. I watched as his chest rose and fell slowly from behind the peaks of my pillow. Sun flickered through the needles of the Douglas fir billowing beyond the window. The storm had moved out. His scarlet lips parted slightly as he exhaled faintly. His thick lashes, so long, quivered with the delicate movement behind his sleeping lids. I couldn't look away. He was beautiful.

What did angels dream about? I wondered. He looked so peaceful I didn't dare wake him. This was the most time I had spent this close to him, able to stare unabashedly at his grace and splendor.

His features were so otherworldly, they were better suited to be seated on Mt. Olympus among the gods than beside me here or having sonnets written by a brilliant poet recited in gardens for kings somewhere. And then it occurred to me—they probably had. I'm sure at some point songs had been composed as a result of someone witnessing his beauty or perhaps sculptures had been minted of him. And suddenly, I felt small. Unworthy of his affections. A mere mortal weakly pining at the feet of Apollo.

Despite it making me feel gloomy, the impulse I felt to run my fingers through his hair and trace the whiskers of his jaw was overwhelming. Thinking about it awoke the ache in my chest.

I bit the inside of my cheek and pulled my fingertips back, when suddenly, he let out a slight moan and his right forearm began to glow. He was dreaming. His halos barely ignited, and his eyes moved beneath his lids seeing some distant vision. The rings brightened slowly in intensity, and I watched enchanted as faint streaks of white-blue lightning fired feebly across his nerves.

I sat up, cross-legged, rapt by the phenomena as they pulsed and began to fade and recede.

"Do you like it?" He was staring at me. I hadn't noticed he was awake and watching me. I looked away, embarrassed.

"I didn't mean to stare." The lock on the bedroom door now made sense. You couldn't have someone walk in and see *that*.

His fingers traced a scar on my knee closest to him.

"Juniper bush the first summer I lived here."

He moved to touch the scar on the right side of my hand.

"Broken pint glass, breaking up a fight outside a bar junior year of college."

His thumb smoothed over the jagged pink scars on my bicep.

"August's bird shot, afraid of butterflies last month." I shook my head and rolled my eyes. "Do you…have any scars?"

A small smile played on his lips, and he shook his head no.

"Delicate."

His smile grew and his fingertip tapped my knee.

"Can I ask you something?" I had been meaning to learn as much as I could but every time I happened to be near him, he either stepped away or there were too many other ears listening.

"Yes."

"Why can I feel you? Is it because you're you?" I still struggled with the word *angel*.

"I have my *ideas*." I stared at him, coaxing him to continue. "I'm worried if I tell you, it'll upset you."

I silently reached toward his forearm where the blue glow would slowly burn. Pressing gently, I could feel the cool band of something beneath the surface of the skin.

"Why would it upset me?" I asked.

"For that, you would have to understand my place in this world. Guardians and our *purpose*." He was ashamed, but I couldn't pinpoint why. "Humans view us as loving sentinels, to watch over the world and protect those in need, but that's not very accurate. Think of it more like a warden." My eyes flashed at the word recalling how Tristan said I used it before killing the Scribe. "I thought that would pique your interest. We're also required to purge the most pernicious of beings." I cringed at the thought of his words. "It would be hard for you to fathom the intricacies of our ways. Beyond that, we *never* intervene."

So much of his hesitation to get involved with me made sense now. But was he supposed to have executed me in a past life? Was that why I'd been reborn? Because he had failed somehow? It sounded absurd. I remembered the night Gabriel had tried to kill me and thought of the fearful faces unwilling to approach me after fighting him off. The concerned panic of Tristan when he heard my stories of a previous life and having known the dreaded Hesperia. The intrigued concern he had when I struggled with the smoke bomb in the guest hall of the house.

"There's nothing wicked or vile about you. I think my brothers are using this as a rationale to end you."

"But shouldn't Ecclesias and Aurelius be more sympathetic to your plight having been in your position before?" After all, they had been involved with humans previously. One would think *they* would understand.

"To the contrary, they would be leading the charge. Upset if any exception had been granted when they were denied one. It would also explain how you knew our forgotten names in the hot spring that day. An aged soul from another time. But it doesn't explain how you were able to *call* to us." His face crinkled in thought, speaking the latter to himself.

"Then why is Zacarius so hellbent on hating me and killing me if I'm not evil?"

"Zacarius is strong-willed. He sees the world in black and white. In his mind, the solution would be simple. End you, and we end this feud. I also feel Jarrett's death was retribution for killing his Scribe. He struggles, at times, within the confines of our edicts. Going rogue will not go without impunity," he spat darkly and I shuddered at the power boiling below the surface of his voice.

"But why is everyone afraid of Hesperia?" I was determined to learn as much as I could. To get the answers I was beginning to think I needed. Maybe then I could understand why Jarrett had to die. Why they were willing to senselessly kill him. An innocent in all this.

"Tristan theorizes you could have been her sister," he said sternly. "But I don't know."

"Sister? Why would anyone be afraid—"

"August is awake. She's growing worried she can't find you. I'll see you this evening."

It was clear these were all the answers I was going to get for now. I needed to do some research. Secret research. And there was only one person I knew who could snoop better than anyone. August Beau Bayne.

20

Curiosities

"I 'm in." August shrugged and marched off in some unknown direction.

"That's it?" I stared incredulously. I'd thought it would take more convincing and a serious bribe to get her help. "Don't you think we should come up with a plan first?"

"I have a plan." She shrugged again as if this were obvious.

"You came up with a plan in all of the fifteen minutes it took me to tell you everything?" I shut the door of her bedroom as she kept trying to exit.

She sighed impatiently. "They murder what they dub 'wicked,' right? Because it's supposed to protect humanity. Eli thinks you might have been wrapped up in something like that a gazillion years ago, but he says you aren't evil, and every time you mention this Malaria chick—"

"Hesperia," I corrected.

"—who might've been your sister. They panic and get all owl-eyed." She held her eyes wide with her thumbs and index fingers. "My guess is she must have been one of these foul meteors to humanity, and they took her out. Maybe their sin radar isn't precise, and now they're thinking you are *her* reborn? Or maybe they were supposed to protect

220

you from her and they failed, and now they're worried you're going to exact your revenge! Who knows, but we're going to find out." She crossed her arms and propped her chin on her fingers as she scrunched her face sideways in thought. "Now, the tough part is finding what region she lived in. My guess is because you're drawn to Eli she had to have lived in his region when she was alive. And because the only possible timeline we have is based on you seeing a picture of her in a gross book, it had to be around 1300 to 1500 AD."

"How would you possibly know that?" I asked.

"Because earlier books in the Middle Ages were printed in monasteries by hand on calfskin, with wooden leather-bound covers like you described. It was common practice in the Medieval ages before the invention of the printing press."

"You learned that in college?"

"Trivia night at the bar. Since Eli and his brothers rotate, she could have been in several places during that period of time. Did you happen to catch what language it was in?"

I stared incredulously at her.

"It's fine. Don't worry about it. That means first we'll have to break into the cottage and steal the book. Then if we can't decipher the language using the internet, we'll break it down by most obscure regions first while cross-referencing active monasteries in that time period." She gave a sharp nod.

"Sometimes August—"

"Oh, please, I wasn't approached by multiple agencies in tenth grade after my aptitude test because I'm an idiot." She swatted my hand away, "Now c'mon, let's go find out who this Malaria is!"

"Hesperia."

She turned to shush me as she peeked down the hallway.

* * *

I acted as a lookout while August not-so-quietly broke into the cottage and looked for the book I described. It didn't take long for her to burst through a side entrance, motioning for me to run after her, with the outline of a giant square tucked into the back of her pants under her shirt.

A huge grin spread from ear to ear on her face, and I smiled seeing her truly happy for the first time in nearly a month. Nothing like a little B and E to lift the spirits of a Bayne.

August hadn't been herself since the funeral. She may have fooled everyone else, but I knew her. Despite her tough facade and pulled-up bootstrap attitude, she was hurting. I also knew August liked to focus her hurt. Fuel it into a purpose. I liked to swallow mine. She liked to harness it.

This was exactly what we both needed.

"Stay right behind me in case someone comes up," she stage-whispered over her shoulder.

She was walking with a pigeon-toed shuffle, and she had her hands below her butt holding up the edges of the book stuffed down her pants.

I awkwardly walked only a foot behind her as she veered left under the stairs down the long main hall and was about to descend into the basement when Amelia, the Saint from my horse-feed fiasco, was leaving the library.

"Menses mishap," August shouted and skipped frantically down the stairs.

"We're going into the lower level?" I leaned around her as we jogged.

"No, that's through the old door next to the study. This is the lower ground floor where you came through with Tristan." She'd made herself right at home. She sped to a stop in front of a wall of glass and yanked on a tremendous black handle, opening a door. Once inside the dark room, the air felt cool and dry. I noted a digital thermostat on my left measuring temperature and humidity.

"The book will be safe in the back room." She reached with her left hand and flicked a switch, causing recessed lights in rows and rows of horizontal wine racks to light up. "The wine cellar is the perfect place to do our snooping. I doubt anyone will come looking for us down here. No one's had any fun since..." She, too, couldn't bring herself to say Jarrett's name yet.

The mere mention of it made us both stop cold. The first week after he died, we spent nights out on the balcony in stunned silence, clutching glasses of wine staring into the flames of the fire pit in disbelief.

I would peak out the windows, afraid Zacarius was beyond the treeline watching me. Waiting. Plotting his next move. Conspiring to take us out one by one.

Eli was withdrawn afterward. Giving me the impression he didn't want me there anymore. Tristan reassured me he was only trying to make sure something wouldn't happen again. August agreed and brought up a crucial point.

"He's probably more worried than ever they'll hurt you again," she quietly said one evening over her glass of wine. "I think we all got a little too comfortable and started living naively."

I couldn't do any of this without her. I would have been lost in my own head over everything. Never wanting to get out of bed. August always had a way of easing tensions and softening the hard moments in life.

Since Ethan was now gone, if I didn't have her at my side, I didn't think I could find the will to keep pushing forward through all of this. I smiled at her determination and loyalty as we moved toward the back of the wine cellar. Friends like August were rare. *People* like August were rare.

"Set it here." I pointed to a table situated in the little room behind the walls of wine and pulled a chair across the brick floors to sit beside her.

"Okie dokie. Let's see if you're a little Antichrist who is going to end the world." She turned the pages. "Oh, thank goodness. It's French and Latin. We should be able to figure this out pretty easily. Wait…" She looked confused as she turned the pages more quickly.

"What?"

"There aren't any pictures in this book," she said.

I grabbed the book from her grasp and frantically began turning the pages.

"They ripped them out. They ripped out the pages with Hesperia!" I shook my head in disbelief. Examining the binding where the missing pages had been. "Why would he do this?"

August looked at me sympathetically. "Maybe, he doesn't want you to worry?"

My mouth was agape. I was speechless. What was he hiding from me? I turned the page to and fro where the missing pages had been, willing them to reappear.

"You only hide stuff if you have secrets. What is he not telling me?" I asked.

"I don't know." August closed the book gently and turned to hide it among one of the racks.

"August…" I looked at her, afraid, tears welling in the corners of my eyes. "What's wrong with me?"

"Am I stupid?" she responded, suddenly off-kilter.

"What?" I looked at her sideways.

"Am I stupid?" she asked more slowly.

"Reckless maybe…"

"Am I a poor judge of character?" She raised her brows in question.

"Well, there was Sweater-Vest Dalton…"

"Except for Dalton," she quickly interrupted.

"No, not stupid, and not *always* a bad judge of character." I could see where she was going with this.

"Then believe me when I tell you this, Lily. There isn't a vile bone in ya." She smiled reassuringly. "There's something we're missing here. And I'm not quitting until we know." She squeezed me tight. "Nope, the only thing wrong with you is your constant aversion to a good time. And Sweater-Vest Dalton was nice, mind your mouth."

"He was pretentious and smelled like matches." I grimaced.

"Shh. You're upset. You're not thinking clearly." She pushed her tiny palm to cover my mouth.

"I think I am." I smiled with a muffled response.

***

I sat cross-legged on the bed and watched out the window patiently. I wasn't sure if Eli was going to sleep here again tonight. I found myself hoping he would appear, but it was already past eleven and the house had gone quiet over an hour ago. The feeling coupled with conflict since Jarrett. What if they switched up tactics and decided to kill Eli? Was that possible? I shook the thought from my head. I wasn't going to lose anyone else in this.

Perhaps, Eli had gone back to sleeping in the cottage? Maybe my intrusive line of questioning this morning had scared him off.

Every time I felt like I was chipping away at his hesitant exterior surrounding us, he would pull back. I wanted to believe August and Tristan. Eli was just worried, now more than ever, his brothers would hurt me again. No one thought they would be willing to attack a human. We were wrong. The cracks in their desperation were starting to show. They wanted us apart and me gone at all costs. The question was, why?

The fire in the wood stove had burned to near embers, and I was about to retreat under the sheets when the doorknob softly turned at the base of the stairs.

I nervously smoothed my hair.

"Did I wake you?" Eli was surprised to find me upright in the bed.

"No, I…" *Was nervously waiting for you like an idiot, which now feels foolish.*

"Are you having trouble sleeping again?" He promptly came to sit on the edge of the bed, his face awash with concern.

"I was waiting for *you*." I looked away embarrassed. "I had hoped you would sleep here again tonight."

"If you'd like that." He smiled.

I nodded, feeling my cheeks flush red. Then I carefully scooted to the head of the bed and pulled my knees to my chest. Watching as he stood and went to the leather chair and began to unbutton his shirt with his back to me. He laid his clothes over the edge and walked to the bathroom before returning in his classic drawstring pants.

I caught his palm as he rounded the corner. "Can I ask you something?"

He peered down at my face. "I'm not going to answer your questions regarding Hesperia until I can give you more."

"No. I was wondering"—I wasn't sure how rude of me it was to ask, but I had debated this all afternoon—"if I could see something?"

He was surprised by this and nodded. Sure I would follow up on this morning's questions .

"I've been having nightmares about Zacarius and that night." His face was pained as I uttered the name. "And I was hoping I could try and replace them. I was wondering if I could see…your sword? I was hoping it would make it less scary."

He closed his eyes in anguish. "I don't want you to think about that. I don't want us to be these things haunting your nightmares." He pursed his lips and exhaled through his nose. Then he calmly positioned me to sit on the end of the bed. "There's been something I've wanted to show you though. Perhaps it will make us less frightening. Can you cover your ears?"

I nodded and did as I was told, looking up at him with my palms clasped on either side of my head. He took a step back to stand in the moonlight of the window, inhaling deeply. Closing his eyes he stood still.

A deafening *crack* suddenly broke the silence echoing through the house. His wings blew wide, the span nearly touching either wall of the elongated attic.

I had never seen them so still, in such a calm space, so *close*.

He looked to meet my eyes nervously and quickly looked away. Like standing before a lover naked for the first time. Abashed of their thoughts on your vulnerability.

I carefully approached his left wing, making sure to watch his face for any sign of uncomfortable intrusion. The flames of the fire refracted off it and sent a light across my eyes, I shielded them quickly with my fingers.

"Sorry," he murmured, and he angled the light down with his wing.

"They're reflective," I breathed, like the sun off a polished watch face. But you would never know by looking at them.

At first, they appeared white, but upon closer inspection, they were what I could only describe as the color of snow in the evening glow of a winter sunset. An alabaster with blue tinges and no origins of the sapphire.

I inhaled slowly and reached cautiously to run my fingertips across the propatagium. He shivered at my touch and let out a sigh. Watching me as I ran my fingers along the edge. It felt impossibly light, practically nonexistent. A mix between a rabbit's fur and cashmere, but softer.

Gradually, he began to relax them, folding them inward. I faced him.

Our eyes met and a small smile was on my lips.

"They're extraordinary," I whispered. I couldn't find the words. I had never witnessed something so incredible.

His breath was growing weak. He moved closer to me. I could taste the want behind his lips.

"Can I—"

"Yes." And I pulled his jaw to mine. My lips parted against his. His tongue tasted like vanilla bourbon, and he smelled like cherries in wintertime. The ache below my collarbone, which had been dull for weeks, suddenly cleaved open and the freight train was rushing towards him.

He reached to my thighs and hoisted me to sit atop his hips and I wrapped my legs around his waist. My forearms rested across his broad shoulders, and I twisted my fingers into his hair that was black as pitch.

A current burned down my spine, and *he* let out a shaky moan. My bones began to thunder under my skin. The ache to be closer to him was palpable in the air around us. The fire crackled louder in the stove and the glass of the window began to tremble.

He abruptly stopped, setting me down, and pulling away. "Why is this happening?" he groaned, running his fingers through his unkempt hair, clearly distressed.

"I'm sorry." I turned toward the bed and pulled back the sheets. I could feel the tears brimming on my bottom lashes from his rejection.

"No, that's not what I mean." He placed a hand on my upper arm to pull me back to him. "The effects happening when we *interact*. I don't understand them."

"Isn't it because you're an angel?"

He chuckled. "No. Can you also feel them?" he asked incredulously.

I nodded. "So the streetlights exploding after our first kiss was—"

"Unusual. It's almost as though when I'm kissing you it feels like…"

He searched my face for the right analogy.

"We're resonating with an invisible frequency?" I smiled impishly.

"Exactly." He shook his head. "That's exactly what it feels like. When that shiver ran down your spine, I could feel how much you wanted *more*. Like I'm attuned to you."

"Is this because I'm human and you're not?" I responded quietly.

"No, the Condemned sleep with mortals often, and no one speaks of such things. I don't know. This has to be because you're one of the Reborn, but I can't be sure."

"So every time we kiss, we're going to cause power outages?" I played with my fingers in my lap while he drifted toward me.

He laughed through his nose. "Why don't we test that theory?" He was sitting on his hip with his knee cocked palming the bed. He reached up with his free hand and pulled me gently toward him by the nape of my neck. He brushed his lips against mine, and I leaned into him. Moving our lips delicately trying not to awaken the ache, and before it could resurface he backed away.

"See? No outages. Maybe it's about practice." He smiled. "Now come sleep. I have something else I want to show you tomorrow."

One thing was becoming clearer to me: I didn't want to lose Eli too. I wanted more. But the energy of our kiss exhausted me, and I couldn't fight the urge to sleep any longer. Instead, I peacefully dreamt of Eli's wings and snow-covered cherries the entire night. A nice reprieve from the monsters who'd been haunting me for so many weeks.

21

Edmund Blevit

The heat of the summer sun was beginning to fester, setting up for a hot August day. Those sticky ones that make your tee cling to your back and strands of hair run currents of beaded sweat down the nape of your neck.

"Why did you bring me here?" I asked skeptically. Eli stood opposite me in the small meadow down the hill from the cottage. A place where the trees thinned and a rocky outcropping swelled upwards beyond the timberline to the south. I liked being alone with him. It was easier when he was around to forget all the terrible things that happened to me. To feel safe.

"I felt some privacy would be more appropriate for what we're going to do," he said.

He had led me here in the light of the morning.

"After talking to Tristan, we believe it only makes sense you have a paladin. These beings are unique because they can be *called* from any distance. I want you to call out to them." He stared at me.

"You want me to call out to some super knight?" I raised my brows skeptically. "How the heck am I supposed to do that?"

I didn't hide the incredulity in my voice. Six weeks ago, I couldn't figure out how to get home on my own drunk from a bar, and now an angel I was with was asking me to call out to another mythical being I was struggling to believe in. I wish I could have August's unwavering faith and acceptance, but it was harder for me. Trust wasn't something I doled out readily.

"Paladins can be summoned under great duress. As you get better at it, it can be something whenever you're in need. You don't have to use your voice, but because today is going to be your first effort, it'll be the simplest way." He came to stand directly in front of me.

"But we don't know who it is?" I was dumbfounded. How on earth could I call out to some person bound to me, some personal fighter, when I didn't even have a name to utter?

He looked intensely into my eyes. "I want you to think about when you were drowning, who did you think of initially?"

Flashes of the moment I had been sucked into the hot springs of the grotto flooded my memories and shuddered. I would have died if Eli hadn't saved me that night.

"There were half a dozen names I thought of and tried to shout. That's not helpful," I replied dejectedly.

"What about when Jarrett had been attacked? Was there a name or feeling you felt compelled to reach out to?" He spoke with calm and soothing tones. Patient in his effort to help teach me.

"Yes. *You*," I whispered.

A small smile played across his lips, and he gently came to place his hands on the points of my slumped shoulders. "I think it was because you knew I was the closest. You probably reached for someone initially, but it might have seemed irrational to you. Perhaps August? But you knew she was at the bar and so you ran to me."

I shook my head. "I don't remember. I just remember trying to help"—my mind choked on Jarrett's name—"him."

I anxiously twisted my shoulders. I was overwhelmed. When Eli asked me this morning if he could teach me something to help keep me safe, I thought he meant how to dodge magical machetes. Not to take me out to a serene clearing to summon who knew what. Everything was happening so quickly, and my entire life had been chaotically overturned.

I also didn't want to disappoint anyone. I already lost one person. I didn't want to fuck up. I wasn't willing to lose someone else, especially Eli or August. I winced at the painful thoughts. But I was growing frustrated, and Eli could see it. He backed a step away and looked into the trees in thought.

"Lily, a Paladin would be incredibly beneficial. If we could find yours, it would mean someone who is completely beholden to you and your wishes would be near you. I wouldn't have to worry about distrusting this person. They would be exceedingly difficult to defeat, only matched by my or my brothers' strength. They're ferocious in a fight. I've never encountered one, but if we could bring yours into the light, it would make this entire situation much safer. It would make *me* feel calmer knowing you had someone at your side if I couldn't be." He was softer when he spoke the last part. Aching in his words. He was worried too about the incident with Jarrett and wanted me to be safe in case of his absence. After all, I couldn't be his only concern. He had throngs of people in his region to look after.

"So, I'm supposed to call out to this person, who could be anywhere, and have this vicious attack dog at my side to sic on anyone?" Lovely. I didn't know if I wanted such a person nearby. I had enough terrifying things surrounding me. "I thought August could have been my Paladin?"

"She could be. And this person wouldn't be *anywhere*. They're naturally drawn to the thing they guard, so they'll be relatively close. And they aren't just for protection. They often provide comfort, friendship, and camaraderie if they connect with their person. Can I try something?"

I nodded.

"Please don't be angry with me. Close your eyes." I did as I was told. "Open."

I jolted backward in dread, practically falling over. Standing before me was Zacarius. The face I feared. His flaming red hair and freckled pallor appeared yellowish pink in the morning light. He was wearing the same shirt and slacks Eli had been in only moments earlier. His face was staring calmly at me.

I began to step backward. I readied my voice to scream out in horror. I wished desperately I had brought a weapon with me. How foolish to implicitly trust I'd been safe.

Terror seized my breath, and I blinked in panic at the tremendous monster of a man in front of me. Before hatred erupted from my throat like a geyser, and I could feel my face twist in rage. His features quickly melted for a moment before shifting back into Eli.

"Please don't be upset. I needed your instinct." He looked away, ashamed. The fear and loathing on my face were something he could barely meet with his eyes. "Who did you want to call out for?" he asked quietly.

I was stunned. It had been a cruel trick to get me to find my Paladin. Anger boiled in my mouth. "I don't know," I replied coldly.

"I'm sorry. I know it was extreme." He looked into my eyes pleadingly. "But I'm worried. I'm…I'm…scared." His shoulders dropped. "I'm afraid they'll kill you, and I won't always be with you. It's not feasible, Lily."

He was ashamed of his actions, unable to meet my gaze. My anger slowly dissipated, and I could feel his guilt for using such extreme measures. Forgiveness took over. "You're right. We don't have time where we can afford to be gentle," I said.

"We'll find another way to call your guard." He looked at me apologetically. "Come on, I'm going to show you something."

I didn't want to admit it as we walked away from the clearing. I thought it through twice before allowing it to fully form in my head. But there *had* been a name—not a name, more a feeling towards a name—rising from the depths within. An instinctual calling to a person for help in a fleeting second of terror when I saw the face of Zacarius.

But I wasn't going to tell Eli. I wasn't going to entertain the thought, because the idea of it, this person, terrified me.

* * *

We stood outside a room I always assumed to be a closet in the basement. The door wasn't very big. When he pushed it open and pulled the string of a light dangling above, I actually thought it *was* a creepy closet at first. A tiny stone cellar large enough for two people.

He asked me to come inside, closing the door behind me. Carefully, he reached around and locked the knob before taking my hand and pulling me through a small archway off to one side. It was hidden behind a wall, and unless you were standing in the room looking directly at it, you would miss it. I felt a cool temperature drop. Then a breeze blew across my lips. It sounded like the ocean's waves were crashing against the wall somewhere. It had me feeling disoriented.

"Where are we going?" I asked tentatively as I navigated the uneven stone floor. The dangling light from the closet grew dimmer and dimmer in our wakes as we made our way down the blackened hallway.

I wasn't sure how this would help me with my Paladin.

"My armory," he stated quietly over his shoulder.

I paused before trotting up quickly to keep pace with him.

I could taste the brine of the ocean in the air and feel the salty breeze drafting over my cheeks. He rounded a corner, and beyond a bend, barely distinguishable, was a tarnished metal door. Out of place but for the elderly castle veneer surrounding it. We weren't in the lower level anymore. In fact, I was beginning to wonder if we were in the house at all.

He removed a lantern carrying the scent of kerosene from a hook on the wall and set a match to the wick before he handed it to me. He then lit a golden tray of oil for himself, holding it high with a loop around his index finger.

Whispering something I couldn't hear into the keyhole, the lock behind the door gave a medieval clang before creaking open slowly.

The room was small, no more than eight by ten feet. It didn't feel like we were underground anymore.

"It smells like the ocean." The room was eerily quiet, and I wondered if it had been intentional.

"It is the ocean. I don't keep these in the house. Or in my region." He turned and set down the flickering flame he held on a low stone table against a wall.

"We used an aperture? From inside the house?" I said, surprised. "Won't someone be able to use it?"

"Yes. Don't worry, no one can use it except for you now. All my brothers hide our weapons." He ignited a narrow trough of oil etched into the walls high enough that the room gently rang with light.

Suddenly, on the wall gleaned the leviathan of a sword that swung from his back and sang when he wielded it. It was frightening. The only time I had seen it up close I had suffered enormous blood loss. My memory of it was an injustice.

"I thought about what you said, and you're right." He sighed heavily. "I don't want you to villainize us and *this*." He motioned to the weapon. "I don't want you to be afraid of *me*."

"I'm not afraid of you…all the time…" I whispered. His expression was pained by my admission. "I watched you kill someone. Andy, that

Residual you tricked and called a traitor—"

"He was. You shouldn't pity him. He'd planned on killing you for Zacarius and Aurelius. He'd been feeding them information regarding you for days. He was going to do it that night." He watched me to gauge my reaction to this revelation. I wasn't going to tell him about the things I had overheard Tristan saying when I had been at the lake with August and her brothers. I was still skeptical and decided to keep watch on Tristan for any other signs of disloyalty myself. My gut told me he was good. I didn't want to sign his death warrant and be wrong. I didn't want August to know the grief of a love lost if I didn't have to. I wanted to be sure I was right before pointing the finger, but nothing connected to what I had witnessed that day.

"It's strange to hear someone was planning to murder me. Almost as strange as seeing a sword that could massacre a herd of buffalo, wielded by angels, hanging behind you. Who made it?" I changed the subject.

He started telling me about the origins of his sword and when it was predominantly used, but I had stopped listening. Eli's back was to me, and I had spotted something which captured my attention much more. There on the opposing wall, in a delicate velvet case, was a dagger. A *mortal* dagger. I recognized the thing immediately. But I didn't feel afraid, only intrigued and drawn to the weapon that nearly cost me my life.

Gently, I lifted it from its haven and twisted it in the light. It was surprisingly heavy. Made of some heavenly alloy I'm sure I would be unable to identify under a microscope.

Then the strangest impulse bubbled up. Like suddenly wanting to leap from the edge of a cliff you peeked over despite knowing it would kill you. I felt the desire to draw the blade along my arm. From everything Eli had told me, it should kill anyone shortly after it pierced you, and despite knowing this, I still felt compelled.

I clenched the blade in my right hand and spread the fingers of my left wide while exposing my palm. Without thinking, I slowly pushed the dagger into the meaty part of my hand below my thumb and twisted.

"No!" Eli roared, and it echoed throughout the gothic keep.

I jumped, alarmed by the change of silence in the stone room.

He looked from my hand to my eyes and back again in horror. I drew back the dagger and a bead of blood began to bubble from the tiny puncture I had made.

"I'm sorry." I set it back into its case and licked the blood quickly from my hand.

He was quiet for several minutes.

"How is this happening?" he whispered before pulling my hand into the light to see the wound better. He was worried. Afraid.

"I don't know why I did that. I think I was curious," I murmured, not wanting to upset him further.

"I need to show you something." Eli was twisting my palm to and fro in his hands, turning it over to see the wound. "Would you come with me?"

It didn't take long for us to extinguish our flames and head back to the house. He kept eyeing me, waiting for the dagger's effects to take hold, but I felt fine.

"How come you don't keep the door locked?" I asked once we were back in the basement hallway.

"I do." He smiled. "It's like the door to my room. It only opens for those who have permission."

He whispered something in what I could only assume was a dead language through the keyhole of his room one morning and then gently touched my hand to the brass knob. The door opened effortlessly from then on, and he proved my safety further by showing me August couldn't enter unless I let her in. And Tristan couldn't wrench the door if he tried. He told me there were three rooms in the house that were sealed, the entrance to the armory was the second. I didn't ask what the third was.

"I'm going to show you how to use the apertures." He was smiling now as he came to stand by two innocuous trees midway down the beaten path to the cottage. No one paid us a mind as we moved about the house and grounds.

"The back doorway we took to go meet with the weird priest in Georgia?" I was feeling skeptical and a little worried. But also excited. Every scientific fiber of my being wanted to know how this worked. Moving through space and time in a matter of moments. My college science professor, Mr. Gamble, would be slipping his chained bifocals on beside me and peering down his nose with an enthusiastic smile if he were here. The curiosity of what could be eclipsing the fear of the unknown.

"It would give me comfort if you knew how to navigate them in my absence. They're the fastest means of escape over reasonable distances." He walked a little way off the path, and I paid close attention to note anything that could help me. A rock, a misshapen tree trunk. Nothing had given me a hint on how to use the indistinguishable paths. "Apertures are the thinnest parts of the veil. Don't think of the Garden and your world as separate but coexisting at once on different planes. Residuals stand on both sides, but we're going to use only one side. Moving through the weakest areas."

"I can't even see them. How am I going to *use* them?" This was far more intimidating than any Bayne game. "They're invisible."

He chuckled. "Not entirely. Think of them more like a mirage in the distance or the heat waves resonating off a hot surface. You can see them at a particular angle and feel them if you're close enough if you know what to look for. The hard part won't be finding them. It'll be using them correctly. It'll take some time to build a cognitive map of which ones go where and you'll understand it the more you use them."

"Yeah, wouldn't want to end up in the middle of a war zone in a foreign country," I grumbled. I was already feeling discouraged.

"That's not my biggest concern. You have to be careful, Lily. If you use them incorrectly or too quickly, you can suffer something similar to decompression sickness. And don't try to hide in one because it will attempt to expel you. Think, a car wreck. At a high speed. Against a wall. It will rip you from the pathway." Well, if that was ominous enough.

He stopped in front of three cottonwood trees in a little triangle. "Many apertures have unique shapes for a doorway. A configuration of trees, a twisted boulder, and a room with seemingly no purpose. Come here." He pulled me forward to stand near him. "What do you see in those trees ahead?"

I stared at the trees, looking for any anomaly or feeling that alluded to what he was saying, but I didn't see anything. I furrowed my brow and focused on the space in the middle of the trees harder, but still, nothing.

"Remember, like a heat wave or a mirage," he murmured gently.

I took a breath and closed my eyes. The afternoon sun was hot, and it felt warm as it washed my face. A soft breeze made my ponytail sway, and I let my fingertips graze my thighs below where my shorts stopped. I heard it to my right and back a little. The ringing was barely audible above the forest sounds, but it was out of place. Among the leaves in the breeze, the birds chirping happily above, and the bugs calling out, an abnormality resonated. Like a power line. I opened my eyes and turned focusing on it, moving towards it in a fluid motion, it grew louder, but only just.

I stopped when it was ringing in both my ears and the air felt only slightly warmer beside me. I noticed a Douglas fir with a thick branch leaning in an arc against the side, a doorway to some fairy-tale wonderland. I eagerly walked toward the ringing and without hesitation stepped carefully and slowly through.

Once the ringing diminished, I stopped, carefully looking around. Deciduous trees were everywhere, and the forest floor had grown grassy and soft. Maples and birch surrounded me, and I felt proud I had managed to succeed on my first attempt. *Is this what Lucy felt like discovering Narnia for the first time?*

"I did it!" I grinned at my success. Turning, I felt a pang of fear when I didn't see Eli in my wake. "Eli?" I called softly. "Eli!" I repeated more frantically.

"I'm right here." He appeared beside me. "You did amazing. I told you, like a mirage."

"I followed the ringing and looked for something that could be a gateway and here I am." I beamed, proud of my success.

"Wait, you could *hear* it?" He was stunned.

I nodded happily.

"You could *hear* the aperture?" he repeated, bewildered.

My happiness diminished and a feeling of self-consciousness took over. I nodded again more timidly.

"What did it sound like?" He searched my eyes incredulously.

"A high-pitched ringing, kind of like power lines? I really had to listen." I whispered the last part, looking away. I felt more and more insecure at my successful attempt now. Every time I did something, it surprised people. It made me feel self conscious and *weird*. I didn't like that outcast feeling. The notion of being different. The anomaly.

"First the dagger and now… You continue to astonish me. No one can hear them. Perhaps this is why you and I tend to create shock waves in our romantic endeavors." He smiled gently. "I was worried when you went through without me…"

"I went at the pace you and I have always taken. I hope that's alright.

Where are we?" I asked.

"You did splendidly. Welcome to New York." He read the surprise on my face. "We aren't far from a little township called Glen off the Hudson River. Please?" He motioned forward with a palm and began to move through the trees.

The sun was lower in the sky here, closer to late afternoon or early evening. At first, it was a little disorienting, like waking up after a longer-than-expected nap, but I quickly adjusted.

We were deep in the forest here, the blaring buzz of cicadas above, while pollen floated with cabbage butterflies gently in the air around us. He walked into a small opening in the trees where the ground gently recessed, and he purposefully headed towards the northern side of the small clearing.

"I wanted to show you this." He stood staring down at a decayed and barely visible tombstone. The wording long weathered away.

The clearing held only a handful of matching stones. We were in some worn, or more likely, forgotten cemetery.

"His name was Edmund Blevit. A physician's son and promising alchemist. He had a brilliant affinity for understanding how some things worked far ahead of his time. He was a quiet boy. He liked the farmer's daughter who sadly died of the flu one fall." He was distant while he spoke as if he could see the boy standing there in front of him. A sadness enveloped his words.

"I'm sorry. How did you know him?"

"He was the first human I had to extinguish," he said sorrowfully.

My breath caught in my throat and my eyes grew wide.

"My brothers have had several, but he was my first." He was troubled when he spoke, as though he were recalling a painful memory. "I tried everything to correct his path. Posing as those close to him and trying to influence his behaviors. But nothing deterred him. He had discovered a means to weaponize influenza and use the local meat market and his father's practice to spread it. It would have decimated humanity. I believe the farmer's daughter was his first test subject. No matter my means, he persevered. He wanted to watch the world burn. There was no greater glory for him. No misguided notion of elitism. He assumed he would die, and he simply didn't care. People like that exist often, but rarely are successful in such grand means." He winced at the memory. "He thought he had slipped and caught a branch walking home through the woods not far from here. I was fast. He didn't have a chance against my dagger. I caught him across the shoulder." He turned his face away and closed his eyes.

"I thought I was protecting my region—all the regions. But after my brother's determination in ending you, I can't..." He inhaled through his nose. "Something doesn't feel right. I find myself questioning everything I've ever known. Our mortal daggers were created for a reason. A painless and quick end to a human so determinedly harmful they simply could not keep existing. Not even beyond. In the Ethoes. Their souls must be extinguished." He came to stand in front of me and stared into my eyes. Searching for answers perhaps?

"How many people have survived a cut from a mortal dagger before?" I asked. Although sure I already knew the answer.

"Only you." He looked at my palm again. "And not once, but twice. You should be gone, and I wish I had more answers. But I fear all paths are beginning to lead to only one reason." He closed his eyes and let out a defeated sigh. "You must be Hesperia's sister."

"What does that mean?" I was frightened, more so when I saw the pain behind his stare.

"That we're all Condemned. And there would be nothing I could do to stop you," he whispered with his forehead to mine in an agonized tone.

Stop me? From what?

So I *was* the wicked one...

22

His Inamorata

I walked quietly behind Eli toward the house. He had let me find the aperture to return home. Again I was able to listen for it, and again I could hear the ringing. He smiled in approval when I was able to identify two other apertures and correctly find our way. I hadn't a clue where they led, but I was able to single out the sounds, which made it surprisingly easy. I wasn't sure if I would fare so well in a city where frequencies would be much more prescient.

I had been too afraid to ask more about Hesperia after seeing Eli's anxious demeanor. I had more questions than I could put together and no idea if I really wanted the truth anymore. Was I evil? When was Hesperia alive? How had she died? Why was everyone afraid of her? They ran through my head on a boundless loop.

It was twilight out and the house was awash with the citrus sunset. I could hear deep voices conversing in the stable and someone cooking in the kitchen beyond the wall of windows on the porch.

"Eli?" I stopped beyond the fringe of the trees.

He turned to look at me.

"Can we go for a walk?" I asked tentatively.

A smile warmed his face and he nodded.

We slowly made our way along the middle of the road past the end of the driveway. It felt nice to be away from the house. I didn't want to go back yet.

"I know you won't answer all my questions, but I do have some I need answered." He was hesitant. "How did you know my dad used to cook me that dinner when you took me on our first date?"

He laughed, not a chuckle, but a *real* laugh. "I must have seemed quite mysterious to you. You don't remember? The night I found you intoxicated coming home from the bar. You had plenty to say that evening. Unfortunately, it wasn't where you lived, but I was able to figure it out eventually. You told me your dad used to make it for you when your mom was away with clients. You also said you were craving it."

Well, that was a lot less remarkable than I initially envisioned. There went August's guess he was able to read minds.

"But the invitation… I changed it from what you suggested at the last second. How did you already know the time?" I squinted.

Another smile. "Coincidence."

"So you can't read minds…" I replied feeling disappointed.

"Unfortunately, no. It would save me a great deal of time trying to understand you." He smiled. Walking casually, he was glancing up now and again at the stars barely twinkling in the indigo skies overhead.

"Do you…" I took a deep breath. I'd been meaning to ask this question for weeks but was too afraid and not quite sure how to phrase it. "Do you really *like* me?" I felt ridiculous uttering the word. It was too trivial a term to describe the level of attraction we held for one another, or at least I harbored for him.

It was more than like for me. More than some primal urge. It was words I had only ever spoken aloud one other time to someone. Jarrett. And I felt like if I said them again to Eli I would be betraying Jarrett.

That what we had together wasn't real and I was just avoiding what I had been feeling for Eli this whole time. But I couldn't pretend I wasn't feeling what I'd been feeling either. It was consuming me. Slowly burning like a low ember in my chest. A constant need for more.

The relief his face brought to mine. The calm serenity his voice evoked within me. The safety he exuded. He was much more than someone I simply *liked*. And if I was being honest with myself, I think it happened long ago and I had been running from it. Hiding in Jarrett from it. The fear of what it would mean.

But sometimes I also had the feeling I was more intriguing to him than anything.

I was looking at my feet as I walked, blushing too hard, and feeling too insecure to meet his gaze. I had fallen in love. And I couldn't tell you when it happened. Maybe the moment I was in his arms crashing to earth? Or seeing the relief in his face when I came to after drowning. When he said nothing, I looked up to discover he'd stopped walking. He was standing staring at me from about ten feet back. I turned to look at him.

"*Like* you?" he asked incredulously. "Lily...you're worried that I don't have feelings for you?"

"Not in the way I do for you at least," I whispered.

"I've been with women before from the Garden. But I've never felt anything for them and definitely never anything for a *human*." He closed the gap between us, "the only reason I've kept my distance is because of your love for the Bayne guy. I had hoped my brothers would concede. See you weren't interested in *me*. I was wrong, and I'm sorry. I didn't want to be disrespectful of your mourning. If you think my distance is for lack of attraction..." His eyes were troubled, and he pulled my hand to his chest to cup it between his two large palms. "I don't think of you as some little pet. The things I want to do to you." I could feel his heart pick up pace. "The things I fantasize about…"

"You fantasize about me?" I asked in a small voice.

"What man wouldn't? You're the embodiment of desire. Your lips are irritatingly distracting. You smell like a mix of cherry blossoms and apples. Your eyes shine like emeralds, and your skin is the shade of moonlight." His voice was growing husky as his eyes gazed down the length of my arm.

"What do you want to do to me?" I bit my lip playfully. The hot summer night was making the air feel sultry. And me emboldened.

"Well, you're the first human I've kissed, and it's more challenging than I imagined. You're more delicate than any member of the legion. You're warmer than any Residual. And Marcus and Tristan agree from a distance you could fool anyone into thinking you're one of us. Your beauty and attraction have not just been noticed by *me*. And when you bite your lip like that…" His blue eyes practically glowed in the night. I could feel the sensual desire growing in his fingertips trailing upward toward my neck.

"You're the first angel I've kissed, and I've got to say, it's appealing." My foot tapped the ground nervously. "But there are things I think about doing too." I couldn't meet his gaze. "Like spending time alone with you where people don't intrude constantly. To get to know you. Before it's the middle of the night, and I'm dead on my feet."

A wide smile broke across his jaw. "Come on." He grabbed my hand and walked quickly up the road.

Most people had gone to bed when we arrived back at the house. I could barely see a little fire burning on August and Tristan's balcony. Eli rushed into the house and down to the basement. He towed me along gently before coming to a stop at the double doors to the hot spring bathhouse.

"How about we go swimming? What's the point of owning the

private rights to a hot spring if I never use it?" He grinned and locked the doors after we entered. "No intrusions."

I pulled my shirt over my head and tugged my jean shorts away, tossing them to the tiled floor. I wasn't going to waste a minute. The only lights that illuminated the room came from the pools below. He was wearing a pair of black boxer briefs and nothing else as he slipped into the water I gently waded into.

"I'm all yours." A small smile pulled up the corner of his mouth.

"My personal guardian angel. How does a girl get so lucky? Or maybe the better term would be *blessed*."

"What do you want to know?" He dipped his head into the pool and broke the surface, steam rising from his sculpted shoulders.

"How old are you?" I swirled to sit on the underwater ledge.

"I believe humans would say *eons*," he replied sarcastically. "How old are you?"

"Twenty-five. But I guess I don't really know, second life and all." I shrugged with a sideways glance. "Where do you go when you're not here?"

He rolled his eyes. "It's not that interesting. Sometimes I'm checking on one of my charges. Sometimes I resolve disputes among members of the Garden who reside in my region right now. And sometimes I'm following up on information that might help me understand *our* situation better. But those leads are fairly thin." He swam backward and sat on a bench opposite me. "Can I ask you something? What did you mean I didn't have feelings in the way you did for me?"

I was thankful the steam was masking the real shade of my cheeks. "It just feels unlikely a guardian angel who was dreamt up in literal Elysium could possess a real attraction to me. My vices alone—I smoke, drink, I swear, and I attract deadly legions of murderers. I'm not exactly someone worth pining for."

"Love is fickle like that. Sometimes it chooses the people even when they have other ideas." He gave a sarcastic roll of his eyes.

I tried to hide the smile on my lips as I watched him raise a well-muscled arm to the pool's edge and the tendon of his neck feathered with the movement.

My heart beat harder.

"Who did you spend your time with before I occupied most of it?"

"*Most* of the time I was alone, but my brother Lucian and I were close. He was forged shortly after me, and I enjoy spending time with him now and again. He's the most troubled by all of this."

The look he gave made my heart ache. I wanted to fix this feeling of loss for him. I was trying to find the right words to comfort him, but nothing felt like enough.

"Or were you referencing lovers?" He had taken my silence to have a different meaning. "I don't want you to think about that." He swam close and sat beside me. "You're the first girlfriend I've ever lived with." He smirked.

"Girlfriend?" I sputtered, surprised at the word.

"Did I not use it correctly? Paramour? Inamorata?" A dubious smirk turned up his lips.

"Is that what I am to you? Your girlfriend?" I eyed him skeptically and inched closer.

"No," he murmured above the swirling waters. "You're more than that. My desirable…my human…*my* Lily."

His hair was dripping beads of hot water. His lips were a deep scarlet in the heat of the pool and his smell was seductive, like a pheromone perfectly composed for my liking. My chest ached for him. The same ache I tried to ignore and fill with Jarrett. The same ache I tried to run away from into Ethan's arms.

He waded slowly to me before his massive hands reached around my waist and lifted me to sit on the edge of the pool. He stood in the water nearly at eye level with me. He was so god-like he could have been Poseidon rising out of the depths. The allure was growing, and we could feel it.

He pressed both hands to the stone tile on either side of my lap and leaned in to put his mouth to mine. I walked my hands back, and he mirrored my movements. Kissing me fervently, I let out a weak moan. I could hear him hum in approval. My head rolled back, and he made his way down my neck and across my collarbone. My hands found his shoulders and he continued down my sternum, the length of my stomach, and across my left hip. He glanced up at me from beneath his thick lashes, and he pulled off my underwear and dropped the soaked cotton to the floor beside me.

He ran his hands the length of my thighs before grasping my calves dangling in the water and pulling them up over his shoulders. Slowly, he kissed the insides of my thighs and then carefully ran his tongue around my sweet spot, gently sucking and caressing. My hands gripped the edges of the pool, and my body shook from the motions. His tongue drew rings of pleasure before he drove it inside of me. An involuntary moan blew past my lips and the lights in the pool flickered.

He pulled me by the hips forward suddenly and brought his mouth to mine. He had one hand around my waist and another beneath my thigh as he lifted me to straddle him in the water and we walked back into the depths.

I kept my arms in a tight embrace around his shoulders, and my mouth explored the length of his neck. I could taste his excitement vibrating in my bones and feel the blood rushing to his groin.

The dense steam thickened around us and crept along my flesh, marinating my lungs with the heavy mist.

"Are you alright?" His deep voice resonated in the tiled room.

I nodded, but I was struggling to breathe. He could tell I was strained and took two large steps out of the water using the submerged bench and carried me into the unused sauna separated by glass. The room was cooler, and he shut the door to keep out some of the steam. He had my back to the warm pane and quickly ripped my bra from my chest. I let out a sensuous moan this time, and the glass vibrated hard against my back.

"Lily," he growled, "is this okay?"

"Uh-huh," I panted, weakly.

He dropped me to my feet, and I stood tiptoe to keep kissing as I began to pull his soaked boxers away that clung to him. It wasn't the first time I had caught sight of Eli naked, and I knew what to expect. I bit my lip at the sight of his dick swelling.

"Lily..."

"Hmmm?" I breathed.

"Lily?"

"Yes?" I whispered.

"Lily!" a voice called softly, like an echo and my hands shook.

I opened my eyes and Eli was still lost in kissing my neck. I immediately pushed my hands to his chest and leaned back to search his eyes.

"What's wrong?" he whispered. "Am I hurting you?"

"Did you just...?" I trailed, suddenly stern. The voice calling my name hadn't been Eli's.

I felt the octaves resonate again and my head shot sideways looking to the door.

Eli followed my gaze. "What is it?" he asked fiercely.

I wasn't thinking, only reacting. I ran and grabbed a robe from the hook, cinching it around my waist as I pulled the doors to the room back. I looked in both directions of the hallway and all was dark.

A nude Eli pulled me behind him. One hand protectively shielded me as he scanned the cavernous hall.

"I don't know..." I whispered.

I ducked from behind his hand and slowly walked up the stairs. No one was in the main hallway. I passed through the empty living room and ascended the main staircase. Eli stood at my side studying my face with concern. I walked quietly into the guest hall and nothing. All was silent.

I paused, thinking over what happened and looked at my hands. I could tell Eli was growing more and more worried.

"It's been a long day, perhaps a shower and some rest is a good idea. I've been pushing you hard today." He sighed, his brows still furrowed with concern.

I nodded slowly and followed him up to our bedroom. I'm sure I looked insane. I assured him I was fine though.

I replayed the moment in my mind and couldn't shake the feeling in my hands and back. Like someone trailing a fingertip across your skin lightly, evoking a shudder.

I made up my mind after rinsing off. Rushing, I pulled on a pair of jeans shorts and my favorite navy T-shirt. Eli was surprised when I emerged from the bathroom fully dressed. He was lying relaxed in bed.

"You asked me not to run off again a month ago in the middle of the night, so full disclosure, you can either come with me or I'll go alone," I affirmed with a sharp nod.

He pulled on a pair of pants and began buttoning up a shirt. "Where to?"

"My apartment. I think." I tapped my lips in thought.

* * *

I didn't argue when he insisted we take his Fisker. It was electric and would make anything easier due to its quiet nature. I sat in the passenger seat eyeing the dark windows of my apartment. Nothing seemed amiss. Eli was silent beside me.

"Stay here," I whispered. I pulled the key from my back pocket and slid from the vehicle before jogging to my front door. I listened intently while turning the key but heard nothing.

Eli waited for me from beside the vehicle. I assured him it was fine, but I could tell he was not so easily convinced.

Once inside, everything was as we'd left it. Nothing seemed out of place.

I walked to the living room while listening intently. My white tennis shoes were practically phosphorescent in the dark. I should have opted for something more covert. And then I heard it, a soft shuffle to my right coming down the hallway. Large footsteps inching closer.

I didn't move. I stared into the pitch and breathed slowly and determinedly.

"Lily?" he whispered.

He stopped at the end of the hallway and my face scrunched in aching pain. Ethan was standing in the dark apartment holding his spare key at his side. His beautiful blond curls were softly reflective in the glow of the moonlight, and his hazel eyes were worried. Whiskers cast a shadow across his jaw and his beautifully tanned skin looked flawless in the poorly lit room.

"I'm sorry I didn't reach out sooner. August told me about Jarrett. I didn't think you'd want to see me after, so I left you alone. I'm sorry," he said sorrowfully. "I've missed you like hell, Harper. I came by here a few times, but it always looked like no one was home."

He continued his anxious explanation while tears began to flow over my bottom lashes and freely down my cheeks. I was shaking my head, unable to reconcile what was happening. I felt so much happiness to see him after so long and so much devastation under the given circumstances.

"Don't cry. I'm not mad. I was being an asshole. I love you, Lily.

You're my best friend, and I don't care if we're together. I want—no, I *need* you in my life," he pleaded.

I choked on my tears when he used the word need.

He wrapped his arms around me in effortless comfort. The comfort that made me feel safer than anyone had made me feel. He smelled like that familiar scent of cotton and bergamot, and I cried harder into his chest.

"Hey…hey, don't cry." He pulled me back to look in my face. "We can get past anything right?"

"Ethan." I pulled myself up to my full height and forced the courage I didn't feel through my teeth. "I stopped to pick up a few things. Maybe we can talk this weekend?"

He was hurt, but he nodded and hugged me again.

I offered to walk him out, and it took everything in me to wipe away the tears and follow him. He couldn't see me like this, or he would never go.

"Listen, maybe I can get you breakfast at that little Mexican place you love so much. Take a trip up to the boulders and hash things out?" He nodded sweetly.

"I'll call you later this week."

He tipped my chin up to meet his eyes using his thumb and index finger, and I had to fight to keep a brave face. I gave a resolute smile.

"We'll get through this." He smiled his signature warm smile. The one that made me happy when nothing else could.

I slowly turned and made my way back to the living room on shaky legs. I waited until I heard his truck rumbling down the road before I sucked in an aching breath, collapsed, and let out a broken sob. Eli was through the door picking me up from the floor in mere moments.

He pulled me up to look at him.

"It's him." I choked through unrestrained sobs. "It's Ethan."

"What did he do?" His voice was harsh as looked in the direction

Ethan had gone.

"He's…" I didn't want to say it. If I said it, it would be real, and I would have no choice. Then this all would be real and everything the Scribe said in the cave mattered. Jarrett's death wasn't some coping hallucination, Eli *was* a Guardian, and I was probably evil. I couldn't have him be a part of all of this.

"*He's* the name. The name I called. I heard him calling back to me. He's…my…Paladin." I collapsed to the floor weeping and choking on sobs.

Eli's face filled with understanding and pain. He knew what I didn't want. What I couldn't bear to fathom.

Another love pulled into the devil's path.

23

Fighting a Ghost

"It can't be him. Please," I pleaded. "Not him."

"What happened to Jarrett wouldn't happen to him. Paladins are…" He spoke softly, searching for the right words.

"Ethan's not. He's sweet. He makes me kill spiders in the shower! You don't understand!" As if Eli had any choice in the matter. His face was plagued with sadness. I could feel how helpless he felt.

"We won't involve him if it's what you want." He pulled me gently into his chest. "I've never wanted to make something stop so much for one human. I'm going to end this. I promise," he murmured into the crown of my head.

The idea of Ethan fighting any one of the monsters I'd come to know horrified me. The image of the sword plunging through Jarrett's chest flashed across my mind, and I cringed at the memory.

"I can go if you want me to." His hands dropped to his sides. "Sleep somewhere else tonight." He was wracked with guilt and barely met my eyes.

"No," I groaned. "That's not what I want either. I…" I had never told him this. "When I'm not with you, I don't feel right. It's worse than grief. *I'm* not right. Like I'm not all there."

255

He put his forehead to mine. "Me too."

"Let's go home," I whispered. I was ready to leave the apartment. Nothing about it felt familiar anymore.

* * *

We were quiet on the drive back, and I was anxious. I knew he wanted to ask me something, but I couldn't pinpoint what.

He chivalrously opened my car door and pulled me forward with a cool palm.

"In the spirit of honesty and *getting to know each other*, I want you to know something." He hung the Fisker keys on a hook. "I *loved* it when you asked me to take you *home*."

My heart quaked. I guess I'd come to think of the House of Roosevelt as home. Despite the dangerous company milling about the actual house, I felt safe here.

"I couldn't leave August—"

"I think August and Tristan have already staked their claim," he noted quietly, glancing in the direction of the second primary bedroom.

"It's not weird?" I asked feebly.

"I don't want to be presumptuous, but I do feel better when you're here, and I'd like it if you continued to stay in *our* room. But I understand if it's too much." He stopped to face me on the driveway.

"I hoped I could reason with you still." A mild voice called from the dark and a young man, maybe late twenties, strolled forward. He was wearing a wine-red button-up shirt and black slacks. It was Lucian. Eli's favorite and most beloved of his brothers. He had olive skin and a prominent dimple on his chin. But despite his beauty, I knew his strength was below the surface.

Eli pulled me to his side, and I could hear the cracking of joints in his shoulder blades.

"I'm sorry, Lucian." His eyes narrowed. "I can't. I don't want to stay away from her." He was saying more with his words, but now was not the time. He spoke out of the corner of his mouth to me. "Lily, wake Tristan, and take August to our room."

I was rapping on the bedroom door at the end of the hallway without a second thought when Tristan swung it open.

"Lucian," I stated, breathlessly.

Tristan reached behind the door pulling out a small sword and pushed past me jogging down the corridor.

"Wake August. Get to your and Eli's room," he called over his shoulder, and then he was down the stairs before I could respond.

August was sleeping face down in a white T-shirt and red knit shorts. She looked like a sleepy lifeguard.

"August, get up." I rocked her shoulder quietly. Her hair smelled like faint wisps of a bonfire. "Lucian's here!" I whispered urgently into her ear. "We have to go."

August's eyes blinked wide suddenly, and she stumbled sideways off the bed. "Let's go." She was wearing one sock, and her eyes were pink with bloodshot.

I was pacing once we had gotten to my bedroom, and she was lying across the end of the bed.

"Aren't you more worried?"

"Not really." Her head lolled sideways to look at me. "If you can spook off Gabriel, then I'm guessing Tristan and Eli will do fine with whoever decided to make this house call." Her words were slightly slurred, and her eyes were unfocused.

"Are you drunk?" I scoffed.

"If I was, would that make this situation better or worse?" She moved to sit up and face me cross-legged, a lazy smile on her face.

Great. Towing a drunk August around when an enemy is at the front gate.

"Jesus, everything is a joke to you. You just run around here with your boyfriend and worry about nothing. We could die, do you get that?" I could feel the annoyance in my tone and didn't care.

She rolled her eyes and leaned back with her palms against the mattress, a look of apathy staring back at me.

"Are you serious? Aren't you worried?"

"I'm not Eli, and I'm not going to *edit* what I tell you because of guilt. But you should know." She skeptically raised her brows at me. "Almost everyone who attended the meeting that night or left here is dead or seriously worse for wear. The ones who are alive are in hiding. Anyone who has information on you, or this"— she gestured in an arc with her hands— "is being hunted. Do you remember Quinn Adams?"

"The bartender from the pub near our house?"

"He's been missing for two and half weeks. The police are saying he's a lost hiker. It's terrible. His mom died of breast cancer last summer. Tristan said it was because you were talking to him one night before spending some time with Eli."

"We didn't *spend* time together! I was drunk and mad. I was venting to Quinn about it. Eli found me too drunk to get home, and he made sure I was okay. *Oh my God*." I rubbed my palms down the length of my face. "I thought they wouldn't hurt humans!"

"You're still not getting it, Harper. They want you dead. And they've been coming at you from all sides trying to get anything valuable for themselves. They're desperate now. Because for some reason, they can't kill you." She snapped her fingers at the end.

"What about your brothers? Ethan?" I was beginning to feel sick.

"They keep watch on our family. And I don't know why they leave Ethan alone." She shrugged.

I did. Someone or something was telling them to stay away from him knowing he was my Paladin. They didn't want to start a fight they may not be able to see the other side of. I cringed at the idea of Ethan facing any one of them.

"So to answer your question, I'm terrified. I don't know what I would do if I didn't have Tristan. I don't think I would get out of bed most days. I lost the job I love and can't go back to my great apartment. I hardly see my best friend, my brother was killed, and some of us didn't have an angel to make that pain go away. So yes, I'm a little drunk, and I'm tired." Tears were sparkling in her eyes. "And I'm scared. So sorry if I stole from your boyfriend's posh wine cellar. I'm a little stressed *too*." She lay back and closed her eyes, letting the tears spill over her temples. "I'm also helping *you*. Getting to know the people living here. Tristan said I have a knack for seeming innocuous. I've managed to deduce at least three people we should be leery of. Andy was one of them. So you're welcome."

I sat quietly next to her on the bed. I'd been terribly selfish about how this was affecting her. I was wrapped in my feelings toward Eli and my grief toward Jarrett. I had been so lost in my own problems lately that I hadn't stopped to consider what this was doing to her, how this was hurting her.

"I'm a terrible person," I murmured. "I'm so sorry. I couldn't have done any of this without you. I love you, August. And"—I took a deep breath and closed my eyes—"I miss Jarrett. I know they did their voodoo on me and it makes that nerve less exposed, but if I look at it, think about it, remember it for a moment, the pain is all there." I pictured him. "Sometimes I dream about him. I can see his face so clearly and he's so happy. I miss him. I miss his voice and that one crooked smile he had when he was up to no good. I miss the way he would put his thumb along my jaw when he would hold my neck…his smell." I choked on a sob. "Oh God, his *smell*." The tears freely flowed. "If I didn't have you or Eli, I would be completely broken too. I'm so grateful for the two of you getting me through this."

Her arms were around me, and we both were crying. Our shoulders were shaking from the mutual pain. I lay my head on her tiny shoulder and cried until the tears wouldn't come anymore. I should have talked to her weeks ago.

We must have drifted off because an abrupt knock at the door jostled me awake. I glanced at the white numbers of the wooden clock. It was after midnight. August was sleeping next to me, and I slipped from the bed to let Tristan in. Crisis must have been averted.

"Lydia?" The Residual with the long white hair and albino-like pallor was standing at the door. The same one who Eli strangled in the stables after she had accidentally grabbed for me. I stepped forward into the hall and closed the door behind me so as not to wake August.

"Eli sent me. He wants you at the cottage," she spoke quietly.

I was still wearing the shorts and T-shirt I had come home in. "I'm gonna let August sleep."

I looked through the front windows apprehensively as we passed, seeing if there were any signs of a fight that had taken place with Lucian. Nothing was amiss. It had been over an hour since he appeared, and I hadn't heard anything.

"What happened with Lucian?" I tugged on my tennis shoes and stood from the chair.

"I'll have Elijah tell you." She walked on the path calmly beside me. "We'll cut through the stables to be safe."

It must've been bad if she wasn't able to tell me *anything*. Maybe I should have awoken August? No, she needed rest.

Lydia stopped in front of the main door of the stables, standing in the amber crescent of light being cast through the opening.

"You know the day I touched you I learned something. I haven't told them yet," she whispered, "but I know *what* you are." She was standing uncomfortably close.

"Okay," I said slowly. She made me feel a little uneasy.

"I could be welcomed. Revered even. They might forge me into the Legion," she pondered aloud. "I could finally be whole. Do you know how someone becomes a Residual?"

I didn't respond. I was leaning away from her now.

"It's someone who dies out of their time and is killed by one of the Ethereal beings of the Garden. I died before I was supposed to, murdered by some soldier from Ophinam's region. I believe you met him? He carried you to the Garden."

I had. He was the ebony warrior with the surprising smile who looked as though he had been plucked straight from South Sudan.

"I was a fisherman's daughter and people would bring us gifts because they thought I was an angel," she snickered. "When I saw the soldier, he was beautiful. It wasn't hard for him to lure me away. He strangled me after he raped me. I was punished for being beautiful. And now the only people who can touch me are from the same plane of existence as that soldier. A sick joke. But now I have an opportunity to be more. When I touched you I knew the truth. I know what you're looking for—"

I suddenly felt an eager twinge to know more. To understand what the purpose of all of this was. Forgetting my uneasiness, I timidly stepped closer.

"And if I killed you, I would be worshiped. Elijah is the oldest of all the Guardians and the lore of his fighting is legendary. I was afraid to go against him and I didn't know if I could get you alone, but they're killing us. *I* knew if I was patient, I could lure you in the same way that that soldier had lured me. With kindness…"

I had forgotten the rule. The only rule Eli constantly pressed time and again. *Trust no one.* I had fallen into a habit and idiotically believed he was waiting for me somewhere and wandered off into the arms of a devil.

I had no idea how to fight a Residual. Was that even possible? The last time she had touched me I nearly died, and that was only for mere moments. My only hope would be to run. I didn't hesitate. I bolted straight down the center of the stable along the brick running past her.

I heard nothing at my back and decided to steal a glance over my shoulder in hopes she wasn't following me, but I was wrong. She was silent in her movements, and I was able to look just in time to watch her wrap a fist through my hair and pull me back to the ground. I smacked the stone with a *thud* and let out a breathy cough.

There would be no winning for me. But I wasn't going to make this easy for her. August had insisted after freshman year of college to take self-defense classes, and I was going to rely on that right now. Except how do you incapacitate an attacker you can't touch?

Surprise them.

"Eli!" I belted as I twisted to push myself up using my palms on the dusty floor.

A boot came with a punishing blow from above, and I felt a swift kick to the face. Instantly, my nose and cheek cracked, and I cried out. My right eye immediately went black. I could taste the blood from my right nostril running over my upper lip.

Keep your distance.

Using my elbows, I pulled myself across the floor on my belly trying to put some space between us. I felt another blow to the right side of my head, and I slammed into a stall door.

Be confident.

"Not as easy to kill as you thought, huh?" I was channeling my inner August as I spit the blood pooling in my mouth from the broken teeth I now felt.

Keep it easy.

I pulled myself to my feet and got her in the sight of my good eye. I was hoping I could land a kick somehow, but I was concussed and could only halfway stand before feeling like I was going to collapse.

"Let me take your hand and you won't feel a thing." She reached out her palm.

"Never." I spit a spray of thick blood in her face.

A shotgun blast came from my blindside and her head snapped suddenly to the right from the blow. Her opacity shifted, and the outline of her body momentarily became hazy. She turned quickly and another blast caught her in the chest. I saw Tristan holding the shotgun Eli had given me the night of the meeting. Apparently, those tarnished copper shells were capable of inflicting harm on a Residual.

She stumbled back again when her shape fluctuated after the second shell. This time she drifted through the stable door at her back, and I started at the sight. A scream tore from her throat, and she clenched her mouth and rolled her shoulders, forcing the misty state of being forth and walked back through the stable door again. Shifting in and out of her corporal form.

She purposefully marched towards Tristan and yanked the barrel from his grasp, hurling it to the ground, and she pushed an angry claw to his face. He took in a sickening breath and his eyes immediately rolled back.

I slid down the boards at my back, and my chin dropped to my chest. My neck and jaw throbbed painfully and the vision in my left eye was graying out. I must have been bleeding more profusely somewhere, and I tried to lift my hand to my face to feel for lacerations when I realized I couldn't move my right shoulder. I couldn't see it completely with my left eye either, but it appeared to be hanging limply from the socket.

Another shrill scream drew my attention back to Lydia.

"Eli." I smiled. The right half of my face felt as though it was drooping with novocaine.

Eli looked at me and his face contorted with rage. He seized

Lydia, and she was thrashing against his grasp. Again where his skin connected with hers began to turn ashen.

He had explained to me on one of our walks how Residuals inherently soak up life around them, but when they try and draw the life of a Guardian, it can only weaken, never kill.

He bent to the ground and picked up one of the shells laying next to Tristan's unconscious body and crushed it in his palm before pressing the powder to her exposed collarbone. She writhed from the pain, and her skin began to decay and bruise a deep plum.

He plucked another of the loose shells from the ground and crushed it, this time pulling her flush against him and forcing the powder into her tightly pressed lips. Then he clamped a hand across her mouth, and the searing decay spread over the rim of her lips.

He let her go and she staggered backward.

"You're going to need to take some soon, Lydia." He walked slowly after her as he spoke calmly.

She shook her head back and forth, a slight shudder in her gait. She inched toward me in the smallest of efforts.

"Don't touch her again. I should have killed you the first time you did." His deep voice was punishing. He was terrifying in his slow approach.

She gave an irritated growl and reached a vague hand quickly through the gate of the nearest stable, laying a palm on the shoulder of a beautiful Hanoverian.

The horse let out a broken neigh, kicking and seizing. She clenched harder as it thrashed and staggered into the door. She was draining it of life. Her face grew firm, and the purple was receding. When the horse dropped, she gave a rotten smile.

Eli's leap was that of a Spartan warrior. He had her on her back by her throat before she could move. Her fingers clawed at his clenched grasp. She had soaked up enough life to be killed.

"I will cut down *every* person who comes for her." And with a swift thrust of his arm, her neck snapped and all the life she had siphoned from the mare bled from her. Her head dropped to the brick stone.

He left her on the floor, and I watched in disgusted amazement as she rapidly decayed in a ghostly fashion.

"Lily? Can you hear me?" Eli kneeled beside me, and I smiled with the working half of my face. "Don't speak, I need to get you back inside the house."

My right hand was laying limply in my lap, and I could see blood staining my favorite shorts. My knees and right thigh were already forming blackened bruises.

"Marcus! Help Tristan!" Eli called into my black periphery. I heard footsteps approaching and shuffling against the brick. "Lydia tried to kill Lily. Her collarbone is broken, and I think her brain is hemorrhaging. I need to help her *now*!"

I didn't hear the response. Eli's soothing arms were carefully lifting me to his chest, and I let my head rest against his broad shoulder. My right arm was swinging as he jogged with me back to the house.

"I'm sorry," I slurred.

"I should have come to check on you after Lucian left. I was checking on Ethan. I'm the one that's sorry." He shoved through the back doors. He was lying me across the table, which had been used so frequently as an operating table. I could hear August in the distance and Marcus somewhere close by. Bjorn was jogging into my good periphery holding a familiar silver tin and white cloth. I had a feeling I wasn't going to be coherent much longer. "He's fine. I wanted to make sure it wasn't a ploy."

He had checked on Ethan for me? My heart welled at the thought.

I screwed up with Ethan. I hadn't said all the things I should have to Jarrett when I'd had the chance. I'd lost so much until now.

I wasn't going to leave this unsaid. I knew how I felt. I needed to tell him.

"I love you, Elijah," I garbled unintelligibly through my broken teeth. I wanted him to know. In case this time I didn't wake up. In case this time the magic elixir didn't work.

He turned suddenly and bent close enough to meet my gaze. "I love you too, Lily."

24

The Garden is Everywhere

I fluttered my eyes and found myself staring at the beam of Eli and my room. My mouth felt dry, and I looked through the glass to see it was dark outside. Eli was pondering out the window while he sat in his deep leather chair.

"How long was I out?" I murmured. It had probably been at least a week with the state I had been in.

"Six hours. It's nearly morning." He lowered himself beside me on the bed. He looked serious.

"How bad is it?" My fingertips skimmed my eye and cheek. Although dreamy in focus, I could see out of both of my eyes. I rolled my shoulder, and it felt good that that side of my body was working.

"Lily." Eli took my hand in his. "I've been thinking. I can't keep you in the dark anymore. Some small part of me hoped all this could end harmlessly. Things could go back to the way they were. I've been foolish, and it nearly cost you your life tonight."

He had felt the same way I had. In some way, all of this would end without some mass casualty and life could resume. Just as I had held onto Jarrett, he had held on to my innocence.

"I keep telling myself, I'll just do this one thing or cross this one small line and we can still go back. I can still fix this. But the line keeps moving. And part of me thought not telling you everything would somehow keep you safe. As long as I didn't do that, it would be alright. But tonight on that table"—he palmed the side of my face and ran his thumb across my cheekbone—"I broke those rules and moved the line again. You were going to die. That Residual had nearly paralyzed you and no human intervention like CPR was going to save you this time."

He was referencing how he had intervened with me when I had been drowning in his forest spring. How he had performed mouth-to-mouth to bring me back from the unknown cusp.

"I relied on the strength of my halo to burn and heal you. But to do such a thing is sacrosanct, so I must admit the truth. There's no going back." He leveled his gaze with me. "I *do* love you. And across the millennia I can honestly say I've never told a woman those words. I'm in love with her." He exhaled through his nose and looked away. "August is right…"

"She does that sometimes." I smirked.

"Time and time again I withhold things from you, afraid you couldn't digest the truth. Worried it would be too far and we couldn't go back. But all it's done is put you at risk of them taking advantage of your innocence. I may not be able to have you at my side at all times, and you need to know how to move in my world. How to protect yourself, because trusting no one is not enough."

"Okay." I was nervous. "Am I going to learn how to fight?"

He chuckled. "Let the foot soldiers be fodder right now. Warfare is first and most importantly fought on an intellectual front. One you can't fight if you're blindfolded. Lesson one—know your enemy. Today you're going to learn something no humans know about. The Garden."

***

I was seated in the office of the cottage. It was a larger room with a circular ceiling at one of the high points of the house.

"It's like we're in Hogwarts." August beamed beside me at the table, vibrating in her chair.

Eli, Tristan, and the Condemned-angel Marcus stood talking in hushed tones at the other end of the room. Marcus was all sly smiles while Tristan appeared serious.

"Tristan's worried that we're giving you the keys to the nuclear codes. You know…in case you end up being"—her eyes got big and she growled the words through gritted teeth—"evil Lily."

"So much faith. How nice," I replied trying to hide how uneasy I felt.

"Okay, ladies." Tristan came to stand in front of us. "I'll be your professor today."

August gave a catcall whistle, and Tristan smiled.

Marcus laughed while leaning against the frame of a nearby door. Eli stood rigidly at the back of the room with arms crossed. No matter how much he felt this would be necessary, there was no hiding how conflicted he still was.

"The most important thing you need to know about the Garden is that you cannot hide from it." Tristan turned and began to write on a piece of glass with a dry-erase marker while August's hand shot up.

"Yes, August?" Tristan gestured to her.

"Is this the Garden of Eden?" She cocked her chin sideways in question.

"Why don't we let Tristan finish the lecture and we can ask questions at the end?" I smiled politely at her. I had forgotten how eager she could be regarding all things academic.

"No, and great idea, Lily. The Garden is what most humans might refer to as paradise, the hereafter, nirvana, or—"

"Heaven," I whispered to myself.

"Precisely." Tristan pressed his lips together earnestly. "But it's an inaccurate sentiment, as you know, because no one but Ethereal beings can reside in the Garden. After a human soul expires, it is whisked away to the Ethoes to be among the dead. The Garden, however, is our home like this plane is yours. It exists everywhere at all times and is teeming with all types of Ethereal. It is ruled by the nine Guardians who are tasked with overlooking your plane and making ours run smoothly. It is infinitely larger than this plane. Even as I stand here now, I am within its rights.

"There are limited means to enter the Garden and any entrance made must be an exit taken. For instance, if Eli were to enter the Garden from this space, no matter how far he traveled within its landscape, he could only return and exit on *this* spot." He gestured to the area he stood.

August's hand shot up again beside me, and I reached over and lowered her arm while nodding for Tristan to continue.

"Which is why, August, Eli had to bring Lily back to the spot in the forest where his brothers had taken her from. There is no way for a human to enter the Garden." Tristan exchanged a look to the back of the room and Eli gave an infinitesimal headshake no. "So, my love, don't try to find some scheme to break in." He smiled fondly at her as her shoulders dropped and her face saddened.

I didn't think that's what Tristan meant to say, but I let it go, happy to be learning this much. It did confirm my suspicions, however. They still weren't planning on telling me everything.

"The Guardians and soldiers of the Legion can scale the Garden using their wings. It's how they can come and go. Residuals are on both sides all the time, as though they're a part of the veil. Fallen and Condemned are forbidden from entering." Marcus snorted. "And the Garden's nobility can use one of the apertures to gain access.

"Eli and his brothers, the Guardians as we refer to them, spend most of their time living in their region before they exchange locations.

When they need to convene for any matter, they meet in the Garden's locus. Where only *they* can enter and render decisions. That's where they intended to execute Lily.

"The Guardians are dictated by, and enforce, the edicts written in our ancient writs. Lily, you know about those because the priest and I gave you a little insight. A lot of the writs have been lost over time, either stolen by people trying to rise up within the Garden, destroyed in times of war or"—he took a breath—"have never been interpreted because they predate the Garden and the Ethereal beings that could translate its texts."

August mouthed the word *predate* and scribbled down another question.

I remembered the book with the strange glyphs given to me by the priest in Georgia and how I had been able to understand it. Did this mean Hesperia and I came from a time *before* the Garden? When and how did the Garden come to fruition?

"Scribes are the official word. They are the ones who write down the texts. They can see the past, the present, and the future if it's loud enough. They'll dictate the writs when they appear to them, and only a *true* priest can translate them. Unfortunately, most scribes these days are a watered-down version of what they once were and are faulty in their predictions. The decent ones who come to be are either killed or kept captive for personal gain. Priests fell out of use a thousand years ago and rarely has anyone, human or Ethereal, seen one, so consider yourself quite lucky, Lily, your boyfriend was able to smoke one out. They're killed and hunted at a stunning rate. Which equally makes them the most coveted. And before you write it down, Ms. Bayne, it's simple. Kill the thing that can tell everyone what the laws say, and you have leverage. Kill the thing that predicts the law, and now you can make your own laws."

It would be hard to kill something that can foretell you're coming, so kill the next best thing—the priest who can read it. I understood Eli's motivation behind killing the Scribe. She wasn't just a provocation for Zacarius. Eli was killing two birds with one stone. By eliminating Josephine, he was eliminating Zacarius being able to know anything about our strategies. He had been right. He was keeping a lot of things from me.

"...which is the region we're currently in."

Uh-oh. I hadn't been paying attention. If we were back in college, I would ask August after the fact, but I felt that wouldn't suffice this time.

"I'm sorry, Tristan." I shrunk as I raised my palm in question. "Could you repeat that last part? I was trying to process."

"There are nine regions total the brothers look after. This is the occidental region. One of the largest, but generally the most peaceful. Human war zones can be much more consuming for their Guardians—"

"Where's Aurelius?" I interrupted.

"The Northern East region." Tristan could see I didn't know what this meant. "What you might call Russia and the Middle East."

The intimidating tyrant struck fear in my gut whenever I saw his face flash through my mind. I couldn't imagine him taking charge of any other place.

"Unfortunately, the history of Ethereals is long and riddled with conflict. Lower branches of our kind have warred before. And once, before you were born, some of the high beings from the other side did as well." I noticed August's worry as she nervously wrote down another question. "But don't worry. It's unlikely for the brothers to engage in strife. Although they can and will fight when necessary, never once has there been a war between them since they were Forged.

"Which is why we feel it might be beneficial, after careful discussion, if Lily accompanies Marcus and me." Tristan pursed his lips and tapped the desk we were seated at with his marker.

"To where?" I looked to Eli for answers.

"To work. Despite Eli's disagreement between him and his brothers, he is still obligated to maintain the order of his region." Tristan folded his arms and leaned back against the wall across from us.

"But won't they wonder who I am? Or know?" I gripped my chair and could feel myself defensively tensing. The idea of being away from Eli made me nervous. Especially after what had happened with Lydia in the stable the night before.

"We have a workaround for that. Any other questions?" Tristan looked at me and then smirked at August's notepad.

"Just three." August smiled innocently. "First, you said some of the laws predate the Garden. Who enforced those before Eli and his psycho band of brothers were Forged?"

"That will be a lesson for another day," Eli voiced from behind us.

"Okay. Second question, you said the brothers had never been at war before, but some of the higher beings on the *other side* did years ago. What did you mean by the other side?" She was giving her best *not getting out of this one* face.

The room remained quiet.

"It meant there must have been a war *in* the Garden." I shrugged, not following the line of thinking she was now on.

"No, there wasn't," August replied evenly. "Otherwise they would call it the Garden. You mean the other side as in the *opposite side*."

I still wasn't following.

"The opposite side of *them*." She turned to me. "He was referring to hell." She turned her shoulders back to squarely face Tristan. "I'm right, aren't I? The 'higher beings' in hell warred years ago. Who would the higher beings of hell be? Kings…" She tapped her chin and scanned the floor in thought. "No, bigger. Something lowly couldn't initiate a full-blown war… It had to be…" She drew in a sharp breath and her eyes got wide.

"What?" I was startled by the revelation I was clearly missing out on.

"The devil! He's real! Of course he is! It makes sense. They're angels, and he was a Fallen angel. Oh my God! Hell's real! Hell's real?" She was speaking a mile a minute.

"That's enough." Eli came to stand beside a rigid Tristan.

"I told you she was quick." Tristan raised his brows insinuating how clever August was. "We might as well give them the truth on this one. Otherwise, she and Lily will commit more theft from the cottage library while we're away."

Eli let out a rough sigh and gestured to continue.

"There is no such thing as hell. But just as there is the Garden exists the Forest. A harsh landscape where the souls of the damned wander. But unlike the Garden, it was ruled by one being…until he took a wife. When she fled to be with her lover, the king and legions of hell began to hunt them. It lasted for nearly five years until the death of—"

"That's quite enough, Tristan," Eli interjected with an air of finality. Tristan picked up on the tone and backed away quietly. "And to answer, what I'm sure is your final question, August: no, you may not accompany them today. You will be coming along with me for an errand."

August slumped in her chair clearly bummed she couldn't be a part of *bring your girlfriend to work day*.

Tristan leaned forward and tore the page August had scribbled her questions on and tossed it in the crackling fireplace on the side of the room. Nothing would be evident our class had taken place.

I was anxious and something else. Scared perhaps. What task would be so great a Guardian would need to settle it? My mind immediately began to race through the possibilities. A witch? That sounds ridiculous. But then again four months ago, I would have said all of this would have been ridiculous.

But despite learning about the Garden, Eli's brothers, literal hell, and the actual devil, one thing kept replaying over and over again in my head.

If I was alive in another life and did *predate* the Garden, why now? What made me choose to come back to this time? Surely if I had some unfinished matter I needed to resolve, as Eli had stated when I confessed my dreams to him weeks ago, it would have been in that lifetime or close to it? There was nothing I could do in this day and age.

Anytime I felt we were getting answers or going in the right direction Eli shut it down.

And all I could think was that he was keeping a very big secret. One I was afraid to know the answer to.

25

Extradition

Eli faced me with a stern set to his jaw as we stayed behind a moment before I took off with Marcus and Tristan. I could feel the concern coming from him.

"I want you to take this with you," he said firmly.

"Your mortal dagger? I thought these were only to be used by you and your brothers?"

"I don't care. You know what it can do. It will work against Ethereals too. Now listen to me, you do *exactly* as Tristan and Marcus tell you to. If they say run, don't hesitate." He cinched something around my thigh and slid the dagger into the sheath at my hip. "You'll be safe with Marcus and Tristan."

"I don't understand why *you* can't come with me," I pleaded softly. "What if your brothers come again?"

My mind began replaying the horrors that could possibly take place. A ghost nearly took me out. There was no way I could win in a fight against one of them.

"They would never think that I would let you out of my reach. And I can't come, as much as I want to, because you need to learn how to manage without me. And as much as this is killing me"—he put his forehead to mine and pulled my face to his by the nape of my neck—"I can't always be there," he whispered.

He was right. If I was adamantly refusing to involve Ethan and Eli was busy deflecting the attacks coming from all sides, at some point, they would find a chink in the armor. They nearly had already. I was lucky to have escaped or had help in the situations I'd come across thus far.

Eventually, one of these times my luck was bound to run out. And I needed to understand his world better to protect myself against it.

"And I know if I'm there. I'll be worrying about you and putting myself between you and it instead of letting you learn how to swim. This is necessary. No matter how agonizingly uncomfortable it is for me."

For us both. I'd been a part of his world for a couple months now, and I still felt as confused and lost as I had when I initially encountered him.

"I also know it *feels* like I'll be there to stop it, but the loss of August's brother has shown me their reach and level of desperation to stop this is far more than it ever has been before. I, myself, am struggling to understand it.

"If Evelyn, the newly Condemned, hadn't been with me at the time I wouldn't have known about Gabriel until it's too late. If Tristan hadn't smelled your blood coming from the stable, he couldn't have sent Marcus to get me when the Residual was hurting you."

"But can't you feel when I'm in distress? I can sometimes feel it with you," I murmured in a small voice.

"It would seem one of us is braver than the other. Your distress only appears to peak when you're nearly beyond saving. You have too much nerve for your own good."

"Yet another thing that landed me here in the first place."

He smiled, pressed his lips to my forehead and pulled me to him.

His arms wrapped around my shoulders gently and he sighed heavily through his nose.

"There's a lot of things we need answered. Know that I am trying to find those for you."

I pulled back to look him in the face, "I know," I replied sincerely.

* * *

"I say we just kill him." I was pulled from my thoughts by the raised tone Marcus used.

"If only it were that easy." Tristan smirked as he readjusted the large duffel he had slung over his shoulder.

"If someone had dealt with this earlier, I wouldn't be trekking through a desert in Bolivia in a minute." Marcus was riled up.

"If we handed out final judgments every time a member of the Garden goes rogue… Well, I think we both know the discord it would create." Tristan was frustrated.

Marcus cared very little about giving anyone a second chance. What had he burned for that cost him so dearly? I didn't dare ask. It felt like asking someone what they were doing time for.

"Fuck 'em. Half the beings in that damn Garden should spend a few centuries among the mortals. Give them some perspective and perhaps some free will and we wouldn't be hunting a rapist." Annoyance blanketed Marcus's face.

"Unfortunately, I think some are determined to break the rules. Perhaps soldiers better suited for the Forest and less the Garden," Tristan grumbled.

"Rapist?" I interrupted as Marcus, Tristan, and I stepped out of the aperture. Struck immediately by the dust in the air, I blinked in the haze.

They'd told me we were dealing with interference. Someone was violating the laws and needed to be handled. But I wasn't sure who and what it meant.

"He's been suspected in multiple assaults, but this is the first human victim he's had," Tristan explained.

"And the first evidence he's left. Can't fucking wait for him to fight back." Marcus laughed as he donned a pair of dark sunglasses.

"Pretty soon we won't have a choice, Marcus. I'll take a peaceful day over this shit every time," Tristan scoffed as he pulled glasses from his shirt pocket and handed me a pair.

"How are we in Bolivia? Wouldn't that be outside of Eli's region?" I worried a little.

"Think of it like extradition." Tristan pulled on black latex gloves, and Marcus pulled out a tin of tobacco before stuffing a hearty dip in his lower lip.

"I say we give them the final rest," Marcus reiterated, thrilled at the prospect and Tristan rolled his eyes.

"He'll be imprisoned longer than humanity has existed," Tristan explained as we struggled up the shifting desert sands beneath our feet.

I pushed myself to the dune's peak and paused at the sight ahead of us. The surrounding sandbanks sheltered an oasis and lush greens blanketed the shores of its small lake. There was no sign of human inhabitants breaking the wild peacefulness. Birds darted from the canopy as a scream tore through the air.

"They're here." Marcus surged forward.

As we followed, another cry broke the silence and Marcus reached toward something before disappearing into an aperture up ahead under a large palm, only to come flying back out a moment later with a small body wrapped in his arms.

"Bastards!" he growled as he dropped the body and rushed back inside.

I gasped as she hit the ground limply. Her hair bounced around her, and her legs fell at odd angles.

"Two of them!" Tristan said this as if it were the answer he'd been waiting for.

Tristan and I rushed forward, with a side-glance at the girl on the ground. He ran to the entrance and disappeared.

She was still. I crouched next to her bloodied frame. She couldn't have been more than fifteen. Warm golden-bronzed skin and almond eyes. Strong and beautiful features, but swollen and bleeding. The blood gushing from her head wounds caked in her black curls and slowed to an ooze as her heart ceased to continue.

Hate bloomed in my chest as I looked on indignantly. Fresh tears trailed down her filthy temples and dropped into the sand. They had raped this child, beaten her, and as a result, she was dead. This was someone's daughter.

"I'm sorry," I whispered. "Women and girls shouldn't have to live in fear, especially for those tasked with protecting us."

Fury pushed me into the aperture. The humidity blanketed my skin as I passed the threshold. It was some kind of wetland swamp. The kind I remembered from my spring break in Florida with August. The air smelled of soil and decay. The savagery of the fight inside the new surroundings echoed through the mangroves and fueled my hatred. Tristan knelt over the smaller of the two men, his fist already starting to bruise from the force he used.

"You were already warned, Oscar!" Tristan yelled as he landed another hit to the man's jaw and slipped on the wet vegetation under his knees.

Preoccupied with each other, I kicked the nearest man in the back away from an unsuspecting Marcus before he could attack and quickly turned to see the man's shocked expression matching my own.

"Well, shit," Marcus blurted in appreciation from behind me.

"I don't…" I began to tell them I didn't understand the strength I was feeling, but the man rolled to his stomach and pushed up onto his hands.

I reacted and my boot sank heavily into his ribs with a sickening crack as he was forced back to the ground.

"What the fuck?" The man laughed before he turned to look at his sidekick quickly.

"You broke the law, Simeon." Marcus shook his head.

"She wasn't even worth it." He referenced the dead girl lying alone in the desert.

"Shut up." I swallowed back the bile rising in my throat and steadied myself on my usually clumsy feet. "What is happening right now?" I looked down at my boot, which was caked with blood and muck.

A *thud* sounded beside us, and I saw Tristan tumble into the foliage. Leaping at me, the man howled, and I dropped to my knees to avoid being tackled. He flew over me and crashed at my heels, sending mud flying around him. It had to be the aftereffects of the silver stuff?

Tristan rushed around me and pulled Oscar's arms from under him, bending them up to his shoulder blades like an officer subduing a criminal. I snagged a piece of chain that had been dropped and scrambled to wrap it around the man's wrists.

"New girl's quick," Oscar said as I stood up.

"Best Pollock we've got." Marcus grinned at me.

A Pollock, I had learned, was a mimic. They could mirror the form of inanimate objects and living things, but rarely could they get humanity right. I was one of the best, for today, apparently. It was how we were going to "hide me in plain sight."

"She's quick, but her eyes aren't dead enough." The monster smirked.

"She's good because she hasn't been tortured," Marcus said and turned away.

"Yet," he replied as he lunged towards me the moment Tristan jerked him to his feet.

"You couldn't break her if you used the force of all nine wardens of the Garden." Marcus laughed as the man was wrenched to his knees by a push from Tristan.

The man sucked his bottom lip between his teeth and tilted his head to look at me. "You'd beg me to," he sneered.

I felt rugged fingers unwrap my balled fist, and a smooth stone was placed in my hand.

Tristan pried Oscar's jaw open as Marcus yanked the unconscious legion warrior over his shoulders.

It was a silencing stone, Tristan had explained on the way here. Looking at the rock as I brought it to the laughing face and awkwardly shoved it past his lips, I relished the sound of his breaking teeth as I thrust it as hard as possible. I felt satisfaction in his defeat. I was serving justice for that girl and possibly countless others.

I sighed as I turned to pick up the duffel bag Marcus had brought along.

Tristan let Oscar fall to the ground, and we ignored his gurgling curses of pain.

"Let's get this over with." Marcus trudged forward through the wetland around us.

Simeon's eyes were closed, and blood trickled from his wounds. I wondered vaguely if they felt pain the same as I did. Was he struggling to breathe, as I had when my ribs had been broken the previous night? Was he afraid? I hoped so. I hoped he felt the same irreparable damage she felt.

"Will they feel the torture?" I asked.

"Honestly, no," Tristan shared.

"They'll feel it physically, but not emotionally," Marcus snorted.

That wasn't a very comforting thought, and he must have picked up on my annoyance about it.

"Not all of the things lurking in the Garden go bump in the night," Marcus countered.

As we reached a small clearing, a pair of giant trees greeted me. The bark looked smooth but buckled upon itself. Gradients of warm, rich browns peeked from behind patches of lichens and moss crawled up the titanic trunk. The two trees towered over us, emerging from the sky down.

"These are fairly young." I could barely speak the words as awe trampled the anger in me at the sight of the beautiful timber.

"Hmm, then it shall make a nice prison." Tristan smiled.

"I'm getting hungry, so let's finish this." Marcus grinned. "And hang these dicks."

Oscar and Simeon were dropped against the tree's roots.

"Simeon was a surprise today," Tristan shared. "But something told me Oscar couldn't pull this off on his own."

"So they'll just be chained here for awhile?" I frowned. It seemed so inadequate for something so heinous. I had wished they would starve or atrophy. Slowly deteriorate and rot in agony.

"Rules are rules." Marcus shrugged.

"Right." I nodded.

"Li—" Tristan cleared his throat. "Toss me that lock." He nodded toward a large rusty padlock.

Picking it from the duffel bag, I walked it over to him. It was heavy and ancient. It must not have been man-made.

With the key around his neck, he opened it and looped it through the links of the chain before securing it.

"Enjoy your stay, boys!" Marcus laughed as he saluted the prisoners.

"Let's get home," I said.

"Are you alright?" Tristan asked as he caught up to us as we exited the aperture.

"No kidding. I knew you were tough, but that was next-level ass-kicking, sweetheart." Marcus grinned.

"I'm not your sweetheart," I replied with a smile.

"Pollock Lily could be." He waggled his brows at me.

"No."

He laughed loudly and Tristan smiled, but I felt them both tense beside me.

As we trekked away from the swamp back through the oasis and out of the dunes, I was looking forward to going home.

***

Tristan pulled me back as we were getting closer to the house and nodded for Marcus to continue on.

"Are you okay? Seeing a child violated by those here to protect... It would breed resentment from the best of us." He had picked up on the things I was thinking. "You needed to see the other side. It's difficult to kill Ethereals." He searched the forest floor for the right words. "A lesson I was asked to *specifically* withhold from August. Anyone can inflict pain on Ethereals, but only other Ethereals can kill one another. And even then, there are still rules."

"But that means..."

"There is no chance to win this with sheer mortal determination." He smiled empathetically next to me.

"I've always been human, Tristan. So I'm sorry to say, but we will lose if provoked." I sighed.

He took a deep breath. "You aren't just a human."

"How is that possible?" I challenged.

"I don't know. Theories and legends aside, none of us know really." He was displeased. "But we believe in you and Elijah."

"Why?"

"I think the Garden is evolving and those within it want something different. You and he could be that. And he will protect you above everything else."

"That's the only thing I'm sure of." I sighed, "I just wish he would tell me what the theories and legends are."

"They don't matter to him, and the reality is, he might not *want* to believe them because it might mean he has to let you go." He continued forward.

I mulled on what he was telling me as we moved up the back steps of the house. I wasn't sure why he would have to let me go or how I was going to get through any of this. But looking at my best friend, bubbly and chattering away as she was cooking dinner inside, I knew I needed her with me.

"Oi, brought you something." Marcus whistled as he strolled toward me in the kitchen with a tumbler of whiskey.

"Good. Shut off that big brain of yours." Tristen smiled softly. "It's been quite a day." He pushed a hip into August.

I shot the whiskey back as I felt Eli's cool palm pull me to his side and his lips against my temple. "I'm proud of you," he whispered.

"Those biscuits smell delicious." Tristan inhaled while closing his eyes.

"Bayne biscuits. Family recipe." August grinned while she pulled out the edge of the pan with a dish towel.

"We'll have to pass it down to our kids."

I paused with the glass to my lips.

"I'll make Bayne biscuits with you anytime." She winked at Tristan. "Our *biscuits* would be the cutest damn things you ever saw."

"I can't wait until this is all over, woman, and we can have a litter of biscuits." He chuckled and retied her apron strings.

"Could you imagine?" Marcus gave himself another strong pour of whiskey. "The human-Ethereal bloodline continuing on for the first time in ages?"

"Just like the legends of the ancient times," Eli whispered.

"Except scarier than any Ethereal because they would be half August," I chimed as I sank onto one of the stools.

She would be the biggest force anyone could reckon with, in my opinion.

"You're just jealous because they would look like Cherubs!" She hopped up and down as she popped biscuits into a basket to go with dinner.

Marcus cringed.

"The cute human kind, not like the creepy one buried out back by the cottage!" she said with a flick of her hand as she set the table.

We chuckled. Only she could make a joke like that.

26

Venus Intervenes

August wanted two things growing up—a sister and a squished face cat she wanted to name Gus. Her parents got her the cat when she was three and the thing hated her, would scratch her when she tried to pet it, and always slept with Bennett. Bennett loved that cat until it passed away shortly before I met August. She now just refers to it as the furry devil who stalked her ponytail her whole life.

But her wishes to have a sister never abated. She loved makeup and dressing up. She loved to do my hair when I let her or helped me pick out outfits. And she absolutely adored anything that sparkled.

"This is the date!" August chittered from inside the closet.

"Is this gonna be weird…because of Jarrett?" I asked quietly.

There was a pause before her head poked out.

"You said he's in that place where all the souls go right? That it's happy there. *He's* happy there." She huffed a sigh. "I like Eli. He's funny." She smiled before it faded.

Funny? She went back to what she was doing. I think it was easier for us both not to think about it. What all got us to this moment. How far we had deviated from the life we had known.

She planned the date with Eli while I was off chaining the sex offenders to a tree in some Floridian swamp. I actually smiled at the thought. I had a hard time understanding the closeness August and Eli shared from the very beginning. She read him better than I could, and he told her things I wasn't privy to. She always had a way with everyone.

"While you played bad cop with my boyfriend, I remembered this flirty little dress that'll be perfect for tonight." She darted between sections of clothes, pulling out hangers to examine the garment on them. All I could see were lengthy, flowing skirts. "You haven't told me how it went, by the way."

I shrugged.

"Tristan said you were pretty angry." She glanced over her shoulder at me.

"I don't understand. How does that happen?" I shook my head as I remembered.

She turned slowly and sat next to me on the bed. "They don't all care about humanity. Hell, a lot of humans don't care either. You just want them to." She sighed. "You always have been like that."

"Like what?" I didn't see her point.

"I think you always expect people to care because of who or what they are." She shrugged. "But they don't. Most people only think about themselves. It bothers you because of what happened with your mom. It's why it makes you angry. When they don't meet you at the bar you've set or do what you think they should do, you get upset and give up on them."

I didn't give up on people.

My mother was never there for me like she should have been after my dad died. My college boyfriend was a dick. And friends never clicked until I met August. I was cutting out toxic people. I wasn't abandoning everyone. Was I?

"Shit." I really hated when she was right.

It was a banner day for realizations.

She patted my shoulder in solidarity. "I've always known, Harper."

"Thanks for sharing," I grumbled while frozen in thought as she sauntered over to the closet again.

"This one," she said as she swung around with the dress in her hands.

My mouth dropped a little when I saw it. Gorgeous, emerald, gossamer tulle shaped the base of the dress. The top was black, and the front was a deep V that reached the cinched waistline. The bottom reached my ankles, and the thin straps would leave me sleeveless.

"Look at these slits!" August purred as she brought it to me to show off the full-length slits on each side of the bodice and skirt.

"I can't pull this off August," I scoffed wistfully.

I *wanted* to pull this off.

"Bullshit. This is perfect. When are you going to see that you're pretty?" She turned the hanger around to show the same deep V in the back. "Show off that sexy tattoo you got."

"It's a scar."

"It's incredible." She shoved the dress into my hands. "No bra."

I took a deep breath and examined the dress. In the green of the waist, there were minuscule vines embroidered into it.

"Just like my scar," I whispered as I ran my finger over the intricate work.

"See? Perfect."

I looked into her bright eyes and smiled softly. "You're right," I said.

"I know." And there was that cunning smirk of hers I hadn't seen enough of lately.

Stepping into the dress, I ran my hands over the material as I hesitantly came to stand in front of the antique mirror in our room. It reminded me of the pictures I'd seen of Greek goddesses.

"Did you help Eli get dressed too?" I questioned with a side glance in her direction as she dug through a jewelry box.

"Oh, that man does not need my help to look good. I mean, he's no Tristan, but look at his closet. You can only buy suits like that in Milan. He's *exactly right*." Her fingers mimicked a chef's kiss as she spoke.

I laughed loudly, and her giggle followed. It felt good to be us again for a second. Just best friends helping get ready for a date.

"Maybe this shadow?" I showed her a palette of radiant golds.

"Oh yeah, that middle one." She pointed.

Bringing over a few pieces of jewelry, she set them on the bureau beside the mirror and began to drape delicate necklaces around my neck. With a yay or nay, we whittled it down quickly. In the end, I was adorned in the gold of ancient Greece to match my eyes.

"I found the jewelry in that swanky room with the velvet couches. It looked expensive," she said in awe.

"Stop stealing from him," I chided.

"He's nervous," she whispered with a smirk.

"Why?" I asked.

"He's all in with you, and he's never felt this way before." She shrugged as she slipped wide-cuffed gold bracelets on my wrists. "That's it."

I *looked* like the goddesses of old, and I'd never felt so beautiful before.

"Now the hair!" She hopped in excitement.

"You have to have a daughter someday." I laughed as I sunk into an upholstered bench at the end of the bed.

"I don't care what I end up with. I'll do all their hair," she declared as she wielded a brush at me.

I closed my eyes and let her work.

"Okay. I got you a few things for tonight." She slipped a small pouch into my hand.

Sliding it open, the first thing I saw were condoms.

"Always prepared." I laughed.

"Date three is your thing." She shrugged.

"We've never gotten through a full date," I challenged.

"Treetop dinner," she began.

"Being followed by his brothers," I shot at her.

"Riverside picnic," she continued.

"Brothers again *and* Ethan showed up!" I guffawed.

"How long have you been sleeping in the same bed?" She glared at me.

I bit my lip. "Touché."

I hadn't told August yet that every time Eli and I got together the world started shaking.

"Tonight will be great. I've worked it all out, so if it leads to *things*, so be it." Her tone was convincing enough to make me smile.

"Too bad we don't have a pink boa for the door." I chuckled.

"Just like in college." She let out a wistful sigh.

"You're crazy." I laughed.

"Crazy awesome." She winked.

* * *

As I stepped out of the house, I watched him take me all in. I saw him swallow and the widening of his eyes made me smile slowly. He was uncharacteristically readable this evening. The sandals August had picked out made it easy to stroll toward him, and I made my appreciation of him obvious as I looked him up and down. A simple linen, collarless button-down in deep navy, black slacks, and simple loafers. The corner of his mouth quirked as I reached him.

"Hello there," I whispered as he dipped his mouth to mine quickly. A chaste kiss as his arm went around my back, freezing at the skin he found there.

"You look lovely." His voice was deeper than usual.

"Your partner in crime picked it out." I laughed softly.

"We should go." He smiled.

"I think we can do what we want."

"I have plans for us, Lilian. Don't tempt me," he warned.

"Where do we start?" I looked up at him innocently.

"With dinner, of course." He grinned.

Slowly dragging his fingers from the skin of my back, he wrapped my hand in his and we headed across the property.

The sun was still high in the sky as we walked, and I took the opportunity to ask him about the things he collected.

"I save a lot of things." He nodded toward the jewelry I wore.

"Is it okay I borrowed it?" I asked.

"They were made for you. I happened upon those at a market. They were the work of a twelve-year-old boy who later invented the gold leaf process," he explained.

"Wow," I whispered.

"The dinner we're about to have is full of recipes passed down by the only surviving bloodline of Pompeii," he said as he came to a stop behind a row of trees.

I could hear the buzzing of the aperture ahead of us and stepped in without hesitation.

"They've come to expect me on occasion." He smiled.

"Ah, bring all your dates here?" I smirked

"Dates? Because there have been so many." He shook his head.

I squeezed his hand. I was nervous too. Not only being with him, but I was afraid of letting him down. He had never dated a human, and what if I wasn't what he had hoped for?

"There's a small festival this time of year, and they eat, drink, and socialize late into the night." He was remembering something from another time.

"I can't wait." I smiled as he guided me through to our destination.

* * *

Stepping into the night, with city lights below, I gasped at the beauty. The shore was bright from the twinkling lights of the many docks lining the coast. Closely knit buildings glowed along the crescent beachfront.

"Naples," Eli whispered, his eyes downcast, nervously awaiting my reaction. "And Vesuvius across the way."

"I've only seen pictures."

"When this is over"—he struggled to get the words out—"I'll show you everything."

"I'd love that." I brought his hand up to my lips and kissed the pulse point at my fingertips. I loved he felt we could win this, but secretly, I was thinking I wouldn't be able to get out of this alive.

"But tonight we feast with the Grey Friars and Poor Clares of Santa Chiara." His voice held such reverence it made me nervous.

"Friars and nuns?" I was surprised and already felt ashamed as I cast a glance at my all-too-revealing dress.

His chuckle vibrated through me.

"They'll find you stunning." His lips grazed my cheek, and it burned red. I would always react to him.

I softly swallowed and tried to believe him.

Our meal was something served to the elite. The bouquet of deep red wines bloomed between us as we laughed and spoke with ease. I didn't ask him the questions burning through me night after agonizing night. And neither did he. On the contrary we were discovering each other the way we should have that first night in the treetops.

I relished in the traditional pasta, delicious breads, and the cheeses.

I laughed heartily as he told me stories from his past. How he detested the smell of mushrooms and how he taught himself to play the viola. He shared his favorite places to visit and how he could never live without a good bottle of cognac.

I sipped and smiled into my wine glass as he told me all about the time he lived by the North Sea and laughed when he told me about how he found himself with some whalers in the mid-nineteenth century. I was getting to know *him*.

"You laugh, but during those weeks I was finding myself just as superstitious as the rest of them. I couldn't whistle for months following that endeavor." He pointed his fork at me in earnest.

"I don't want any of this to end. This place..." I smiled as we made our way to the roof of the monastery.

"Once a place of death and sorrow, and yet one of the most peaceful places I've ever been. It's evolved. Perhaps, so have I..." He looked to meet my eyes for a moment as he held my hand, and we strolled down to the stone walkway by the water. "It's the only place I ever really *feel* mortality." He didn't look at me as he spoke.

My heart broke for him. It was hard to imagine how lonely immortality could make someone.

"How many years have you come here?" I asked softly.

"I saw the first stone placed," he replied, seeing some distant memory.

I pulled him to a stop as we stood in the dark, and turned to face him. "You're not alone this time."

His eyes softened and he framed my face with his hands as he leaned his forehead against mine.

"For now," I barely heard him whisper it before he covered my lips with his.

I pulled away. "Will this conclude our evening?"

He swallowed, shook his head no, and then let out a deep sigh.

"Next...Syria." He was too enthusiastic about this.

I pursed my lips together. "Syria? In the middle of the night?" He couldn't be serious.

"I can't show you the surprise when they're all awake and on edge." He smirked.

"Sneak"—I gulped—"into a country currently in the throws of war…"

"We'll be safe," he assured me as we stepped across the roof.

"I don't doubt that really, but I am not great at sneaking." I remembered how easily Tristan found August and me on our weak attempt at espionage.

"We'll be fine." He turned to face me at the edge of the roof and smiled.

I agreed unbelievably.

"Come here." He gathered me in his arms, scooping me to his chest.

I interlaced my fingers behind his neck.

The distinctive crack of his wings startled me as my feet left the ground. I inhaled and closed my eyes. I could hear the wind around us and feel the rush of his wings as they beat, but my eyes stayed closed. The last time I took a flight with Eli, I wasn't in the best of health.

"You're safe with me," he murmured. "It's beautiful, and we're almost to the aperture we need," he encouraged gently.

Be brave.

My eyes popped open, and I turned my chin to look. The lights of the cities were far below us. The darkness around us was interrupted only by the minimal light reflecting from his wings. It was colder up here, but so much quieter. I saw why Eli and his brothers kept this as the preferred method of travel. I felt like how I felt when I rode my motorcycle. Free.

I watched as his wings swelled upward creating a soft parachute between them, and we gently dropped to the ground.

"I can hear it," I replied as I looked in the direction it was radiating from.

He placed my feet to the ground gracefully and shrugged, putting away his heavenly assets.

"We'll have to get you used to that I think." He smiled as he swept a tress of hair away from my face. "The aloft travel. I've never had someone with me before..." He paused. "Besides, I like having you in my arms." He didn't smile as he said it, but I felt the heat behind the words.

My heart fluttered at his intensity, and I had to look away, unable to meet his gaze.

"Onward to your gift?" He smiled.

"There's a present for me in Syria?" I asked.

"Yes." He turned to walk ahead and wrapped his fingers around mine to guide me.

I followed him silently.

* * *

Red emergency lights lined the corridor we walked through. As Eli moved forward, I hesitated at the abrupt change in surroundings. I could hear the rapid popping of automatic weapons in the distance. The dust infiltrated every pore.

I coughed lightly, and suddenly, Eli pressed himself in front of me, my back against the wall. Voices sounded down the corridor, growing louder as someone made their way toward us. My heart raced and my mind braced itself for a fight. I tried to focus on them and the possible nearing danger, but he was against me. Eli was very careful to maintain a reserved distance when we were together. Most nights he came to bed after I had fallen asleep and was often gone before I awoke. His kisses were cautious and his manners in place.

He hadn't been willing to make a move on me after our passionate interlude in the sauna. Interactions with humans were forbidden—

imagine sleeping with one.

He smelled like an erotic mixture of mandarin, jasmine, and cedar. Lost in his arms, I didn't notice the fading of the voices or the relaxation of his hold.

"We need to go that way." he whispered.

I nodded mutely.

As we made our way through the red haze, there was only the sound of our feet on the dust-covered floors.

This is crazy, I told myself. *Where the hell are we?*

Two turns were all it took for us to reach the room he was looking for. He gently nudged the handle and the lock snapped, allowing the door to swing open with a low grind from its hinges.

We're going to die here. A war zone at night. Without any credible identification. As an American, I was fairly convinced this was violating some international law somehow.

Eli strode inside and through a second and better-preserved door, closing it behind us.

A light bulb blinked on at the ceiling and I was startled by the sudden brightness. The ground around us shook as an explosion sounded above our heads.

"Fuck," I breathed.

"We're fine. They'll be busy for a while," he assured me calmly.

"Fine? We're in the middle of a war zone, Elijah," I whisper-yelled at him.

He held in a laugh.

"I heard you discussing lost antiquities with Tristan and August a couple weeks ago." He moved aside crates to expose a safe in the wall. "And how you would like to see one of the great pieces lost to time."

"And you know where one is?" I laughed through my nose.

"Hopefully a lost DaVinci will suffice." He easily pulled open the safe and withdrew a small wrapped item.

As he uncovered the linen meant to protect it, he faced me.

"It's the *Medusa* shield."

My breath stopped cold, and I took a step forward. I instantly knew what I was looking at. The daughter of a museum curator, I had heard about all the great pieces and works growing up. And all the myths and legends too.

The paint was still clear, and despite the poor light of the room, I could make out the entire work. An art piece that had been lost in time, so shrouded in myth it was rumored not to have been real. No person had ever seen it, and few today believed it ever actually existed.

"He painted it on the wood of fig trees. You said you wanted to see it?" He scanned my face for a reaction.

I opened my mouth to speak, but nothing came out. This was unbelievable.

"You and August were drinking on the balcony, and I overheard," he admitted.

I laughed.

"You always know things." I eyed him.

"Observance is kind of my thing," he joked.

"I love you." It fell from my lips without thought and his eyes lit up.

"And I, you," he replied.

I leaned up to kiss him soundly. I felt one arm come around me, as the other moved to place the painting down carefully. His lips were firm but gentle against my own. The crates creaked from our energy, the buzz illuminating once again from our contact. My eyes closed softly. His hand dragged across my smooth skin as it slipped beneath the fabric of my dress. Trails of heat wound up my spine, and I pressed closer, fitting tightly against him. His hand slipped further down and below the waistline of the dress, where he just grazed the edges of the white lace I wore there.

"Can we go home?" I asked with a gentle tilt against the swelling in his slacks.

Heat rushed through my core as he stilled at the contact.

"Not home." The pressure of his fingertips gripping the fabric was firm. "Somewhere...*private*."

I took a deep breath to slow the pounding of my heart and ease the burn spreading from his hand and up the delicate scar along my spine. I could feel its pattern, as though warm water ran upwards. His left hand cradled the nape of my neck, and when he moved away from me, the chill of the underground air dimpled my skin, causing me to tremble.

Opening my eyes, I could see the brightness of his halos. There was a warring intensity in his eyes I'd never seen before, and I brought my hand to his face, skimming my thumb over his lips. As his hands left my skin, the heat dissipated, and I felt an ache take its place.

With a deep breath, he turned and grabbed my palm heading for the exit. I couldn't move fast enough to wherever we were going, and speech was lost to me. Moving through the halls, every gentle touch branded me, and every absence pierced me. Jumping from aperture to aperture, we stepped out into a dimly lit cave.

"The edge of the property is right outside," he mentioned, "and we're close to the grotto."

Torches lined the cavern sparsely, and the orange glow of their fires reflected off the rivulets of moisture draping the walls. I smiled in appreciation as I paused to take it in for a second.

"You amaze me." Eli was suddenly next to me, taking my hand in his.

"Why?" I laughed.

"The look on your face when you love something," he began. "I've never seen that look before."

Never? He'd *never* seen it before? "You've been alive so long and never—" He leaned down quickly and interrupted me with a kiss.

The softness of his lips against mine infused my skin with fire, and I clung to him. Each time he'd let himself do this, I felt the thrall that connected us grow stronger. My fingers twisted into his shirt and we both paused when buttons tinked softly against the floor of the cave.

"Thank you," he whispered as he stepped back.

"For what?" I looked into his eyes and his lips turned up as he looked back at me.

"Looking at me that way." He took a deep breath, "Should we go?"

"Yes," I replied breathily.

Pulling me to the exit of the cave, he swept me up into his arms and descended to the forest floor in a soft leap. The sun was low in the sky as we dipped beneath the trees. Debris tickled at my open toes, and the fabric of my skirt caught lightly on protruding branches. I couldn't wipe the smile off my face as my mind raced with what was happening.

It wouldn't stop me, but I worried it could be dangerous. Would we be okay? He was an Ethereal being after all.

"Is this really alright?" I whispered.

He turned to look at me quickly and tightened his hold on my hand.

"We can stop if you're not sure," he said lowly.

"I'm sure." I nodded. "I just don't know what to expect."

"We'll take it slow and find out together." He paused.

He tilted his head to the sky.

I couldn't stop the confidence sweeping through me, and I could feel his desire for me amplifying inside my bones. I peeled off his shirt while letting my dress pool to the mossy floor.

His hand went to my waist, and he lifted me to his lips before leaping over the edge of the hot spring. Our personal grotto.

Gripping my behind slowly, he bit at my clavicle with a groan.

I was ignoring everything. I didn't care about the buzzing. The creak of the trees and the rushing of the wind growing. I wanted him.

His body was a divine masterpiece, and unthinkingly, I bit my lower lip at the sight. My eyes were drawn down to his impressive dick from the perfect Adonis belt he donned.

His groan vibrated through my veins, and I wrapped a sure palm around his thick shaft, stroking with intention. His breath dropped, and he leaned down and let his tongue slide along my jaw as he moved across the forest floor.

Lowering to his knees, he spread my thighs and drove himself into me slowly, he closed his eyes and his halos ignited with a vibrant spark that lit up the entire cavern. Like lightning rushing up his thick forearms and biceps, across his shoulders and back down his spine.

He shifted his mouth to the peak of my nipple and rolled his tongue against it.

"Oh fuck," I thought, then felt him smile as my hands reached to tangle in his hair.

Had I said it aloud?

A sound left my throat somewhere between a sigh and a groan.

"Oh my God," I breathed. My hands drifted to the back of his neck and pulled his head up. I could feel the electricity roaring between us, the pull tearing at my chest to get closer to him.

"Stop?" He struggled to say the words as his face rose to mine and his body followed.

"No!" The words left my lips a second before his mouth covered my own.

His hips crashed into mine, thrusting my legs wider and him deeper.

Around us, lightning cracked with every movement. The air circled above us as his hands trapped my wrists over my head at exactly the moment I wished for it. Rushing, hot, and thick. Waves of pleasure soaked my nerves. The cavern shook with us. Raining stones down.

Was this him?

No.

The thought hit me.

It was *us*.

The vibrating electricity which ignited when we would kiss had grown into an audible resonance around us and could easily be heard for some distance.

As he broke a kiss, I moaned again, and a nearby tree near the opening above splintered at it's base, resounding throughout the forest as it crumbled against the floor.

When he wanted me on my knees, I moved without hesitation. I knew what he craved. Could hear it. Taste it. Feel it inside my chest.

In the recesses of my mind somewhere, I could hear the trampling of distant feet as screeches of the fauna thundered through the forest. What was that?

As he moved his hands to my hips, pulling me down the full length of him, crushing my clit against his flawless skin, I let out a whimper from the rising pleasure, watching the intense blue light of his halos brighten and bleed across the room.

He growled my name into my ear and pulled me to his chest as we both came. I let go and arched against the pleasure he inflicted, letting out a breathy uninhibited moan.

He was always cautious before, but in the rush of our mutual orgasm, he felt something else.

Panic.

"They were right," he croaked in disbelief as we slowed. "The kiss and the pull and…" He gasped. "But then I…" He stiffened. "This can't be…"

"Eli?" I was worried at whatever revelation I was suddenly missing.

He eased away from me, searching my eyes and face for the answer to a question I didn't know.

"Who was right?" I pulled my dress up around my chest, feeling insecure for the first time.

"How can this be happening? But then…you're…" He shot a stunned glance to my face and I felt fear rip through his chest.

"Eli, you're scaring me. What's going on?" We had connected so intensely it was as though we were operating on the same frequency for the moment. My senses were erratic, and something was breaking in my chest. Like the awakening of a familiar feeling.

Before I could get my questions answered, we heard a faraway scream break the confusion. A flurry of yells and crashes erupted in the distance and Eli's face filled with rage.

He hugged me tightly as his head turned to the sky. Something was here…or *someone*.

"I *do* love you, but I need you to stay here. I'll come back for you." He gently turned me to face him, and I complied easily. "Get dressed, stay quiet, and Lily, "—he turned as he was climbing with his clothing fisted in one palm—"hide."

"I will. I love you too." I didn't try to stop him as he leapt away.

It was something I would think about for months to come.

27

A Lost One Rises

I was trembling all over. Eli's face had been a mixture of confusion and shock before the distant chaos erupted. I, myself, couldn't explain what happened, but I felt more scared than ever.

I looked at my palms trying to understand what was going on now. I felt as though my skin was buzzing like a power line. I could taste the iron of the river water in the mist floating through the forest. Sense the animals and something else in the surrounding trees, where they were in relevance to me, and how they were moving. Something ominous was closing in. Something sinister.

A twinge of fear hitched in my chest, and my eyes snapped open instinctively scanning the surroundings as I tugged on my dress. I knew exactly where Eli was headed. He was jogging at a good clip, heading northwest. The farther he moved from me, the more the draw to follow poured over the crown of my head like hot liquid, running the length of my neck and spine. His worry was growing when suddenly, I heard a loud crack of trees about half a mile in his direction and fear clutched his chest.

I took a breath and did as he asked. Wait. He would take care of whatever it was. But the sounds were growing, and the commotion was building. Coming from multiple directions. The fear surged through my veins and became bitingly painful in my palms and out beyond my sides, like the pain of phantom limbs.

And then the archaic voice resonated inside me, and Eli's voice rose within my chest.

Lily...run!

I didn't hesitate. I couldn't explain it, but I knew I needed to get to Marcus and Tristan and get help. Something had harmed Eli. Something was happening.

We had been half a mile from the house as the crow flew. Some new sense told me many things were between me and it, and I was terrified. I jogged, watching my footing and giving silent arcs to the dark things I knew were lurking nearby.

I escaped behind a tree when I sensed something coming toward me and pressed my back against the bark. Slowly, with dragging footfalls, whatever it was moved past. It was large and reeked of something incredibly sweet. I had such a surface understanding of some of the creatures from the Garden, but I'm sure Tristan and Eli kept me in the dark about most of the frightening things or their capabilities.

When it had moved far enough away, I stepped onto the trail and cautiously began forward. The sounds that erupted earlier near the house and in the direction of the cottage dwindled. Maybe they had sent another Cherub? Perhaps two this time, and it was what was behind the discord.

What would I do if I came upon something I needed to fight? Run? And if I couldn't... Well, I wasn't going to think of that right now.

"Fuck, there you are!"

Carrying his rifle from his work truck and a handgun holstered on his hip, his blond locks shined in the moonlight. He was donning a white T-shirt and jeans. He must have been sleeping.

"Ethan?" I had done it without realizing it. I had called to him the moment I didn't understand what was happening with Eli. My subconscious had summoned my Paladin.

"Nice dress. I don't know how I knew you needed help or where you'd be, but I *did*. Shit has been weird for me lately," he replied breathlessly. I reached toward him and instinctively wrapped my arms around his waist.

"Monroe, I'm glad you're here." And I was. Because if Eli was right, no one was more equipped to be at my side right now than him.

There would be no use in trying to keep him out of the fight. My innermost instinct called to him when I needed him most. I was worried he was going to get hurt. But I had to trust Eli was right. If Ethan was as strong as they suspected, he was exactly what was called for.

"I'll explain everything later. Right now we need to get back to the house. The one August and I have been staying at. I need to get to Tristan." I rocked back on my heels and met his eyes. "I think there are things here trying to kill me. If I tell you to shoot something, can you do it?"

"Yup." And he gave me one brisk nod before immediately falling in step beside me.

We made it a few paces before we stopped cold in our run coming face to face with Tristan. "Lily, thank God I found you!"

"Tristan, there are these things crawling the forest… Wait why do you look like that?" Ethan began to lower his weapon.

"Shoot it!" I screamed.

Ethan didn't hesitate. He raised the rifle and dropped Tristan with two in the chest and one in the head.

"That wasn't him." I could see them for what they were. Whatever was rising up inside me helped me recognize the things closing in around us. "Pollocks. They can disguise themselves as anyone."

It looked like an inky cloud of obsidian moving toward us. Sounding like Tristan but slightly off.

Ethan stood with his back to mine. The brumes of several beings were closing in on us.

"We need to keep moving!" I called over my shoulder.

"Keep to my wake." Ethan spun and bounded over a small log. He knew this forest better than anyone. He could get us there blindfolded. "Count my rounds!"

"Three o'clock!" I shouted and he fired immediately.

He bobbed and weaved, and I followed. All while feeling Eli's terror grow in the distance to my right.

"Overhead!" I shouted as a red-ringed member of the Legion was plummeting through the trees, cracking branches as they fell.

For every one he shot down from the sky, another crashed into the earth nearby. I could feel the horde of killers at our backs, descending on us from the Garden.

"Reload!" I yelled.

I was running for my life.

We both were.

The uproar was surrounding us, and I knew then what was happening. This was their attack. And they were sending *droves*.

The lights of the house came into view and safety tugged at me. Only to be quickly erased when we got closer. The odor of blood was overwhelming. It reeked with a bitter stench. Bodies were scattered about the forest floor as we slowed our approach.

Ethan and my measured breaths were the only audible sound. The monsters following us had eased off and I couldn't understand why until—

"Apex predator," I murmured to myself. "They're backing off because something more dominant is nearby," I answered Ethan's confusion at my utterance.

A groan broke the silence, and I moved around the curvature of the house slowly.

Looking in horror. "Tristan?"

He had what appeared to be railroad spikes nailing him to the stone wall of the house. There were two below his collarbones impaling his upper chest, a pair in each of his triceps giving him the look of a bloodied scarecrow. He was dangling and coughing a wet cough.

"What the fuck happened?" I heaved.

"The Guardians—waiting." He drew in a rattling breath. "They felt the shift…"

He was soaked with so much blood I couldn't tell what color his clothes were supposed to be, and his body was so lacerated that it was difficult to discern the source of all the liquid.

"Where is everyone?" I panted frantically.

I could hear a lone sword fight beyond the treeline and the roars of two weakening men.

"Dead. They took August…" He retched.

I picked up his short sword at his feet he had dropped when they crucified him.

"I'm going to get her back—"

"I'm coming with." Ethan was reloading his rifle.

"No! Get Tristan down! He can tell you how to help him."

They were drawing me to them using August. That was why they hadn't hurt her. They were biding their time. Waiting. Watching. Planning. Since their first attempt failed to take me out. They'd been stalking the periphery like lions in wait.

I couldn't put anyone else in front of me anymore. I needed to face the inevitable head-on. I needed to be brave no matter what was going to happen.

I leaned up and kissed his cheek, leaving without another word.

This was it. I was going to face Eli's brothers. They had taken August and had done something to Eli. I could feel it. And I could feel something else climbing up from the pit in my stomach.

Rage.

I wasn't sure what I was going to do but I was going to do something. I may not be human—hell, I could be a woodland nymph for all I knew—but whatever was happening to me, I was planning to use it. They feared me. I had seen it the day Tristan learned I knew who Hesperia was. Saw it in Eli's eyes when the smoke bomb August's brothers set off affected me. And finally when I used the lightning lighter against Gabriel. Time and time again, I saw the looks they gave.

They were afraid of *me*.

I heard voices up ahead through the trees and moved faster.

"She'll come. We have *him*." Aurelius's voice rang out and my chest boiled with ire.

I took one deep breath and moved into view from behind a tree.

The brothers were covered in blood, spitting and wiping their faces from the massacre at the house. I examined the group to get my bearings. The eight brothers faced me. Some catching their breaths. All with their grotesquely massive swords dragging through the dirt at their sides.

I searched the faces when I saw the dark-skinned man, who had taken me to the Garden, with his thick hands wrapped around August now. I winced at the sight of her and had to square my shoulders with resolve.

They'd brutally beaten her. Her beautiful face was a deep plum and swollen while blood oozed from her mouth hanging agape, but she was alive.

Relief washed through me at the sight of her tiny breaths. I wouldn't let them take her. The molten anger sweltered in my neck.

I would do whatever I had to do to stop them.

Though the bodies were obscuring him, I could see Eli. He too appeared battered. He was face down in the dirt and his wings were outstretched in their full glory, hammered with spikes into the ground, the same spikes they had used to pin Tristan. They weren't human-made.

I swallowed against the ire I felt bleeding from my bones. The immense urge to thunder forward and help them both.

A sick smile grew in Aurelius's cheeks, "Lilian, you've joined us. And you brought a weapon. Intending to free your lover, no doubt." He gestured to Eli. "Very noble of you. I'm sure by now you can sense these forests are teaming with the Legions. You're outnumbered."

His cold voice was maddening, and the undertone of his threats was making it increasingly difficult for me to focus. I wanted to fight. Even if I died in the process I wanted to *hurt* him. I wanted to rip August and Eli free and tear through them all.

"It didn't stop me before," I said as I decided to hedge my bets and rely on a theory I had had for a while now.

"You remember?" His face grew dark. "Before I was Forged, I saw you from a distance once, fighting."

His words sparked a memory, but I quickly dismissed it. I needed to focus on this right now.

"The War of Mesopotamia. I came close to you. The *ancients*—dreaded among the legions…" He looked away, reminiscing for a moment.

"I wasn't sure if it was you. But after the lightning with Gabriel, no one could wield that and live. Not even me.

"So if the legend holds water, we must separate you from your mate. Zacarius quickly discovered it wasn't the man from Washington. He was mortal and for that…"

Aurelius made fleeting eye contact with two of Eli's brothers. They grabbed Zacarius suddenly by the upper arms and wrenched him to his knees.

"What are you doing?" The red-haired man who breathed hate into my every fiber looked stunned at the turn of events unfolding around him. "Let me go!"

Aurelius, with his silver hair and olive skin I now recognized in Tristan, came to stand in front of him. "You killed a human. You're treasonous and no longer fit to wear the crowns of our kingdom."

Aurelius placed two palms encircling Zarcarius's neck and squeezed, his halo brightened with ferocity and a ringing buzzed so loud I winced before a crack echoed.

"I will not be a member of the Fallen!" Zacarius growled.

"No. You will not. *You* are being censured," Aurelius replied calmly.

Horror took over the red-haired man, and he began thrashing violently against the men holding him. Screaming "no" at the top of his lungs repeatedly.

What happened next was something I would remember until the end of time. Aurelius clenched the broken halo beneath the skin of Zacarius's neck and pulled it through an open wound one of the brothers made in the front of his throat. As he pulled forth the piece, the metal dimmed more and more. Then, using their daggers, they plunged the blades beside the blue glow in his forearms and thrust them underneath, prying the luminous bits of metal from beneath the skin upwards over his wrist like a bloodied bangle. I looked away when they moved to his calves. His screams were something you might hear in the torture chambers amidst the bowels of a medieval castle.

I turned back to watch as the man collapsed in a heap onto the ground. Unconscious or dead, I didn't know.

Aurelius handed the metallic rings to Lucian and came back to face me. His hands were stained with the blood of what I now guessed was his *former* brother.

"This all could have been avoided had you died in the Garden as I'd planned. I guess not all myths can be true."

He went to stand near Eli who I could see clearly on the ground. Deep gashes were cut into his shoulders where swords came down onto him. He'd tried to save August when he arrived.

Lifting his head from the dirt by his hair, Aurelius murmured just loud enough into his ear for me to hear, "And if you had stayed away from her as I'd asked, none of this would be happening." He dropped his head and it hit the dirt with a sickening thud. He was barely conscious. It had probably taken all of them to ambush and subdue him.

Loud cracks erupted and their wings ruptured from their backs. One by one they took off as Aurelius moved toward the warrior gripping a limp August. The man pushed her into Aurelius's waiting grasp and leapt into the air before launching himself upwards with his wings.

"Now Lilian, if you just allow us to leave with Eli, I will not hurt your rather vocal little friend here." He smiled caustically.

They wanted to take Eli. If they couldn't kill me, they were going to abduct him to end what was between us. To keep us away from one another. I needed to triage the situation. He was immortal. August wasn't. I slowly lowered my sword.

Two of Eli's brothers pulled the stakes from him and gripped each of his wings, rising slowly into the night. Soaring with my unconscious lover dangling between them into the blackened sky.

I would save him. If I had to scale the heavens myself, I would get him back. But in that moment I remembered something Eli had said to me in the days following Jarrett's death.

Know when to fight and know when to harness your wrath.

"She's my *sister*," I spat darkly.

"I knew your sister, and Hesperia would have killed this girl in her bed if it came between you and her." He looked upwards over his shoulder.

We were alone now.

"Let her go." I felt like I could have burst into flames and light him on fire with my stare.

"No."

He withdrew the dagger from his hip and swiftly pulled the knife across her throat.

It happened so fast I didn't register the act itself. He mounted a tree close by and leapt skyward before I had the chance to raise my sword.

August crumpled into a heap. The wound in her neck so wide and deep, he almost decapitated her. Her head was at a disjointed angle to her shoulder.

Her fingers twitched twice, and a gurgle bubbled in her throat before her eyes fixed. Unable to see me as I clamored to her. A pool of blood as thick as motor oil made me slip while dropping to my knees beside her. My eyes searched her face for any semblance of hope. A shred of...*something.*

"No, no, no, no..." I pulled her into my lap, frantically wiping the blood from her eyes. Clutching her head as my own blurred with the tears of the inevitable truth my mind was refusing to accept.

Death wasn't like the movies. It wasn't loud or climactic. It was silent. Still. The crickets and chirps of the night bugs hummed around me. The fireflies' intermittent glows flared unaware of the trauma unfolding in their midst.

"This isn't happening." I wiped the tears from my cheeks with a bloody forearm. There was no one to run to this time. No one to get help.

I swallowed hard and closed my eyes, shaking with fury.

"Oh no," I whimpered. Unable to look at the body in my lap.

They had taken Eli.

Tristan may be dead.

And the man to my right had taken Jarrett from me.

Now they had just killed August.

My August.

My friend. My family. My *sister*.

The electric hum burned in my stomach, and my nerves seared. A metallic taste foamed on my tongue, and I could feel something twist in my chest. It felt stronger than the first time I kissed Eli or when we made love. It wasn't anger or hate.

Looking at her pale beaten face and lifeless still body, it was over. And they had taken her from me. I couldn't put this into my box. I couldn't compartmentalize this.

I felt *wrath*.

Clenching my fists, I pushed them into the dirt and grass at my hips. The tears streaked my cheeks. The wind blew around me and my hair whipped against my neck. The tree tops creaked.

My body slowly contorted against the distress.

It wanted out.

The forest fell silent. A power was present in the atmosphere and nature could sense it.

Cracks of electricity sporadically bolted through the open air around me, and I pulled my shoulders blades together. I groaned and writhed from the reaction taking hold inside me. Tendrils of furious force threaded through my muscles.

The evil they so feared was rising.

My bones resonated with the feeling. It was consuming, and my throat felt raw as it built inside me.

Suddenly, I threw my head back and let it erupt from my depths like a supernova. The vibrations that trembled inside me when I was with Eli. The noise in my nerves. The pain in my chest from the loss of Jarrett—and now August. The hate for taking her from me. I held her name in my mind fueling my ire.

A scream so loud the very ground quaked and ruptured around me creating steaming fissures. The bark peeled away from my sound waves as the trees broke at the base, crashing to the ground, as though the force of an atomic bomb fueled my octaves.

I wanted it out of me. All of it.

The stars shook in the sky and torrents of rain exploded from the cloudless night around me. I dropped my gaze to the trees ahead and let loose my scream on them as they ignited with a vicious wildfire.

The entire Garden and all its inhabitants would feel my wrath. I knew they were cowering at what they had just awakened. I could feel it. And whatever it was inside me, it had risen. And as the explosion that was me receded, and an apprehensive calm replaced the forest around me, one thing was final as I sat here in this epicenter holding August's lifeless body.

I was going to kill everything in heaven.

The End.